LINE
OF DUTY

Books by Terri Blackstock

Emerald Windows

Cape Refuge

Cape Refuge
Southern Storm

Newpointe 911

Private Justice
Shadow of Doubt
Word of Honor
Trial by Fire
Line of Duty

Sun Coast Chronicles

Evidence of Mercy
Justifiable Means
Ulterior Motives
Presumption of Guilt

Second Chances

Never Again Good-bye
When Dreams Cross
Blind Trust
Broken Wings

With Beverly LaHaye

Seasons Under Heaven
Showers in Season
Times and Seasons
Season of Blessing

Novellas

Seaside

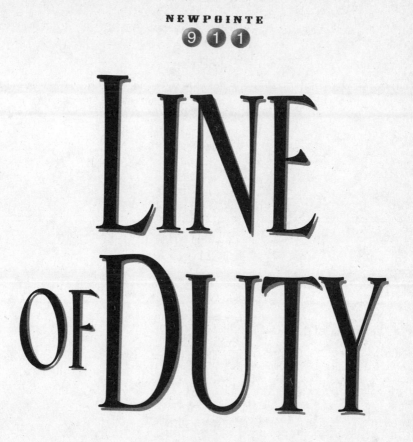

NEWPOINTE
9 1 1

LINE OF DUTY

TERRI BLACKSTOCK

ZONDERVAN™

GRAND RAPIDS, MICHIGAN 49530 USA

ZONDERVAN™

Line of Duty
Copyright © 2003 by Terri Blackstock

Requests for information should be addressed to:
Zondervan, *Grand Rapids, Michigan 49530*

Library of Congress Cataloging-in-Publication Data

Blackstock, Terri, 1957–
    Line of duty / Terri Blackstock.
      p. cm.—(Newpointe 911 ; bk. 5)
    ISBN 0-310-25064-1
      1. Women lawyers—Fiction.   2. Missing persons—Fiction.   3. Fire fighters—
Fiction.   4. Skyscrapers—Fiction.   5. Bombings—Fiction.   6. New Orleans
(La.)—Fiction.   I. Title.
PS3552.L34285L56 2003
813'.54—dc22

                                                      2003014625

Published in association with the literary agency of Alive Communications, Inc., 7680 Goddard Street, Suite 200, Colorado Springs, CO 80920.

Interior design by Jody DeNeef

Printed in the United States of America

---

03 04 05 06 07 08 09 /❖ DC/ 10 9 8 7 6 5 4 3

This book is lovingly dedicated to the Nazarene.

Acknowledgment

As many of you know, I fully intended to end this series with Book 4, *Trial by Fire*. But on September 11, 2001, as I mourned the loss of so many firefighters, paramedics, and police officers in the line of duty, I was overwhelmed with the need to say even more about those men and women who are among America's truest heroes. For the work they do day in and day out, keeping us secure and saving our lives, they have my deepest gratitude and admiration.

And for all of those readers who wrote me and encouraged me to continue the Newpointe 911 series, thus convincing my publisher that it might be a good idea after all, I thank you. Without such loyal readers, I'd still be searching the want ads for a "real job" to support my writing habit and trying to get out of jams that my daydreaming got me into. You have validated my neurosis and given focus to my fertile imagination. I thank God for blessing me with you.

LINE OF DUTY

Chapter One

● ● ●

Ashley Morris sensed the doom in the Icon International Building. She had listened to the news reports of layoffs and the company's crashing stock value with the detached interest of a sixteen-year-old, but it was hard to ignore the reality now. In the lobby, grim-faced employees spoke in low voices. Some wiped tears as they carried boxes out to their cars. Reporters with camera crews waited outside, interviewing exiting employees who'd just gotten the ax.

She'd picked a lousy day to hit her mother up for money.

Popping her gum, Ashley got onto the elevator with two women and a man. One of the women gave her a look as if she had just parachuted out of a UFO. Ashley looked right back at her and blew a bubble. The woman looked away.

Ashley grinned and looked down at a chipped fingernail. She had to admit, she had dressed for the occasion. Her bright orange T-shirt—two sizes too small—clashed with her burgundy hair. She had cut the sleeves off at the seam and frayed the edges, so that her tattoo of some Chinese word she didn't know was more visible. The shirt didn't quite meet her jeans, and her belly-button ring sparkled against her pale skin. Her jeans had been slit in parallel lines down the fronts of her legs, revealing other tattoos—a butterfly and a rose. And she'd worn a chain from her nose ring to her earring, just for added effect.

"Sarah got canned," the man said. "She's cleaning out her desk."

"I'm next. I know I am. And my whole retirement's gone. Where am I going to find another job at my age?"

"They're saying they're going to indict Merritt in the next day or so," the woman who'd stared at Ashley muttered.

"They ought to take him out and shoot him."

When the others got off on the tenth floor, Ashley leaned back against the elevator wall. This could be serious. Her mother was the administrative assistant to Donald Merritt, the corrupt CEO. And if things weren't looking good for him, Ashley's mother was probably taking the brunt of it. She would be in a terrible mood and wouldn't have much patience for her daughter.

Yeah, her timing really stank.

She stepped off on the thirtieth floor, her hiking boots squeaking on the tiles. A large, opulent Christmas tree blocked the view of Canal Street. She wondered if her mother had been responsible for decorating it this year. She remembered so many years past, when she had come here with her mom on a Saturday and helped dress the tree. Ashley had hung some of her own cheesy handmade ornaments among the expensive balls and lights. Her mother had given them spots of honor.

Ashley walked through the door to the executive office suite.

The suite that housed the CEO, president, and CFO looked much like a hotel lobby. She remembered when the company had moved into this building. Her mother had been irritated at the amount of money spent on the decor. But some designer had really racked up on it.

There was a sitting area on either side of the door, with leather sofas and homey easy chairs clustered around oriental rugs. Lamps created a soft glow around the room, making it look less like a place where deals were made and schemes were laid than a place of comfort and rest.

The walls were painted in a rich jade green, and artwork, which Merritt had picked up on one of his junkets to Paris, graced the walls, illuminated by inset spotlights.

Three doors marked the offices of the men who ran the company, and outside their doors sat their administrative assistants, who did all the real work.

Her mother sat at her desk now, just outside the CEO's door. She was deeply engrossed in whatever filled her computer screen and hadn't seen Ashley come in. She looked as if she'd aged ten years since Ashley had last seen her a week ago. Deep lines seemed etched around her eyes and into her forehead, and she looked as if she hadn't slept in days.

Ashley wondered whether she was responsible for that, or if she could blame it on Icon.

"Hey, Mom," she said.

Debbie Morris looked up, and a smile flickered on her face. "Ashley!" She seemed glad to see her daughter, even though her eyes swept over Ashley with critical dread. She got up and hugged her. "What are you doing here?"

"Just dropped by to say hi."

Her mother's face tightened. Clearly she knew better than that. She glanced toward the closed glass doors of the conference room. Ashley could see people inside. "Honey, I've asked you—begged you—to try to look a little more conservative when you come here."

"I'm not changing my look for a bunch of judgmental snobs. If they don't like the way I look, they can turn their heads." She ran her fingers through her mousse-tousled hair. It stuck up all over, just as she liked it.

Debbie sighed. "It's not a good time for a visit. It's chaos around here, and I'm trying to hold it together."

Ashley picked up a paperweight off of her mother's desk and rolled it around in her hand. "I don't know why you want to hold things together for that crook."

"Ashley!" Her mother took the paperweight back. She looked around, making sure no one had heard. The CFO's assistant seemed to be concentrating on the file on her desk, and the president's assistant was talking on the phone.

"Lower your voice," her mother whispered. "He's right in there with a lawyer who's suing him. Trust me, he's in a firing mood, and no one's job is sacred."

"He wouldn't fire you. You know where all the bodies are buried."

She thought her mother might faint. "Come with me, young lady," she said through her teeth. She grabbed Ashley's hand and started pulling her toward the door.

"What did I do? I need to talk to you. Are you throwing me out?"

Debbie pulled her into the hall and turned to her. She was shaking. "It may not have occurred to you that I need this job, Ashley. There are already plenty of reasons I might lose it without my daughter's mouth getting me fired."

"Sorry," Ashley said, raising her hands innocently. "I didn't know you were so touchy. I was just kidding."

Debbie blew out a heavy breath and started toward the exit sign. "Come with me. I need to get a printer cartridge out of the twenty-ninth-floor stockroom."

Ashley knew her mother just wanted to get her off the floor before she said something else to embarrass her. Amused, she followed her. "I really hate that you're ashamed of me."

"No, you don't. You work too hard at it." Debbie opened the door to the stairwell and started down the steps. Halfway down, she turned and regarded Ashley again. "You're a beautiful girl, Ashley. Why you insist on having things hanging from you and stamped on you—"

"Oh, I forgot to show you this." Ashley stuck out her tongue, revealing the gold stud in the center of it.

Her mother gasped.

Ashley laughed. "Get used to it, Mom. I'm an individual, with my own style."

"No, you're not, honey. You're a clone of those friends of yours. And they're out to destroy you. Making you drop out of school and leave home to live in some kind of commune—"

"Mom, this is not the sixties. Several of us just share a house to help with expenses."

"You're sixteen, Ashley! You should be living at home with me!"

Ashley considered a smart-aleck comeback but then remembered that fifty bucks she needed.

"I didn't come to fight with you, Mom. I came because I got a speeding ticket and if I don't come up with the fifty-dollar fine by this afternoon, they're going to arrest me."

Her mother stopped on the landing and gave her a skeptical look. "Ashley, I'm not giving you money. I told you when you left home that you can't expect me to support you financially. Not until you come back home."

"Fifty bucks, Mom. That's all I need. Come on, please. I make minimum wage. I didn't count on a stinking speeding ticket this month. Do you want me to go to jail?"

Debbie opened the door onto the twenty-ninth floor. The light caught a tear in her eyes.

"Well, do you?" Ashley demanded.

"No, I don't want you to go to jail. I don't think they put people in jail for speeding tickets."

"They do if you don't pay your fine."

"All right, Ashley. Let me get the cartridge I need, and when I get back to my office, I'll write a check to the municipal court."

Ashley might have known her mother would pull that. "Mom, they don't take checks. I need cash."

Her mother wasn't buying. "You're not using this to buy drugs, are you? I want to see that ticket."

Ashley grunted. "Well, it's not like I carry it around with me."

"Then I'm not giving you a dime."

Ashley rolled her eyes and followed her mother toward the stockroom. Her mother had read too many books about tough love and parenting prodigals. Some author who probably didn't even have kids was dictating their relationship now. Ashley resented it.

"What do I have to do to convince you that I'm not a drug addict?"

Debbie reached the stockroom door and turned back to her. "Come home. Move back in and go back to school."

"Mom, come on."

Her mother opened the door. "Ashley, I'll give you the fifty dollars if you'll come home tonight."

Ashley could agree to that. She didn't have to follow through. "It's a deal."

"Don't lie to me, Ashley."

"Mom, come on. I'm in a hurry."

Her mother flicked on the light . . . and gasped.

A crude machine sat at the center of the floor, surrounded by ten-gallon watercooler jugs. Wires ran from the contraption to a digital clock on the floor next to it.

"Whoa, what's this?" Ashley asked. "Is that a bomb?"

Her mother froze. "Ashley, get out of here. Take the stairs and get out of the building."

"It is a bomb!" Ashley just stood there, staring as if it were a joke.

"Leave!" Debbie reached for the phone on the wall. "Ashley, get out!"

Ashley knew she wasn't kidding. "Mom, you have to come, too."

"I will," her mother cried, punching numbers into the phone, "but I have to tell security so they can evacuate the building! Go! I'll be right behind you!"

The numbers on the digital clock changed, second by second. . . .

"Answer the phone!" Debbie cried, her back to Ashley. "For heaven's sake, pick it up!" She turned and saw Ashley still standing there. "Ashley, for once in your life will you do what I tell you?" she screamed.

Ashley took off. She burst through the exit door and started down the stairs. Twenty-nine floors. What if the bomb went off before she could get out? What if her mother didn't make it before it exploded?

She thought of the Twin Towers and the Pentagon. And she began to take the stairs two at a time.

Chapter Two

● ● ●

Donald Merritt fit his reputation.

Jill Clark Nichols had hoped that the rumors she'd heard about him weren't true. After all, it took brains and integrity to build a business from the ground up and make it the fifth-largest communications company in the world. But whatever integrity he had begun with had long since been bartered away.

His good-ol'-boy charm wore thin when coupled with his condescension. Ever since she'd arrived to take his deposition this morning, he had treated her as if she were some country-bumpkin attorney who'd cheated her way through the bar exam. Not a good attitude when she represented twenty-five former employees and shareholders who'd filed a civil suit for a long list of fraudulent bookkeeping schemes. Any day now, the Grand Jury was likely to indict him, and the Securities and Exchange Commission was expected to file civil fraud charges sometime this week.

Jill didn't intend to let her clients down.

"Mr. Merritt," she said, glancing at Wanda, the court transcriber she'd brought with her, making sure the woman wasn't missing anything. "On the morning of April thirtieth of this year, you held a stockholders' meeting, did you not?"

He flipped through his day planner. "Yep. That's right."

"And in that meeting, isn't it true that you misrepresented company earnings for the previous fiscal period?"

"Mrs. Clark—"

"Nichols," she said. "My name is Nichols."

"Of course. A fireman's wife." He stretched his legs out in front of him, crossing his cowboy boots at the ankles. Folding his arms over his chest, he laughed. "Why do they need a paid fire department in a podunk town like Newpointe, anyway? Looks to me like a waste of taxpayers' money. What did you say your husband's name is?"

Jill wasn't biting. "I didn't say. Mr. Merritt," she said, passing him a copy of the minutes of that shareholders' meeting, "I'd like you to turn to page eight of these minutes and read aloud the earnings figures you gave to the stockholders on that day."

He cleared his throat and shifted in his chair, and his lawyers leaned in with him to find the passage in question.

He had lied that day, and she had audit reports to prove it.

"Mr. Merritt, we're waiting. Please read the section I've marked."

A shrill, piercing sound blared overhead, startling her. Her transcriber jumped to her feet.

"Is that a fire alarm?" Jill asked.

"Yeah," Merritt said in that lazy drawl of his. "Bad timing, huh? Guess we'd better get outta here."

Jill didn't stand. The man was slick. She had to hand it to him. He had probably told someone to sound the alarm at exactly 10:20 A.M., right about the time Jill would be asking the tough questions.

"Should we go?" Wanda asked, already starting to load her transcribing machine into its case.

Jill touched her hand, signaling for her to stay put.

One of the lawyers got up and went to the window. "No sign of smoke."

"Probably a drill," Merritt said, stretching up out of his slump. "But you can never be sure. Guess we oughta go."

Jill looked through the conference room's glass doors into the reception area. She could see two women getting up from their desks, looking around as if trying to decide what to do.

The phone on the table buzzed, and Merritt snatched it up. "Merritt. Yeah." He stood up. "The stockroom? That's right below us. Yeah, we're going."

Merritt hung up the phone, his face suddenly serious. "Bomb threat. We have to get out." He pointed through the doors. "Head for one of the exits. Don't take the elevators."

Jill was still skeptical, but she didn't wait for further instructions. She grabbed her briefcase and pushed through the glass doors. The two administrative assistants still in the office held the doors for them, and Jill let Wanda pass her to head for the exit.

"Leave everything!" Merritt called out. "Just go! Hurry up! Down the stairwells. Now!"

His voice sounded panicked. Jill was not inclined to trust him. Still, his face had changed with that phone call. He'd said something about the stockroom. Did that mean they'd actually found a bomb?

She headed for the north exit, behind a few others who'd come from offices across the hall. Merritt and the others rushed for the other one on the south side of the building. As she stepped through the exit door, she heard hundreds of feet filling the stairwell beneath her, people laughing nervously and chattering as they descended. There was no panic, and no particular rush.

No one seemed to be taking the alarm all that seriously. Yes, Merritt had probably set the whole thing up. If that was the case, she would make him pay.

It probably wouldn't take too much digging to find out who'd sounded the alarm and why.

She reached the twenty-seventh floor, then the twenty-sixth.

Thoughts of how she could prove it raced through her mind. Maybe she should go back up right now and check the twenty-ninth-floor stockroom. She paused and turned back. . . .

An explosion above her shook the building.

With a searing whoosh, it lifted her off her feet and slammed her into the wall. She dropped her briefcase and tried to cover her head, but the stairs beneath her crumbled, and she fell with them, grabbing and clawing until she hit solid footing.

She heard screaming above her.

She tried to think. A bomb had gone off. People were hurt.

She looked up and saw fire crackling like a taunting monster, its sound like sheets being shaken in the wind. Smoke was thickening the air, filling the stairwell, choking her. She heard a crack, and a flaming ceiling tile dropped down next to her, almost hitting her.

Jill forced herself to her feet. Beneath the debris, it looked as if the stairs below her still held. She didn't know what floor she had fallen to, but she doubted that anyone behind her had survived.

She started down, pulling the neck of her blouse up over her nose, trying to get as far from the smoke and flames as she could. She caught up with those below her. They all looked shell-shocked and glassy-eyed, desperate to make their way down.

Suddenly, a girl came running up, against the flow of traffic, fighting the people in her way.

"Mom! Mom!" Terror undulated on her voice. *"Mama!"*

Jill caught the girl to keep her from going higher. "Honey, you can't go up there. There was an explosion."

The girl tried to wrestle herself free. "My mother's up there! I don't think she got down! I have to go after her!"

"No. There's fire and the ceiling's caving in. The stairs have collapsed. You have to go down. We have to get out."

The girl broke free and kept going up, until she reached the wall of smoldering debris. She started to cough.

Jill looked down, torn between saving herself and going back up to stop the girl. Finally, she turned. "Honey, please! Come with me."

"I have to find her!" the girl sobbed. *"Mama!"*

The terrified scream tore through the stairwell, reverberating off every surface, vibrating in Jill's chest. She reached for the girl. "Honey, come with me, please. We have to get down. It's dangerous here."

"I don't care!"

"Maybe your mother went down the other stairwell," Jill cried.

The girl looked down at her now, hope seeping back into her smoke-stained face.

"Come on, sweetheart. We'll look for her at the bottom."

Still sobbing, the girl nodded and started down. They made it down two more flights and caught up to the others on the stairwell. Thousands of employees were trying to evacuate, glutting the small space.

A man sat on the steps, bottlenecking the traffic. People yelled for him to move, but he didn't get up. When Jill reached him, she bent down. "Sir, are you all right?"

He shook his head. "My leg. I can't get up."

"You have to. Come on, I'll help you. Hurry!"

He tried to stand, but she saw the pain on his face. "Go around me," he said. "It's okay. I'm going to slow you down."

"No. You can do it." She slipped her shoulder under his arm and tried to lift him. "Here, lean on me."

"No," he said, "just go. It's okay."

"I'm not leaving you!" she shouted. "Now get up and lean on me!"

He got up and did as he was told. She put her shoulder under his armpit on the side where he'd hurt his leg and tried to help him walk.

How would she get him down alone?

Then the sobbing girl turned and looked up at them. Wiping her face, she came and slipped her shoulder under his other arm.

"Thank you, honey," Jill said. "We can do this."

For the first time Jill noticed the girl's multiple piercings and tattoos. Tears streaked the smoke soot on her face.

The man winced with pain as they pulled him with them.

"Between the two of us you're going to get out of here," she said.

He looked behind him, as if the flames pursued them.

"Don't look back," Jill said. "Look down and let's move as fast as we can. My name's Jill Nichols. What's yours?"

"Gordon Webster," he grunted.

Jill looked at the girl. "And yours?"

"Ashley Morris."

"Okay," Jill said. The air was getting thick with smoke, and she was starting to feel dizzy. "Gordon, I know it hurts, but we've got to move faster."

Her pep talk seemed to work. He tried to help.

But the stairwell grew even more crowded, and wailing people tried to make their way down with breakneck speed. With all her might she tried to support the man's weight.

"It's no use," he said. "I can't make it."

"Of course you can," Jill said. "Come on, Gordon, we can do this! You don't want to die in this building."

They were practically dragging him down the stairs, and she looked at the girl and wondered if she should tell her to leave them and go. At this pace, all three of them could die here, if the top floors began to collapse further. Ashley started to cough, and Jill longed for clean air.

She concentrated with all her might on getting down, one step at a time.

She wondered what floor they were on now. She couldn't have fallen more than one or two flights, and she'd come down two or three flights since the explosion. That would put her somewhere around the twenty-first floor, maybe. Then she saw the number *18* on the door of one of the landings and started to count again. They reached the seventeenth, the sixteenth . . . and an urgent prayer ran through her mind. *Lord, please save us. Don't let us die in this building.*

Chapter Three

• • •

Ray Ford heard the yelling from his office at Newpointe's Midtown Fire Station and went to his door. Several of his firefighters stood at the entrance of the TV room, watching a news report.

"Somebody call me?" he asked.

"Chief, you gotta see this!" George Broussard called out. "They got a fire at Icon. Sayin' it was a bomb."

Ray pushed through his men and turned up the volume. The cameras were fixed on the upper floors of the New Orleans corporation. Smoke and flames billowed out in red and black fury, engulfing at least the top five floors. There would be massive casualties, he thought. Maybe even hundreds killed.

"You think it'll be a five alarm, Chief?" George asked.

"Could be." Only forty minutes from New Orleans, Newpointe was among the departments expected to respond in a five-alarm emergency. There hadn't been one since the protocol had been set up, but after September 11, big cities across the country had prepared for catastrophic disasters.

He went to a telephone, dialed the number for the New Orleans chief. The line was busy.

The second he hung up, it rang. George, who had house watch duty, grabbed it up. "Midtown."

Ray looked at him, waiting.

"Will do." George hung up. "Five alarm. They need every ladder and engine in the area. Ambulances too."

Organized chaos followed as the men pulled on their turnout gear.

"Terrorists," Cale Larkin said. "Gotta be terrorists."

"Get every available tank and mask," Ray shouted. "And I'm calling in everybody we've got. Let's go!"

• • •

Painting someone else's business wasn't exactly the way Dan Nichols would have chosen to spend his day off from the fire department. But Mark Branning was his best friend in the department, and he and Allie had been desperately trying to sell the Blooms 'n' Blossoms. A potential buyer was coming from Lafayette to look at the place tomorrow, and the front room needed a coat of paint. Mark had asked Dan for help in getting it done.

Ordinarily, Dan would have spent the day hunting or fishing or hiking through one of the wildlife refuges outside of town. Or he would have hit the road and run seven miles instead of his usual five. He might have gone to the gym and picked up a game of basketball. Then he would have taken his wife to lunch. He knew Jill would have a lot to talk about when she finished deposing Donald Merritt.

But this was probably going to take all day.

"I really appreciate this, buddy," Mark said as he rolled the wall opposite him. "It's above the call of duty."

"Yeah, well. You owe me." Dan glanced back to see how much Mark had gotten done. He had already covered half the wall. Dan rolled faster.

Justin, Mark and Allie's three-year-old son, picked up a brush and slopped it into Dan's paint tray.

"Justin, what am I gonna do with you?" He threw his arm around Justin's waist and lifted him out of harm's way.

"I wanna help!" The brush dripped from the child's hand, pale yellow. Not a color that Dan would have chosen.

Mark took Justin from him and carried him like a sack of flour. "Allie, he's dripping paint on the floor. Quick. Grab a wet rag."

"Justin!" Abandoning the wreath that she was putting together for a funeral, Allie came into the front room and kissed his exposed round belly, eliciting screaming giggles. Mark set him down.

"You can't help Daddy paint right now," she said. "I told you, you need to stay in here with me."

"I can do it!" Justin cried. "I paint good."

"But the Wiggles are on. Don't you want to watch?"

Distracted, Justin settled down.

"I think we should let him help," Dan offered on a chuckle. "He can have my roller."

"That could be dangerous." Mark went back to his paint. Dan's competitive nature kicked in again, and he began to roll as if his time was running out.

In the other room, Justin's whining had turned to giggles.

The sound of a child's laughter was music to Dan. He couldn't wait to have one of his own. He and Jill had been praying for pregnancy for the last few months, but it hadn't happened yet. When they'd first married, he'd wondered if he even had it in him to be a good father. Since his own parents had practically abandoned him to a series of nannies paid to love him, he'd had no real parental models.

That is, until Mark and Allie had shown him how easy it was to love a child.

Even though their lives seemed to revolve around that little bundle of energy, they were happier than he'd ever seen them.

Instead of hiring sitters or slapping him in day care, they dreamed of selling the flower shop so Allie could stay home full-time with Justin. But there were no buyers. She had to keep the business viable and profitable if she had any hope of selling it, so she came to work every day, bringing Justin with her, and spent more time pulling him out of trouble than she did making the floral arrangements that kept her afloat.

He heard the volume come up on the television that played softly in the background most of the day, and suddenly Allie called out, "Oh, no! Mark, come here! Hurry!"

Dan rolled faster. He had the advantage now.

Mark went into the other room, then cried out, "Dan, get in here!"

Something was wrong. Dan put the paint roller back into its tray and went into the other room.

"What's going on?" Then he saw, on the TV screen, the Icon International Building with flames shooting out the roof and clouds of black smoke billowing out the blown-out walls on the top few floors.

"Some kind of explosion," Mark said.

The sight paralyzed Dan. He stared at the screen as his heart slammed against his chest. *Jill!* She had gone there this morning!

He clutched the wall and searched around for the phone. Where did they keep it? He'd been in here a million times. Finally he remembered the cell phone he kept on his hip, and he pulled it off its belt clip and dialed Jill's cell phone. It rang.

"Where was she?" Allie asked him. "What floor?"

Jill wasn't answering. "The top one," he said.

It kept ringing. Allie went into Mark's arms, and they stared at him in horror, waiting.

Finally, he hung up and dialed her office. Maybe she hadn't gone. Maybe there was traffic, or the meeting had been cancelled.

"Hello!" Her secretary shouted the greeting.

"Sheila, this is Dan."

"Oh, Dan, it's terrible, isn't it? Just terrible."

"Sheila, tell me where Jill is. Was she in that building?"

"Yes!" Sheila cried. "She was on the top floor. That's where the meeting was at ten o'clock, and they're saying the bomb went off at ten-twenty."

He fell back against the wall and cut the phone off. Mark and Allie stared at him. Justin had suddenly gone quiet, as if he sensed the terror building in the room.

"I've got to get to her."

Mark let Allie go. "Let's go to the fire station, buddy," he said. "We can get information there."

Dan didn't answer. He rushed out of the flower shop and sprinted as fast as he could the two blocks to the Midtown fire station, with Mark on his heels.

··· ···

Nick Foster and his wife, Issie, had arranged their schedule so that they both could be off today. The firefighter and paramedic sat in Nick's pastoral office at the Calvary Bible Church, sifting through paperwork that he had been putting off for weeks. Issie had never been a secretary and did not want to be one now, but she figured her EMT skills came in handy for the paperwork triage that would free her husband from some of his responsibilities. It was tough being the wife of a bivocational pastor, but she had to say that the worst of the days since she had married him had been better than any of the days before.

"So where's the prayer request clipboard?" she said. "Lisa Manning had a request that came in Sunday."

Nick reached for the clipboard hanging on his wall and tossed it across the desk to her. The radio station he listened to that played Christian music twenty-four hours a day crackled, then beeped as a news alert broke in.

"Ladies and gentlemen, we have a news bulletin from Canal Street in New Orleans," the disc jockey said. "It seems that an explosion occurred at ten-twenty this morning at the Icon

International Building. The bomb seems to have originated on one of the top floors in the thirty-story building. It is not yet known how many people were killed or even if they have been able to evacuate the entire building, but we would ask that our listening audience please pray for the people in that building and the rescue workers trying to get them out."

Nick stopped what he was doing and looked up at Issie. She was staring at the radio as if she could see the announcer. "Nick, we've got to go help," Issie said.

Nick nodded. "You read my mind."

Together they bolted out of the office and headed for their car.

··· ···

Dan and Mark were just getting to the Midtown station as Nick and Issie drove up. The whole shift was throwing on turnout gear, and the trucks were already idling. Dan didn't wait for orders. He grabbed his own gear and started pulling it on.

"Five alarms!" Ray said. "I'm calling everybody in!"

Mark and Nick grabbed their gear and jumped into the truck, and as it started moving out of the bay, Dan climbed in. Issie got into the rescue unit that sped off in front of them.

Dan wiped the sweat from his forehead. Even in the cool of December the air seemed sweltering. He pulled his cell phone out and dialed Jill's phone again. Still no answer.

"It's going to be all right, man," Mark said.

Dan gritted his teeth. "She was on the top floor. Ray, where was the explosion, exactly?"

Ray shook his head. "I don't know, Dan."

Dan kept the phone to his ear as a sick feeling swirled in his stomach. He thought of Jill trapped above that fire, helpless to escape. *Please, God . . .*

Nick patted his knee and began to pray out loud. "Lord, you know where Jill is. Protect her. Put her in a bubble. Help her to get out of that building. We're gonna need a ton of miracles today. One for every person in that place."

The phone kept ringing, ringing, ringing. Either she didn't have her briefcase with her, or she wasn't able to answer it. "Oh, God, don't let anything happen to her."

The siren on the truck almost drowned out the ringing, but Dan didn't give up.

· · ·

Ray talked into his own cell phone as they crossed Lake Pontchartrain heading for the South Shore. NOFD had set up a command post in the lobby, he learned, and dozens of firefighters had already started up by foot, carrying at least sixty pounds of gear each in hopes of attacking the fire.

As they hit Interstate 10 heading into the city, they could see the black plume of smoke marking the tragic spot.

He wondered if any survivors had made it to the roof. Was a helicopter rescue possible, or were the flames too high? With all the black smoke he could see around the top of the building, was there any source of fresh air?

Ray looked behind him at the men straining to see. "I was told that the building's standpipe system should be working, so there should be a water source on the upper floors. But the elevators are dead. There's a north wind, so we have to watch the buildings south of Icon. We're looking at an inverted burn. We're not sure how far down it's gotten yet."

"Did they evacuate before the explosion, Ray?" Dan yelled up to him. "Were there people on those floors?"

Ray wished he had good news for his friend. "They don't know, Dan. They believe there were people trapped."

· · ·

The closer the Newpointe truck got to Canal Street, the more glutted traffic became. Panic had broken out in the streets. Sirens blared and horns honked as other emergency vehicles from neighboring towns tried to thread through the bumper-to-bumper cars. The traffic lights weren't working, and uniformed police stood directing traffic and trying to help the emergency vehicles through.

"Looks like the power's down in the whole area," Ray said.

Dan hung on as George drove the cumbersome truck around a corner.

The smell of smoke hit him before he could even see the building. Still blocks away, people with soot-covered faces ran toward them as if getting as far from the inferno as they could. As the truck flew past, he saw two women collapse on the sidewalk in fits of coughing. Maybe Jill had gotten out too. Maybe she walked among the refugees, out of harm's way.

"Looks bad," Ray said as the fire came into view.

Dan leaned over to see out the opposite window. The smoke was thicker here, blurring their view, but he could see the raging fire engulfing the top floors. Flaming debris fell through the air, threatening anyone on the ground.

The gravity of the situation hit him. Just being on the same block could prove deadly. No one would be safe, least of all the firefighters heading into the fray.

As they turned onto Canal Street, he saw that the road had been cleared. Only emergency vehicles were allowed through. Blue and red lights flashed all around them, and the smell of exhaust from the enormous vehicles mingled with the smoke.

People still poured from the building—some burned, others bleeding, all gasping for breath. These would be the ones from the upper floors, he imagined.

He thought of jumping out, grabbing one of them, and demanding to know what floor they'd come from and whether they'd had an evacuation alarm before the bomb went off. If they had, maybe Jill had survived.

Lord, please help me find her.

"We're reporting to Battalion Chief Breaux," Ray yelled as the truck came to a stop. "His command post is in the lobby."

Dan leaped off the truck, got his gear, and headed inside. He found the command post in a corner of the lobby that looked spit-polished and untouched. From here, you would never know that tragedy devoured the top floors.

He got his orders, then headed up the south stairwell. The evacuees came down single file, leaving the right side for the firefighters going up. Lugging a hose, a pickax, and an extra tank, he scaled the stairs, checking each face he passed for his wife.

Chapter Four

● ● ●

Jill was almost to the fifteenth floor when the second blast shook the building. It came from somewhere below them, shaking the stairs beneath them and knocking them off their feet. She lost her hold on Gordon and he tumbled down several steps.

Ashley's screams echoed Jill's, and she reached for the girl and tried to cover her as the stairwell wall just below them caved in, covering the stairs. Gordon hunkered against the wall that hadn't crumbled, his arms shielding his head.

"Come on," Jill cried. "Everybody up!"

"Where we gonna go?" Ashley screamed. "We're trapped. We can't get through!"

Jill smelled the gas fumes rippling on the heat. She looked back up the way they had come. The flames were eating the floors one by one, and soon, the new fire from the second explosion would begin to climb. She didn't want to be sitting here when the two forces met.

Maybe the stairs beneath them hadn't collapsed. She hadn't felt the floor fall away. If they were still intact, maybe getting down was just a question of clearing the rubble out of their way.

But the fallen wall had blocked their way, and she knew they might not have time to dig their way through. No, going back up was the only answer. But how far would they get before they encountered those licking flames? And how would they drag Gordon up? It had been hard enough when they'd been going down.

She regarded the older man, whose face twisted in pain. He was breathing heavily and rasping asthmatically. Black soot stained his face just below his nose and around his mouth from breathing the smoke. Ashley's face was streaked as well. Jill supposed that she looked the same.

"Come on, Gordon," she said. "Get up. I don't know where we're going, but I know we have to move."

Gordon gritted his teeth against the pain and tried to get up. "The other side," he grunted. "If we go up to the next landing and go across to the other stairwell, it may be open."

She had forgotten the other stairwell. Maybe it hadn't been affected. Maybe it was still clear all the way down.

They hoisted him up again, taking the stairs up one at a time. Finally, they reached the next landing and touched the reentry door. It wasn't hot, so Jill pushed it open. The floor was smoky but provided clear passage to the south stairwell. Gordon slowed them, but they dragged him mercilessly despite his pain.

Gordon was struggling for breath when they reached the exit door on the south side. Before testing the door, Jill let him go and quickly shrugged out of her blazer.

"Here, this can filter out the smoke." She tied the arms around the back of his head.

He fought her. "No, use it for yourself or the girl."

"Don't argue with me!" she shouted. "There's no time." He allowed her to secure the blazer around his face, but veins popped out on his forehead as pain racked through him.

"Leave me," he said, his voice muffled through the cloth. "I can't make it. There could be another bomb. You have to get out of here as fast as you can."

"I will not leave you!" she shouted. "Don't you understand there's fire above and below us? You can't stay."

Ashley started to cough. She let Gordon go and doubled over.

"Pull your shirt up over your mouth," Jill said, doing the same.

"You don't have much time before it spreads this way," Gordon said. "I'm slowing you down."

"Come on, Ashley!" Jill shouted. "Let's get him down." She tested the exit door into the south stairwell. It wasn't hot, so she flung it open. The stairwell looked clear. Could it be that the bomb had only hit the other side of the building?

Maybe they would make it down, after all.

They managed to get Gordon down one flight, then two, when she heard something crashing behind her. She looked up and saw the flames licking through the wall.

She had never felt more helpless.

The closer they got to the tenth floor, the louder the screams grew. There were people trapped on that floor, but she couldn't see them and didn't know where to look for them.

Please, God. Help them.

The building felt unstable. She could hear crashing and flames crackling, and she felt the shiver of the stairwell as if it might fall out from under her.

We're going to die. The thought came to her suddenly, unbidden, and as she dragged Gordon down the stairs, she felt an overwhelming sense of sorrow.

I never got to be a mother.

She remembered herself and Allie, years ago, talking about Jesus' return, and she'd stupidly said that she hoped he didn't come back until she'd had the chance to be a mother. Allie had laughed and told her that she suspected heaven would be better than motherhood and that she doubted she would even remember not having that family when she stood in the presence of God.

Maybe so. And if she were a more mature Christian, she should look forward to the end of her earthly life. As Paul had said, "To be absent in the flesh is to be present with the Lord." But she wasn't there yet. She and Dan had so many plans. She wanted to see the look in his eye when he held his baby for the first time. She wanted to know what it was like to nurse a child. She wanted to change diapers and potty train and videotape that first day of kindergarten.

Was that dream dead now? Just an arrogant human plan that had nothing to do with God's purpose?

Ashley started coughing again, so they had to pause for a moment. The heat was more intense here, and she had the sense that they were approaching more fallout. Despair seeped through her, and she thought of giving up, sitting down on these stairs, and letting the end overtake her.

She didn't know what floor they were on or how far they had to go.

"Come on, Ashley," she said over the girl's coughing. "We have to keep moving, sweetheart."

Ashley managed to stop hacking and began pulling her weight again.

Then she heard footsteps, and her heart leaped. They had caught up to other survivors! And they were still moving, which might mean that the stairwell was clear—that they could get out this way.

Except that the footsteps seemed to be getting louder, as if they were coming toward them, instead of moving away.

As they reached the next landing, she heard a man's voice yelling to someone else. "Check all of the offices as you reach each floor. Make sure nobody's left!"

"We're here!" she shouted. "There are three of us! Is the stairwell clear?"

"It's clear!" a voice yelled. She heard someone running up toward them—and then she saw him. A firefighter, loaded down with gear, wearing a mask and oxygen tank.

Relief assaulted her, and she started to cry. If firefighters had made it this far up, she knew they would get out.

"This man is injured!" she cried. "Please, can you help us get him out?"

The firefighter came the last few steps and took Gordon from her. "Need help up here!" he yelled back down the stairs. "Got an injured man!"

Ashley started coughing again, and he nodded toward the girl. "You two get out of here now. We'll take care of him."

"We'll see you outside, Gordon," Jill cried behind her as she took Ashley's arm and started down the stairs.

The old man only nodded and waved.

Chapter Five

● ● ●

"What floor are we on?" Ashley's words came between fits of coughing.

"Four, I think." They ran down, side by side. "We're going to get out. I can feel it."

They turned on the landing. Two firefighters had just entered the stairwell, carrying a man in a wheelchair. They blocked the way, making it impossible for Jill and Ashley to get by.

She thought of yelling for them to move, but then she heard the man's asthmatic wheezing and realized he had probably been left there, terrified, as everyone else got out. She slowed down and put her arm around Ashley.

Ashley was trembling all over. Jill thought of the girl's mother and prayed that she would be waiting outside for her. But she feared the worst. If her mother had been on one of the upper floors, it was doubtful that she had survived.

The firefighters carried the man rapidly, but they stopped on each landing to let more firemen pass them on the way up.

Finally, they reached the first floor. They burst out of the stairwell, past the firefighters carrying the wheelchair, and into the lobby. Daylight broke through the smoky air. Ashley coughed and gagged as Jill pulled her along beside her.

She ran across the lobby, keeping the neck of her shirt up over her nose. Except for the haze of smoke, the lobby looked as clean and inviting as it had when she'd arrived this morning. One would never know that just a few floors up people were dying.

Rescue workers had set up a command post on one corner of the floor, and a stream of firefighters in bunker gear headed for the stairwells to search for stragglers.

Ashley stopped coughing as the front door came into view, and together they headed for it. Bursting outside, they both gasped for air.

She could hear the flames above her now, and she looked up. The top seven floors were engulfed in flames, and more smoke poured from a hole around the tenth, where the second explosion had occurred.

Debris fell like bombs around them, crashing on the pavement. She didn't know which direction to run.

The south side of the building looked safer, so she headed toward it, pulling Ashley. Emergency vehicles blocked the street, and firefighters just getting to the scene leaped out of their trucks and headed toward the door she had just come out.

Half a block from the building, she looked back to see if they were out of harm's way. Debris dropped closer to the flaming structure, but not near them. "I think we can slow down now," she said.

Ashley started coughing again. Jill bent over and tried to clear her own lungs.

She looked around, trying to determine where they should go. Maybe an ambulance somewhere was providing water or oxygen. She pulled Ashley toward the vehicles. She passed a fire truck from Slidell, one from Mandeville—

And then she stopped cold. She saw two Newpointe trucks.

Her heart tripped as she turned back toward the building and wondered how many of her friends had gone in. Thank God Dan was off today.

Or was he? She'd never known Dan to miss a big fire. He would have gone to the station as soon as he'd heard.

Besides, he would have been worried about her. He would have come just to make sure—

She ran between the idling trucks and saw Marty Bledsoe changing tanks. Ashley followed her, still hacking the soot from her lungs. "Marty!"

He turned around and looked surprised to see her. "Jill, you're okay!" He looked hard at Ashley. "She needs oxygen. Here, take this. Sit down, honey."

Ashley sat down on the truck's bumper and took the mask.

Jill started to cough again, but she wasn't going to take Ashley's tank. "Where's Dan, Marty?" she choked. "Did he come with you?"

"Yeah, Dan's here," he said. "He went up to help the evacuation."

Dread almost knocked her down. She looked back at the building. Already it swayed, as if it might fall down. One more bomb, another crumbling wall, flames eating through a floor, could bring it all down.

And when it did, it would bring Dan down with it.

Chapter Six

● ● ●

It was slow going. Sweltering heat battled with the black smoke pouring through the stairwells as Dan climbed higher. Breathing through his mask, he stopped for a moment to shrug his tank off, then slipped out of his turnout coat. He tied it around his waist and pulled the tank back on.

He was still too hot. The fire was spreading so quickly that there was no escape from it, and the farther up he went, the hotter it got.

Around the eighth floor, he'd encountered vicious flames and a pile of debris in the south stairwell, and he'd had to cross to the north stairwell. He hoped that when they got as high as they could go the standpipe system would still be working.

On the radio snapped to his belt, he could hear the broken transmissions from those who'd gotten to the upper floors.

"Twentieth is as high as we can get."

"Anybody ... higher?"

"No way. Top ten ... fully involved."

"Any injured ... ?"

"Haven't found any.... Looks like the floor was evacuated in time."

Dan wiped the sweat from his forehead and kept going as possibilities raced through his mind. If an alarm had sounded before the first blast, then those on the top floors might have made it down several flights before the bomb went off. Jill could be outside even now, trying to get to a phone.

"Chief Breaux here." The voice sounded distant and broken. The radios didn't work all that well in high-rises. Fire departments all over the state had lobbied for better equipment, but so far the bureaucracy hadn't coughed up the money. "What side of the building are you on?"

Crackling lingered for a moment. "North side, Chief."

". . . top twelve floors of the north side are involved . . . guys need to get out of there . . . down and sweep the floors for survivors as you go."

The men in front of Dan paused, as if trying to decide whether to keep climbing. Sweat poured from their faces. The guy directly in front of him was about thirty pounds overweight and looked as if he would need rescue himself if he climbed another flight.

Dan tried to get around him.

"I want to know who's on each floor . . . how many injured are being brought down," Breaux said. "Give me a roll call. Who's on nineteen?"

"Miller and Jackson. We're the only ones, heading down."

"How about eighteen?"

Dan kept climbing. He had reached sixteen when he encountered six guys heading down.

One of them stopped him. "Wrong way," he said. "Chief said to head down."

"I heard the transmission." Dan wasn't daunted. "I have to get up there anyway."

"Hey, son. Breaux's in charge here and he meant what he said."

Dan looked past him and adjusted the hose he carried on his shoulder. The guy was slowing him down. "Look, my wife was on the top floor. If there's any chance she's there—"

"We got injured!" One of the New Orleans guys burst through the reentry door. "Need help in here!"

Dan couldn't ignore the call. He glanced up the stairs one last time, then headed onto the floor. A ceiling on the north side had caved into one of the offices and a wall had collapsed. Several people lay trapped. Some were dead.

Dan went to a woman who lay on the floor. "Please, help me," she coughed. "I think my leg is broken."

The break was visible. She would have to be carried. Several more men were coming onto the floor. "Grab a chair," he shouted to one of them. "Help me get her down."

The firefighter, who wore a NOFD T-shirt under his open turnout coat, grabbed a rolling secretarial chair with sturdy arms. The two of them lifted her into it.

"Hold on, now," Dan said. "Try to stay in the chair and we'll get you down."

The woman was sobbing. "I should have gotten out earlier, but I thought I had time. I had to back up some of my data. How could I be so stupid?"

"Calm down, ma'am. You'll be okay."

They each grabbed an arm of her chair and carried her to the stairwell. Other firefighters on the way up turned sideways to let them down.

Dan thought of handing her over to someone else, but there were other injured. And even if he traded places with one of the other guys, he wasn't likely to make it much higher.

Oh, God, please let Jill be safe.

The woman in the chair began to cough, and he handed her the extra tank he had on his back, helping her breathe. "You'll be all right, ma'am. We're going to get you out of here."

They got her to the ninth floor, the eighth, the seventh ...

A blast shook the building, knocking the chair out of his hands. The woman went flying, and Dan dove for her. She hit the next landing and lay unconscious where she'd fallen. Blood ran through her hair.

Dan yelled for help, but all was chaos behind him.

"Evacuate immediately!" the radio voice shouted. "Evacuate! Evacuate! Get out of the building now!"

The floor began to sway, like some trick foundation in a carnival horror house. Cement rained from the ceiling above him. He tried to cover the woman with his body. Debris knocked against his helmet, hammered into his back . . .

He heard a rumbling thunder that seemed to pick up volume and velocity, and the building trembled like a shed in a hurricane.

"It's coming down!" someone shouted.

The thundering grew louder. He pulled the woman up onto his back and started down the next flight.

The wall next to him began to crack . . .

And the stairs crumbled beneath his feet.

He dropped her and fell forward, cement and steel shattering like thin ice beneath his feet. Rock and metal battered him, buried him, crushed him beneath its angry weight.

I'm going to die.

It was his last thought before the world went black.

Chapter Seven

● ● ●

It's going to fall!" Ashley's scream turned Jill to the building, and she saw it swaying.

The top floors began to collapse in on themselves. For Jill, it was her life coming down, her hopes and her dreams, every plan she'd ever made. Dan was in that building.

She screamed.

Ashley grabbed Jill's arm. "Run!"

In the split second between paralysis and action, Jill made the decision to live. She would not stand here and be buried alive, and she would not let this girl die.

She took Ashley's hand and ran. A stampede of other evacuees scattered in all directions. She heard a violent tornado sound behind her, popping her ears and burying her screams.

Debris crashed in their path. A wind of heat whooshed through them, then swallowed them in a mushroom of smoke and ash as it sucked the oxygen from the air.

She couldn't breathe, couldn't cough, couldn't speak . . .

She shoved Ashley under a car, covered her with her own body. Sheltering her head with her arms, she waited for it to end, the awful train-rumble and the tsunami wind, the horror of smoke and dust running them over, suffocating them, blanketing them.

In the eye of her terror, she once again cried out to God for help.

Chapter Eight

● ● ●

Forty minutes away at the Blooms 'n' Blossoms in Newpointe, Allie watched the television with horror as the third bomb exploded.

"They're telling us to get away from the building!" the reporter on-site shouted. The camera shook as it followed him away from the scene.

The screen shifted to a broader view and an instant replay of the explosion. "Looks like this one came from one of the bottom floors," the anchor said, clearly excited. "This does not look good for the evacuees or for the firefighters already in the building. Bill, tell us what you're seeing."

Allie slapped her hand over her mouth and cried out. Was Mark in the building? Had Newpointe even gotten there yet?

"Mommy?"

Her child's face looked tentative and frightened, and his bottom lip quivered as he started to cry. She was scaring him.

She picked him up and turned back to the screen.

The screen went black, then switched to a wider angle, filmed from a helicopter. The building was falling into itself, shrinking floor by floor as a brown cloud replaced the concrete and metal. It seemed to move in slow motion, erasing everything in its path.

"Oh, God, no!" Allie cried. Justin started to scream.

"It's okay, honey!" She was trembling, trying not to drop him. "Mommy's going to close the store, and we're going to run down to the fire department and make sure Daddy's okay."

She hoped Justin didn't understand. Her heart slammed against her chest, beating out a warning rhythm. *The building is down. Firefighters are dead.*

It couldn't be. Newpointe was probably stuck in a traffic jam, unable to get through. Mark was probably sitting in the truck, watching the whole thing from a distance.

God, please get him out of harm's way!

Quickly, she turned off the set, locked the door, and took off on foot the two blocks to the fire department from which her husband had left over an hour ago.

He had called her from his cell phone on the way out of town. She had told him to be careful, never imagining what danger awaited him.

Justin wailed as she ran, and she held him tighter. She passed City Hall, the police station, then crossed the grass and headed up to the fire department.

She saw two off-duty firefighters pulling up into the small parking lot. Ignoring them, she raced inside. She found Slater Finch in the empty truck bay, donning his gear.

"Slater, do you have any news on Mark and the guys?"

"None," Slater said, "but the building just fell and I'm goin' over. I was off duty but I came in soon as I saw."

Johnny Ducote burst in through the door on the parking lot side. "We gotta get over there, Slater!"

"Let's go," Slater said. "We'll take my Jeep."

Johnny grabbed his turnouts and started out to Slater's Jeep. Allie walked out to the parking lot as Lex Harper pulled up. "Wait for me!" he cried.

Allie followed him in and watched him gather up his gear. "Lex, I need to hear from Mark. If you see him, please tell him to call me. If you have any word at all ..."

But Lex wasn't listening. Arms laden with his coat, pants, and boots, he headed back out the door. Sobbing, Allie buried her face against her child.

"Allie!"

She looked up to see her friend Celia, tears staining her face as she clutched her own daughter. "Mark's there, isn't he?"

Allie nodded, and Celia drew her into a hug.

"What's happening?" Allie cried. "It's like nine-eleven all over again. The crashing building, the firefighters . . ."

"Stan just left to go help. Honey, he'll call as soon as he knows something. He knows how worried we all are." She pulled Allie into the station, where the television still blared. The crashing building replayed on the screen.

Allie set Justin down and watched it again as if for the first time. "How can people do such a thing?" She wiped her tears and wondered if there were terrorists watching the coverage. Were they calling each other in celebration over the crumbling symbol of corrupt capitalism? Was it Al-Qaeda? Bin Laden himself? Or was it some localized cell of hate-mongers who'd been biding their time, waiting for today to strike?

"It's going to be okay," Celia whispered. "We just have to have faith."

But Allie knew that the Lord took the lives of the faithful all the time. Devoted Christians grieved. Lovers of Christ often suffered.

Faith was not always an umbrella of defense. Today, good people had died.

She prayed desperately that her husband wasn't one of them.

Chapter Nine

● ● ●

Jill couldn't breathe. Coughing the fallout from her lungs, she crawled out from under the car and rubbed the powder from her eyes. Silence had fallen over the street, like the morning after a snowfall. But it wasn't snow; it was a yellow ash that coated the street and the cars and hung foglike in the air. Ashley slid out from under the car and bent double to clear her lungs. Tears rivered through the powder on her face. She walked back toward the building as if in a daze.

"Ashley, we should stay back," Jill choked out.

But it was as though Ashley couldn't hear.

Jill followed her. Others stood frozen in the street, covered in yellow-white. Some coughed and gagged, others threw up. A cluster of firefighters convened quietly around a fire truck so covered in ash that you couldn't see the color beneath it.

There was a reverent hush, as if no one dared yell or cry out. Shock had dropped its covering over that block.

Jill searched for that Newpointe truck she had been standing beside with Marty, but now all she saw was rubble and knew that the debris had buried it, right where she had stood just moments ago.

Ahead of her, she saw the yellow fluorescent stripes of a fireman's coat glowing in the smoke. Hope stirred from her despair, and she headed toward it. She touched the firefighter's arm and he turned around. It was Ray Ford, Newpointe's fire chief, his black skin covered with white and his eyes shell-shocked and dazed.

"Ray, it's me, Jill."

Recognition flickered in his eyes. "Jill!"

"Have you seen Dan? Do you know if he got out?"

"I ain't seen anybody, Jill," he said, "but I'm going back, and if he's in there, I'll find him."

He started to walk, and she followed behind him. The smoke was thicker here, and the air was thin and tainted. She coughed again.

"Jill, you get out of here," he said quietly. "There were already three explosions before the building collapsed. We don't know if there are more bombs. You get to where it's safe."

She sucked in a breath. "I can't. I have to know if my husband's alive."

"You know I'll do everything I can to find him." He started trudging through the debris. She started to follow him, but a pair of hands grasped her from behind and she swung around, thinking for the briefest of seconds that it might be Dan. But it was only a New Orleans police officer.

"Ma'am, I have to ask you to leave the block. It's too dangerous here."

She collapsed in a fit of coughing again. "You don't understand . . . my husband . . . a fireman."

"There's a school three blocks away that we've set up as a command post. We're sending victims over there. You can wait there in the gym for word about your husband. Go down three blocks and take a right. You'll see it."

"I don't want to leave here," she choked. "I can't."

"Ma'am, your husband's life might be at stake, and we need to work as fast as we can. We can't have extra people milling around."

"I can help." She started to cough again. "I can dig. I can do whatever you need."

"You can't even breathe," he said. "Go to the treatment center and wait."

She looked around, searching for someone else who could help, and saw Issie standing across the street, covered with soot and ashes. Her face was wet and streaked with tears.

"Issie!"

Issie ran to her and threw her arms around her. "Jill, are you all right?"

"Yes," she cried, "but where is Dan? I can't find him."

"I don't know," she said. "Our guys went up to help evacuate the building, and then it collapsed. Maybe they got out."

Jill looked toward where the building had stood. The cloud of smoke still hung in a phantom outline of the structure. "They told me I have to go to the school three blocks away and wait for word. You want to come?"

"No," Issie said, "there are too many wounded." She looked helplessly around. "It seems to me like the end of the world. Doesn't it to you?"

"Yes," she said, "only Jesus is supposed to come riding in on a white horse and take us away."

"I don't see any white horses," Issie said. "Maybe it isn't the end. Maybe the worst part of all of this is that it has to go on."

Chapter Ten

● ● ●

Jill had lost Ashley when she had wandered off into the fog. Hoping the girl had been told about the treatment center, Jill decided to follow the stream of victims heading that way.

They were all like her—dazed, soot-covered, choking souls, walking in a grim parade down Canal Street to the school the police directed them to. She wondered if Wanda, her court reporter, had made it out. She was in the clear stairwell. Maybe she had gotten down long before Jill.

Her eyes burned as if handfuls of hot sand had been flung into them. Those around her had bloodshot, swollen eyes, and Jill knew hers probably looked the same.

The crowd began to move into the high school, where the air was clear. Outside, people who weren't covered with filth handed out bottled water. She took one thankfully and went in. They were directed to the gym just down the big high school corridor. A "Tammy For President" sign hung on the door next to "J.D. for V.P." Inside, the brick walls were papered with Tempra-painted signs—"Tame Those Dawgs" and "Falcons Fly" and "We're Number One."

The place smelled of sweat and mold, but the flood of survivors brought the scent of smoke with them.

"Ma'am, do you need to wash out your eyes?"

She turned and saw a young woman in a Red Cross shirt holding two tiny cups of water.

"Your eyes look bad. Here, wash them out."

Jill's hands shook so hard that she feared she would spill the cups. Still, she took them. "Thank you."

"Over here," the girl said and led her to the bleachers lining the wall. Jill sat down, and the girl knelt in front of her.

Jill washed out each eye and let the tepid water run down her face. It gave her relief, but her corneas still felt lacerated. She wished she could step into the shower and let the spray run over them. The girl gave her more water. "Are you hurt anywhere?"

She hurt all over, but she didn't have time to think about it now. "I don't think so. I need a phone. I . . . lost my cell phone." The enormity of her loss crushed down upon her, and she started to cry again. "I have to call . . . try to find my husband."

The girl set a comforting hand on her shoulder and directed her attention to a line forming at the corner of the room. "We have a phone over there but there's a pretty big crowd waiting."

Jill squinted at the line of people waiting to use that phone. Despair ripped through her, and she covered her face in anguish.

"Where is he?" the girl asked softly. "At home?"

"No," Jill said. "He's a firefighter. He was in the building when it came down. I have to know if he's all right."

The young woman pulled a small cell phone out of her pocket. "Here, use mine."

Jill caught her breath.

"I wasn't going to tell anybody I had this, but your husband was in there and all . . ."

Jill's face twisted in gratitude, and she touched the girl's face. With a trembling hand, she took the small phone. "Bless you."

"Sure. I hope you can hear. It's pretty noisy in here. You might want to step into the hall."

Jill went back out into the corridor and found a quiet place. She dialed Dan's cell phone number. It rang once, and then a recording clicked on.

"The customer you are calling is not available at this time."

Not available. What did that mean? Dead? Injured? Buried? The recording that had always played on his phone when he was out of range had a myriad of possible new meanings. She breathed out a sob, then hung up and dialed the Midtown station instead. Maybe someone there had heard from him. Maybe there was someone keeping a count of who had checked in. She prayed as it rang.

"Midtown Station, Andy Sweeney." Andy was the new kid on the block, the one just out of the firefighter's academy, still on probation and probably holding down the fort since everyone else was here. She had represented him once on a DUI charge, when he was still in high school.

"Andy, this is Jill Nichols," she said. "Please, can you tell me if you've heard from Dan?"

"Ma'am, I ain't heard from anybody," Andy said. "I've been sittin' here waiting for somebody to call so I could find out if I could go help with the rescue effort, but I can't get in touch with anybody."

She leaned her head against the wall and started to sob. "I have to know if he's all right," she said. "You must be able to radio somebody. Isn't there anybody who's answering their radio calls?"

"Nobody, ma'am," Andy said, "not since the building came down. I watched it on TV, hoping and praying that nobody we know is in there."

Jill swung her fist at the air. "They *were* in there," she cried. "Don't you understand? They were. Dan was in that building."

"Ma'am, Mark's wife is here if you want to talk to her."

"Allie?" Jill wiped the tears off her face. "Yes, let me talk to Allie."

She heard voices, then, "Jill, thank God you're all right!"

Jill could tell that Allie was crying. She clutched the phone. "Allie, I can't find Dan. Ray told me he was in the building when it collapsed—"

"Jill, did you see Mark?"

"No," she said. "I don't know where he was when the building came down. I saw Issie, and she said our guys had gone in."

There was a moment of silence, broken by strangled sobs on the other end. "Was she sure?" Allie's voice quivered. "Maybe they got out."

Jill leaned her forehead against the wall. "I don't know. Maybe."

She heard low voices, then the phone changed hands. "Jill, this is Celia. Where are you?"

"In the gym of some school on Canal Street," she said. "It's where all the victims are kind of coming to wait for word and to get help."

"Honey, can you get home?"

"No. My car was in the parking garage, under the building. I'm sure it's history. Besides, I don't want to leave here. I want to stay close by." She squeezed her eyes shut and banged her fist against the wall. "I just want to know that Dan's okay. But they've blocked off the street and won't let any civilians in there, only emergency workers."

"Jill, we're coming down there, okay? We'll find you and wait there with you. Is there anything you need?"

"Yes," Jill said, "a change of clothes. I'm filthy."

"I'll go by your house," Celia said. "Do you still keep a key under that pot by the back door?"

"Yes."

"Honey, you sound awful. Are you all right?"

"Yeah," she said. "Just a little smoke inhalation."

"Okay. Just wait there for us," Celia said. "We'll get there as fast as we can, probably less than an hour, okay?"

"I'm not going anywhere. I'll be here."

"I love you, honey. It's going to be all right. And would you do me a favor and call one of our cell phones if you find out any news about the guys?"

"If I can get to a phone, I'll do it," she said. "I promise."

• • •

As Celia got off the phone, Allie fell into her arms. The television replayed the scenes of the building falling down and
people fleeing as if they were in some kind of third-rate movie.
But it was no movie. It was real.

Where had Mark been when that building crashed? Did it
make a difference what floor he'd been on? How close to an exit?
She wanted to scream out, collapse in anguish, start lashing out
at anyone near her. But she couldn't. She had to get to New
Orleans, fast.

She heard voices in the truck bay and turned to see Celia's
eighty-three-year-old Aunt Aggie hurrying in, with teary-eyed
Susan Ford, the chief's wife, on her heels.

"Where my boys at?" Aunt Aggie demanded as she trod in,
wearing a pair of Nikes she had spray-painted gold, and a gold
velvet wind suit.

Susan went to Allie. "Where's Ray? Has anybody heard from
my Ray?"

"Yes!" Allie said. "Jill said she saw him."

Susan cried out in exultation and hugged Aunt Aggie.

"But I don't know about Mark."

"I'll go find 'em, *sha!*" Aunt Aggie declared, her Cajun form
of *chère* meant to comfort. "I'll go there myself and pull ever' last
one of my boys outta that mess!"

No one was surprised by Aunt Aggie's declaration. She, after
all, was the one whose mission in life was to cook three meals a
day for the firefighters of Midtown and care for them like a protective mother.

But Celia intervened. "Aunt Aggie, what we really need from
you right now is a baby-sitter. Would you keep little Aggie and
Justin while I take Allie to New Orleans?"

Susan grabbed her arm. "I'm coming, too."

Aunt Aggie didn't like it. "Call that Jolene girl to baby-sit. I got to be there!"

Allie pictured Aunt Aggie raising a ruckus at the bomb site, hindering the rescue effort and winding up in jail. It had happened before. "Aunt Aggie, please. I'd feel so much better if Justin was with you. It may take all night. He and little Aggie could sleep at your house. We can get Jolene to help, but she can't do it alone."

Aunt Aggie's face changed, and she reached out and took her great-niece from Celia. "Awright, I guess I can do that."

They piled into Celia's minivan to take Aunt Aggie home and swing by Jill's house.

Allie leaned down to close Justin's seat belt over him. "You're going to Aunt Aggie's, okay? Will you be a good boy?"

He nodded and wiped her tears. "Don't cry, Mommy."

She took his hand and kissed it. Still holding it, she looked out the window. Afternoon sun still shone, clear and bright for a December day. It seemed as if it should be the dead of night. "Please God," she whispered, "let him be all right."

Chapter Eleven

● ● ●

Jill had never felt more alone.

The school gym where they'd congregated held a crush of people, all of whom had life-or-death issues in common. Some were survivors with soot-stained faces, coughing smoke out of their lungs and guzzling water. Others were volunteers who'd brought food, water, blankets, cots. Family members streamed in with haunted expressions, searching for their loved ones.

She sat on the floor and leaned back against the wall, staring out into the noisy crowd. Each survivor had an escape story to tell, and everyone engaged in nervous chatter. Jill longed for silence so she could think.

But thinking was probably not the best idea. Her mind was dragging her into a panicked, desperate state, and she had the sense that she would explode just like the building, leaving only a burning mound of unidentifiable rubble.

She forced herself to concentrate on the door where Allie and Celia would come in.

A cluster of new victims stumbled in, coughing and crying, and she wondered where they had been. Had they been wandering the streets in a daze, or were they pulled from the rubble? If they had been, could Dan have been among them?

She watched the faces that came in, one by one, and caught her breath when she saw the burgundy-haired teenager who had helped her with Gordon. Ashley looked like a war-waif, her eyes glazed in round, dull shock. Jill saw the same desperate panic on her face.

As the girl's bloodshot, swollen eyes darted quickly around the room, Jill knew that she was looking for her mother. She hoped to God that she found her here.

She watched her go to the sign-in table and, bending over, search the list of those who'd come here.

Clearly, her mother wasn't listed, and the girl straightened and turned back to the crowd, her face twisting in a fresh wave of anguish.

Sympathy pulsed through her, and Jill got up. "Ashley!" she called through the crowd. "Ashley, over here!"

The girl heard her name and swung around, cruel hope on her face. Her eyes met Jill's, and that hope crashed. She started to cry and backed against the wall.

Jill crossed the room and pulled her into her arms. The girl coiled into herself as sobs racked her. "You didn't find her?"

"No!" Ashley cried. "Where is she?"

"Come on," Jill said. "I'll walk around here with you. If she's here, we'll see her."

The girl looked so vulnerable, even with her tattoos and just-out-of-bed hairstyle, and the chain connecting her ear and nose rings. She was a child, Jill thought—a child who'd just been through a battle scene and may well have come out an orphan.

When they'd covered one side of the building to no avail, Jill thought of something. "Stop," she told Ashley, and the girl turned her wet face to her. Jill ran her fingers through the girl's tousled hair, dusting out the ashes that were disguising the color. "Not everybody has hair this color," she said. "If we can get these ashes out, maybe your mother will spot you."

The girl looked weak. "I don't think she's here."

"Maybe not yet. But she will be, eventually."

"I think she's dead." The words tumbled out of her. "She was with the bomb."

Jill stopped dusting her hair and looked into her face. "With the bomb? What do you mean?"

Ashley wiped her face, smearing the soot. "I was up there to get some money from her, and she had to go to the stockroom. I went with her, begging for money like some kind of brat . . ."

"Go on," Jill said.

"And we opened the stockroom, and there was the bomb. This big thing with wires and stuff, and all these water jugs around it . . ." She got the edge of her T-shirt and wiped her nose. "Mom made me leave while she called security. She promised she would come right behind me after she called, and I heard the fire alarm and people started filling the stairwell, and then . . ."

Jill knew before she said it. "The explosion."

"I don't think Mom got out." The words squeaked out of her. "She couldn't have. I would have seen her on the stairwell when I went back up."

Jill pulled the girl into her arms and held her as she wept. Her mother may well be dead, just as Dan could be. But they couldn't give up. Neither of them could surrender to that fear.

"Come on," she said. "Let's walk around some more. We'll find her. I'll bet she's looking frantically for you."

Ashley acquiesced and let Jill pull her along. They pushed through clusters of people and stepped over those sitting on the floor. But Ashley's mother wasn't there.

Finally, Jill found a place near a wall where they had a good view of the door. "Come on, let's get you some water and just sit down and rest where we can watch the door. When she comes in, we'll see her."

Ashley wearily slid down the wall and sat on the floor, her eyes glued to the front door.

Please, God. Let her mother walk in.

But all they saw were more victims, coming in one at a time, shock clearly showing on all their faces.

Chapter Twelve

● ● ●

The ride to New Orleans was quiet, except for the ongoing radio coverage of the mayhem around the wreckage. The buildings adjacent to Icon were burning now, and reporters speculated on when they would fall.

Allie was glad that Celia had offered to drive. She didn't think she could have managed to do it herself, with that mental footage of the falling building reeling over and over in her mind.

Celia had finally heard from Stan, who hadn't found any of the Newpointe guys yet. For all she knew, Mark could be dead.

How absurd that this would happen today. It had started out so beautifully. Justin had gotten them up earlier than usual, and Mark had made pancakes. As Allie got ready to go to the flower shop, he had bathed the syrup off their son.

She had heard them singing together, Justin giggling with delight, and she couldn't resist sticking her head into the bathroom.

Itsy bitsy spider went up the water spout . . .

Mark knelt beside the tub, his arms and shirt soaked from bathwater, and he walked his fingers over his head with the zeal and animation of a preschooler. The three-year-old copied him, his eyes bright with glee.

Like father, like son.

She had wondered how they could possibly be more blessed.

Who would have suspected that this beautiful, perfect day would become the worst day of their lives?

It was supposed to be his day off. He probably still had yellow paint on his hands.

Allie stared out Celia's window and listened to the radio reporter's account of the collapse again. To the media, it was a great news day. Careers would be made by the coverage today.

Allie glanced out the back window. Susan had decided to bring her own car, in case they had to leave at different times. She drove with tears streaming down her dark face, and her mouth moved in vigilant prayer for the missing.

Allie pulled her cell phone off of her belt and looked down to make sure she hadn't missed a call. Sometimes the ringer wasn't loud enough. She had set it to vibrate with every ring, so she would feel it if she didn't hear it. But no calls had come.

Mark, where are you?

She should have reminded him to take the cell phone with him. He had rushed off before it had occurred to her.

"I'm going to park here," Celia said, pulling into a public parking lot a few blocks from Canal Street. "I don't think we'll get any closer. We can walk to the school."

Allie tried to see over the buildings to the place where Icon had stood. All she could see was thick smoke, still sweltering up from the rubble. How could anyone have survived that heat?

She felt weak as she got out of the car, and the thick smog assaulted her.

Susan pulled into the spot next to them and got out. "Honey, did you hear anything on the way?"

"Nothing," Allie said.

"He's all right, darlin'. Remember that Nine-Eleven video, where those filmmakers followed that fire department around? Every firefighter in that firehouse survived. It's gonna happen to our men, honey."

That was easy for her to say, Allie thought. She already knew Ray was fine.

She started up the block in the direction of the school, her eyes still fixed on that smoke cloud over the site. The roads surrounding the Icon block were closed off, and emergency vehicles glutted the street in haphazard configurations. There were no firefighters in sight. They were all there, right in the middle of things. . . .

They reached the school, where several radio stations were broadcasting. One of the correspondents stuck a microphone in front of them. "Ladies, could you tell us why you're here? Are you waiting for word about loved ones?"

Allie waved them off, and Susan and Celia put their arms around her shoulders as they pushed through the door. They found the gym just near the front entrance and pushed inside. The noise level sounded like that at a basketball game, and Allie looked around and saw the fallout of the day. People with dried blood on their clothes and faces, mingled with soot and despair, sat around the room with stunned looks on their faces. Others, like them, who had obviously not been in the building, watched the door as if hoping that someone they knew would walk through.

"We'll never find Jill," Allie said. "So many people."

"She'll find us," Susan said.

She was right. They hadn't stood there longer than a minute before Allie heard her name called through the crowd. "Allie! Celia! Susan!"

Allie saw Jill standing against the wall next to a rough-looking teenaged girl. She caught her breath at the bedraggled sight of her best friend and started to cry as she cut through the crowd.

They grabbed each other in a desperate embrace.

"Honey, are you all right?" Celia asked.

"Fine," Jill said.

Allie wondered if Jill realized just how bad she looked. Besides the soot that covered her, she had bloody scrapes on her face and arms. Her clothes were torn and filthy, and a white powder covered her hair.

"Have you had any word yet?" Jill asked.

"Nothing yet," Allie said. She started to weep, and Jill clung to her in kindred grief.

Chapter Thirteen

● ● ●

Anybody here?" Mark Branning's voice cracked through the silence, almost startling him in its clarity. He had gone down with the building, hanging on to the railing of the stairwell between twelve and fourteen, and had ridden the surf of cement, glass, and steel until it came to a crashing halt.

He lay in darkness now and stared up at the opaque black. Was he alive or in some twilight-zone death stage before the light revealed itself and drew him home?

He hadn't expected to feel so alone at death. Weren't loved ones supposed to meet you? Usher you into a place of beauty and peace?

He felt around beneath him. He lay on an uneven bed of crushed cement, but he wasn't pinned or trapped in any way. Several inches of powder covered him, gritting into his eyes and ears, his nose and mouth.

He shook his face to clear them, rubbed his eyes, but his hands just brought more grit. But that was the least of his worries.

Nothing seemed broken, and he felt along his limbs in the darkness. He felt pain, but not so much that it hindered his movement. Miraculously, he was all right.

So he'd lived. But would he get out of this place? Had God saved him just for a last moment of reflection?

He pictured Allie clinging to little Justin and watching coverage of the collapse of the building. She was probably a wreck. He hoped someone had come to be with her.

They had walked through the valley of the shadow of death before, and the Lord had seen them through. They had survived bullets and fire and the day-to-day struggles of life. Had it all been so they could come to this?

He had a flash of Allie at a funeral visitation, wearily greeting those who came to say kind things about him. He saw his father, skinny and drawn, reeking of Jack Daniel's and trying to act respectable.

The picture made him angry. He wasn't ready to die. Maybe God had placed him in this precise pocket because he did intend for him to live. Maybe it wasn't over yet.

He called out again, "Anybody there?"

This time he heard coughing and a movement of rubble.

"I'm here," a voice croaked.

Mark's heart jolted, and he sat up. Powder showered from his hair into his face. "Man, am I glad to hear another voice!"

"Mark, that you?"

He recognized Nick's voice and began to laugh, softly at first, a tickle at the back of his parched throat.

"I wouldn't call this funny," Nick muttered.

Mark shook his head and tried to clear his throat. "No, not funny. Not funny at all. Are you all right, man?"

"I think so." Nick's voice came from his right.

"I thought I was dead. It wasn't like you promised, buddy." He started to laugh again. It wasn't a normal reaction. He couldn't remember ever succumbing to a laughing fit when he'd been in crisis before. Maybe it was hysteria. A shrink would have a field day with this. He hoped he got the chance to tell it.

"What shape are you in?" Nick asked.

"I'm okay."

"Are you trapped?"

"No, man. Looks like I fell right into a pocket."

"Me too. Probably the same one. I think I'm under part of the stairwell," Nick said. "I can't see a thing, but I think I could crawl out if I knew which way to go."

"Help me." It was a third voice, one Mark didn't recognize.

"Who's that?" Mark called out.

"Sam Shelton," the voice grunted. It seemed far away, below Nick. "My legs are buried. I need help."

Mark tried to see through the blackness. Nothing. He got on his knees and felt in front of him. Slowly, he moved toward the voice. He cut his knee on a sharp edge but kept going.

"I have a flashlight on my key chain. Can anybody see the light?"

Mark strained to see. "No, buddy, I don't see anything."

"Now?"

Mark still didn't see it.

"I see the light," Nick yelled. "Just barely."

"Where? Where is it, Nick?"

"Not far beneath me. Mark, try to move toward my voice."

He crawled to the right, careful not to disturb the rubble beneath him. All he needed was for the bottom to drop out again.

He heard a brushing away of debris and crawled blindly toward the noise.

"Where are you?"

Nick's voice sounded close. "Right here, man. Reach toward me."

He felt Nick's hand grabbing for him.

"Hey, Preacher." Mark hugged him, then looked down and saw the small dot of light.

"We see you, Sam. We're trying to get down to you. Keep the light on."

They crawled toward it, carefully moving over girders and beams, broken steps and steel rails. The light's circle grew bigger, making it easier.

When they finally reached the man, Mark winced at the pain he must be in. He lay beneath a heavy sheet of concrete, about six feet long and four feet wide. It lay across his lower body, crushing him from the waist down.

Mark's emergency training kicked in, and he crawled next to the man and began to take his pulse.

"How you doing, buddy?" Nick asked him softly.

"Been better."

"Feel any pain?"

"Are you kidding me?"

The man's pulse was racing. "Would that be a yes?" Mark asked.

"Yes!" he gritted out. "Please, get this thing off of me."

The pain was good news. Mark glanced up at Nick. His face was streaked in black soot, and his temple was scraped and bleeding. He wasn't wearing his glasses. Mark guessed he had lost them. "Any ideas?" he asked him.

"We can try to lift it up, but I doubt he can slide out from under it. And there's not enough room to move it."

"Let's try," Mark said. Nick nodded, and they each took a side of the cement slab. "One, two, three . . ."

Mark strained to lift it, and it gave a few inches. "Move out, Sam," he grunted.

The man used his arms to slide upward—but not far enough.

"Little more," Nick said through his teeth.

The man ground his teeth together and, with a herculean effort, dragged himself free of the slab.

They dropped it back in place, and Mark tried to catch his breath. He wiped the sweat from his forehead and looked down at the man. His legs looked mangled, useless, and thick veins strained against the skin of his forehead. His eyes locked on Mark, as if he knew he could get him out of here.

Mark wasn't so sure. He took the light and held it up, looking around for an escape. It couldn't be much past noon, yet there wasn't a sign of daylight through all this debris. How would they ever find their way out? Did anyone know they were here? Or were they just among hundreds also buried?

"Take the light," the man groaned. "Take it and find your way out, then come back for me."

Nick looked at Mark. "I'll stay with him," he said. "You go."

Mark nodded, relieved. He needed to do something besides sit here in this tomb and wait. He took the light, held it up, and decided to move up where the stairs had been. The stairwell had been next to an outer wall. If he could just find a breach in it, see daylight coming through . . .

"I'll be back," he assured them and started moving upward, over the mound of debris and twisted steel.

He glanced back and saw that Nick had begun to pray over the man. Something about that made him feel better.

He climbed upward from steel girder to steel girder, testing his weight with every step. Thankful for his gloves, he grabbed whatever looked like it would hold and pulled himself along.

It was clear why this pocket had not collapsed. Because it was near an outside wall, there were more steel girders, and instead of toppling over they had bent, forming a barrier network above them. He hoped he could penetrate that ceiling when he reached it.

He climbed as far as he could, then shone the light around, searching for another pocket that would offer him passage. He saw a slab of concrete much like the one that had trapped Sam. It was split down the middle, making a V-shaped ditch he could crawl through. He put the light in his teeth and pulled himself through.

It took him into another cavelike hole, only big enough to slide through on his belly. He shone the light around, praying for a pin-light of day indicating he was near the top.

A flash of flourescent yellow glowed from under a pile of powderlike debris, reflecting back his light, and he crawled toward it.

It was the arm of a turnout coat.

His heart began to hammer, and he thought of all his buddies who'd fallen with the building. It could be Dan or George or Ray. . . .

He started to dig with both hands, clutching the light between his teeth. He uncovered his chest, saw the NOFD emblem on his black T-shirt.

Not one of his own comrades, but still a brother. He dug harder to uncover his head. The man lay limp, lifeless. Quickly, he touched his neck for a pulse.

There was none.

Mark just stared at him for a moment, and the enormity of what had happened caved in on him like the building itself. Had he survived only to be found later, like this man, buried beneath a tower of rubble?

He propped himself on his elbows and started to cry. His anguish came up in a slow trembling, convulsing through his body, constricting his heart with sudden and inescapable fear.

If he could just see the light of day. Even a hint of gray, suggesting that light was nearby. If he could just know that there was someone on the other side of this debris who knew he was here. Someone who hadn't given them all up for dead. Someone who still had a rescue left in him.

God knows. The knowledge hit him like a lightning bolt, electrifying him, fortifying him.

God knew he was here—and had the power to rescue him.

There was still hope, as long as he was breathing.

He forced himself to leave his fallen brother and crawl on. He got to a dead end, carefully dug through with his hand, shifted through wood and Sheetrock and crumbled cement. And then he saw it.

A slit in the darkness. The daylight he had longed for.

The sight almost paralyzed him, but he pulled himself toward it, fighting everything in his path, swimming through the devastation.

"Anybody hear me?" he shouted. "Help! Anybody there?"

There was no answer, but he kept going. He reached the slit and pushed through.

Daylight washed over him, but it was thick with smoke. He pulled himself up, expecting a crowd of rescuers to cheer as he emerged.

But all he saw was a battlefield. He got to his feet in horror and looked around him. He stood on a mound of rubble, but there were other mounds, testifying of death and destruction, as if a fleet of planes had rained bombs down upon them. A building adjacent to the mounds burned in lavish, licking flames, the heat of which undulated around him.

He saw no one.

Had anyone survived this mayhem? Was he the only one who'd made it out? Had they taken the whole city?

He collapsed to his knees and cried out.

Suddenly a figure emerged in the smoke, another firefighter, coming up over the mound. "Need help over here!" the man shouted.

Before Mark could get up there were others running toward him. He wept harder at the sight of them.

"There are others," he made himself cry out. "At least two survivors in the pocket I crawled through. We have to hurry."

"We're with you, buddy."

Together they began to widen the breach that he had crawled through, as he switched gears from victim to rescuer.

• • •

When he and Nick had put Sam into an ambulance, Mark saw Ray Ford running toward them.

He threw his arms around both of them and clung to them as if he'd never expected to see them alive again.

"Where's Issie?" Nick asked. "Have you seen her?"

"Yeah, man. She's okay. Looking for you."

Relief melted the tension on Nick's face. "God is good," he said.

"Who did we lose?" Mark asked.

Ray pulled back and rubbed his trembling mouth. "I haven't been able to make contact with Dan, George, or Junior. I think Jacob's missing too. Man, I'm glad to see you two alive."

Mark stared at him. "They gotta be all right. They're around here somewhere, don't you think? Dan, he's tough. If anybody could survive this, he can."

"He was in the building when it came down, just like you guys." Ray's voice was hoarse with emotion. "How many pockets could there be?"

"A lot," Nick said. "They're not dead, okay? We'll find them. They're probably sitting in a hole somewhere waiting for us."

"They were in the same stairwell we were," Mark said. "They couldn't be that far from where we landed."

They joined the others, digging and sifting through rubble, moving cement and steel and computer parts and tabletops with an urgency Mark had never felt before. Heat whirled up from the smoke and sweltered through their clothes.

"Nick!"

Mark turned around and saw Issie running over the mound toward them, tears streaming down her black-sooted face.

"Issie!" Nick cried, and he dropped the concrete he held in his hand and took a few steps toward her. She flung herself into his arms, and he crushed her against him.

"I thought I'd lost you!" she cried. "Oh, thank you, God!"

"I was so worried about you," he said. "Were you clear of the building when it came down?"

"Yes. There are so many injured, Nick. And so many dead."

Nick kissed her, then let her go. "We have to work," he said. "We have men missing."

"Two paramedics missing too," she said. "Karen Ensminger and Steve Winder. They're not responding to our radio calls. I'll help," she said, and she got beside them and joined in the process.

They formed a brigade, passing debris from hand to hand, digging carefully so as not to collapse any pockets that might contain survivors. Mark looked up at the cloud of smoke still hovering around them. The whole French Quarter was probably enveloped in smoke. He wondered how many bodies lay beneath this rubble. They would find many dead today. He didn't know if he was up to the task, but he kept digging as fast as he could, praying with all his heart that he would find Dan and his other comrades alive.

Chapter Fourteen

● ● ●

The gym had gotten more crowded as family members of the missing began to add to the numbers already there. Allie clutched her cell phone in her hand, desperately praying that it would ring.

Jill had taken a shower in the locker room and changed clothes, and her cuts and bruises were more evident with the soot washed off. Her eyes still looked injured.

Ashley, Jill's teenaged friend, refused to shower, for she feared missing the moment that her mother walked in. Susan had used her own cell phone to check area hospitals for the girl's mother. No one by the name of Debbie Morris had been admitted anywhere in the area, but Allie suspected that a number of patients were still unidentified.

She wondered how many of them were firefighters.

Her phone vibrated in her hand, and she heard her distinctive Charleston ring.

"It's ringing!" Jill said.

"Oh, God, please . . ." Allie clicked it on. "Hello?"

Jill moved closer, trying to hear.

"Hey, honey."

"Mark?" Relief exploded like a nuclear bomb inside Allie.

"Yeah, sweetheart, it's me. I'm still at the site, but I'm okay. You must have been praying."

"Oh, Mark! Thank God!" She wilted into tears. "Are you okay?"

"I am now."

She looked up at the others. "He's okay! Mark's okay!"

"Find out about Dan," Jill cried.

Allie pressed her finger to her ear. "Mark, Jill wants to know if you've seen Dan."

"Jill's okay?" he asked. "Oh, that's good news. We were worried about her." He got quiet for a moment. "Let me talk to her, honey."

Allie's stomach tightened with dread, and she handed Jill the phone.

• • •

Jill knew it wasn't good news. If Dan was okay, Mark would have blurted it out to Allie. She looked at Susan, then Celia as she took the phone. The dread on their faces mirrored her own.

She brought the phone to her ear. "Mark? Where is he?"

Mark's sigh spoke of his own despair. "Jill, I think Dan's missing."

A fog of dizziness weakened her knees, and she slid to the floor. "Oh, no, please say it's not true." Susan fell beside her and hugged her arms around her.

"Jill, you can't give up. Nick and I were buried when the building came down, but we got out. He could be in a pocket like we were. They've gotten several survivors out already. We're digging as fast as we can. And we're not sure he's buried. He could just be in a different part of the site here, trying to rescue others. We don't know for sure."

It was difficult to hear in the crowd, and she thought of screaming for everyone to shut up.

"Weren't you with him?" she asked. "Wasn't he where you were?"

"I don't know where he was," he said. "He could have been helping someone out of the building. He may not have even been inside."

A tiny bud of hope sprang up in her heart. "Do you think so?"

"Could be. I just don't know. But I swear to you, we're doing everything in our power to find him. And if I see him, I'll let you know immediately. I won't let a minute pass."

Jill handed the phone back to Allie and melted into Susan's arms. Celia joined them, and the women wept together. She looked up and saw Ashley watching her with her own tears streaming down her face. She wished she could comfort her, but there was no comfort in sight.

"Come here, sweetie," Susan said in that sweet, maternal voice. She reached a hand out and drew the crying girl into their circle. "We'll pray for Dan and your mama too. God knows where she is, just like he knows where our Dan is."

Ashley complied and came into their circle, but she didn't take her eyes from the door.

Chapter Fifteen

● ● ●

It had been awhile since they had pulled out any survivors, so the paramedics busied themselves treating the rescue workers with their breathing and eye problems. Issie stood over a firefighter who looked old enough to be retired. The whites of his eyes were bloodred, and he wheezed like an asthmatic. But he couldn't wait to get back to the digging.

"Medic! We've got one." Issie turned and saw that the voice came from a mound next to where Mark and Nick dug. "I'm going!" Issie called and abandoned her patient. She dashed up the mound, heart pounding. *Let it be one of ours!*

Other medics had gotten there before her and were already pulling a civilian woman out of the rubble. Her dress was tangled around her legs, and blood congealed on her face. She was unconscious.

"She's alive," one of the paramedics cried. "I need a board over here, stat—and a neck brace." Issie waited as they passed the spineboard to them. If they'd found one alive here, maybe there were others. Karen and Steve, maybe, or Dan, George, Jacob, or Junior.

She felt woefully unequipped. Her own rescue unit had been crushed in the collapse, so none of the things that they needed for a catastrophe such as this had been available until rescue units from other towns had come to help.

She watched as they quickly strapped the woman to the board and moved her into an ambulance. The firefighters and police officers resumed their digging.

"We got another one over here!"

Issie took off toward the voice and watched as they uncovered another one. But she knew without checking that this one hadn't made it. Burned beyond recognition, it wasn't clear if this one had been a man or woman, a firefighter or civilian. She breathed back a sob and told herself that she had to stay strong. There was no time to fall apart now.

She tried to find a place on the body where she could feel a pulse, but there was none. She couldn't get any words out, so she just shook her head.

The grief in the faces of the workers looked as thick as the smoke still floating over the place. Issie just sat there, waiting for someone else to be uncovered, praying that the next one would be alive.

Chapter Sixteen

● ● ●

It was 11:30 when Stan came home from the Icon site. He was dead tired, and his body ached from digging for his buddies. But he had been called back to help with the investigation. The FBI had asked all of the surrounding police departments to be on the alert for anyone suspicious and had given them a long list of information they needed about citizens in their towns, businesses that might have sold to terrorists, and witnesses who could provide any evidence. He had come home to shower before going to the station.

Celia—who had come home just moments before—had greeted him like he'd been raised from the dead. She drew a hot bath for him to soak the soreness out of his muscles. He lay in the hot tub, wishing he could relax and drift off to sleep.

But Dan was still missing, and so were so many of his other friends.

How dare he relax when his colleagues were still there?

The phone rang, and he heard Celia answer it. Knowing it was probably for him, he got out and wrapped a towel around him.

"Hello? Yes, he's here." Celia brought him the cordless. "The station."

He took the phone. "Yeah?"

"Stan, we got a tip that there are three Middle Eastern men staying at the Best Western over on Huey Long Boulevard. The manager said they checked in tonight and were acting suspicious. Thought you'd want to know."

"Yeah. How long ago did you get the tip?"

"Just now. We dispatched four cars."

"I'll be there in a few minutes."

He hung up and rushed into his closet for some clean clothes.

"What is it?" Celia asked.

"Possible bombing suspects at a motel." He stepped into a pair of pants, then pulled on a shirt.

"In Newpointe?"

"Looks like it."

He pulled on some shoes and started through the house, buttoning his shirt.

"Have they made the arrest yet?"

"Not yet." He slipped his shoulder holster on.

"Stan, be careful!" she cried.

He slowed down and kissed her. "Don't worry. Lock the door," he said as he bolted out of the house.

He got to Huey Long in just a few minutes. Blue lights flashed in the Best Western parking lot, and he saw that officers already had the three suspects. They looked young, no more than nineteen or twenty. They were clean cut and appeared to be scared to death.

Stan went to the car to question one of them.

"We did not do anything!" the kid spat out in a heavy accent. "You are arresting us because of our nationality! You have no evidence against us."

Sid Ford—the fire chief's brother and the other detective on the force—leaned into the car. "Hey, Stan, we just got the warrant to search the car."

Stan nodded and turned back to the kid. "What're you doing in Newpointe?"

"We are exchange students at the University of Louisiana at Monroe. We were coming to New Orleans to help with the rescue but could not find a hotel there, so we had to get one here.

We were in class this morning, three hours north. We have dozens of witnesses."

Stan would see about that. "Where are you from?"

"Iran," the kid said. "But we have respect for the American people. We are not terrorists."

Stan instructed some of his colleagues to take the men back to the station to await questioning while he and Sid searched the car.

Chapter Seventeen

● ● ●

Since the gym was overcrowded, those in charge asked anyone who didn't need to be there to go home, thus making room for the ones who would be there all night. Celia and Allie had decided to go home and rescue Aunt Aggie from their children, or vice versa. But Susan had stayed there with Jill, intent on holding her hand all night and getting her through this horror.

People from local churches had been bringing cots and mattresses all night so that everyone had a place to lie down. One by one, the survivors had left to go home to their families and had been replaced by family members waiting for word on loved ones who had not been accounted for.

Ashley still hadn't showered. She lay coiled on her cot with her arms hugging her knees, her eyes constantly scanning the faces, as though her mother could have slipped in without her seeing her. Jill knew it was no more likely that Ashley's mom would come through that door than it was that Dan would.

As the night grew old, Jill sat on her little mattress against the wall, alternately praying and crying. Susan dozed on the cot they had given her. Jill forgave her. She knew that she was exhausted after such an emotional day. She couldn't blame her for not being able to keep vigil with her tonight.

Jill got up and paced in front of her cot. Allie had called Susan's phone to check on her twice since she'd left, but she'd had no news about Dan. Aunt Aggie had called a prayer meeting, she'd been told. The church was praying for Dan and the others who were missing.

But God didn't seem to be listening.

If Dan were alive and able, he would have contacted her by now. She knew he'd been buried under several stories of concrete.

Were his bones crushed? Had his neck snapped? Was he bleeding? She took some comfort in realizing that if he was conscious, he was praying to the same God as she. Wouldn't she know if he were dead? Wouldn't there be some feeling in her gut that her soul mate was no longer on this earth?

The waiting was killing her. She was useless here. One more set of hands might make them reach him faster. If she could just get to the site, she knew she could find him.

The idea took hold in her mind, and she wished she had thought to get Celia and Allie to bring her one of Dan's T-shirts with NFD on the front and back, so she could pretend to be a firefighter and join in the rescue. Maybe she didn't need it. Maybe by now they had stopped turning people away and needed more help. Maybe they would let her in.

She leaned over to Ashley and whispered, "I'm going out for some air."

Ashley's red eyes were dull as she stared across the room. "There's no air," she whispered. "Just smoke."

Jill recognized the commentary on the girl's life. She stroked her filthy hair. "I know. But I need a change of scenery. If Susan wakes up, tell her I'll be back."

Ashley didn't respond, so Jill cut through the cots. She could hear sobbing from different beds around the room. So much anguish. She went to the registration table where the volunteers had finally gotten organized. They were keeping lists of those who were accounted for, the living and the dead, and they updated them hourly.

She got in the line of people waiting, and when it was her turn, she bent over the table. "Has there been any word on Dan Nichols?"

The woman—who looked as weary as she—did a quick search on her laptop. "No, ma'am. No word."

Jill almost felt sorry for her. Almost all of the news she was giving out was bad. Earlier in the day there had been times of celebration for different groups around the floor, when someone had been discovered alive. But those celebrations had become fewer and farther between as the night went on.

"What about Debbie Morris?" she asked.

The girl scanned her list. "No, I'm sorry."

Jill got out of line, her chest as heavy as if someone's foot was wedged on top of it, stomping the life out of her. She went to the front door and stepped out into the night.

The air was still heavy with smoke, and she could hear machinery working just three blocks away as they dug for people. She hoped they weren't just bulldozing through the rubble. She hoped they were digging carefully.

She walked up to Canal Street, in an area she would never have ventured alone after dark. Just blocks away, the seedy French Quarter probably carried on as usual. Bars were probably still open, bands still played, and ladies of the night probably peddled their wares as if nothing significant had happened that day.

But there was no one hanging around here. Thugs and muggers didn't expect unsuspecting tourists to be in this area, and the smoke was a deterrent. Besides, what greater danger could befall her than what she'd already survived?

She slowed her step as the war zone came into view. Beacons and spotlights hung from various heights around the site, lighting the areas where rescuers worked, illuminating the fallout.

She froze, staring at the horror that lay before her. As she looked up at thirty floors of rubble compressed into the height of three or four, she realized how unlikely it was that Dan—or anyone else—would be pulled from it alive.

She wished she had died under that rubble herself.

"Ma'am, are you supposed to be here?"

She turned around and saw a police officer shining a flash-light into her face. Why wasn't he helping to dig? "I . . . I came to help with the rescue effort," she said weakly.

"I'm sorry, ma'am, but we've got all the help we need. We're asking all civilians to stay out of the way."

"I'm not a civilian," she lied. "I'm a firefighter from New-pointe. I was off-duty, but I thought I might be needed."

He clearly didn't believe her. "Ma'am, do you have any identification?"

She knew she'd been caught. She didn't have anything that said she was a firefighter, nothing to convince them to let her stay. "I forgot my ID. Look, I just want to help. We have people missing."

"We need experienced emergency personnel, ma'am, and if you don't have ID then I can't let you go in. Too much is at stake to have inexperienced people digging through there, possibly endangering the lives of those who could still be saved. And if you're media—"

"I'm not media," she said. "I told you—" Her voice broke off, and she realized what he'd just said. *The lives of those who could be saved.* "So you do think some could still be alive?"

"We're hoping," he said. "Now, please, you'll have to leave."

She could see the trauma on his own face. He'd been through a lot today, maybe even more than she had. She didn't want to make his job harder for him.

She stood a moment, staring at the expanse of destruction. She might be just yards from where Dan lay. Tears assaulted her.

The cop's face softened. "You're not really an emergency worker, are you?"

There was no use continuing the lie. "My husband's a fire-fighter. He's in that rubble somewhere." She caught her breath on a sob.

He dropped the light, allowing her the darkness. "My brother's in there, too."

It was clear that he knew what she was going through. But it wasn't the same, because he was able to stay. If they pulled him out, dead or alive, he would be here.

"I could help!" she cried. "I'd be another set of hands, so they could dig faster. Time is critical. Please—"

As she spoke, a dump truck came through, its headlights illuminating the road in front of it. She froze at the sight of a line of bodies, laid out in the dirt. "What are they—" Her voice caught in her throat. "Oh, no, they're dead, aren't they?"

"Ma'am, I really need you to—"

She jerked free of him and went toward the corpses. The headlights passed, but there was enough residual light for her to see a yellow fluorescent stripe from a turnout coat. She stumbled toward it. The man, burned beyond recognition, was too small to be Dan.

"Ma'am, I asked you to leave!"

She saw another dead fireman and lunged toward him. He wasn't Dan, either.

Dan hadn't been wearing his NFD T-shirt. He'd been off duty, and had been wearing something else. What? What had he been wearing? If he'd taken off his turnout coat because of the heat, he would look like anyone else.

The cop followed her as she went from body to body, searching all the faces of the dead for her own husband until she got to the end of them. He wasn't among them.

"Okay, now let's go." The officer's voice was gentler now. "Please, ma'am."

Nausea roiled up in her, and she turned and retched onto the dirt.

Someone touched her back. "Jill, you shouldn't be here."

Jill turned, saw Issie, and threw her arms around her. The two of them wept together. "Isn't it horrible?" Issie said. "They're all dead, Jill. We couldn't save any of them."

Jill pulled back and grabbed Issie's shirt. "Where is Dan? Where is he?"

Issie's face twisted, and tears left mud trails down her face. "Don't give up hope, Jill. We've pulled a few survivors out. They're not all dead."

"I want to help," Jill said. "I want to dig!"

Issie put her arms around her. "It's very tedious, careful work."

"It doesn't look careful, with all the dump trucks and machinery around here."

"It is, though. The ones working on the mounds have a bucket brigade, and they're passing debris—just a little at a time—in buckets. That way they can make sure that they're not overlooking anything. Then the debris is dumped into the dump trucks, and the trucks haul it off for the forensics teams to go through, looking for evidence. The heavy equipment helps lift the steel beams and slabs of concrete. We've found several pockets. They're doing it with the best possible care, Jill. Just let them work."

Jill watched as several brigades on the rubble worked in just the way Issie described. "But what about where they aren't digging? There are hundreds of people in that gym who could come and help. We could start our own brigade."

Issie put her hands on Jill's face and made her look at her. "Go back and wait with the families, Jill. I know it's hard. You're not alone, are you?"

"No, Susan's with me."

"She let you come over here by yourself?"

"She didn't know. She dozed off." Jill shook Issie's hands off her and turned back toward the site.

"Jill, I don't want you to put yourself through this. It's the worst thing I've ever seen."

Jill looked back at the line of bodies, wondering if she would ever get that image out of her mind. Muffling her anguish, she said, "What are they going to do with them?"

"Transport them to a place where they can be identified," Issie said. "But for now, as we pull them out, we're just lining them up. We don't have enough rescue units."

Suddenly Jill felt the fatigue of the day pull at her, and she realized she hadn't eaten since this morning. How could she be nauseous with nothing in her stomach? She turned to throw up again. Issie waited, then put her arm around her shoulder.

"Ma'am, you're in no condition to deal with this," the cop said. "Please go back."

"Come on, Jill," Issie said. "I'll walk you back to the end of the block, and then you have to go, okay?"

Jill finally nodded and let Issie lead her to the end of the street.

She made her way back to the school and went back into the gym. So many people, unable to sleep, watched the door or stared up at the ceiling. How many of them would have found their loved ones in that line of corpses?

She thought of the verse in the Bible that said God kept our tears in a bottle. How many bottles had he lined up to catch the tears of all these people? Most of them would have funerals to plan this week.

She met Ashley's eyes across the room. She was still watching the door, waiting. Behind her, Susan still dozed on her cot.

When she got back to her bed, Ashley sat up. "You were gone longer than I expected. You didn't go to the site, did you?"

She thought of Ashley running out of here, seeing those bodies. . . . It would haunt her for life. "No," she lied. "They wouldn't have let me in, anyway." She sat next to her. Ashley's eyes were vacant and distant as she stared toward that door.

"She's gone," Ashley whispered.

"Maybe not. Maybe my husband's in a hole somewhere taking care of her. He would do that. If she was injured, he'd be seeing to her."

Ashley was silent for a moment. "I never said good-bye."

Jill hadn't said good-bye to Dan either. She'd been in a hurry that morning, and he'd been getting ready to go help paint the floral shop. She'd run out with nothing but a kiss on his cheek and a plea for him to pick up their clothes from the dry cleaners.

"I should have stayed with her," Ashley said, "but she was screaming for me to go."

"Thank the Lord," Jill said. "If she hadn't, you might not have gotten out."

"I wish I hadn't," Ashley said. "I wish I'd stayed with her."

Jill wanted to tell her she had just had the same wish, but there was no point. "Where's your father, Ashley?"

"Died when I was five. Car accident. My mom raised me by herself."

Jill felt sick again. What was going to happen to this girl, if indeed she was an orphan? "How old are you, honey?"

"Sixteen."

"Isn't there anyone you can call to come get you? Or someone who can just be here for you?"

Ashley shrugged. "I don't have grandparents," she said. "No aunts and uncles. I never knew my father's family, and my mom was an only child, like me."

"What about friends? Surely there's someone who could come hold your hand while you wait."

"Yeah, right. If my friends pushed up in here, this whole group would start grabbing their purses."

"Rough crowd, huh?"

"Yeah. They're probably all stoned by this time of night, anyway. Riding some kind of high because of all the drama. They wouldn't be that helpful. Most of them wish their parents were dead. They wouldn't get it."

Jill studied her for a moment. "Why would you hang around with people like that?"

"I *am* people like that," she said. "If my mother wasn't missing, if I hadn't been in that building, I'd probably be smoking a joint and laughing about the news coverage. I wouldn't get it, either."

On the television across the room, Jill saw a news alert. "Look," she said, "It's about the bombing."

Ashley rose up and moved closer to the screen. Jill followed for lack of anything better to do.

"Three Middle Eastern men were arrested an hour ago at a motel in Newpointe, Louisiana. The FBI is investigating their possible role in the Icon International bombing today, as well as rumored ties with Al-Qaeda."

Ashley let out a rabid curse.

Jill closed her eyes. Al-Qaeda . . . Middle Eastern men. How could they get away with this again? She wanted to go down to the police station, wherever they were being held, and look them in the eye and scream out that her husband was missing, that all of her hopes and dreams were on the brink of disaster, that nothing in her life would ever be the same. She wanted to ask them how they, as humans, could do this to other human beings.

But she would never be able to get close enough to tell them anything—and besides, she couldn't leave. Any minute now they might pull Dan out and call Issie and her colleagues to come and jump-start him back to life—or line him up in the string of corpses on the side of the road.

The night would be long, and there would be no sleep for her.

Chapter Eighteen

● ● ●

Aunt Aggie Gaston had moped long enough. It was time to take care of her boys.

She had gone to the prayer meeting at the church and taken a big ol' pot of stew. She'd laid it out in the fellowship hall with homemade bread and a big pot of rice, as well.

No one had partaken. She wondered how any of them could call theirselves Christians, eating like that. It was clear in the Bible that folks were to eat when they got together under God. There practically wasn't a story in the Old Testament or New when somebody wasn't eating something. Why, even the elders on Mount Sinai ate a meal after God gave Moses them tablets.

Jacob ate with Esau when he'd been about to nuke him after he'd come back with his feuding wives. And hadn't Abraham ate with that Abimelech fellow who thought Sarah was Abe's sister?

She had brought that up at the prayer meeting, only to be told that this was a serious occasion. Like she didn't know that. Like her boys weren't buried under a thirty-story building, waiting to be dug out.

Implying that she was some crazy old woman who thought food would solve everything! She knew it wouldn't solve nothing, except send up a soothing aroma to the Good Lord who invented beef stew in the first place. And it would soothe them grieving souls while they prayed.

But she couldn't stuff it down their throats.

But she knew where her food would be appreciated. That was why she'd loaded the pots of food into her lavender Cadillac and commandeered Celia's stroller to carry it to the site. Her boys from the Midtown Station in Newpointe would miss her cooking. The Lord knew they'd been working their fingers to nubs trying to get their buried brothers up out of the ashes. She hoped they didn't have some misguided idea that they had to starve themselves like the praying saints at church to save their brothers.

It was getting to be 1:00 A.M. by the time she got to the city, and she found a parking place as close to the ruins as she could get. She got out and set up the stroller, then loaded the pots of stew and rice into it, along with the baskets of bread.

She had worn her black wind suit with a black turtleneck, just to look less conspicuous. She'd added gold lamé tennis shoes and a red bead necklace to the ensemble, just because a girl needed a little splash of color. After all, she had her Miss Louisiana image to keep up. She'd been the prettiest girl in the state in 1938, and she'd worked hard at her looks ever since.

The fact that she was eighty-three was no excuse to start letting herself go. After all, Sarah had been quite a looker at age eighty, when Abraham lied about her being his sister so some king wouldn't kill him over her. And even if she did say so herself, she could still turn heads at her age.

She saw a couple of police officers standing on the outskirts of a glut of police cars, fire trucks, and ambulances, and she lifted her chin and kept pushing that stroller like she knew where she was going.

"Excuse me, ma'am. You can't go any further."

She smiled that Miss America smile at him, hoping he realized she still had her own teeth. "It's okay, darlin'. I got me some food to take in. Here, have yourself a roll."

The cop was too skinny for his own good. How he thought he could chase down criminals with that scrawny frame baffled her. But he didn't appear to be hungry. "Ma'am, we've had volunteers bringing us food all night. We don't need any more, and I'm not allowed to let you near the site."

Time for the big guns. She took the top off of the stew pot. The smell wafted up on the smoky air. "You tell me—you had any food smells like that? Krystal burgers and chicken nuggets ain't real food. My boys need some strength! I cook for the Newpointe station every night of their lives, and I ain't about to stop taking care of my boys now."

The second cop came closer at the smell. "Maybe it would be okay to take it in. But we'll have to do it for you."

Incensed, she slammed the top back on the pot. "What it gon' hurt for me to go set it up? Them boys got better things to do than serving food. I can dip it out, hand it out, clean up after."

"Ma'am, I told you, you can't go."

Aunt Aggie stood there a moment, her Cajun temper rising up inside her as she stared past them. She couldn't see the wreckage from this vantage point, so there was no way to get in touch with Mark or Ray or Nick, or any of her other poor brokenhearted adopted sons. She couldn't comfort them or hug them or tease a laugh out of them. She couldn't see the pleasure on their faces as they took their first bite.

She thought of kicking up a ruckus, but then she realized they'd had enough of a ruckus today. She would accept this like the lady she was.

"Awright, then," she said, thrusting the pot at the cop who seemed interested. She took the rice out of the stroller and gave it to the scrawny one. "Remember, it's for my Newpointe boys first. 'Course them other boys need feeding too, so you just tell anybody who's hungry to get some eats. And tell them Aunt Aggie brought it. They'll know me."

She piled the bread baskets on top of the pots, then watched as they headed down the block.

Other cops eyed her, as if ready to drag her into the pokey if she came one more step. She decided it was best not to provoke folks whose nerves were on edge.

She turned and started pushing the stroller back to her car.

"Lord, let it lighten their load," she said aloud as she walked. "That Dan is hungry by now. Stomach's prob'ly gnawing at him. Ole George is probably craving some of Aunt Aggie's eats. You know how that boy can put it away. And the others—Jacob and Junior . . . Karen and Steve—they just as hungry, wherever they are. And they ain't the only ones."

She hoped the Lord was making note of her request. She knew he had control of things, but sometimes it didn't hurt to make suggestions.

She made a whole list of others as she drove back to Newpointe.

Chapter Nineteen

● ● ●

Mark had to stop digging at two o'clock in the morning. He hadn't eaten much since breakfast yesterday, and his throat was parched. He went to the mess tent where restaurants all around the area had been bringing food all night. His stomach felt too unstable for food, but his fatigue reminded him that he had to have fuel.

He turned his back to the corpses lining the road, even though the tent wall separated him from them. He didn't want to think about them. They'd been trucking them off to a makeshift morgue, but every hour a new line of bodies formed. The number of those who had been pulled out of the rubble in the last few hours was probably over a hundred. All but three or four of them were dead, the rest critically, maybe even mortally, injured. He'd pulled several out himself.

But there was still no sign of his fallen friends.

He guzzled down a bottle of water, ate half a sandwich, then left the tent. It had been over fifteen hours since he'd breathed fresh air. Cuts stung on various parts of his body. The one on his knee probably needed stitches, but he would deal with that later.

He stepped out of the tent and looked back at the rubble. He needed to get back.

But he was so tired.

Slowly, he lowered himself to the curb across from the site, resting his elbows on his knees. What he wouldn't give to see Dan coming up over one of those mounds of rubble, full of strength and life. While Mark rested, Dan would have done push-ups to reenergize.

Dan would have hung on Mark's account of his own burial and his long, unlikely journey out. He would have wanted a blow by blow.

As it stood, Mark hadn't had time to dwell on the tomb from which he and Nick had emerged. He had given Allie a brief account by phone, then returned to the site to hunt for Dan.

His friend probably lay in his own tomb now. Was he lying there awake, praying in the dark? Or had he given up his soul the moment the building collapsed?

A rush of tears got a choke hold on Mark, and he slid his hands out of his filthy gloves and covered his face in anguish.

"So you're okay, huh?" The voice startled him, and he looked up.

Eddie Branning—Mark's father—stood in front of him, a one-hundred-pound six-footer who looked as if he'd lived the hardest of lives and barely lived to tell about it. Alcoholism did that to a person.

"Dad, what are you doing here?"

Eddie rubbed his mouth. "I came to help." He looked even skinnier in the borrowed turnout coat he wore. He must have gone by Midtown to get it, after he'd taken a few hours to sober up.

"How long you been here?"

"Couple hours," Eddie said. "I looked for you but couldn't find you. I was . . . worried about you."

Mark wouldn't have expected that. He pictured his father hearing about the building collapse only because the network interrupted Jerry Springer for a news bulletin. He'd probably still been in a stupor from the night's drinking. Had he called Midtown to see what Mark thought of the whole thing? Had they told him that their own men were on the scene and that some of them were missing?

Mark pulled himself up off the curb. Unexpectedly, his father took a step across the pavement and pulled him into an awkward hug. He couldn't remember that ever happening before. He touched his father's back, not knowing quite how to react.

He felt Eddie's body trembling as he held him, and he wondered if it was relief or alcohol withdrawal. The trembling reminded him that the old, retired firefighter was the weaker man, even when Mark was at his weakest.

That old resentment tempered the feeling that hug had induced.

He pulled back. "Well, I guess we'd better get back to work. I've got buddies missing."

Eddie nodded. "I'll follow you and we'll work together, Son."

Eddie followed him back to the line, and they went to work.

• • •

An hour or more had passed when suddenly a voice cut across the night. "Newpointe! We've got some of your men!"

Mark swung around and ran toward where the men were clustered. "Let them be alive," he whispered. "Please, Lord, let them be alive!"

Eddie was fast on his heels. They reached the scene and he saw Ray and Nick trying to push to the front of the crowd.

"Let us through!" Ray cried. "Let us get our own men!" And as the crowd parted, Mark saw the face of George Broussard— bloody, charred . . . and lifeless.

Issie was beside them in seconds, on her knees testing his pulse. After a few seconds, she looked up into Mark's eyes. "He's gone," she said.

"There's another one under him," someone shouted.

They started pulling the bodies out, one by one: Jacob Baxter and Junior Reynolds. Dan would be next, Mark thought.

Rage lifted its lethal wings inside him. They were all dead, every one of them. How was he going to tell Jill, and Jacob's and Junior's wives, and George's little boy Tommy, who had already lost his mother?

He couldn't watch them pull his best friend out. He was no help, so he turned around and started off the mound. His father caught his arm, and Mark raised his hands. "I don't want to see them—" His voice broke off, and he swallowed hard and tried again. "I don't want to see them pull Dan's body out."

"It's okay, buddy."

He didn't want his father's temporary comfort, so he walked off to the side and waited, hands on hips and tears streaming down his face.

Minutes passed . . . then half an hour . . .

His fear of finding his friend dead turned to dread of not finding him at all. Forcing himself to do what needed to be done, Mark went back to work in the very area where the others had been found, thinking that if he had a shot at finding his friend, this would be the place.

Chapter Twenty

Allie's call came at around 3:30 A.M., waking Susan from where she slept on the cot. Jill listened in as Allie broke the news about George, Jacob, and Junior.

Dan was still unaccounted for.

As her friend talked to Allie in a soft voice, Jill lay down on her cot and hugged her knees. She glanced up and saw Ashley, with that porcelain white face, focused on that door, as if her mother could still walk through it.

At what point would both of them have to face the fate of their loved ones?

It was cruel, this night. Crueler than anything she had ever experienced.

They were newlyweds, practically. Their marriage was only two years old. They had been planning a family, had even gotten to the point where they entered each month with expectation and hope.

God, why did you let me find love if I couldn't keep it?

Finally, she heard Susan say good-bye, and then her friend's dark hands were on her shoulders, rubbing and caressing, trying to coax her out of her gloom.

"He's gonna be all right, sweetie. Dan's a big ole tough guy, the way he's always working out. He's in better shape than any of the firefighters in Newpointe. He can make it."

But Jill had nothing to say in reply. She lay still, staring at the air. She imagined that phone ringing again, snatching it up, hearing Dan's voice on the other end. *Hey, baby, it's me.*

He would tell her that he'd been working so hard that he hadn't been able to call, that no one knew where he was, that he'd been all right all along. He would tell her he was coming to get her and take her home.

But she knew that if that phone rang again, it wouldn't be Dan's voice on the other end.

Chapter Twenty-One

● ● ●

They hadn't found any survivors in over six hours, but Mark couldn't give up. After all, if he and Nick had been pinned and unable to move, they would probably still be alive, waiting and praying for rescue. Dan might be doing the same. Knowing him, he'd probably set up some underground triage unit and keep busy binding the wounds of other survivors. Maybe they'd find a whole busload of living, instead of enough dead to populate a graveyard.

He told himself these things, but deep down he knew how unlikely it was. If Dan were alive, he would have scratched and clawed his way out by now. They would have found him in the first few hours.

"Quiet, everybody!"

The digging stopped, and he heard a wave of yells going over the mounds, one person telling another to be quiet. He heard the dump truck engines cutting off, the machinery idling down.

Silence fell over the night, and everyone waited.

It had happened several times tonight as clusters of rescuers had thought they'd heard noise from deep in the debris. The others all froze where they were, waiting for more word.

Please, God, let it be Dan.

"Survivors!" someone yelled. "We got survivors! Medic!"

Mark's stomach flipped with hope, and he saw Issie and several other paramedics rushing toward the scene. He moved closer and saw them pulling out a woman. He couldn't tell if she was conscious.

"There's more!" someone shouted, and the medics got busy at the mouth of a hole.

He wanted to scream out that he needed a description. Were any of them firefighters, paramedics? Did they wear Newpointe uniforms? Were they alive or dead?

He heard the word *Newpointe*, and he couldn't wait any longer.

He rushed down the mound he was working on and toward the crowd around the hole. He tried to push through, to see the faces of those they'd found as flashlights lit them up.

And then he saw Dan, lying unconscious at the bottom of a hole, as if he'd been dropped there in a heap. Workers pulled debris out of the way, and Issie got to him first.

Please don't let him be dead.

"There's a pulse!" The words were the sweetest he had ever heard, and he started to cry as the crowd cheered around him.

• • •

I need a cervical collar!" Issie called. "And hand me my megaduffel." From her perch beside Dan, she reached up for the items she needed. Larry Jenkins, a paramedic from Hammond, brought a spineboard in behind her.

She checked Dan's airway. "Dan, can you hear me? Answer me."

There was no response. His breathing was rapid and deep, his pulse slow and bounding. "He's showing signs of Cushings reflex," she shouted. "There might be some intracranial pressure."

"Unconscious!" Larry shouted up to the team at the mouth of the hole. "Unresponsive. Glasgow score of three."

Carefully, Issie moved him enough to get the cervical collar on him. There could be fractures in his spine, damage to his spinal cord. Moving him out of this hole without doing further damage would be difficult.

But she couldn't get him out until she'd intubated him. It was standard procedure when there was head trauma, just in case there was swelling in his airway. It too would be difficult, since she couldn't move his head back to get the endotracheal tube down his throat.

If they did a nasal intubation, they could keep his neck in a neutral position. She got the tube out of her bag and inserted it into his nose. She trembled as she fed it down through his nasal cavity, praying that it would slip easily into the trachea.

Her prayer was answered, and she felt it go into place.

"Need oxygen!" she cried, and someone handed down the tank. She connected it, then checked his pulse again. It was weaker now.

They had to hurry.

"Let's get him on the board," she said, and another medic crawled down to help them. The hole was wide enough to lay the spineboard out beside him, and carefully they moved him onto it.

It was a miracle that he hadn't been crushed or smothered in the smoke—or burned.

Lord, don't let me lose him now.

They maneuvered him out of the hole, and some of the medics at the top began to run with him down the mound to an idling ambulance. She ran behind them.

"I'm going!" she said as they got him into the unit.

Two other medics followed her in, and they surrounded Dan and began taking his vitals. Another one got behind the wheel.

"Issie, I'm coming too."

It was Mark's voice, and she glanced out at him. "Ride shotgun, Mark," she said. "There's not room for you back here."

Mark jumped into the passenger seat, and as they pulled away from the site, she felt his eyes bearing down on her as she tried to keep Dan alive.

The siren screamed as they flew down Canal Street, declaring waning life and impending death.

And she vowed that Dan would not die on her watch.

Chapter Twenty-Two

● ● ●

Jill hadn't slept yet, but she lay on her cot, curled up under a blanket. Someone had turned the gym lights down, but few of those keeping vigil actually slept.

Occasionally, a cell phone rang and someone answered. They were the subject of everyone's attention for a moment, as if whatever information they were getting might impact them all. Several televisions played around the gym, the main source of their news about the progress at the site.

When she heard the distant siren winding up from several blocks away, she sat up.

Ashley's eyes widened, and she sat up too. "They found someone. They wouldn't need the siren unless they'd found a survivor."

Jill grabbed onto that hope and held it like a lifeline.

Others around the room began to get up as the siren moved toward them. Some of them headed for the door.

"Come on," she told Ashley, and the two of them pushed through the cots and burst out of the school as the ambulance raced by.

The group on the sidewalk cheered, and strangers began to hug, hope animating all of their weary faces. It could be any one of their loved ones, or several of them.

Ashley began to cry again, and Jill pulled her into a hug and held her against her.

"Maybe," the girl whispered.

Maybe. It was a word that held the future in its precarious grip, a word full of hope and life.

"Yes, maybe," she said.

They went back into the gym and crowded around the information table, waiting to learn who had been found.

Suddenly, she heard her name. "Jill! Jill, it's ringing!" Her heart shot up like a rocket from the launchpad.

The crowd parted, and Susan raced toward her and thrust the phone at her.

"Hello?"

"Jill, they found him!" Allie yelled into the phone. "He's alive!"

Jill felt her legs give way; Susan caught her. "He's alive? Is he all right?"

Voices rose around her as the others passed the news that someone had been found alive. Jill couldn't hear, so she pressed a finger to her ear and headed back outside, still unsteady on her feet.

"Mark said he's unconscious," Allie said. "I don't know much, except that they've taken him to the Medical Center. Mark said he looks bad. Head injury, possible neck and back injuries. But he's alive, honey."

"I'm on my way there," Jill cried.

"Me too," Allie said. "I'll be there in less than an hour."

Jill hung up the phone and turned back to Ashley. Tears streamed down the girl's face, and she wore an expression that hovered somewhere between grateful hope and crushing disappointment.

"He's alive, Ashley," she said. "If he is, then others could be too." She framed the girl's face. "You believe that, don't you?"

Ashley compressed her lips and nodded. "Yes. I'm happy for you. Really, I am."

But the sorrow in her eyes said otherwise. Jill understood.

The room had suddenly grown quiet again, and Jill had the strange sensation that the world had moved into slow motion.

"Do you want to go with us?" Jill asked the girl.

"No . . . I have to stay here. I have to wait."

Jill turned to Susan. "Do you have a pen and something to write on?"

Susan dug through her purse and handed her a pen and an old receipt.

Jill jotted her name and number down.

"I'll be praying for you, okay? If you need to talk, I'll be checking in for messages. Are you going to be all right?"

"Sure. I'll be fine."

But Jill knew that wasn't true. It was cruel, leaving her here. Yet what could she do?

"Thanks, like, for letting me hang with you."

Jill managed a smile. "They'll find your mother, honey. I know they will. And it'll be soon."

The girl looked old and beaten, and there was little hope in her eyes. They hugged again, then Jill wove her way through the envious crowd, and she and Susan headed for the hospital.

Chapter Twenty-Three

● ● ●

The Medical Center of Louisiana consisted of Charity and University Hospitals and served as a Level One trauma center for the entire New Orleans area. Jill had once handled a malpractice case against the center. It had been settled out of court, but in the course of preparing for the case, she had learned much that impressed her about the medical staff at the center, which received emergency referrals from eight state hospitals.

If she'd been able to choose where Dan was taken, this would have been it.

Susan dropped her off at the door to the emergency room. The ambulance still idled outside, its lights flashing and its back door open. Dan had apparently been taken inside.

She found Mark sitting in the waiting room, filthy and reeking of smoke and sweat. He rose to hug her. She locked her arms around him and felt the burden of the past hours crushing through her.

"How is he?" she asked.

"Still unconscious, and his vital signs are weak. He's hanging on, though, Jill." His voice broke off, and a look of frantic despair pulled at his face.

Jill refused to feel that despair. Dan couldn't die. He had survived a thirty-story building crashing on him. His organs had been strong enough to get him this far.

"He's gonna be all right," she said, pulling back and lifting her chin. "He'll make it. God wouldn't bring him this far just to let him die, would he? He has his hand on Dan."

"I think so, too," Mark whispered.

"Where is he?"

"In an examining room. They're checking him out. They said they'd come tell us as soon as they know something. Issie's still back there with him."

"I have to see him." She went to the desk where a nurse sat talking in a low voice on the phone. She was heavyset, with a sweet face that reminded Jill of one of her great-aunts, and she wore a red cotton lab coat with little cartoon flowers all over it.

She put her hand over the phone when she saw Jill, and whispered, "May I help you?"

"Yes, my husband was just brought in from the Icon site. Dan Nichols. I have to see him."

"Of course, honey." The woman quickly got off the phone. "I'll go see if you can go back."

Susan came in then and hugged Mark as if he were her long-lost son. "I'm so glad to see you, sweetie!" she said. "We could've lost you."

Mark nodded, unable to speak.

The nurse returned and held the door open for Jill. "Honey, follow me and I'll take you to your husband."

Jill followed the nurse into the cold, antiseptic hall.

"You don't look so good, yourself," the woman said. "Were you in the building, too?"

Jill hadn't even looked in the mirror since her shower. She supposed her bruises had darkened, and the scrapes and cuts on her face and arms must make her look as if she'd been in a fight. "Yes, I got out just before the building crashed."

The woman began to silently weep as they walked, and Jill felt the sudden, weary obligation to comfort her. But she didn't have anything to give.

"What an awful day for you," the nurse said, "wondering if your husband was alive. What a miracle they found him in time."

"Yes, it is," Jill said.

She looked up ahead and saw Issie coming out of a room. "Issie!"

The two of them held each other in silence for a moment. "Come on," Issie said, taking her arm. "I'll take you back."

Issie led Jill into a room where a team of doctors and nurses worked in urgent frenzy. She couldn't even see Dan in the midst of them.

Suddenly, fear overtook her.

"Dr. Hudson, this is his wife," Issie said.

One of the doctors turned. He wore a surgical mask and cap, but he had kind eyes.

"Is he—is he all right?" Jill asked.

"We're doing our best to stabilize him," the doctor said. "He came to for a few minutes, which is a good sign."

"He did?"

"Yes. It's possible that he hasn't been unconscious the entire time. That indicates that his head injury may not be as severe as we first suspected."

"Did he speak?"

"He can't," Issie said. "He's been intubated."

She moved toward the bed, straining to see between two doctors. She touched a resident's sleeve, gently pushed him aside.

And then she saw him.

He looked dead already. His closed eyes seemed sunken in, and his skin was a deadly gray. His lips were dry and cracked. She managed to get to his head, and she bent over him, touching his face gently. "Honey, it's me, Jill."

There was no response, so she turned her wet eyes to the doctor. He was blurred through her tears. "Is he going to make it?"

"The next twenty-four hours or so are critical," he said softly. "He's got a thoracic fracture. We're about to prep him for surgery."

Jill touched Dan's hand. It was cold, limp. "Thoracic fracture," she repeated. "What does that mean?"

"It means his back is broken. Dr. Henderson, our thoracic surgeon, is on his way, and Dr. Grist from Oschner's, who's one of the finest thoracic surgeons in the country, is coming to assist. We have to remove any bone fragments and stabilize his spine so there's no further injury to the spinal cord or exiting nerves."

Damage to the spinal cord? She wondered if that meant paralysis. Suddenly she was gripped with a sense of urgency. Unwilling to delay Dan's surgery, she backed away from the bed. "Whatever you can do," she said. "Whatever can be done."

"After surgery, we'll let you see him for a few minutes, but then we'll move him to ICU."

"Yes," Jill said. "Good."

"Meanwhile, if you'll go with Dr. Clemens, he needs to ask you a few questions about your husband's medical history."

She nodded and let the resident lead her out, but before she left the room, she looked back at Dan.

The horror wasn't over yet, but she refused to believe that he wouldn't come through it. He simply had to live.

Chapter Twenty-Four

● ● ●

Aunt Aggie came bearing biscuits.
She brought enough to feed an army of doctors and nurses, as well as all of the friends who'd begun arriving at the hospital to keep vigil with Jill. There was even enough for the others in the ICU waiting room.

Jill had no appetite, but she ate to appease the old woman. Turning down Aunt Aggie's "eats" was tantamount to slapping her in the face. Jill wouldn't dare.

Allie, who had come soon after Dan went into surgery, sat curled next to Mark. They'd had a sweet reunion, which created a yearning in Jill that brought her to tears. Celia had come with Aunt Aggie and joined Susan in supporting Jill. She firmly believed that the prayer power in this room would pull Dan through.

It was almost six in the morning when Dan came out of surgery. Dr. Grist found her in the waiting room, and her friends gathered around her for the news.

"How is he?"

"We had a few problems during surgery," he said. "Your husband's lung collapsed . . ."

Jill caught her breath and backed away. Was he about to tell her that Dan was dead? She thought of stopping him. Couldn't he let her go on thinking that he could be all right? Just for a little while longer?

But he continued. "We inserted a chest tube and put him on a respirator. Several ribs were broken, but we stabilized his spine, and we had to stop some internal bleeding."

"So . . . he's alive?"

"Yes," he said. "He's very strong, Mrs. Nichols, but he's not out of the woods. The next twenty-four hours are critical."

She started to cry then—from relief or fear, she didn't know.

Susan hugged her. "He'll pull through, sweetie. He's come this far."

Aunt Aggie grabbed her next. "He's tough, that boy is, *sha*. He gon' be awright."

Mark held her shoulders and made her look up at him. "Jill, think of those lungs. Who in the whole state has a better set of lungs than he has? The guy runs five miles a day."

She knew it was all true. He was strong. But would he make it through this?

The nurse led her back to his bed in ICU, and Jill tried to hold herself together as she got her first clear look at him.

He still looked dead.

Black circles shadowed his eyes, and black-and-red bruises marred his white-gray skin.

She leaned over and kissed his cheek. His stubble was thick, and the normalcy in that comforted her. She touched his face. "Dan? Honey, it's me. You're going to be all right, do you hear me? You're going to come out of this."

He didn't respond.

She pulled back his sheet to see the extent of his injuries. Bruises marked his chest and rib cage, and they had bandaged him in places.

But he still looked so athletic, so strong.

Jill thought of all the times she'd teased him about his constant need to work out. The guys on his shift were merciless in their ribbing. She had always asked him what, exactly, he was training for.

Now she knew.

His right biceps was scratched and bruised, but it was still bulky and hard. He was still Dan, not just some shell of her husband.

She covered him back up and pressed her face against his. Her tears dropped onto his pillow. "Lord," she whispered against his skin. "I know you're here. You're in control of all this. You can touch him and heal him."

She wept over him as she prayed, longing for him to open his eyes and tell her things would be all right. But he slept deeply, unresponsive, leaving her to wonder if his brain had been damaged, if his memory would be intact, if he would even know her when he came to himself.

At least he was here, where experts could care for him, and not buried under concrete and steel.

She had much to be thankful for.

Stroking his arm, she began to whisper the Twenty-third Psalm. Slowly, gradually, the comforting words calmed her fears. She and Dan weren't alone. It wasn't up to the doctors and nurses to determine whether Dan lived or died.

It was up to the Great Shepherd, who had led him out of the valley of the shadow of death.

She would fear no evil now.

Chapter Twenty-Five

● ● ●

By midmorning, Jill's body had begun to ache. She didn't remember injuring her knees, her back, or her neck, but that initial explosion had thrown her pretty hard. It would take awhile to work the soreness out.

She moved slowly, fatigue making her limbs heavy. She needed sleep, but anything could happen with Dan. She wasn't sure her friends would wake her at his visiting time if she fell asleep.

Her lungs were congested, and her chest ached from coughing. Dan's doctor had prescribed an antibiotic and something to help her breathing, as well as a mild anti-inflammatory to help with her soreness. Susan, who had been with her all night and was almost as tired as she, had gone to get the prescription filled.

As she waited for visiting time, Jill wondered about Ashley's mother. Had she been found, or was the girl still camped out on a cot in that room full of suffering?

Her court reporter, Wanda, had sent word that she was fine. She had gotten out in plenty of time.

Jill wondered about Gordon Webster. That firefighter who had come along and taken Gordon from them had certainly saved her life and Ashley's, for she and Ashley could never have gotten Gordon out in time. But she wondered if the firefighter had managed to save Gordon . . . or himself.

She hadn't seen them come out, but then, she'd been looking for Dan.

But if they had made it out—wouldn't the paramedics have brought Gordon here?

She slipped out of the waiting room and went to the nurse's station. A very young woman, probably a nursing student, came to help her.

"I was wondering if Gordon Webster had checked in here. He would have been one of the Icon survivors."

The woman typed his name into her computer. "Yes, he's here."

Relief and joy rose up inside Jill. "He made it? He got out?"

"Must have. He's in Room 413." The nurse jotted the number down for her on a Post-it note.

Jill took it as if it were a gift. "Thank you so much."

So it had been worth it. Gordon was not among the dead. She and Ashley may well have helped save his life.

She wished she could tell the girl.

She had to see him. She had to look him in the eyes, see the life there, and know that all was not lost. And she had to let him know that she had made it, too.

She took the elevator to the fourth floor, made her way wearily up the hall, and found room 413. Softly, she knocked.

"Come in."

She stepped into the room and saw the man she had met on the stairs yesterday.

"Mr. Webster?"

He had an oxygen mask on, but he lifted his head and looked up at her.

He looked older than he had the previous day, more frail, and she could tell from the look on his face that he didn't recognize her.

"Jill Nichols," she said. "I met you during the evacuation yesterday. On the stairs?"

His eyes rounded, and he tried to sit up, then collapsed in a fit of coughing. She stood a moment, trying to decide what to do for him. Finally, she picked up the half-full glass of water from the bedside table and offered it to him.

He waved it away. "I'll be all right," he said as the coughing settled. "These blasted lungs. All that smoke."

She knew the feeling.

When he was breathing normally again, he pulled the mask off and reached for her hand. "My lady hero," he said. "I'd be dead now, if it wasn't for you. I owe you big. Never expected the building to collapse like that. Third bomb went off, and the whole thing just came tumbling right down. They'd already got me into the ambulance, and the rush of air and debris from the building's collapse almost turned the thing over."

"We're all so blessed to be alive."

He took her hand, squeezed it hard. "It was sweet of you to come all the way here to see me. A crotchety old man who gave you such a hard time."

"You didn't give me a hard time," she said with a smile. "Besides, I was here anyway. My husband is in ICU."

He sat up slowly. "Your husband? Was he in the building, too?"

"Yeah," she said. "It's kind of ironic that we'd both be there when neither of us work for Icon."

"Sure is."

"He's a fireman and was helping with the evacuation. He was buried when the building came down. But they found him this morning, thank God. He's still in bad shape." Her voice broke off.

She could see the pain on his face as he processed that, and she appreciated it. He dabbed at the tears in his eyes. "Oh, honey, I know what you're going through. I lost my wife to cancer just a few weeks ago. Had her down in that same ICU, living minute to minute."

So he was completely alone. She hadn't meant to cry, but she couldn't seem to help herself. "I'm so sorry, Mr. Webster."

"Gordon," he said, stroking her hand. "Call me Gordon. We've been through too much to not be on a first-name basis."

"All right, Gordon." She sat down in the chair beside his bed. "How long were you married?"

He swallowed hard. "Forty-five years." He looked up at the ceiling, as if seeing happier days. "Had all these plans for traveling when we retired. Only Icon let me go six months before retirement, and when their stock dropped, our retirement just faded away. Then it turned out that they'd gotten behind on paying our insurance premiums, and here we were with all those medical bills. . . ."

Jill felt the blows he must have suffered over the last few weeks. Unemployment, financial ruin, the death of his wife, and unparalleled trauma just yesterday.

And she thought she had it bad.

"How bad is your husband?" he asked, wiping his eyes.

"Pretty bad," she said. "Head injury, a broken back, broken ribs, his lung collapsed, and he may be paralyzed."

Gordon cleared his throat. "You have a long row to hoe."

"Yes, I do," she whispered. "But I know God's in control. He got him out of that rubble. And he's watching over him now."

He patted her hand. "You're a good lady, Jill Nichols."

"No, I'm not. I've been a wreck all night."

"Well, if anyone deserves to have their prayers answered, you do."

She drew in a deep breath. "So how are you?"

He threw back his bedcovers, revealing a cast that went from his foot to above his knee. "Broken in two places," he said.

"Will you be able to take care of yourself when you get home?"

He breathed a laugh. "Won't have much choice, will I?"

"Do you have children who can help you?"

"No, Alma and I could never have any. I don't have much family to speak of, and what I do have is halfway across the country."

How would he take care of himself with a broken leg and lungs that weren't a hundred percent? "Gordon, where do you live?"

"In Newpointe," he said.

She caught her breath. "That's where I live. What part of Newpointe?"

"The southeast area. Broad Park."

She knew the area well. It was an older subdivision populated mostly by elderly people.

"Do you have a church that can help you, Gordon?"

He shook his head. "No, I haven't been to church in over thirty years. All they care about is getting your money. Alma started getting religious before she died, but we never did go to a church."

So he was even more alone than she thought.

But not for long. She would mobilize Calvary Bible Church to minister to this lonely, wounded man. Her friends couldn't help Dan right now, but they could help Gordon Webster.

She got up. "I'd better get back to the waiting room, in case the doctors come by again. But I'll be back to check on you, Gordon. And when you get out, if you need someone to take you home, I'm sure I can arrange something for you. You're going to need help."

"No, don't worry about it," he said. "I'll be fine. You just concentrate on getting your husband better."

"I'll come by again later and see how you're doing, okay?"

"I'd like that." He put the mask back on, and she started away.

"Jill?"

She turned back.

He had pulled the mask back down. "Thank you for everything."

She smiled. "Sure."

Her heart broke as she got back on the elevator and rode back to her floor. What she feared the most—losing her spouse—had already happened to Gordon. Like Job, he'd been stripped of almost everything in his life. He needed help. He needed the love of her church to get him through this.

And she needed to stop feeling so sorry for herself and realize that others had it even worse than she.

· · ·

When she got back to the waiting room, she saw that everyone was gathered around a television set for a bomb site news update. She saw the site of the Icon Building, thirty stories compressed to the height of four or five.

The miracle of Dan's rescue came home to her. She moved closer to the set.

A Fox News reporter stood on the roof of a building that overlooked the site, but as he spoke, the cameras zoomed in on the scene, highlighting the faces of the rescue workers who toiled in the heat of the smoldering rubble, still trying to rescue anyone who could be alive.

"Among the missing is fifty-four-year-old Donald Merritt, chief executive officer of Icon International. Merritt was expected to be indicted sometime next week for fraud and embezzlement, for allegedly 'cooking the books' of the international firm and lying to stockholders about the profits. Today, the anxieties plaguing the Merritt family have little to do with the law."

Allie, who hadn't left here since she'd come early this morning—even though Mark had returned to the site—put her arm around Jill. "Isn't that who your meeting was with?"

Jill nodded. "I would have thought he'd gotten out. I was with him. We evacuated the top floor. If I got out, he should have been able to. And I was slowed down because I was helping Gordon."

"Maybe being slowed down is what saved you. Otherwise, you might have been near the tenth floor when that second bomb went off."

"But he took the other stairwell, and the tenth floor wasn't damaged on that side. He must have been helping people get out, too. I can't believe I was sitting in a meeting with him yesterday, and now he could be dead."

The reporter switched gears, and the footage she had seen a million times of the Al-Qaeda training camp began to play.

"FBI sources tell us that they're looking into a possible Al-Qaeda connection, though they can't yet say for sure that the terrorist organization is behind the bombing. Three Middle Eastern men are being detained in Newpointe today, though the FBI has not yet confirmed that they're suspects in the bombing at Icon headquarters."

Jill went rigid. "How could anyone be so evil?"

The television continued blaring, and Jill listened without watching, knowing that the drone of possibilities and speculations and the ever-changing body count all burned themselves into her subconscious, forever becoming a part of her.

Chapter Twenty-Six

● ● ●

Ashley needed a shower. She had been in the gym all night and all day and still smelled of soot and sweat. She went into the locker room, intent on hurrying back in case any word came about her mother.

Some volunteers from a local church had given her a change of clothes—a pair of jeans, some underwear, and a T-shirt. It was more conservative than what she usually wore, but it beat the filthy outfit she'd been wearing since yesterday.

She showered, then put on the hand-me-downs and stood in front of the mirror. Her burgundy hair stuck up in every direction, just like she usually liked it. But today was a slicked-over kind of day.

She didn't have a comb, so she parted it with her fingers, then finger-combed it into place.

Her mother had hated her devil-may-care hairstyle, almost as much as she'd hated Ashley's nose ring.

Now Ashley wished she hadn't shown her mother her pierced tongue just before she died. She stuck her tongue out now, pulled the gold stud out, and tossed it into the trash. She didn't feel like talking around it as she demanded news about her mother. It had been a stupid thing to do, anyway.

She stuffed her soiled clothes down into the trash can and grabbed her purse. Leaving her hair wet, she went back out.

She had to admit—she did feel better. Earlier, that same church group had shown up bearing Egg McMuffins for everyone. The food had given her much-needed energy.

Now, as she went back into the noisy gym, she saw that a crowd had formed at one of the tables near the door.

There must be a new list of survivors they'd dug out . . . and a new list of the dead.

She stood in the crowd with her heart in her throat, waiting to get close enough to see if her mother's name was on either one.

One family began celebrating and cheering as they saw their loved one's name on the survivor list, and she caught her breath with hope that, perhaps, her mother's was there, too.

She moved up in line. The family in front of her saw the list, and she watched them crumple in tears and embrace each other.

What would she do if her mother's name was among the dead? There would be no one to cry to, no one who could hold her up.

She'd have to endure it on her own.

Bucking herself up, and forcing herself to do what was necessary, she stepped up to the table.

First, she scanned the list of survivors. Her mother's name was not there.

Her hands trembled as she looked at the other list, ran her finger down to the M's. Allen Maeler, Anthony Montgomery . . .

And there it was. Deborah Morris.

Ashley felt her body trembling, felt her knees giving way, felt the ripping anguish in her throat.

It was official. Her mother was dead.

Someone pushed her out of the way, and she stepped back and just stood there, her mind racing with a collage of images that had no connection to each other.

Just fifty bucks, Mom!

You're a beautiful girl, Ashley.

I'm dropping out of school, Mom.

Ashley, what kind of life will you have if you stay on this track?

I'm moving in with this guy who says I can stay there for free.

Ashley, don't break my heart!

Her mother was dead. She wondered how they had identified her. The news had said that they had pictures of the employees and were using them to find the names of the dead.

The dead. She couldn't grasp it. It couldn't be true.

"Honey, are you all right?"

Ashley looked into the eyes of one of the church ladies. Her mouth quivered. "Where ... did they take the bodies?"

"They've set up a morgue for them, darlin'." She touched Ashley's shoulder.

Ashley backed away. "I need to go there. To see my mother."

The woman looked stricken. "Was her name on the list?"

Ashley nodded dumbly and swept her hair behind her ears. "But it could be, like, a mistake. They could have gotten her mixed up with someone else. She has one of those faces, you know? People always think they know her."

"It's about a mile from here." The woman's voice sounded soft, full of pity. "Down Canal Street, behind the New Orleans Bank. You want me to take you, darlin'?"

Ashley shook her head. "No, I'll walk."

"But you don't want to go in there alone, honey. I'll go with you."

But Ashley started away from her, unable to answer. She burst out into daylight and started walking, not even certain she was going in the right direction.

The sky was clear blue, the sun shining so brightly that she imagined her friends sunbathing on the roof of the house they had all been sharing. There was something wrong with that, she thought. On a day full of death, there should be clouds, rain pouring from the sky, thunder like the angry voice of God.

She walked and walked, wondering why she hurried to get to that morgue and see her mother's mangled body. Then she realized that she hurried because the sooner she saw the woman they had identified as Debbie Morris, the sooner she could tell them that it wasn't true. It was some other woman who looked like her mother.

As she turned the corner onto the block where the morgue was, she knew instantly which building it was. Media stood outside the door, doing live remotes from here since they couldn't get to the site of the bombs.

She stopped before approaching them, trying to get her bearings. She could use a drink, or a cigarette, or something to dull this pain. She could use a getaway car. She could use a friend.

Forcing herself, she walked through the crowd of reporters and pushed into the building.

Other family members with red eyes and horror on their faces waited in the front room. Ashley stepped inside and went to the table set up there.

"May I help you?" The woman's voice was kind, and Ashley wondered how many times today she had confirmed people's worst fears.

She swallowed. "My mother's name was on the list," she managed to say. "I need to see her because I'm sure it's a mistake." She burst into tears with the last words.

"Oh, honey." The woman's voice was too gentle. "What's your mama's name, sweetheart?"

"Deborah Morris."

The woman scrolled down her computer list. Standing up, she called across the room. "Johnny, will you please take this young lady to number eighty-seven?"

Number eighty-seven? Her mother had been reduced to a number? Or maybe it was a good thing, since the name could be wrong.

The man approached her with a clipboard, and in a low voice said, "You can come with me."

Ashley followed him around the wall and into a huge, cold room full of bodies lined up on the floor. There were dozens of them, all in body bags.

Thousands of dreams destroyed, thousands of hearts broken, thousands of lives ruined.

Nausea churned in her stomach, but she forced it down. She could do this. It was the only way to show them they were wrong.

He led her to number eighty-seven, then knelt beside the body and began to unzip the bag.

Ashley remained standing, not wanting to get too close. She had never seen a dead body before. She focused on a steel beam on the ceiling.

The man pulled back the bag and got to his feet. "You can look now," he said quietly.

She thought she was going to faint. Tears trailed down her face, and her body wavered. Slowly, she forced her eyes down.

Her mother looked as if she slept, and Ashley stood for a moment, staring, remembering how she'd loved to sleep in the bed with her when she was little. On Saturday mornings, she would stare her mother awake.

"Ma'am, can you confirm her identity?"

Ashley thought of screaming no, that she couldn't identify her, that they had the wrong person. But screaming it wouldn't make it true.

Instead she fell down beside her body and touched her mother's face.

Her face was untouched, but the rest of her had been badly burned. The hair on one side of her head had been singed off, and the skin from her shoulders down seemed melted and mangled.

She held her breath for a moment, locking in the anguish that begged to burst out. Finally, unable to hold it anymore, she let out a loud, "Mama!"

The man put his arm around her shoulders and gently pulled her to her feet. The woman from the front ran back and took Ashley from him. "Oh, honey, I'm so sorry," she said. "So, so sorry."

Ashley almost couldn't walk, but the woman led her to a room with a small table and a couple of chairs. She guided Ashley into one and gave her a box of tissues and a cup of water.

"I hate this job," the woman said. "I volunteered to help, and they put me here. It's a dark day, all right."

Ashley wept into her hands, and the woman sat next to her, patting her back.

"Is there anyone I could call for you, sweetheart?" she asked. "Anyone at all?"

Ashley tried to think of someone but came up empty. "She's all I've got."

"You don't have a daddy?"

"He died a long time ago."

"Grandparents, aunts, uncles?"

"No." Ashley had to get out of here, to leave this place of death. "I have to go."

"Of course, honey. Could you just sign this paper, saying that we've identified her correctly? That way we can have the funeral home come and get her, and you can go ahead and make arrangements."

Arrangements? For what? Was she, a sixteen-year-old girl, supposed to arrange a funeral for her own mother?

She turned back to the table and signed the paper, then started out of the room.

"Honey, we'll send her to Finn and Banks Funeral Home. You just call them, and they'll guide you through it."

Ashley couldn't take it all in. She hurried out of the room, down the row of dead mothers and fathers and husbands and wives, and burst back out into daylight.

Chapter Twenty-Seven

● ● ●

Ashley found her car still parked in the public parking lot several blocks from where the Icon Building had stood. It was covered with ashes, but it looked unharmed.

She found the extra set of keys under the seat and started the car.

It was just after three in the afternoon when she got to her mother's house. She hadn't been here in weeks. Unlocking the back door, she stepped into the kitchen and stood for a moment, trying to get her bearings before she stepped over that threshold, into the home that her mother had made for her. The home to which her mother would never return.

The kitchen light was blaring, as if someone was home, but Ashley knew better. Her mother had a problem with turning off lights. She closed the door behind her and heard a radio on in another room. So many mornings her mother had left it playing when she rushed off to work. Ironic that it had played all through yesterday with news updates about the explosions and the deaths. And now it still played.

She stood just inside the door for a moment, looking around the kitchen, all lit up, polished and shiny, with that music from the radio playing in that other room. For a moment she tried to imagine that her mother was back in the bedroom, that in a moment she would rush out and hold out her arms.

Ashley, you're home!

What did they do when a sixteen-year-old girl was suddenly orphaned? Did they let her keep her mother's house? Did they take it from her?

The empty longing of her grief propelled her further into the house. She looked around the living room. Her mother had left a coffee cup on the table next to the chair where she sat to read her Bible every morning before work. Her Bible lay open on the arm of the chair—signs of life where there was none.

She walked further into the house, past the bedroom she had abandoned when she chose to drop out of school and leave home. Her mother had kept it just as she'd left it, though a little cleaner.

She went back to her mother's bedroom, where the radio was playing, and stood at the entrance for a moment. The bed was made, but her mother's pajamas lay draped over a chair, along with a skirt that she imagined her mom trying on, then discarding, before settling on the outfit she would wear to her death.

She crossed the room, picked up those pajamas, and brought them to her face. "Mama," she whispered.

The praise song playing on the radio grated on her nerves, so she crossed the room and turned it off.

Silence fell over the house. Slowly, Ashley left her mother's room and went back into the living room, sat down in the recliner her mother enjoyed when she got off work and needed to put her feet up. She picked up the Bible and saw her mother's prayer journal beneath it. She grabbed it, too, and opened to the first page. One of her mother's famous prayer lists. Notes to pray for a friend going through cancer treatments. Notes to pray for her pastor's wife who had strep throat, Francis's cousin who had gall bladder surgery . . .

And then she came to her own name, written three times on that list. *Ashley, Ashley, Ashley.*

There was no specific request there. She could only imagine her mother writing down, from the pain in her heart, all the things Ashley had done lately. She could picture her mom contending with God for the soul of her daughter.

She dropped the journal and her mother's Bible into her bag, then went to her room and dug through the drawers for the clothes she would need for wherever she would go.

She couldn't stay here tonight. Staying here alone would be too cruel. She would keep expecting her mother to come breezing in, fussing at her about the nose ring, about the tongue stud. She turned off all the lights and, with a knot in her throat, locked the door behind her.

She went back out to her rusted old Subaru and drove toward town. She needed to find Chris, her boyfriend, and all of her friends. Maybe she would be able to shake this feeling of sudden unbelonging.

Maybe they could help her plan her mother's funeral.

Chapter Twenty-Eight

• • •

Ashley's Subaru rattled into the driveway of the small, rickety house she and her friends rented. For a moment she sat behind the wheel, letting it idle as she stared up at the house that, just a few weeks ago, had seemed like such a haven to her.

There were no rules here, and she could live with her boyfriend and all of her good friends who had the same likes and dislikes as she, and no one could tell them what to do or how to do it.

But it wasn't a home.

Funny how she'd thought that her home would always be there to return to if she needed it. A base from which she could rebel. Now her home was empty. Just a house. And she felt as if she had dived into a free fall and didn't know where she might land.

The door opened, and she saw Chris look out. He had a cigarette in his mouth and looked as brooding as James Dean as he stared out at her.

She got out of the car, pulled her bag with her. "Hey," she said.

He dropped the cigarette onto the ground and stomped it out. "Where have you been?"

Did he really not know? Had it not even occurred to him? "Where do you think?"

"Home? You were going to get money from your mother, but I thought you'd be back."

His ignorance made her angry, and she walked up and looked up into his face. He hadn't shaved in days. That had always been attractive to her before, but now it repelled her.

The feeling was mutual. "You look like death," he said.

That simple declaration birthed a rage inside her, and she stood looking at him, hating him for not knowing what she'd been through in the last twenty-four hours.

"No, this isn't what death looks like," she bit out.

He frowned down at her. "What's wrong with you? Did I do something?"

She let out a long breath and deflated against his Camaro. Looking up at him, she decided that she wasn't being fair. She should tell him what she'd been through. Then she would get his comfort instead of his indictments.

"Yesterday," she said, "I went to ask my mom for the money—"

The door swung open, and she heard raucous laughter inside. Eddie, the twenty-five-year-old out-of-work rock star, leaned out. "Hey, Ashley's back. See, Chris, I told you she hadn't quit you. Hey, I need to use your car, man. I have to make an emergency run to the store for some Oreos."

It was their favorite staple food when they got the munchies after getting high.

Chris tossed him the keys, and Eddie staggered out and got behind the wheel. "Hey, Ash, you're gonna have to move your car."

Ashley just stood looking at Chris, who had already lit up another cigarette.

"Ashley, come on, I'm in a hurry," Eddie said.

Ashley nodded. "Hold tight. I'm going."

She went back down the driveway to her car and started it up. It sputtered and hesitated as she backed it out. She stopped in the street and watched Eddie back out and head off to the store. Chris went back inside.

He was waiting for her, she knew, and she would walk into that house where everyone was high and giggling, and she would tell them about her part in the explosion and how she'd just had to go and identify her mother's remains.

There was no reaction she could imagine from them that wouldn't seem cruel.

Suddenly, she wanted to be anywhere but here, with anyone but these people.

She shifted into drive, and instead of pulling back in, she drove away. She didn't have a clue where she would go.

Who could she count on? Who wouldn't let her down?

She thought of Jill, the woman who had helped her out of the building and stayed with her for most of the night. She didn't even remember her last name.

She pulled the paper that Jill had given her out of her pocket. Jill Nichols, 555-6682. She had said to call if she needed her.

Maybe she needed her now.

It was a Newpointe number, so she got on Highway 10 and headed across Lake Pontchartrain.

She turned on her radio and punched around for the news.

"... *after the Icon bombing yesterday. Sources tell us that there are ninety-seven people confirmed dead at this time. A spokesman for the FBI said that they do suspect terrorism, but they are not ruling out other possibilities...."*

A rage unlike any she'd ever known stabbed through her. She pulled off the road. Gritting her teeth, she grabbed a beer bottle off of the floor and smashed it into the radio. Her beating broke the glass and the plastic plate and knobs, and she kept beating the dashboard until there was nothing left in her hand.

She sat there for a moment, staring at the fallout of her fury.

It hardly mattered who had done it. Whether it was an American or a foreigner or the devil himself....

She sat a moment, weeping out her rage, wishing for something else she could break. She wished for a cliff to drive off. A concrete wall to drive into at eighty miles per hour.

After a while, she pulled back into traffic and headed toward Newpointe.

When she reached the outskirts of the little town, she stopped at a convenience store and looked up Jill's address in the phone book. After getting directions from the clerk, she navigated her way to the Nichols house at the end of Second Street.

It was just after 7:00 P.M. when she reached Jill's house. She parked her Subaru on the street and got out. For a moment she stood in the yard, looking up at the big house. She wondered whether she'd done the right thing. If Jill's husband was all right, then probably the last thing she wanted was someone in misery getting her down again. But she had seemed like such a nice person and had offered help if Ashley needed it.

And Ashley didn't know where else to turn.

She went up on the porch and knocked on the door. There was no answer, so she rang the bell and waited, then knocked again. When no one answered, she realized it was possible that Dan was still in the hospital, that Jill hadn't even been home yet.

Though a storm still raged in her heart, it seemed less threatening here. The thought of going back to her home or her friends was more than she could take. She would wait until Jill got home.

The furniture on the porch looked even more comfortable than that in the house where she had been living. She went to a bench with a cushion on it and lay down. She would just wait here. And while she was waiting, she would close her eyes.

She would wake when Jill's car came up the driveway.

Then she could ask Jill to help her bury her mother.

Chapter Twenty-Nine

● ● ●

Jill felt as gutted as the Icon Building as she drove back to New-pointe that night. Her mind and heart were still at the hospital with Dan, but there had been little change since they'd checked him into ICU. There were things she needed from home, things that would make Dan more comfortable, like a pair of socks, his shaving gear, and his own clothes. She could use a change of clothes herself. She would just have to hurry back to the hospital as soon as she could. Thankfully, Allie and Mark had brought her Dan's pickup that had been parked at their shop since yesterday. Her own car had been crushed under the building.

She turned on the radio as she took Highway 10 over Lake Pontchartrain. Another news update rehashed the accounts of yesterday.

"Sources tell us that the family of Donald Merritt, chief executive officer of Icon International, has contacted police regarding a hidden bank account that Merritt allegedly set up in a Swiss bank. They claim that a large sum of money disappeared from that account yesterday. Sources at the FBI tell us this may be a lead into who planted the bomb in the Icon Building."

Jill's mind raced with possibilities. Who could have gotten access to Merritt's hidden bank account? His accountant? His chief financial officer? Could any of them have been callous enough to grab his money just hours after he was killed?

She wondered what the FBI knew. Was there more to it than simple embezzlement? Could it have been part of the plan that included blowing up the building?

A volatile mixture of grief and rage boiled up inside her, threatening to explode. Could all the destruction really be the result of greed? Did Dan lie on the brink of death because someone wanted to get at Merritt's money? Was there anyone that cruel, that money-hungry, that they could wipe out a hundred people, all for the almighty buck?

She cried out to God that he would expose whomever had done this and let justice rain down upon them. In the last twenty-four hours the world had become an awful place. If only the Lord would ride in on his white horse, right now, and gather his people from the far corners of the earth. Then maybe she could put it all into perspective.

But right now it seemed like someone else was in control.

She reached Newpointe and drove faster than she should through the streets until she came to her own. The house that Dan had lived in when they married was much more extravagant than anything she would have chosen. His parents had deeded his childhood home to him, and since it was paid for, there seemed no reason to sell it. Still, every time Jill pulled onto their street and drove past the exclusive upscale homes, she wondered what on earth she was doing here.

A rusty old car sat next to the curb in front of their house. Had someone's car broken down, she wondered, or was it a client waiting for her to get home? Or worse, a reporter who needed a quote about yesterday? She should have come earlier, while it was daylight. Now darkness made coming home seem dangerous and uncertain. Bracing herself, she pulled her car into the driveway and looked up at the porch. In the light of the gas lanterns on either side of the door, she saw that someone lay curled up on the wicker loveseat, apparently asleep.

She got out of the car and closed her door, hoping to wake them. When the person didn't stir, she moved closer. As she went up the steps, her fears melted away.

Ashley.

She stepped up the front steps and quietly walked across the boards until she came to the girl. Stooping down in front of her, she pushed Ashley's hair back from her face.

"Hey, Ashley. Wake up, honey."

Ashley stirred and looked around, as if she'd forgotten where she was, and then quickly came to herself and sat up. "Hey. I didn't hear you drive up." In the moonlight, the girl looked paler than ever.

"What are you doing here?" Jill asked softly. "How'd you find my house?"

"I looked it up in the phone book. I hope you don't mind that I came."

"No, of course not." Jill sat down next to her, studying her face. There was a chill in the air, and the girl wasn't wearing a coat. She shivered.

"Have you heard any word on your mother, honey?"

Ashley's face contorted then, and she got up and went to the rail, looked out over the street.

"I had to identify her body." The statement came out hoarse and broken, almost too soft to be heard. Jill felt it like an electrical shock, painful and familiar. She got up and turned the girl around, and Ashley came willingly into her arms. Jill just clung to her as they wept together.

"You had to do that all by yourself?" Jill whispered. "Did anybody go with you?"

Ashley shook her head. "My friends are all jerks and idiots." She was shivering harder, and her hands were ice cold. Jill pulled her to the door, unlocked it, and took her inside. The house was just as she'd left it yesterday morning when she'd hurried off to her Icon meeting and left Dan to clean up the dishes. Who could have anticipated the events of the rest of that day?

She turned on the light and looked fully at Ashley. The girl had taken off the chain that attached her nose and ear rings, but her piercings were still adorned with studs and loops.

"Have you eaten anything?" Jill asked.

Ashley shook her head. "I'm not hungry."

Jill didn't listen. She pulled Ashley into the kitchen and opened the refrigerator, searched the contents. "I don't have much. I really need to go to the store."

"Don't worry about it," Ashley said. She looked up at her. "How's your husband?"

That dull feeling of despair fell over Jill again. She closed the refrigerator and turned back to her. "He's in really bad shape."

Ashley looked down at the table. "Bummer."

The word sounded flip, but Jill knew she didn't mean it that way. "Yeah. Big bummer," Jill said. She dropped down into a chair across from Ashley. "I just came home to get some things. I have to get back to the hospital in case he wakes up."

Ashley quickly got up. "You go ahead. I don't want to keep you. If my mom was in the hospital I wouldn't want to deal with people showing up on my porch. I just wanted to come by and tell you . . ."

Jill took her hand, and looked hard into her eyes. "I told you to call if you needed someone. I'm glad to see you, Ashley. I'll help you any way you need."

Ashley struggled with her tears again, then said, "I just don't know how to begin."

"Begin what?"

"Burying my mom." The words caught in her throat. "I don't even know how to start. What are you supposed to do?"

Jill couldn't imagine the depth of the pain this girl was feeling. She remembered the shock and anguish she'd felt when her mother died thirteen years ago. Her father had taken care of everything. She couldn't imagine being sixteen and having to do it alone.

Jill touched her cheek. "I'll go with you to the funeral home. Would that help?"

"Yes." Ashley seemed to relax. "I guess I need to go tomorrow."

"All right," Jill said. "We'll go first thing."

Ashley looked up at her. "Are . . . are you sure you can leave your husband?"

Jill knew it wouldn't be easy. "He's in ICU, and I can only visit him every few hours. We'll work it between visits."

Ashley sighed. "Okay."

"Meanwhile, where are you staying, sweetheart?"

Ashley shrugged. "I don't know. I went to my mom's house, and she'd left the lights on and the radio playing just like she was coming right back. I couldn't stay there. It was too hard." She sucked in a shaky breath. "And then I went to where I've been staying with my boyfriend and some other people. They didn't even know I'd been in the explosion or that my mother had died, and I just couldn't make myself tell them."

"Why not, honey? You needed that support."

"Not from them," she said. "Like I said, they're idiots. They would make me feel worse. I don't know what to do, or . . . where to go."

"You could stay here," Jill said. "We have very comfortable guest rooms. It's embarrassing, really. You can have your pick."

Ashley stared at her for a moment. "Really? You wouldn't be afraid?"

"Afraid? Why would I be afraid?"

"Because I'm not exactly the kind of person people take into their homes . . . not without locking up their silver."

Jill gaped at her. "Ashley, I saw your character in that stairwell yesterday. I know what kind of person you are."

Ashley looked perplexed. It was as if she'd told the girl something about herself that she didn't know. "If you're sure."

"Of course I'm sure. The only thing is that I was going to sleep at the hospital tonight. You'd be here alone. On the other hand, you could stay up there with me, but I'll be sleeping in a chair . . ."

"No, I'll stay here," Ashley said. "I'm alone, anyway, whether I mind it or not. After being in that gym all night, it might be good to have the quiet."

"Well, it won't be quiet for long. My mother-in-law is coming from Paris tomorrow." She led her back to her own bedroom and started to pack the things she had come home for. "I've never met her before, but she'll be staying here, too. Wish I had time to give the house a good cleaning. It's not really company-ready, but somehow I don't think you'll mind."

Ashley managed a weak smile. "Looks great to me."

Jill pulled open a drawer and got the things she needed for Dan. When her bag was packed, she led Ashley into one of the guest rooms. She turned on a lamp and folded back the comforter, making the bed look a little more inviting. She had gotten Allie to help her decorate the rooms last year when she and Dan had housed some visiting missionaries who needed a place to stay. She turned back to Ashley, saw her sitting stiffly in a chair, staring vacantly at a spot on the wall.

"Honey, do you have a church? A pastor who could do the funeral?"

Ashley seemed to shake out of her reverie. "I grew up in church. My mom was real religious. I'm sure the pastor will do it."

"Would you give me the pastor's name?" she said. "I'd like to call him and tell him about your mom. I think he could help us with the arrangements."

Ashley gave her the name. "But I don't want them hounding me. I don't have the energy for it."

Jill sat down at the foot of the bed and studied the girl. "Hounding you about what?"

"About Jesus and all that. They'll think this is some kind of opportunity, you know? Hit her while she's down and all that."

Jill sat there a moment and turned that thought over in her mind. So often when someone faced a crisis, she had prayed that it would be an opportunity for them to discover the Lord. But she'd never thought of them taking it that way.

Jill dug into her purse and pulled out a twenty-dollar bill. "I don't have much food in the house. Why don't you go get yourself something to eat and bring it back here? Tomorrow I'll get one of my friends to run to the grocery store for me and stock the refrigerator for you and Mrs. Nichols."

"Don't worry about it," Ashley said. "I'll be fine. I just need a place to crash, that's all."

Jill set down the money, hoping she'd use it later. "I feel like I'm abandoning you again." Jill hugged her.

"Well, you shouldn't. You've got to get back to your husband. What else can you do?"

"I could call one of my friends to come get you and you could stay with them. I have some great friends. You could stay with Allie or Susan Ford, or Aunt Aggie. Oh, she'd be perfect, and she'd love to have you."

"I'm not up to being with new people right now," Ashley said. "I promise I won't bother anything."

Jill touched her chin and made her look at her. "I'm not worried about you bothering anything. I just want to make sure your needs are met too, and you're going through a really awful time. It doesn't seem like you should be going through it alone."

"I have my car," she said. "If I need anybody, I can go find someone. I really just need to sleep."

As Jill headed back to the hospital, she prayed that God would watch over the girl and offer her the arms she needed to fall into as she grieved her dead mother.

Chapter Thirty

• • •

Jill slept in an ICU waiting room recliner that night, covered with a hospital blanket. Others slept in chairs around her, all of them wanting to be no more than a moment away from their critically injured or ill loved ones. In the hours that she'd been here, she'd gotten to know many of them. Some, like her, were here because of the Icon bombing. Others had unrelated catastrophes.

All had impending grief and precarious hope in common, and each of their lives revolved around their fifteen-minute visits every few hours.

Morning dawned like home at the end of a dark journey. Thankful for an end to the discomfort of night, she got up and showered in the locker room–style facility they offered to families.

There was no change in Dan when she visited him at 7:00 A.M. Feeling her hope fading, she returned to the waiting room and waited for Ashley. She dreaded leaving the hospital for any reason, least of all to plan a funeral. But she couldn't abandon the girl now.

Her own mother's death loomed freshly over her again as she thought through the tasks she would walk Ashley through today.

Jill's mother had been forty when she had Jill, and her father even older. Her mother had died at sixty of a massive heart attack that no one had seen coming. Her father had only made it another five years before he, too, was dead. For his funeral, Jill had been the one to make all the arrangements. Just out of law school, she'd been mature enough to deal with it, but she'd still wept like a child with every decision she'd had to make.

Ashley got to the hospital just after seven, clad in a pair of bell-bottom jeans and sandals and a wrinkled Miller Lite T-shirt. The only concession she'd made to the temperature drop was a hooded zip-up sweatshirt hanging open.

The funeral home sat on a lake in a lush garden that overlooked the cemetery behind it. It seemed like such a place of peace, but Jill knew that the anguish that came into these walls each day was anything but peaceful.

There was a run on funerals today. The waiting room was full of grieving next-of-kin, waiting like Ashley for a meeting with the director. Ashley sat rigid in a chair next to Jill, coughing intermittently, chewing gum, and staring into space. Jill looked around at the other faces. Any day now, she could be in a room just like this to plan another funeral. The latest body count was over a hundred, at least a third of them firefighters.

The air in the room seemed hot and stagnant, as if someone had cranked up the heater to accommodate the cooler weather. Jill coughed too, still struggling with the damage the smoke had done to her lungs. She felt as if she might faint if she sat here any longer, so she got up and walked toward the door. Ashley looked up at her with dull, red, questioning eyes. Jill opened the door, letting the cool air rush her face. "It's hot," she said. "Just needed a little air."

Ashley nodded and coughed again.

Jill gazed out at the sunny day. Christmas lights and holly decorated the lampposts in the parking lot. It looked like a day of hope. She yearned to dash out of this building and get as far from this place as she could. But then she looked back at the girl.

Ashley looked so small sitting in that chair, like some kid who should have been left at home while her parents took care of business. It was clear she hadn't rested last night. Dark circles shadowed her eyes, and she looked so pale and thin that Jill wondered if she'd even eaten in the last two days. Her cough sounded terrible. She needed to see a doctor. Jill never should have left her alone last night. She should have insisted that she stay at the hospital with her.

Jill closed the door and went back to her seat, patted the girl's knee. "You okay?"

Ashley stopped coughing but didn't answer.

The office door opened, and the director walked out with a weeping couple, speaking to them in a soft voice. What a horrible job, Jill thought. He seemed like a decent man. When he went home tonight, would he prop up in a recliner with a chicken pot-pie, or would he curl up in fetal position in some dark room?

When he'd said a gentle good-bye to the couple, he looked their way. "Miss Morris?"

Ashley looked up, as if not certain he was speaking to her. Jill got up, and Ashley slowly followed.

Jill put her arm around her and walked her into the office. The room was comfortably appointed, with plush easy chairs angled toward a desk with a gentle lamp glowing, softly lighting the room. They might have been applying for a loan instead of planning a funeral.

As the director asked Ashley questions, and she answered chewing her gum like it was a pacifier she couldn't let go of, Jill felt a surge of love. She suspected that everyone who saw the girl made judgments about her. But God saw her raw, gaping wounds, and he loved her enough to make Jill love her, too.

She felt very special for being chosen to care for this child.

They set up the funeral for Friday, to be held in the funeral home's chapel unless the church offered to host it. Ashley agreed to contact the preacher.

"Now we need to talk about payment," the man said.

Ashley's big eyes filled up, and she shot Jill a look. "I don't have any money. I . . . can I, like, get it on credit or something?"

Jill took her hand. "I'm a lawyer. I'll take care of her estate and make sure that you're paid. You have my word on it."

He studied Jill for a moment. "And if she doesn't have enough money?" he asked.

"Then I'll pay it." Jill handed him her card. He looked it over and found it satisfactory.

Ashley cried softly as Jill drove back to the hospital. "I'm sorry you had to offer to pay. I know my mom had some money. She was real smart that way."

Jill rubbed her shoulder. "Don't worry about it. She probably had life insurance, if Icon didn't let that lapse too." She looked out the window. Just days ago, she had been filled with righteous indignation over her laid-off clients' plights. It was ironic that every one of them probably counted their blessings now. Being let go may have saved their lives.

When they reached the hospital, Jill expected Ashley to go straight to her car. Instead, she followed Jill in. Clearly, the girl didn't want to be alone. As they went up, that pall of dread fell over Jill again as she shifted her heart from Ashley to Dan.

Chapter Thirty-One

● ● ●

Jill stepped off the elevator and saw the crowd around the receptionist's desk. Susan and Allie stood among them, and she could hear Aunt Aggie's voice rising above them.

"Ain't no use creatin' a commotion now! Dan ain't gon' get any better because o' your yellin'!"

Jill froze. Had something happened?

Ashley touched her arm, as if she sensed it, too.

"I have the right to see my son!" a shrill voice declared over Aunt Aggie's admonitions. "I've come from Paris, and I intend to see him now."

Dan's mother. Jill stepped into the crowd of her friends.

"There now. Jill's here, see?" Aunt Aggie cried. "Y'oughta be ashamed, raisin' your voice like that when there are sick people up in here. I don't care how much money you got, they oughta throw you out."

Clara Nichols gasped and stared at the old woman. "I will have you know—"

"Mrs. Nichols?" Jill burst forward and got between the two of them before it came to blows. Aggie had been known to pack a wallop with her purse.

The woman spun around to her. "What?"

"Uh . . . I'm Jill. Dan's wife."

Mrs. Nichols' chin came up, and she gazed down her nose at her.

Jill felt suddenly exposed, and somehow inadequate.

Clara Nichols looked like an older version of Ivana Trump, with her hair pulled up in a smooth French twist and diamonds dangling from her ears. She looked as if she'd just come from a beauty salon or one of those ritzy spas in the south of France.

"So you finally showed up, huh? My son is lying in there, hanging by a thread for his dear life, and you're … what? Sleeping late?"

Jill felt the heat climbing her cheeks, and she opened her mouth to speak. But nothing came out.

"Mrs. Nichols, Jill was here all night." It was Susan, coming to her rescue again. "She just left for a little while this morning."

"And you think you're so classy!" Aunt Aggie snapped. "Comin' up here like you own the place and slappin' around them accusations. She was out helpin' her little friend plan her mama's funeral. You proud o' yourself now?"

It was getting worse. Jill glanced back at Ashley and saw the girl staring at her feet. She put a protective arm around her shoulder. "This is my friend Ashley," Jill managed to say. "Aunt Aggie's right. I was helping her plan a funeral."

"I see." Clara seemed to grope for the proper comeback. "All I know is that when my husband was on his deathbed, I didn't leave the hospital for four days."

Jill didn't know anything about that. Dan had told her that she hadn't even called him until his father was already gone. She might have been there during her husband's dying days, but she had never been there for her son. Dan hadn't even laid eyes on her in ten years.

But she didn't say that now.

"Mrs. Nichols, we're all under a lot of stress. If you'll just come in here and sit down, you can come in with me at the next visitation time."

"I have no intention of waiting until then." Clara spun back to the nurse's desk and pointed a vicious fingernail in the young nurse's face. "I told you to get the administrator on the phone. I *will* talk to him now. I *will* see my son."

"Yes, ma'am," the girl said. "If you'll just wait in the waiting room, I'll have him come up and speak to you."

The woman huffed out a sigh and started toward the waiting room, her high heels clicking on the floor. Allie caught Jill's eye and mouthed an apology. Jill shook her head as if to say it wasn't anyone's fault. She caught similar glances from Susan and Celia.

It might have been funny at another time.

She gave Ashley a concerned look, but the girl didn't look upset. This was a fascinating diversion for her, Jill suspected.

The crowd of friends left the seats on either side of Mrs. Nichols free. Jill had no choice but to take one. "Mrs. Nichols," she said as she lowered next to her, "visiting time is in half an hour if you could just wait."

"Why should I have to wait?" she snipped. "He's lying in there with nothing to do. It's not like he's in surgery. It's barbaric keeping a dying man from his family."

Jill's face tightened. "He's not a dying man, Mrs. Nichols. Please don't say that."

Clara looked disgusted at the rebuke. "So, you're his wife."

Jill felt as if she'd just been insulted. "Yes, I am."

"The lawyer."

"That's right."

Clara examined a long, manicured nail. "So, Jill is it? What exactly have you done for him, Jill?"

Jill didn't know what she meant. "I'm sorry?"

"Have you demanded the best doctors? Looked into having him transferred? Or have you simply left it all to chance?"

"Mrs. Nichols, he's getting phenomenal care. This is a wonderful hospital."

"Just as I thought." The tone was dismissive, and she sprang up, ending the conversation. Jill didn't know whether to press for more or to be thankful for the reprieve.

"What is taking that woman so long? That's the problem with these university hospitals. They're staffed with nothing but incompetents. You should have taken him to Oschner's, or we could have helicoptered him to Johns Hopkins. But to leave him here is the height of negligence in my opinion—"

Aunt Aggie burst out of her seat again. "You accusin' my girl Jill of somethin'? If you are, you better say it straight out."

Jill sighed. "Aunt Aggie, I can handle this." She got up and faced her mother-in-law. "Mrs. Nichols, Dan probably couldn't be moved now if we wanted him to be."

"So will you at least explain to me what his condition is?"

Jill cleared her throat, swallowed hard, and began to explain what she knew.

"Does he have brain damage?" Clara demanded.

"We don't think so," Jill said. "The scans of his head looked normal, and there's plenty of blood flow to the brain."

"Then why is he on the brink of death?"

"He is not on the brink of death!" The words came out too loudly, and she brought her hand to her forehead and told herself to calm down.

Susan seemed to have regathered her strength, and she got up and touched the woman's arm. "Darlin', Jill's been under an awful lot of stress lately. You know she was in the building when it exploded. It was a real traumatic event. And now to have Dan in the hospital like this, it's not easy for her."

"Do you think it's easy for me to get back here from Paris in record time, to be beside the bed of my son in his last days?"

Jill gritted her teeth. "Mrs. Nichols, I told you—"

"Clara!" the woman snapped. "You're in my family, for heaven's sake. You can at least call me by my first name."

Jill cleared her throat and wished she could step outside for air again. It was suffocating in here. "Clara, my husband is going to live."

"But in what condition?" Clara snapped. "Will he be able to walk? Will he be able to think?"

She wanted to scream out, *What do you care? You've never been interested in his thoughts before!* She thought of running out and finding a place to scream.

How dare this woman do this?

Before she could formulate a reply, a man stepped into the waiting room and called out, "Mrs. Nichols?"

Jill turned around, but Dan's mother lunged forward as if he addressed her. The man headed for the elder Mrs. Nichols.

"I'm Ray Adams, the hospital administrator. I understand you were having some problems about visiting your son."

Jill slowly sank back down to her seat. She looked over at Ashley, who seemed captivated at the turn of events. "You okay?"

Ashley smiled. It was the first time she'd done it since Jill met her. "Is she for real?"

"I'm afraid so."

Somehow Clara was able to convince them to let her go in to see Dan, and Jill realized there was no time to lick her wounds. She had to go with her and protect him.

"I'm coming with you," she told her, brooking no debate.

Clara clicked out as if she hadn't heard. Jill caught up to her in the hallway. "This way," she said and led her into the ICU and around to the cubicle where Dan lay, unchanged.

Clara's anger melted at the sight of him, and in its place came a tragic humility.

Clara hung back, staring at him with a stricken face. Jill went to his side and kissed his cheek. "Hey, sweetheart. It's me."

He still breathed through that respirator, and he slept soundly. She had been told that he had awakened several times and responded to the medical staff, but not yet when she had been present. As much as she wanted to look into his eyes and talk to him, she would prefer that it not be now, with Clara present.

"Oh, my word," Clara whispered. Jill looked up at her and saw real pain on her face. "What have they done to him? He looks like a corpse."

Jill had thought the same thing, but Clara's utterance of that thought revived her anger.

Clara moved closer to the bed and studied her son. Jill saw the struggle on her face and, for the first time, realized that the woman really did care for him in her strange, detached way.

"I had forgotten he was so big," she said in a quivering voice. "How tall is he now?"

The question seemed almost amusing to Jill, as if he'd grown in the last ten years.

"He's six foot four inches," she said. "He's in very good shape. He's kind of a health nut, and he runs and lifts weights. That's playing in his favor now."

There was silence for a moment, and Jill watched her as tears came to her eyes. She hoped Clara's façade would crumble now, and that she would see the mother in her, the woman who had given birth to him. She hoped she would say something—anything—to redeem her for her behavior.

"I told him not to be a fireman," Clara said finally. "Of all the ridiculous careers he could have chosen, to deliberately walk into a building in flames."

That fragile hope died. "He was rescuing people," Jill said. "People are alive today because Dan and the other firefighters went in."

"That sounds very heroic, but look where it got him."

Jill wished his mother would go back to the waiting room and leave her alone here with him. If he could hear, she wanted him to hear accolades about his heroics, not recriminations about his choices. But Clara wasn't leaving.

Against Dan's ear, Jill whispered, "Dan, your mother's here. She came all the way from Paris because she's worried about you."

He moved his hand, and Jill caught her breath. "Dan? Dan, can you open your eyes, honey?"

He didn't move again. Her eyes filled with tears, and she looked up at her mother-in-law. "He's going to be all right. I can just feel it. As soon as they take him off this respirator . . ."

Clara looked so awkward, standing there as coldly as a stranger. Jill suddenly felt pity for the woman. It must be terrible to be a mother without normal maternal instincts. She wondered if Clara suffered regret over the opportunities she'd missed. Jill's heart softened.

"I'm really glad you came, Clara," she said. "It'll mean a lot to him."

The light caught a tear in the woman's eyes. "If he's ever able to realize it."

"We'll just have to pray," Jill said. "It's all we can do. Everything is out of our control."

Clara dug through her bag and found a handkerchief. "It's not out of mine. What we need is better doctors. I have the means to get them here."

Jill almost told her not to bother, but she knew it wouldn't matter. She just hoped she didn't offend the ones who were already working on his behalf.

"I'll go make that call now," she said.

She realized his mother was uncomfortable here. Clara hadn't touched him or even come close to the bed. After stirring up such trouble with the nursing staff, after causing such commotion, after flexing her muscles and wielding her power, she didn't know what to do with her victory.

Jill thought of pointing it out to her, but what good would it do?

Jill kissed Dan's cheek. "I'll be back in a little while, sweetheart," she whispered.

Then she led Clara back out to the waiting room.

Although Celia and Allie had taken Aunt Aggie home, Susan stayed with her. Clara was fidgety and clearly uncomfortable for the next hour, and Jill realized it was going to be a long day.

"You must be exhausted, Clara," she said. "Wouldn't you like to go to my house and rest for a while?"

"Actually, I was considering staying in a hotel."

A surge of hope shot through Jill, but she tried to hide it. "Wherever you think you'd be most comfortable."

"I hate to bear bad news," Susan ventured, "but I heard on the news that the hotels had been closed for several miles around the Icon site. There's still a lot of smoke in the area, so those hotels have had to evacuate. The other hotels in town had to take up the slack. And there's a flood of media and family members who've come to town to see about the victims . . . and all the funerals . . ."

Clara looked insulted. "I might have known. Well, I suppose I'll have to stay in Newpointe then. Since that house was once my home, I guess it might be all right."

Jill's stomach sank. Did the woman expect it to be just as she'd left it? They'd made quite a few changes since she'd married Dan. She hoped Clara would not be disturbed by that.

"That's fine. We'd love to have you." She hoped she sounded sincere. "Ashley's staying there, too." She gestured toward the young girl, who sat slumped in the seat, the back of her neck propped against the back of the chair.

Ashley slowly sat up at the woman's critical scrutiny. "Hey," she said.

Clara Nichols gave the girl a disgusted once-over, but didn't return the greeting.

As if it had made her self-conscious, Ashley got up and raked her hands through her hair, leaving it further tousled. "I have to go to the bathroom."

Jill knew that she was giving them the chance to discuss her behind her back. She watched as she left the room.

Clara snapped around. "I will not stay in the house with that girl. Who is she, anyway?"

Jill sighed. "She was in the explosion with me. I met her on the stairwell, and we helped each other down. Her mother was killed in the blast. She's only sixteen. Her father died when she was little, so she's orphaned now. She needed a friend."

"That still doesn't answer why she's staying in your home."

"She showed up on my doorstep last night," Jill said. "She's got the weight of the world on her shoulders. I told her she could stay with me as long as she needed to."

Clara grunted. "She could be a thief or a killer, for all you know. She looks like a drug addict. Do you want a drug addict living in your home? She could murder us in our sleep."

"She's not going to murder you in your sleep, Clara. She's a sweet girl. Under those piercings and tattoos is a very broken heart."

"You're being conned," Clara declared. "She's going to take you to the cleaners."

Anger flashed through Jill, and she realized she didn't have the energy to deal with this now. "You don't know me very well, Clara. I'm not stupid. I'm an attorney, and I've done pretty well for myself all these years. I'm not easily pushed around, and I'm rarely conned. I made a judgment call about helping that girl, and I intend to do it. You're very welcome to stay in our home, but as you know, there's plenty of room there for you and Ashley, too."

Ashley came back in and plopped back down in her chair. She slid back down to the edge of her seat and threw one leg over the other. Jill knew she was putting on her tough, defiant façade. She resented Clara for putting her on the defensive.

Then suddenly, Ashley switched to offense. "I think I'll head on back to Newpointe." She looked at Clara. "I could give you a ride if you want."

Jill gaped at her, wondering what she was thinking. Was it a dare? Was she only offering because she knew Clara would refuse?

"I was going to rent a car," Clara said. "I planned to have it delivered here."

"You could have it delivered to Jill's house."

Jill looked up at her and suddenly realized that Ashley was trying to help her. It was an act of compassion, to get Clara out of her hair.

She thought of hugging Ashley, offering her a trophy, throwing her a party.

Instead, she accepted the gift. "She's right, Clara. It would be much easier for you to order the car in Newpointe and have them deliver it there."

The woman touched her forehead as if she was getting a headache. Finally, she looked at Ashley. "Oh, for heaven's sake. All right, I'll go with you."

Ashley got up. "Ready?"

Clara Nichols grabbed her suitcase, which she had rolled against the wall. Looking back at Jill over her shoulder, she said, "As soon as I've settled in and gotten the rental car, I'll be back, hopefully before the next visiting time."

Jill said a silent prayer that the woman would not make it back in time.

Chapter Thirty-Two

● ● ●

Ashley knocked aside a Burger King bag and some candy bar wrappers to make room for Clara. She was glad she'd swept the broken glass out that morning. As Her Majesty got into the car, looking as though she might gag, Ashley dug through her bag for a piece of bubble gum and shoved it into her mouth.

"Want some?" she asked, offering Clara the pack of Double Bubble.

Clara gaped at her. "Hardly."

Ashley shrugged and turned the key. The Subaru sputtered and choked, then hummed to life.

As she pulled out of the parking lot, she started to cough.

Clara gave her a disgusted look. "You should be in the hospital yourself," she said. "For heaven's sake, you shouldn't be spreading those germs in public."

"Don't worry, I don't have a disease." Ashley blew a bubble, bit down on it. "You can't catch it. You had to be there."

The woman adjusted her seat and kept her hands in her lap as if she was afraid to touch anything. Ashley wondered if she'd ever been in a car like hers, rusted out and torn up, with her friends' cigarette butts overflowing the ashtrays.

"Are you sure this rattrap will get us to Newpointe?"

Ashley blew a bubble. "Pretty sure," she said, "but if it doesn't, we can hitchhike."

Clara grunted.

Ashley glanced at her. Clara was a pretty woman for someone her age. Sixty, maybe? Ashley hoped she looked that good when she got that age, but she figured it took a lot of caviar and plastic surgery to keep someone in that condition.

Ashley drove for a while, the silence broken only by her coughing spurts.

"What happened to your radio, for heaven's sake?"

Ashley stopped chewing. "Long story," she said quietly.

"Well, at least you're not blaring that rap garbage you people listen to."

Ashley assumed "you people" included anyone under twenty. "It's not garbage," she said, "it's poetry."

"Poetry? You wouldn't know Coleridge from Dr. Seuss. That's not poetry. If you want to know poetry, I'll show you some poetry when we get to the house. That is, if my son kept my library."

Ashley couldn't wait. "So how long since you've seen your son?"

Clara looked out the window for a moment. "It's been awhile," she said.

"Like a year, two years?"

Clara shook her head. "A little longer."

"So is this the first time you've met Jill?"

The woman lifted her chin higher. "Yes, it is. I was out of the country when they got married."

Ashley blew a bubble, popped it with her teeth. "You didn't even come to your own son's wedding?"

"I told you, I was out of the country."

"And it's, like, a big deal to come back for a wedding?"

"Dan understood."

Ashley breathed a laugh. "Yeah, right."

Clara seemed to stiffen. "You're driving too fast, you know. The police are going to pull us over."

"The police have better things to do." Silence settled for a moment. "They're looking for terrorists. I hope they find them. I hope they string them up by their necks and parade them around the streets."

That silenced her for a while. Finally, Clara said, "I'm very sorry about your mother. I know that must be quite a blow."

Ashley stopped chewing again, but she didn't answer.

"When's the last time you spoke to your mother?"

Ashley really didn't want to talk about this, especially to Clara. She couldn't think of anything worse than being that vulnerable to a woman so cold. "I went up to Icon to talk to her that morning," she said. "That's why I was there. My mom's the one who found the bomb."

She felt Clara's cool eyes on her as she changed lanes and passed a slow-moving Cadillac.

"I was a brat that day. But you probably know how that is."

Clara looked puzzled. "What do you mean, I know?"

Ashley shrugged. "You and me, we have a lot in common. I mean, I'm not too happy with the way I treated my mom. And you may never get a chance to make things right with your son."

That chill returned. "I prefer not to discuss my son with you."

"Fine," Ashley said. "Then don't ask me about my mother."

Clara stewed for a moment as Ashley came off the highway and headed up to Newpointe. "I don't know why you think I have anything to make up to my son. We had a perfectly fine relationship."

"So how often did you talk?"

"We spoke as often as we needed to, thank you very much. And I'm here, aren't I? When my son is in need, I'm here."

"But you weren't even here for his wedding, and he was your only child. You would think—"

"I don't want to discuss it, I told you."

Ashley rolled her eyes. "Whatever. I'm just saying that even when I was at my worst, acting like a brat, my mom was there for me. But, hey, if being off in Europe or somewhere is more important than coming to your son's wedding—"

"I don't want to discuss my son's wedding again. Do you hear me?"

Ashley started to cough. She didn't have the energy to fight with this woman. But it griped her that the woman claimed to care about him enough to throw her weight around in the hospital when the truth was that she didn't care at all.

Ashley didn't understand why her mother had been the one taken. Why hadn't God chosen the mothers that didn't do a good job, the ones who neglected their sons and daughters, the ones who caused trouble wherever they went? Weren't there people who made life better and others who only caused trouble and heartache?

Suddenly she wished she could get rid of her gum, so she rolled her window down and spat it out.

"Young lady," Clara bit out. "I would appreciate it if you wouldn't go spitting out of windows with me in your car."

She rolled the window back up. "Sorry, but you didn't seem maternal enough for me to spit it in your hand."

The woman looked horrified, as if she didn't know what she was talking about.

Ashley grinned. "I used to spit my gum in my mom's hand," she said. "She'd drag me into church, and I'd be chomping on bubble gum, blowing bubbles, and she'd get angry and hold her hand out in front of my face. I knew I had to spit it. And then she'd sit there with it, holding it in her hand and trying to be all proper, and I'd start to giggle, knowing that it was melting and sticking to her hand and that it would take her awhile to get it off. I'd watch her try to wipe it onto the bulletin and fold it up in little pieces so it wouldn't stick to anything else."

"Sounds barbaric," the woman said.

"So you never let your son spit his gum into your hand?"

"No, I most certainly did not."

Ashley might have known.

She navigated her way back to Jill's street. When she missed a turn, Clara corrected her. "You can get there at the next left and then go around the corner, and you'll be on Second Street."

"So you used to live there, huh?"

"My husband and I built it. We left it to Dan when we moved away."

"It's a really nice house," Ashley said. "I was surprised when I saw it yesterday. Jill didn't seem like the type who'd live in a place like that. But if it was free, I guess I understand."

"It wasn't free, I assure you. Dan's father and I paid dearly for it."

Ashley pulled her car up to the curb.

"For heaven's sake, don't leave it here," Clara said. "There's a little drive in the back of the house. You can park it back there so no one will see it."

Ashley turned her dull gaze to her. "I'm not ashamed of my car."

"Well, I am. And I don't think my son would appreciate having it parked out in front of his house."

"Really? Jill didn't seem the type to marry a rich snob. I thought he was a fireman."

"Oh, for heaven's sake." The woman got out of the car and started up the sidewalk.

"You going to get your suitcase?" Ashley called after her.

"Bring it in for me, will you?" she said over her shoulder.

"Does it roll?"

"Of course it rolls."

"Well, can you pull?" Ashley asked.

She grunted again and came back to the car. Ashley opened her trunk and pulled it out. Clara grabbed its handle and it toppled over. Stooping down, she managed to right it, then pulled out the handle and began pulling it behind her, her high heels tapping on the concrete.

Ashley was up at the door before the woman could get there with the suitcase. She unlocked it and pushed the door open. The woman struggled to get her suitcase up the porch steps.

As Clara came into the house, she caught her breath. "My word! Everything's changed," she said. "They've even changed the colors."

"Looks nice to me," Ashley said.

"It looks Bohemian. What were they thinking?"

She pulled her suitcase down the hall and found the master bedroom. The bed was not made up and several pairs of Jill's shoes lay cluttered around the floor.

"My room!" Clara moaned. "What has that woman done to it?"

"May have been your room once," Ashley said. "But I think it's hers now." She was glad she hadn't missed this.

Clara harrumphed and pranced down the hall to the guest room Ashley had been given.

"That's where I slept last night," Ashley said. "If you want it, you can have it. I can sleep in another room."

"No, thank you," she said, as if the bed was probably infested with lice. She pranced to the next room and pulled her suitcase in. "This will be quite adequate."

"Okay then," Ashley said. "Well, if you're okay here, I'm gonna take off."

"Take off?" the woman asked her. "Where are you going?"

Ashley shrugged. "I have stuff to do."

"Well, all right. I suppose you'll be back later?"

"Sometime tonight," Ashley said.

"All right then. I'll just call for a rental car."

Ashley shuffled out the front door, glad to be rid of the woman. She hoped the rental car place took their time.

Jill would need a few hours before she was ready to take Clara on again.

Chapter Thirty-Three

● ● ●

They found the last of the Newpointe dead on Wednesday afternoon.

Steve Winder and Karen Ensminger, the two missing paramedics, had apparently died instantly beneath a ton of rubble.

Before pulling them out, they had summoned the Newpointe firefighters, cops, and paramedics still at the site. Mark, Ray, Nick, and the others pulled the bodies out in Stokes baskets and passed them down the line of their colleagues.

When they took them into the temporary morgue tent, Issie collapsed.

Mark watched, wishing for numbness, as the other medics rushed to her aid. Nick lifted her in his arms and carried her to one of the medical tents nearby.

Mark knew the pain she felt. The ache inside of him felt as if it would somehow ignite and consume him from the inside out. His eyes burned and stung to the point that he could hardly open them, and every muscle in his body ached.

He had gotten a couple hours' sleep yesterday at the hospital, but he'd been back at the site by the afternoon and had worked here all night. Knowing some of his buddies were still missing motivated him to keep digging.

But he had hoped they'd find them alive.

He had begun to feel light-headed, so he trudged off of the mound. He stepped into the tent and saw that Nick had laid Issie down on a cot. He was giving her water and whispering softly.

And all at once Mark realized he was sick of this place.

He wanted to be anywhere but here.

He could be at home with his wife and son, curled up on his bed. Or at the hospital, keeping vigil for his best friend. Or at work, with the other firefighters who grieved while they held down the fort.

Oh, for the innocence of Monday morning.

He suddenly started to weep.

Ray came up behind him and pulled him into a fierce hug. "We've got all our people out now," he said. "I'm telling all our folks to go home."

Mark just looked at him. "Are you sure?"

Ray's dark skin was streaked with white powder and tears. "We've all had enough," he said. "They have people lined up waiting to get in on the rescue effort. We need to rest up, clear our heads. Some of us are coughing so bad we need medical attention ourselves. We've got funerals to plan, families to notify. And we have our own town to protect."

Mark nodded. There wasn't much he could say, and as he drank down his water, he looked back up at the site where he knew dozens of bodies still lay undiscovered, but he doubted any were still alive. He felt as if he were leaving a job unfinished, as if someone were in jeopardy, waiting for him to help and he was turning his back.

But he had no more energy to give. Muttering a silent prayer that God would continue the work through the people who were there and available, he waited for the others in his group to head out.

Chapter Thirty-Four

● ● ●

Why are there flowers at funerals? It doesn't make sense, the glorious colors and fragrant scents, surrounding a box filled with death. Yet there they are, those flowers, crammed into the tiny viewing room, spilling out into the larger room beyond, where soft-spoken friends with teary eyes mill around waiting to talk to me.

"It's not her, just a shell of her," someone says, but I feel that it's not me, just a shell of me. I stand outside my own body, thinking how I want to crawl into that box with her and lie down and sleep, and not wake up until she wakes up too.

And then I'm not in the visitation room, but floating above that thirty-story building, looming high above the other buildings on Canal Street, searching for her like an eagle stalking its prey.

I float without wings above it all, and then I spin to my back and find that I'm not above it, but below it. It's falling, falling, and the earth falls fast beneath me, and I still haven't found her, don't know where she is, alive or dead, safe outside or crushed beneath . . .

"Let's get that tube out."

A voice above him pulled Dan from that dreadful dream. He fought his way through networks of cobwebs, clinging to him and pulling him back.

He tried to swing his arms, swim through the webs, but someone held him still.

"There we go. Easy . . ."

He struggled to move his eyelids. Someone had glued them shut. It was hot, miserably hot, and his throat hurt like fire. He gagged and choked. . . .

"Okay, it's out. Respiration seems normal. . . ."

Finally, his eyelids came unglued, and through the small slit, he saw light. A blur of figures moved above him, cold hands probing, poking, pulling his eyes open wider. . . .

They came into focus. No one he knew. No one who would know.

"Dan, nod if you hear me."

He managed to nod.

"We just took you off the respirator. How do you feel?"

He felt as if they'd poured acid down his throat. His chest hurt, as if some vital organ had been ripped out of him. "What . . . happened?"

"You were in the Icon Building when it collapsed. Do you remember that, Dan?"

Despair waged war inside him, and he recalled the dread that had flown him over that building in his dream. "Jill," he managed to whisper. "Oh, God . . . tell me . . . she's not dead."

Another blur, and the voices pulled out of his consciousness, nothing more than those of Charlie Brown's teachers, making noises but lacking words.

She was dead, and those were her flowers at her funeral, and it was her coffin lying there among the fragrant blooms. And he was the shell. . . .

But then he heard a voice he knew.

"Dan, honey, it's me, Jill. Please, wake up, honey. Look at me, and tell me you're all right."

He felt the warmth of tears falling on his face, and he struggled to open his eyes again. Jill? Had she said it was Jill? Could she be alive?

His eyes came open, and he saw the blur of her face over him, and he stared up at her, trying to focus, trying to see.

And then, there she was, more beautiful than he imagined. Not a shell, but a living light, shining his way out of the darkness.

"Honey, I've been waiting so long to talk to you." She sobbed with the words. "Dan, you're gonna be okay. You're breathing on your own."

His heart seemed to burst. He swallowed, the effort scraping his throat. "You got out?"

"Yes, honey. I got out. You were buried, but they found you. Thank God, you're alive."

His arms felt like lead pipes, but he managed to lift them and reach for her. She came into them, sobbing against his bare chest. He felt his own tears warming down his temples. "Were you hurt, baby?"

"No," she said. "I'm fine. I'm perfect. And you're awake!" She touched his face. "Does anything hurt?"

"Throat," he said.

"What about your legs?"

He shook his head. "Legs feel fine. No problem."

She looked up at a man standing across the room. A doctor, he supposed.

The man stepped close to the bed. "Dan, I'm touching your leg. Can you feel this?"

He didn't feel a thing, and a dull alarm went off in his head. "No."

"How about this?"

"Uh-uh."

The doctor did a few more tests as Jill stood beside him, stroking his hair back from his face. "What is it?" he asked. "My legs . . . what's wrong with them?"

"Probably the drugs," Jill whispered. "Just a little numbness."

He saw the look pass from Jill to the doctor. They were keeping something from him. But his mind was fading, and he couldn't hold onto the fear or the thought. Jill was alive. His dream of a life with her was not dead.

And he was so very tired. He could sleep for a week. He tried to tell her that, but the words wouldn't come. He kept her hand in his, warm and comforting, as he began to float again, this time on a warm breeze over bright meadows.

Chapter Thirty-Five

• • •

They were all there, sitting in the waiting room, some of them in prayer, others talking quietly among themselves, all keeping vigil for their friend whom they thought lay dying. Jill came in with tears on her face and looked around at Mark and Allie, Stan and Celia, Ray and Susan, Issie and Nick, Aunt Aggie, and several of the firefighters who worked at Midtown Station.

Mark saw her face and came to his feet. "Jill, what is it?"

Everyone got quiet and turned to look at her.

"He's breathing on his own!" she cried. "He spoke to me. He's going to be okay!" She threw her arms around Mark, and Allie bounced with joy. The others came to Jill, laughing and thanking God, dancing her around and hugging her until she thought she would break.

When she'd told them every detail of their conversation, she finally worked her way to a telephone and called his mother.

The phone rang four times before it was answered.

"Nichols residence." It was Clara's clipped voice, and Jill wiped her face.

"Hi, Clara, it's Jill."

There was a moment of silence, and then Clara asked, "Has something happened?"

Jill laughed. "Yes. Clara, he's off the respirator, and he woke up and talked to me."

Again, a moment of silence, and she wondered if the woman was struggling with her own emotions or if she was simply thinking of something appropriate to say.

"That's wonderful," she said finally, and her voice was quivery and broken. She cleared her throat. "What did they say about his legs?"

Jill couldn't deal with telling her that Dan hadn't had any feeling. "They don't know yet," she said. "He wasn't awake for long."

"I'm coming back to the hospital," Clara said.

"No," Jill said quickly. "They won't let you in tonight. They're watching his breathing very carefully, and they don't want him overstimulated. They asked me not to let anyone else come back."

"Even his mother?" Clara asked.

"I'm sorry, Clara. Seeing you after all these years might confuse or disorient him. It's better if you just wait until the morning."

Again Clara grew quiet, and finally Jill asked, "Can I speak to Ashley?"

"She's not here," Clara said. "She went out."

"Went out where?"

"I don't know. She doesn't report to me."

"Well, did she say she was going home?"

"I told you, she didn't say."

Jill wished her mother-in-law had asked. "Well, if she comes in, will you tell her the good news?"

"Yes, of course."

Jill could tell she was angry for not having the opportunity to see Dan tonight. But as Jill hung up, she knew she was doing the best thing for him. The last thing he needed was to deal with his mother right now. One thing at a time. There would be plenty of time for reconciliation tomorrow.

Chapter Thirty-Six

● ● ●

Ashley pulled into the parking lot at her mother's church that afternoon and checked the men's watch she wore on her wrist. Four o'clock. Maybe the pastor was still in.

She got out of her car and buried her fists deep in the pockets of her denim jacket. She felt sick, as if there were an emptiness deep inside that couldn't be filled by food or water. She pushed through the double doors into the church and stood in the hall looking both ways. It had been years since she'd been here. She'd been twelve when her mother had last been able to drag her to Sunday school.

She walked through those halls, the rubber soles of her shoes quiet on the hard tile. She heard the sound of someone playing a piano in one of the rooms. Voices were exchanged somewhere else inside the building.

She found the preacher's office and stood outside the door for a moment, wishing with all her heart that she didn't have to go in. But her mother deserved a pastor for her funeral, and this one was the only one she knew.

She took a deep breath and stepped inside the office. The secretary looked up and instantly got that guarded look on her face that people sometimes got when they saw Ashley or her friends. That look screamed *thugs*, as if she expected Ashley to hit her over the head and steal the choir robes or something.

"May I help you?"

Ashley swallowed. "Yeah, I need to see the pastor."

"And what is it in regard to?" the secretary asked.

Ashley just looked at her. She knew the woman probably thought she was here for a handout and was trying to keep her away from the pastor who had important things to do, like writing sermons that his congregation would sleep through. "It's about a funeral," she said in a flat voice. "For Debbie Morris, my mom."

The woman's face instantly changed, and she sprang to her feet. "Oh, you must be Ashley! Oh, honey." She came around the desk and put her arms around her. "I'm so sorry about your mother. We've just been grieving here ever since we heard. Pastor Jack saw her name on the list, and we've been trying to contact you ever since."

Ashley shrugged and wished the woman would stop fawning. "Well, here I am."

"I'll get him right away, dear," she said, and rushed to the pastor's door. She stuck her head inside.

Ashley couldn't hear what she said to him, but in seconds he was at the door, reaching out for her.

She didn't want anyone else hugging her, but he did anyway, and she stood there, rigid and cold, desperately trying not to fall apart in front of these people she hardly knew.

"Ashley, come in here, sweetheart. Come sit down."

She followed him across the deep carpet of his office and took a chair across from his desk.

"Where have you been staying, honey? We've been calling all over. We even got the name of the friends you've been living with, and they didn't know where you were, either."

So they knew now, she thought.

"I've been with a friend," she said.

"Are you all right? Is there anything we can do for you?" She shook her head and started to cough. The display of weakness made her angry. They'd probably slap her onto a gurney and rush her to the hospital.

"That sounds bad." He got up and poured her a glass of water from a pitcher on his desk. Handing it to her, he asked, "Have you seen a doctor?"

She drank the cool water, let it soothe her throat. "I'm okay," she said. "I just . . . came here because I need a pastor to preach at my mother's funeral at ten o'clock on Friday. I wondered if you could do it."

"Of course I will," he said. "In fact, if you need help putting the whole thing together, we'll be glad to do it for you."

"What whole thing?" Ashley asked.

"The program for the funeral."

Ashley realized she was in over her head. That nauseous feeling swirled in her stomach again. She wished she'd eaten before she'd come. "I've never even been to a funeral since I was five. I don't really remember what they do."

"Then don't worry. We'll take care of everything. What time is the visitation?"

Ashley shrugged again. "The funeral guy asked me if I wanted one, but I told him that was okay. Just the funeral was fine."

"The visitation is really for you, sweetheart," Pastor Jack said. "It's so you can talk to the people who knew and loved your mother and hear how special she was."

"I know how special she was." The words cracked in her throat. "The funeral's enough."

"All right, then. Do you want to have it here?"

"I already told the guy we'd do it there—at Finn and Banks. I don't think it's too late to change it."

"With so many other funerals, maybe it would be better to have it here. We could seat more people."

"Okay, I guess."

"All right, darlin', and we'll take care of putting it in the newspaper so people will know. We'll have it come out in tomorrow's paper. Is that all right, honey?"

She wished he'd quit calling her by those terms of endearment, like he expected her head to blow off if he used her name.

"What about after the funeral? Do you want us to eat at your mother's house, or should we try to get one of the other members?"

Ashley didn't think she could make another decision. "What do you mean?"

"The gathering after the funeral, when people come by your house to give their condolences. Folks bring food. You'll need someone to sit at your house that day to take what people bring. I can get ladies from the church to help serve."

Ashley couldn't think of anything that horrified her more. A party, after her mother's funeral? Tears crescented in her eyes, and she held her face still to keep them from falling. "I don't want to do that."

"Well, certainly you don't have to if you don't want to. It's all for the comfort of the family, after all. Of course, if you have relatives coming, they may like to do it."

"I haven't talked to any of my relatives," she said. "I hardly know them. I don't think they'll come."

"Well, darlin', you need to let them know."

Ashley started to cough again, and this time she couldn't catch her breath. She doubled over, trying to clear her lungs. He came back around the desk and touched her back, as if that would help.

"Honey, are you sure you're all right?"

Ashley swallowed and forced herself to stop. "Just a little smoke damage."

"Oh, my word," the pastor said. "You were in the Icon Building too?"

Ashley nodded and looked up at him. She saw the concern on his face, as if he thought she'd been through too much. She knew what that would mean. He would try to intervene in her life, maybe call the state to take her into their custody. They would hover over her, maybe force her into foster care.

She stood up and tried to steady her breathing. "Another victim took me in," she said, hoping to head off his efforts. "I'm going to be staying at her house in Newpointe for a while. Her name's Jill Nichols. She's a lawyer."

There, that ought to keep him from worrying about her custody, as if she hadn't already been living on her own.

"Jill Nichols." The pastor wrote the name down. "All right. Is it listed? Can we contact you there?"

"Yeah, it's listed. I guess if I'm not there you can leave a message." She started to the door. "I gotta go."

Pastor Jack followed her, and when they got in the reception area again, the secretary stood up. She'd been crying. "You know, Ashley, your mother loved you very, very much. She had you on every prayer list that came down the pike. You were always on her mind."

Ashley swallowed. Her throat felt raw. "I know," she said. "I'll be here Friday, before ten."

"Nine-thirty would be good," Pastor Jack said.

She nodded and took off out the door. Hurrying up the hall, she burst out into the cool, December air.

She didn't cry until she was back in her car, pulling away from the church.

Chapter Thirty-Seven

● ● ●

The nurse came to get Jill as soon as Dan began to come out of his sleep again, and she rushed to his bedside. He lay with his eyes closed, but the color in his face was good, and his hands were no longer as cold as they had been.

She took his hand and whispered into his ear. "Dan, it's me. Wake up, honey."

His eyes opened slowly, and he stared at her, as if waiting for her to come into focus. Then the very beginning of a smile curved his lips. "Hey, baby."

She pressed her face close to his. "Hey, honey. How're you feeling?"

"Beaten up," he whispered. He took her hand, brought it to his mouth, and squinted up at her again. "Tell me about Icon. Tell me how you got out."

She pulled a chair up to the side of his bed and sat down, leaning her elbows on his mattress. Carefully, she told him about the evacuation and Ashley and Gordon. "I got out just before the third bomb went off."

"The one that got me," he whispered. "How long did it take them to find me?"

"Until four the next morning," she said. "It's a miracle you're alive. I don't even know how you breathed all that time."

"What about the others?"

The question startled her, for she had hoped to head off that question until he was stronger. Trying to evade, she said, "What others?"

"Brothers from Midtown," he said. "Any of them missing?"

She couldn't tell him that some of them had died, so she lifted her eyebrows and tried to smile. "No, no one's missing."

He breathed a sigh of relief and closed his eyes again, and she realized the questions had taken a lot out of him. He didn't have the energy to think through her evasion.

He would have to know later that five of his friends had died. But he didn't have to know now.

She sat with him, stroking his forehead as he drifted back into sleep.

· · ·

Later that night, as Jill waited for Dan to wake again, she called home to see if Ashley had made it back in.

The girl answered instead of Clara.

"Ashley?"

"Yeah." She could tell from Ashley's voice that she'd been crying. She wished she could be there to comfort her. "I called earlier. Clara said you were out."

"I had some errands to run this afternoon." Her voice was dull, metallic. "Then I went to a movie."

Jill wondered if that was true. "Did Clara tell you my news?"

"I haven't seen Clara," Ashley said. "She's locked in her room, probably trying to protect herself from me."

Jill knew the girl wasn't exaggerating.

"So what's the news?" Ashley asked.

"Dan woke up. He talked to me."

Ashley caught her breath, then coughed. "That's great, Jill. I'm really excited for you. Is he, like, all right?"

"I think so. The doctors are saying that he'll probably recover fully from his head injury. He does seem to have some paralysis, though. It's still early. . . ." She got quiet for a moment, realizing she shouldn't transmit her heavy concerns to the girl.

"Honey, we need to get together and make some plans about your mom's funeral. We have to plan a program. Who's going to preach, who's going to speak—"

"It's already done." Ashley's statement cut into her words.

Jill frowned. "Really?"

"Yeah, I took care of it. I went by my mom's church. The pastor's going to plan everything. All I have to do is show up."

Jill felt a surge of relief. Of course her mother's church would want to be involved in the planning. There were people who loved her there. "That's good," she said. "I'm glad they're taking some of the stress off you. Are you okay with that?"

Ashley was quiet for a long moment. "Yeah, I didn't really know where to begin. They know what to do, and they probably knew her better than I did. I never thought of her as having a life. But she had a lot of friends."

Maybe the girl wouldn't be quite as alone as she'd thought she was going to be in the beginning. She hoped Ashley would allow people to love her. "So are you going to be okay tonight? Because I'm not going to be able to come home. I need to be here every time Dan wakes up."

"Sure, I'll be fine."

"I know I haven't been much help," Jill said. "One of the reasons you came to my house was so you wouldn't be all alone, and now you are, except for Clara."

Ashley chuckled lightly. "Actually, I'd rather be alone than be with her. But really, it's not so bad."

"I just wish I could be there for you."

There was a moment of silence, and she heard the emotion quivering in Ashley's voice. "I just needed a place to crash. You gave me that."

Jill realized that the girl thought that was all she needed. She would give her more, as soon as Dan was completely out of the woods.

Chapter Thirty-Eight

● ● ●

Clara had locked her bedroom door and shoved the chest of drawers in front of it, just in case Ashley decided to break in during the night and rifle through her jewelry. One could never be too careful.

She couldn't imagine why Jill would open this beautiful home to a girl like that, even if she had lost her mother. She supposed deadbeats and hoodlums lost their parents all the time. That didn't make them good people, and it certainly didn't make them trustworthy. Jill was making a huge mistake.

She thought of her phone call with Jill earlier tonight. Dan was awake. He was going to be all right.

Relief had flooded through her, and then a sense of dread. She knew she should have rushed up there and insisted on talking to him. But the truth was that she didn't know what she would say. It was easier standing over his bed when he was unconscious. Now to have an actual conversation with him ...

She felt inadequate. She had never been good with sick people. She didn't suppose Dan wanted to talk to her, anyway. In all these years, he'd hardly ever called unless there was some major life event that he needed to notify her of. He had called her when her brother died and, later, when he'd gotten engaged.

He had a lot to deal with if he was going to be crippled. She certainly wasn't equipped to help.

Still, she couldn't contain her overwhelming relief that he wasn't dead and that he no longer needed the respirator.

She went into the bathroom adjoining her room, took a sleeping pill, then rummaged through her things for her eye mask. She climbed into bed, slid the mask over her eyes, and lay staring up into the self-inflicted darkness.

Maybe it was enough that he was alive. Maybe she should think about going back to Paris sooner than she planned.

Chapter Thirty-Nine

● ● ●

It was quiet, too quiet. Ashley wished she had a stereo in her room and could turn it up so loud that she couldn't hear her own thoughts.

But Clara would freak and call the police.

Now that she thought about it, it didn't seem like such a bad idea, but Jill didn't need the drama. And Ashley owed her more than that.

She pulled her mother's journal out of her bag, then kicked off her shoes and slid onto the bed. Crossing her legs in front of her, she stared down at the journal. Her mother had written in it every morning, and sometimes at night.

She put you on every prayer list that came down the pike.

Her wayward daughter was, no doubt, the subject of many of these journal entries. Yet there was more. Her mother did have a life and friends and things other than Ashley to worry about. And now Ashley wanted to know what those things were. It was a way of being close to her mom, a way of pretending that she was still alive.

Her hands trembled as she opened the entry to one of the middle pages.

Another round of layoffs today. I wasn't in the bunch—at least not this time. I guess as long as I'm Donald Merritt's secretary, my job will be secure. The problem is, how long will his be secure? Sounds like he might be in some pretty serious trouble, if what the news reports say is true. But to look at him, you'd just think that everything was going along hunky-dory, like he didn't have a care in the world. All those people losing their jobs, their stock, their retirement, and he's still got women sneaking into his office for long, private lunches, flashing diamonds on their fingers, dragging their minks behind them. And him driving that Jaguar that probably cost a hundred grand, and his wife in that Navigator she flits around town in.

I should quit, but I don't have any money saved, and my 401K is shot. I'm still putting money away for Ashley's college, and I won't stop doing that no matter what. Even if I have to sell the house, I'm going to keep funding her college account.

Yeah, I know that she says she doesn't want to go to college. She's said a lot of things. And it's possible that I won't be able to make her go. I can't seem to make her do anything else, including live at home. But at least she'll have options. Options are important things to have.

Someday, she might realize that the life she's chosen is a dead end and want to turn around and go in another direction. You said you answered prayer if we had faith, didn't you, Lord? I have faith that you'll change her heart one day.

Lord, you've been a husband to me since Jim died eleven years ago. And you've promised to be a father to the fatherless. You know that Ashley needs a father. She'd never admit it, but I know that her father's absence has created an empty hole right in the middle of her. She needs you, she just doesn't know it.

Ashley's throat tightened, and she stopped reading and closed the journal. Tears burned her eyes, and she pressed her lips together. Her mother must have been so disappointed in her.

It had seemed like a game before. Shock your mother, amaze your mother's friends. Let them all know that you're going to be anything but what they expect. Never do what she asks, and flee from what she wants.

Only now she was gone.

Ashley got off the bed, pulled a pad out of her bag, and opened it to a clean page. Lying down on her stomach and propping her head on her hand, she wrote, *Dear Mom.*

Her pen froze on the paper as she tried to formulate the words she wanted to say to her mother. But her brain seemed just as frozen.

I'd give anything if you were still here. I'd throw away my nose ring and cover my tattoos. I'd color my hair back to my natural color, if I could remember what it was.

Empty words, she thought. They hardly mattered now.

I wish I could go with you, be where you are. I'm too much of a coward to do anything painful. But if I could just fall asleep and never wake up . . .

She started to cry then, too hard to finish her letter, so she flung the pad across the room and smothered her face in her pillow to muffle the sound of her sobs.

Chapter Forty

● ● ●

*I*n *Dan's dream, he was running the fifth mile, up Jacquard Street, past the Walgreens and Joe Sigrest's Hardware Store, the Baskin-Robbins, and Louisiana Bank's drive-through branch. Sweat soaked his head- and wristbands as he made the last block, past Sheri Hartman's Dance Studio and the Blooms 'n' Blossoms. His side hurt and his thighs burned as he made the corner on Purchase Street, passed City Hall on one side, the Police Station on the other, and ran up the wide driveway to Midtown Station.*

He came awake, still in the hospital. Monitors hummed beside his bed, creating a monotone score for this new phase of his life. He looked around for Jill, who had been there when he'd drifted off. He saw her at the doorway to his area, heard her talking quietly to someone. She turned and saw that he was awake.

Quickly, she came to his side. "Dan?"

"Hey," he whispered.

She glanced back up at the person who stood at the entrance. "Dan, there's someone here to see you."

"The guys?" he asked.

"No. Your mother, Dan. She came all the way from Paris."

For a moment, he thought he might still be floating in that twilight state between sleep and wakefulness. Not his mother. She wouldn't have come. "My mother?" he repeated.

"Yes. She's here, Dan."

Jill stepped back, and he saw Clara take her place next to him. She was smaller than he remembered and had her hair up in one of those Hollywood styles, like something out of a magazine.

He stared up at her.

"Hello, darling," she said.

Her voice was strange, unfamiliar. She sounded like Bette Davis in *All About Eve*. Cold and above-it-all. Even a little nervous.

He realized he had to say something. "Mother?"

Her smile was tight, strained. "I was in Paris when I heard the news," she said. "I thought I'd never get a flight out. Then when I got here they wouldn't let me see you except for a few minutes every few hours. How are you, darling? Do you feel like yourself?"

It was a crazy question, he wanted to say. Who else would he feel like? Instead, he said, "You look different."

She smiled and smoothed her hair. "Do I? Younger, I hope."

Younger? No, he wouldn't say younger, though he had to admit that she carried her age well. She'd probably had as much cosmetic surgery as Michael Jackson. Sometimes people had more money than was good for them.

"Thanks for coming." It was all he could think to say to this woman who'd played such a minor part in his life. He couldn't imagine why she had come. He would have expected her to feign concern from a distance and keep all her Botox appointments.

"Don't worry, Danny. You'll get the best of care. I'm going to see to it."

It was awkward, the way she just stood there looking at him, as if she were some stranger who'd been pulled in from the hallway.

"It's just so awful about the Icon Building. You're so lucky to have lived through it, both you and Jill. So many people didn't, you know. And all your firefighter friends and their wives have been so diligent to be here, even when they have all those funerals to attend."

Something tightened in his chest, and he caught his breath. "What funerals?"

Suddenly Jill was back at his side. Her face was red, and he recognized her anger as she took Clara's arm and tried to gently push her away. "Honey, she just meant—"

"What funerals?" he demanded again, louder. "Jill, who died? Did some of our men die?"

"Honey, calm down."

He knew then that she was keeping it from him. They had lost someone. Who had died? Mark? Nick? He tried to rise up, but he couldn't manage it. "Jill, tell me."

"For heaven's sake, Jill," his mother snapped. "He's not a child."

Jill shot the woman a silencing look, then turned back to him with tears in her eyes. "I will. I'll tell you. Just a minute, honey."

He watched as she ushered his mother out of the room. He squeezed his eyes shut and braced himself for the worst news of his life.

· · ·

How dare you?"
Clara spun around and glared at Jill. "How dare I what?"

"How dare you say that to him?" Jill started to cry. "He doesn't know that any of his friends died. He has enough to deal with! I didn't want him to be upset in this condition. It might set him back."

Clara looked defensive instead of apologetic. "Well, you should have told me. How would I have known that?"

"Common sense," Jill said through tight lips. "Please, just go."

"You will not throw me out of my own son's room!"

"I'm not throwing you out," Jill said. "I'm asking you to let me have some time with him to tell him about his friends."

Clara backed off then. "Very well. But I expect to see him again after that."

Jill watched her prance away, and she squelched the urge to throw something at her. She had to tell him now. She had to go in there and list the friends he had lost.

She couldn't do it alone. "Clara!" she called out, stopping her.

Clara stopped at the double doors leading out of ICU. She jerked her head back, that haughty I'll-show-you look on her face. "What?"

"Please ask Mark and Nick and Stan to come in here. Tell them Dan needs them."

"So you're going to crowd his room with those people, but you'll banish his own mother?"

Jill didn't have time for this. "Forget it! I'll do it myself."

"No," Clara said. "I'll do it. Go back in there."

Jill waited as Clara huffed out. Leaning against the wall beside his door, she told herself that she had to pull together. His mind was probably going wild about his closest friends dying. She should have planned this better.

Nick came through the doors, Mark and Stan on his heels. "Jill, what is it?"

"He knows," Jill said. "His mother let it slip that some of our guys died. We have to tell him who it was. I need help."

She led them in and found Dan lying there with his hand over his eyes. Tears ran down his temples, and his face twisted in pain. "Who, Jill? I have to know."

"Okay, honey." She wiped the tears off his face. "But look who's here."

He looked beyond her, and she saw the relief washing over him. He started to cry harder as Mark, then Stan, then Nick surrounded his bed. Mark leaned over and gave him a rough hug, then he reached for Nick. Stan took his hand, squeezed it hard.

"You guys are okay."

"Yeah, you're the one we've all been praying for," Mark said.

"Then who?" He looked at Jill again. "Who died?"

Nick took Dan's other hand, and Dan looked up at him. "Dan, we lost George Broussard—"

Dan sucked in a hard breath and covered his face. "Oh, dear God . . ."

"And Junior Reynolds, Jacob Baxter—"

"Oh, no."

His reaction was just what Jill had feared. She half expected the heart monitor to send out a Code Blue.

"Who else?" he demanded.

"Steve Winder and Karen Ensminger."

He folded both arms over his face, hiding his anguish from those who watched him. "So many. How could we have lost so many?"

"But we didn't lose you, man." Mark's voice was broken, hoarse.

Jill came to him and he folded her into his arms and held her against his chest as he wept. His friends just stood around him, wiping their own tears.

Finally, Dan let Jill go and pointed up at Stan. "Stan, you find the maniacs who killed all these people, and you make them pay."

"The FBI has the case," Stan said. "But we're holding three men who might be connected. If they're not the ones, we will find out who is. And when they do—"

"I've got to be on my feet by then," Dan said. "I've got to be standing when I spit in their faces."

But Jill feared that standing would be as impossible a hope as bringing his friends back. She didn't know how she was going to tell him about his legs.

Chapter Forty-One

• • •

Clara was ready for a fight when Jill emerged from ICU. But when she saw her tears, and those on the faces of Dan's friends, she decided that her confrontation could wait. Maybe it wasn't the time.

Allie, Celia, and Issie went to comfort their husbands. "What happened?" Allie asked.

Jill wiped her face with a balled-up tissue. Why that girl wouldn't use a handkerchief, Clara couldn't imagine.

"We told him about the ones we lost. He was very upset."

Clara watched Jill go from one sympathetic pair of arms to the next, and suddenly she wished she had kept her mouth shut. Had Jill been right? Had the news set him back?

"How is my son?" she demanded.

Jill gave her a grudging look. "He's sleeping right now."

"Are you sure you're not just trying to keep me from seeing him?"

Jill just gaped at her, and Clara knew she'd made a mistake. "Clara, I wouldn't have left his side if he hadn't fallen asleep. Tears take a lot out of a person, especially when he's weak to begin with."

Clara sat back down. Now she knew Jill was lying. Dan wouldn't cry. His father would never have allowed it. In all the years that she'd been married to the man, she had never seen him shed one tear. It wasn't in his genes.

It couldn't be in Dan's either.

On the other hand, she didn't really know him as an adult. His level of sensitivity was something she couldn't gauge. And he had suffered quite a blow.

But she hadn't meant to upset him. For heaven's sake, if Jill hadn't wanted him to know, why hadn't she briefed Clara on what not to say? It was absurd, her standing there mute while Clara floundered for something to say. It was almost as if she'd set her up.

And she resented it.

"Well, I can see that I'm not needed here." She got up and slipped her bag over her shoulder. "I'm going home."

"To Paris?" Jill's question was a little too hopeful.

"No. To Newpointe."

"Oh, of course."

She started to formulate some kind of tart comment that would put her daughter-in-law in her place, but there was no one here who would appreciate it.

She wished her husband were still alive. She could use an ally . . . and a friend.

Jill stood there with her own friends, their arms draped around her shoulders, as if their strength was what held her up.

Clara felt suddenly cold. She picked up her sweater, draped it around her shoulders. "If Dan awakens, let him know I'll be back before the next visiting time."

"Clara, it's okay."

She looked back at her daughter-in-law. "What is?"

"That you told him. He had to know. It's all right."

The fight in Clara withered, and she didn't know what to put in the place of her anger. Not saying a word, she simply walked away.

As Clara left the hospital, she felt her own tears pushing to her eyes. Whether they were for her son or herself, she wasn't sure. But she didn't plan to give it another thought.

She had neither the time nor the patience for tears.

Chapter Forty-Two

● ● ●

Stan Shepherd found the coffeepot as soon as he got to the station and poured a cup that some rookie sergeant had made hours ago. It was too weak, but it would have to do.

He took the cup to his desk and looked down at the chart he had scribbled on Newpointe Police Department letterhead. His detective's mind tried to puzzle through the things they had learned about their three Middle Eastern detainees. So far, their alibis had checked out. They were indeed students, and several witnesses said they had been in class that morning when the bombs had gone off.

"Excuse me. Officer Shepherd?"

Stan looked up and saw a familiar blonde standing in front of him. It took him a second to remember her name.

"Amber?"

She smiled, pleased that he recognized her. "I didn't know if you'd remember me."

"Well, sure I do," he said, "but I haven't seen you since you went away to college. What's that been, six, seven years?"

She smiled. "Yeah, something like that."

Amber Williams was the daughter of two of his friends from church. She'd been raised in their fellowship and had been baptized when she was ten years old. Stan had taught her in Sunday school when she was in tenth grade.

"Look at you, all grown up." He pulled a chair up to his desk, and she sat down. She looked nervous.

"What brings you here?"

She looked down at her hands. "Uh . . . there's something that I need to tell you, but . . . is there somewhere we could talk in private?"

Stan frowned and realized that she wasn't here for a social call. This was police business. "Sure." He stood up and looked at the interview rooms at the back of the squad room. One of the doors was open, indicating that it was vacant. "Come right back here and we'll talk."

As he led her back to the room, he reeled through what he knew about the girl. She must be twenty-two or twenty-three by now. Certainly not a kid anymore, she looked like she could be a magazine model. She carried herself with an air of confidence that she hadn't had when she was younger. But the expression on her face said clearly that something important was troubling her.

He closed the door and pulled a chair out for her. "So what's wrong, Amber?"

She waited for him to sit down across from her. "Detective Shepherd, I probably should have gone to the FBI or the New Orleans Police, but since I know you . . ."

His eyebrows came together. "Go ahead."

Tears glistened in her eyes. "This is hard to say. If my parents found out, they would just die. But I guess they're probably going to."

His mind raced ahead, trying to figure out what she might be getting at, but he couldn't settle on any one thing.

"I've been having an affair with Donald Merritt."

His heart plunged, and he sat up straighter, staring at her. "Donald Merritt, the CEO of Icon?"

She nodded. "I know it's horrible. He was a married man and he had children, and I knew better. I really did. But I got caught up in that power thing and all his money. He took me on vacations with him and bought me nice things, set me up in a beautiful apartment. It was like living in a fairy tale."

Stan thought of all those Sundays when he'd talked to the girl about Christ. Had her sincerity just been a show?

She leaned forward, her eyes locking into his. "When he disappeared in the explosion, I was devastated," she said. "I started thinking this was my punishment for being with him. Maybe his punishment too."

Stan shook his head. "Amber, I still don't understand why you've come to me."

"Because . . . I don't think he's really dead."

Stan's eyes narrowed. "Why would you say that?"

"Well, at first I was sure he was," Amber said, "but then when reports started coming out about hidden bank accounts and that so much of his money was missing, that his family didn't know where it had gone, I started thinking."

She got up and began to pace in front of the table. "Okay, he was in a lot of trouble, right? I mean, he was probably going to go to jail. He was waiting for an indictment any day now. Former employees were suing him because their 401Ks had vanished and their severance packages weren't being paid. Stockholders were suing him because he had cooked the books. And he knew he was in serious trouble."

She stopped and turned back to him. "To top matters off, the day before the explosion I told him I was pregnant."

"Pregnant?" This was getting worse and worse. He thought of her poor parents and the scandal this would bring to their family.

Her eyes filled, and she looked up at the ceiling. "I was so stupid. I gave him an ultimatum. I told him that I wanted him to get a divorce and if he didn't tell his wife about us, I would."

Stan sat back in his chair and rubbed his mouth with a finger. "So he stood to lose his wife and children, too." He tried to process it all. "So what are you saying, Amber?"

She still looked like the little girl he knew—not a harlot or a home wrecker.

She swept her hair back behind her ear. "Look, I could be wrong. Maybe he really is dead and lying under that building somewhere. But on the news, there were witnesses who saw him running down the stairs. If they got out, then maybe he did."

Now it was becoming clearer. "Are you suggesting that he vanished on purpose?"

She sat back down in her chair and pulled it up to the table, her eyes intent on Stan's face. "Think about it. If you were in that much trouble, about to lose your fortune, your freedom, your family, everything, and you saw a way out, wouldn't you take it?"

Stan stared at her.

"I think he walked out of that building that day and realized that if he never checked in, they'd think he was dead. I think he's the one who took the money out of his bank account. It was secret, so he probably thought no one would ever realize it. I think he's waiting somewhere until everything blows over. They can bury him and we can all mourn his loss, and then he can skip the country and start a new life."

"Amber, why would you give yourself to someone like that?"

She wiped the tears running down her face. "Because I'm stupid, that's why."

"Do your parents know about the baby?"

She squeezed her eyes shut then and twisted her face. "Oh, that's the stupidest part! There never was a baby. I lied. I made it up to manipulate him." She slid her hand down her face. "I know what you're thinking of me. Believe me, it's nothing I haven't thought about myself already."

Stan shifted in his seat, then clasped his hands in front of his face. "Well, I appreciate your telling me this," he said. "It may all be relevant." He studied her face for a moment. "Amber, do you think there's any possibility that Donald Merritt could have had something to do with the explosion?"

She closed her eyes for a long moment, then finally said, "It's crossed my mind."

"Then he was capable of that?"

"He might have been."

He felt the urge to throttle her and ask her why it had taken three days for her to come forward. "All right, Amber. I'm going to need some details, and then I'm going to call the FBI, and they're going to need to interview you."

"I understand," she said. "I was just scared, so I came to you. I thought it might help—your knowing me and all."

He shook his head, still reeling. "How did you meet him, Amber?"

She studied her hands again. "When I got out of college, I couldn't find a job so I started working for a temp agency. They sent me to Icon. I guess I caught his eye. I was flattered by the attention from somebody so important."

In his head he mentally calculated the age difference. It had to be at least thirty years. He'd seen Merritt's wife and children on the news, and his heart had ached for the pain in their faces. He wished they would never have to know, but it was going to be hard to keep this from the press.

If Donald Merritt was alive, Stan hoped he was there when they caught him.

Chapter Forty-Three

● ● ●

Now let's talk about why I can't move my legs."

Jill froze beside Dan's bed. "What?"

"You've been keeping a lot of bad news from me." He took her hand, brought it to his lips.

There was no indictment in his eyes. Only questions that she couldn't evade.

"Let's just get it all over with," he said. "Lay all the cards on the table. I promise I won't kill the messenger. Is this paralysis permanent?"

Jill sighed and pulled up a chair. "Dan, the thing is, we don't know yet. You had a spinal cord injury, and they're giving you drugs to help with the swelling. Until the swelling is completely gone, we can't know for sure."

His face tightened. "So what are my chances?"

She tried to look hopeful. "Honey, your chances are good. I'll bet within a few weeks you'll have all the feeling back, and you'll be back on your feet. They're not going to keep you down."

He looked at her for a long moment, as if testing the confidence on her face. She must have satisfied him, because the tension relaxed from his face.

"You look tired," he said.

She smiled. "I am."

"I want you to go home tonight."

"No, I'm staying here like I've done every night."

"But I'm out of the woods and in good hands as long as I'm in ICU. Besides, my mother's here."

Jill seized the opportunity to get his mind off of his legs. "What do you think about that?"

He moaned and shook his head. "I can't imagine why she would come."

"Why?" Jill repeated. "Because she thought you were dying. She was worried about you."

"Come on. What's the real reason?"

Jill grunted. "Dan, that is the real reason. She came storming in here demanding to see you, wanting to change your linens and hire doctors halfway across the world."

"So where is she staying?"

"At our house. With Ashley."

Dan almost laughed. "Ashley, the sixteen-year-old? My mother is staying there with her? At our house?"

"That's right."

"Has she called the decorating police yet, since we ruined her color scheme?"

"I'm sure it cramped her style," she said. "I think she would have opted for a hotel room, but they were all booked up. She's a little scared of Ashley, I think."

"Scared of her? Why?"

"She's a little ... uh ... different. She sort of has a lot of piercings and tattoos."

Dan almost looked amused. "You're kidding me. And my mother is really staying there with her?"

"She's a great kid," Jill said. "She's got a lot on her. And like I said, your mother didn't have much choice."

"Oh, get me out of this hospital so I can see this for myself," he said. "My mother with a sixteen-year-old punk rocker. That's priceless."

"I think they're just staying out of each other's way."

"Then you definitely need to go home. Those two probably need a buffer. Besides, in a few days I'll be in a private room, and you'll be able to stay with me all the time. Get a good night's sleep while you can. Please, go home. I'll rest easier if you do."

"Are you sure? Because I don't want you to wake up in the night all depressed and worried...."

"Even if I do, they're not going to let you in here," Dan said. "Not in the middle of the night."

He was right. "Well, okay, if you say so."

"I do."

He looked tired, and that haunted look came back over his face. He looked down at his legs.

"Honey, it's going to be all right," she said. "I know it is."

But she knew Dan wasn't convinced.

Chapter Forty-Four

● ● ●

The FBI agents who came to take Amber's statement acquiesced to her request to allow Stan to stay in the room. His presence calmed her, she said, and she was nervous.

Mills Bryan, the agent in charge of the case, had come himself, since he had already considered the possibility that Merritt could be involved. Amber's story could be pivotal in resolving this case. Stan hoped so. The sooner they nailed the culprit, the sooner the grieving families could begin to heal.

"When you saw him the night before the bombing, did he say anything to indicate that he was going to do something drastic?"

"No," she said. "Nothing at all. I mean, he was angry and really depressed when he left. I thought he might dump me. But there was nothing about a bomb."

"When the two of you traveled together, Amber, did Merritt use his own name?"

Her eyebrows sprang up, as if they'd finally hit on something. "Actually, he did have a credit card under the name of Donald Miller. He used to check into hotels under that name sometimes. Come to think of it, he had checks under that name, too."

Stan exchanged looks with the agents.

"Would you by any chance have kept any receipts for anything he bought with that credit card or those checks?"

Amber thought for a moment. "I don't think so. But I guess it's possible that he might have thrown something away. I've been so stressed out that I haven't emptied my wastebaskets in the last week. Also, he used to shove things like that into his pockets, and he left some of his clothes at my place. I could check the pockets."

"We're going to need to search your apartment," Mills said. "Will you give us permission to do that?"

Amber looked up at Stan, as if asking him if she should allow it. He nodded. She looked down at the tissue in her hand. She had shredded it into little cords. "I want to cooperate," she said. "But I'm worried about word getting out. I don't want my parents to know."

"We could get a warrant," Mills said.

Amber drew in a deep breath, as if she knew that there was no way out of it. "All right, you can search my place. But do I need a lawyer? Am I in some kind of trouble?"

"You haven't broken any laws," Mills said. "You're doing exactly what you should do. You came forward as soon as you realized that things were not as they seemed. You're certainly welcome to consult a lawyer, but I don't anticipate any charges being filed against you."

That seemed to satisfy her, but those tears still glistened in her eyes. She looked up at Stan. "You must think I'm awful."

Stan wished he could sit down with her and talk to her about the laws she had broken—God's laws. He longed to ask her what she believed about Christ if his sacrifice for her sins had not been enough for her. He longed to ask her if those days when she'd seemed so pure and zealous for the Lord were just an act.

He would have to do that later.

"We're not here to judge you," Stan said quietly. "If Merritt had anything to do with blowing up that building, we need to know all of this. You've done the right thing today, Amber."

"Too little, too late," she whispered. "I'd been feeling so proud of myself. So sophisticated and glamorous. My friends didn't know who I was seeing, but they envied me because he spent so much money on me. I loved that."

"You're not the first young woman to be taken in by a rich and powerful man," Mills said.

Those tears escaped and ran down her face, leaving a mascara trail on her cheeks. "I can't believe he would deliberately do that. So he cheated on his wife, lied, stole money from his company . . . but he built that company from the ground up. That building was like a monument to his dream. And those people were innocent . . ."

The agent who'd been taking notes handed her a box of tissues, and she grabbed three out and pressed them against her face.

"I feel like I helped cause this," she cried. "I feel like maybe I pushed him too far and he snapped. But those other people should not have to pay for my stupidity."

Stan watched her as she sobbed into her hands, and he could see traces of the girl he used to know. She did have a conscience. Maybe now she would stop ignoring it.

Chapter Forty-Five

● ● ●

The phone was ringing when Ashley came back to her mother's house. She didn't answer it, but when the answering machine picked up, she stood frozen as a concerned woman's voice asked for Ashley by name. She listened as the caller said she'd heard about Debbie's death and wanted to know if she could help with the funeral.

The funeral home had called her at Jill's earlier, asking Ashley to provide some pictures of her mother. She hadn't had any with her, so she had been forced to come back home.

She looked around the house, realizing for the first time that every framed picture was of her. Debbie hadn't had any made of herself. She was always the one behind the camera when snapshots were taken.

Why had it never occurred to Ashley to take the camera out of her mother's hand and turn it on her?

She rifled through the drawer where her mother kept her snapshots, always planning to organize them chronologically and put them into a scrapbook. There were hundreds of photos of Ashley, chronicling every stage she'd ever gone through, from her pixie stage at four to her compliant stage at five. Later she'd become a tomboy who wouldn't wear anything but pants, then a girlie-girl who only wore dresses. Then she'd discovered the joy of denim, then spandex, then Salvation Army vintage.

She didn't know what stage she was in now, but whatever it was, she wished she could move past it and step into new skin . . . be someone else.

She flipped more quickly through the pictures, growing frantic. Of those few of Ashley's mother, none flattered her. She was such a pretty woman, and Ashley wanted everyone to know it.

She found one of the two of them together when Ashley had been only six years old. They'd been on a riverboat on one of their rare vacations, and another tourist had taken their picture with their faces close together.

Ashley hardly recognized herself now. She had almost forgotten that her hair had been that rich shade of brown, her teeth so white and perfect before she'd begun to lose them and replace them with oversized permanent teeth. Her mother's face glowed in the picture, thrilled that her daughter was enjoying riding the Mississippi.

She would give them that one. They could blow it up, and then when the funeral was over, she'd have it to keep.

She dug further, found a couple more that would do, and stuffed them into her bag.

She found a duffel bag in the closet and dumped the rest of the photos into it. She wanted to go through them one by one, reflecting and contemplating, trying to find her mother among them. But she didn't want to do it here.

If she fell apart in this house, she would scatter like shrapnel and never be able to put herself back together again. No, she had to do it on neutral ground.

She thought about the funeral tomorrow and what would be expected of her. Stepping into her mother's bedroom, she stood in front of the mirror.

She looked like a bad reproduction of one of those horror house characters at Halloween. Smeared mascara darkened the circles under her eyes, and she couldn't remember the last time she'd washed her hair. It stuck up the way she usually wanted it to, but today it just looked silly and sad.

She wore a pair of wrinkled black stretch pants and a black stretch tank top under one of her boyfriend's big flannel shirts.

Her frayed denim jacket, a find for ten bucks at Goodwill, was shorter than the plaid shirt. Her shoes were brown hiking boots that laced up to the ankles.

It was how she'd wanted to look, carefully designed to make the statement she wanted to make.

Yet now she couldn't remember what that statement was.

She couldn't go like this to her mother's funeral. Her mom deserved better. For once in her life, Ashley would conform.

But what would she wear? She hadn't put on a dress in at least two years. Her mother had bought her things that she'd never worn, but Ashley didn't know if any of them still fit. She went to her room and scanned the clothes still hanging in the closet. She found a classy-looking black dress that still had the tags on it. Her mother had bought it for her less than a year ago, hoping she could lure her back to church.

It was dorky, Ashley had said at the time. It looked like something a schoolmarm would wear, and schoolmarm was not in her repertoire. Her mother had held onto it anyway, as if she expected Ashley to change her mind.

She took it down from the hanger and held it up to her in front of her dresser mirror. It had a scooped neck and a high waist and little white buttons down the front. She pulled off her clothes and slipped it over her head.

It still fit. She closed her eyes and wondered if it had ever occurred to her mother that she had bought this dress for her daughter to wear to her funeral.

Not in a million years.

But again her mother had provided for her.

"I'll wear the dress now, Mama," she whispered, and carefully took it off and laid it on the bed to take back to Jill's house. She rummaged in the closet until she found a pair of black pumps that her mother must have bought to go with the dress.

She rummaged in her dresser drawers until she found a pair of pantyhose. The phone rang again, and she grabbed the dress, the duffel bag with the pictures, and the shoes, and went back to the living room.

The machine kicked in after four rings. "Ashley," the voice said, "this is Sara Jean."

She could tell that her mother's friend had been crying. The woman had been laid off from Icon just a month earlier. She should be counting her lucky stars.

"I just read the obit in the paper. It's the first I knew for sure what had happened to your mama, and I just wanted to tell you, honey, that I'm so sorry, and if I can help you with anything, please call me. I'll come to the funeral early tomorrow and see if you need anything." She left her number.

Ashley wondered how many other messages there were on the machine. She would have to listen to them eventually. But she wasn't up to it right now.

She loaded her car and headed to the funeral home to give them the pictures.

When she finally got back to Newpointe, Clara's rental car sat in the driveway at Jill's, but she was apparently locked in her room again when Ashley went in.

Quietly, Ashley slipped into her room. As she closed the door behind her, she realized the absurdity of her being here at all. She hadn't known Jill more than four days, yet she had moved in with her like she was an old friend. But Ashley couldn't explain, not even to herself, the inside-out feeling in her soul, the desperate, sick feeling that kept her from going to her friends or reaching out to anyone who knew her mother.

She climbed to the center of the bed. Carefully, she dumped out the contents of the bag she had brought with her. Pictures of herself and her mother lay faceup like a mockery of the life they had led. She wished it had been she who had died instead of her mother. It would have been only right. After all, it had been Ashley who had been disobedient and rebellious, with her death-defying stunts and her careless abuse of her body.

She thought of the time she had ridden standing up in a friend's topless Jeep, or the time she had climbed on the hood of a friend's car and held on for dear life as he pulled out into traffic. Both things had given her a rush, but either of them could have gotten her killed. Her mother had probably never done anything like that in her life. In fact, she probably spent a lot of time on her knees asking God to protect her careless and reckless daughter.

That image of her mother on her knees reminded Ashley of the prayer journal she hadn't been able to finish reading yesterday. She took it from the bed table and began to turn the pages. Almost every page had a plea about Ashley—a prayer that she wouldn't quit school, then later, after she had, a prayer that she would go back.

> *I come to you in tears today as the mother of a prodigal. And, Lord, it's not drugs or sex, tattoos or piercings that have me the most afraid for Ashley. What I'm most afraid of is that she may never turn her life over to you. If there's only one prayer you'll answer for me, Lord, only one I could ask for the rest of my life, let it be this one. Please make yourself known to my sweet Ashley. Take the blinders off her eyes, shine your light in her darkness, and send her godly people who can love and guide her. I'm asking for a miracle, Lord.*
>
> *Trusting you,*
> *Debbie*

Tears dripped off of Ashley's chin as she turned the page and read another entry ... then another. Her mother's prayers marked events in Ashley's life. So many of them had been answered.

Many more had not.

She heard the door closing, and voices as someone came into the house. Had Jill come home? She closed the prayer journal, then stacked up all the photographs and put them into the bag. Lying back on the bed, she listened for a friendly voice.

Chapter Forty-Six

● ● ●

Jill was glad to be home.

She stepped inside and looked around for any sign of Clara or Ashley. They both seemed to be in their rooms. She wondered if they'd been carefully avoiding each other since yesterday.

A door at the end of the hall opened, and Clara came out, wearing a long white robe with fur around the collar and wrists. "What are you doing home?"

Jill swallowed her instinct to react sarcastically. "Dan urged me to sleep at home tonight. Since he's doing so much better, I decided it wouldn't hurt." She went into the kitchen and set her bag down on the table. Clara followed her. "So how are you?" Jill asked.

Clara got a glass out of the cabinet and filled it with water. She threw it back, as if it were a shot of liquor. "I'm doing very well, considering."

Jill knew she was still angry. "Look, Clara, I'm really sorry about this morning. I hope you understand why I didn't want Dan to know that so many of his friends had died."

Clara just stared down at her glass. "I don't know why I even came here, really. Everything I do is apparently wrong."

Jill began to make a pot of coffee. "Actually, it turned out all right. Now it's over with. He knows, and he's okay."

"Then you should thank me for being the only one who was honest with him."

Jill bit back her chagrin. Being gracious was one thing—thanking her was another. "Where's Ashley?" she asked.

Clara snapped her chin up. "I am not that girl's keeper. I have enough on my mind without trying to chronicle her comings and goings."

Jill's face tightened. "Is she here or not?"

Clara went back to the sink and filled her glass again. "I heard someone come in. I assume it was her."

Jill got up then and left the woman standing alone in the kitchen. She didn't know why Clara couldn't find an ounce of kindness within herself. Why couldn't she see how much Ashley was hurting? Why couldn't she care?

She wished Clara would just get on a plane and go back to Paris. It would be such a relief.

She knocked on Ashley's door. "Ashley?"

"Come in."

Jill opened the door and saw her sitting in the center of the bed, her legs crossed and her elbows propped on her knees. She'd been crying.

"Are you okay, honey?"

"Yeah." Ashley wiped her cheek, and Jill went to the dresser, got the box of tissue, and handed it to her.

Ashley tore one out. "Sorry."

Jill smiled and sat down on the bed, face to face, knee to knee with the girl. "Honey, don't apologize for grieving. It's natural."

Ashley nodded and wiped her nose.

"Where are your friends, Ashley? I know you have some."

"They're around somewhere."

"Have you told them yet?"

Ashley swallowed. "They know."

"How?"

"The lady at the church was looking for me. She got the number where I was staying and called them."

"Do they know where to find you?"

She shook her head. "I don't really want to talk to them."

"Why not? They could help you through it. You wouldn't have to be so alone."

Ashley looked up at the ceiling. "I guess I just figured . . . what if they handle it wrong, you know? Like, what if they don't understand how important it is and they say something stupid and I lose it?"

"It's okay to lose it with your friends."

Ashley shot her a look. "You don't know my friends."

Jill took her hand. "You're right, I don't know them. But maybe they'd surprise you. Maybe they wouldn't know exactly the right thing to say. Nobody really does. But they could hold your hand, walk beside you."

"Maybe." Ashley stared down at the wadded tissue in her hand.

"Would you like me to talk to them for you?"

Ashley laughed. "Yeah, I can just picture that. You could drop in at the Fixation Tattoo Parlor and tell Chris that I need him. He'd drop everything and come running to rescue me."

"Who's Chris?"

"My boyfriend," she said.

"Doesn't sound like you like him very much."

"Yeah, well." She tore out another tissue. "Guess nothing feels the same anymore. Four days ago I was just like them. No responsibility, no rules. Just fun. Whatever feels good. That's our motto. I can't blame them, really."

"How did your mother feel about them?"

New tears rushed to Ashley's eyes. "She couldn't stand them. Thought they were leading me straight to hell. When I moved out to live with Chris and some of the others in this house our friend Eddie rented, she went ballistic. Reported me as missing to the police. They came after me and made this big deal. I went back home, but I didn't stay." She sucked in a sob and pressed the Kleenex to her mouth. "I don' t know why I tried so hard to do what she hated. Why couldn't I just make her proud of me one time, instead of ashamed?"

Jill reached across and kissed Ashley on the cheek, stroked her ruffled hair. "I'm sure she was proud, Ashley." The girl seemed so small, sitting here on this bed. And her grief seemed so big.

"When's the last time you've eaten, honey?"

"I don't know."

"Well, I'm ordering some Chinese takeout. It's a little beneath Clara, but if she's hungry she'll eat it. Got any favorites?"

Ashley shrugged. "Not really."

"Then I'll get a little of everything." She slid off of the bed. "I'll call you when it comes. And tonight we can just hang out, maybe watch a movie or something."

Ashley looked up at her. "So you're staying home tonight?"

"Dan insisted."

Ashley gave her a weak smile. "He must be doing really well."

"Yeah." Jill looked at the floor, wondering whether she should tell the girl that he still couldn't move his legs. There was no need to bring her further down.

"It's kind of a miracle, isn't it, that he'd be buried like that and be one of the few survivors and still be all right?"

"Yeah, kind of a miracle." Jill turned and saw the snapshot of Ashley and her mother lying on the dresser. She picked it up. "Is this you?"

Ashley looked at the picture with her. "Yeah, I was six. They copied the picture at the funeral home so they could use it tomorrow."

"Good. That's nice."

"I didn't have anything recent. That was the best I could do." She took the picture from Jill's hand and gazed down at it. "I wonder why my mom didn't get a miracle. She was a good person.

She loved God and prayed all the time. How come some people get miracles and some don't?"

"I don't know the answer to that," Jill whispered.

Ashley just stared down at that picture. After several moments, she looked up. "Sweet and sour chicken," she said. "Can you order some of that?"

Jill smiled. "I'll let you know the minute it's here."

Chapter Forty-Seven

• • •

W e've been interviewing survivors and witnesses, and so far have twenty-plus people who saw Donald Merritt in the stairwell that day." Mills Bryan stood at the front of the room, listing the facts on a dry-erase board. "Five say they saw him exit the building."

Stan jotted that on his legal pad. The other detectives who'd been assembled from police forces across the region took it all in, each one hoping they'd be the one to find the missing CEO.

"Guy's alive," Sid Ford whispered. "He's so guilty I can smell it."

Stan looked at his friend, the only other detective on the Newpointe force. "Yeah, but don't forget the three guys we arrested." They were still being detained in the Newpointe jail. Even though their alibis had checked out, the FBI had instructed them to keep holding them awhile longer, primarily for their own safety. If they let them go, some grieving, angry soul would probably gun them down before they got out of town.

"It's critical that we ascertain what kind of bombs these were, where the material came from, how it was detonated. Witnesses may have seen the bombs being taken up and not realized what they were. That's why we've asked for your help."

Mills flashed up a slide of the inside of a warehouse that looked to be the size of a football field. "As you know, the rescue effort is still ongoing. Workers are carefully digging through rubble looking for bodies. All of the debris is being moved in buckets and dumped into trucks, and we're transporting it to this warehouse. We have forensic chemists on the scene, and we need all of you to help sift through the rubble. We're looking for timing mechanisms, debris from blasting caps, explosive materials. As you know, the parking garage was full, and since the biggest explosion occurred there, there's quite a bit of metal. We have arson experts searching for metal that may have come from the vehicle that held the explosives."

Stan had hoped they needed them to interview witnesses. Digging through ashes was not his idea of important investigative work. But it was clearly needed.

"I know it's not glamorous work," Mills said, "but we can only use trained detectives for this. We can't take the chance of having any pertinent physical evidence overlooked, and we have to keep a careful log of every single thing that could be important."

"I'm in," Sid whispered. Stan nodded that he was, too. They both had a personal interest in this case, since so many of their good friends had died. But he supposed the others in the room had come for the same reason. To do this, they would have to put some of their own cases on the back burner. But it was worth it if they could avoid another attack like the one at Icon.

"When do we get started?" Stan asked.

"You can start right now," Mills said.

Stan was ready to get his hands dirty.

Chapter Forty-Eight

● ● ●

Ashley was quiet as they ate. But Clara was not.
"I think what we should do is to move Dan to another state," Clara said. "Possibly to Rochester, near Mayo, where the best doctors in the country can treat his paralysis. I won't accept that he won't walk again. The right doctors could do the right kind of surgery."

Jill had begun to consider taking Dan to a hospital that had made progress in spinal cord injuries. But he would have to be a part of that decision.

"He can't walk?" Ashley said.

Jill touched her hand. "We're still hoping for the best. It's early yet—"

"We have to move quickly, Jill," Clara spouted. "We can't just wait."

"The doctors are moving," she said. "I don't think it will be necessary to move him out of state. This could be a very long process. He should be at home while he does rehab."

"For heaven's sake, Jill, you have to think of him instead of yourself. Maybe it is inconvenient, but if it enables him to get the best medical care—"

"I think he is getting the best," she said. "His doctors seem very capable, and they're consulting with other orthopedic surgeons."

"Things are not always what they seem. What do they care if my son is crippled?"

Jill just gave her a dull look and thought of telling her that she didn't know why she would spend so much time being anxious over his care now when she hadn't given it a thought when he was a child.

But she bit her tongue and told herself that she only had to endure Clara for a while longer. Surely she would grow bored and return to Europe soon.

When Jill finally retreated to her room, she luxuriated in a long, warm shower. When she got out, she sat on her bed, hugging her knees, and prayed for God to heal Dan's legs before he realized how serious—and how permanent—his paralysis might be.

Then she curled up under her comforter and drifted into a deep sleep.

Chapter Forty-Nine

● ● ●

"Mama!"

Jill sat bolt upright at the scream and groped for her lamp. "Mama, no!"

Ashley. Her scream was piercing, chilling, and reminiscent of that day on the stairwell.

Jill ran out into the hall and saw Clara looking out her door. "What on earth is happening?"

Jill threw open Ashley's door and saw her writhing on the bed, covered with sweat and still screaming.

"Mama, no! Help! Somebody help!"

Jill pulled the girl up and tried to shake her awake. "Ashley! Ashley, you're dreaming. It's a nightmare, honey. Wake up. Come on, honey."

Ashley fought her off, sobbing and screaming, and finally, she opened her eyes and focused on Jill. Her fighting stopped.

Jill put her arms around her. "You're okay. You're here at my house. Remember? You're with me."

Ashley wilted. "It happened all over again." She sucked in a sob. "I heard that explosion, and we were in that stairwell, and the smoke was filling up . . ."

"I know, honey," Jill whispered.

". . . and I knew my mother was dead. People were screaming and running down, and some of the faces around us were blotted out because they were the ones who were going to die."

Jill held her tighter. She had to protect her somehow. She had to help her banish these memories. She looked back at the door. Clara stood there, hands at her sides, her black eye mask pulled up to her hairline.

"Would you get her some water, Clara?"

The woman disappeared.

Jill looked around for the box of tissues and found it next to the bed. She pulled one out and began to dab at Ashley's face.

"It's okay," Jill said again. "You and I are probably going to have these dreams for a long time. It was a traumatic thing that happened."

Ashley was soaking wet with sweat, and her body shivered as if she was freezing.

"Oh, I hate this!" Ashley cried, pressing her hand against her forehead. "I hate this so much!"

"I hate it, too."

Clara came back in with the water and handed it to Jill. She sat Ashley up and made her drink.

"If she had only run with me," Ashley said when she had emptied the glass. "If she hadn't stayed to call security ... I shouldn't have gone without her, and maybe she would have come...."

"Don't do that, Ashley. Honey, you did what she told you."

"First time in years." She sucked in a sob. "I'd rather be dead with her than having to go to her funeral."

Jill understood that. If Dan had died, she would have felt the same way. She wiped at her own tears and looked up at Clara. The woman just stood there, watching as if she'd just witnessed a bad wreck. Jill wished she would go back to bed.

"I'm glad you're alive, though," Jill whispered. "I'm glad you're here."

The girl clung to her, hiccuping her sobs, and Jill sat there for a long time, stroking her hair. She couldn't explain the bond she had with this girl. It was like mother-love. She'd never felt like that before.

Slowly, the girl stopped shivering and her breathing settled. Her sobbing stopped.

"I'm okay now," she said.

"Are you sure?"

"Yeah. Go on back to bed. You need your sleep."

Jill let her go. "You call me if you need me, Ashley."

"I will."

Jill kissed her cheek and started to the door.

"Jill?"

Ashley's voice turned her around.

"What, honey?"

"She probably didn't suffer, did she? I mean with the explosions so close to her, she probably died instantly, don't you think?"

"Probably."

"Because all those hours when we were waiting to find out . . ." Her voice broke. ". . . I just pictured her lying there buried somewhere and suffering all that time. But it probably wasn't true."

"No," Jill said, "it probably wasn't."

Ashley sniffed and nodded. "Good night."

"Good night, sweetheart."

When she left Ashley alone in the room, she saw Clara standing near her door, her face pale. "That poor girl," she whispered.

The comment surprised Jill. "She's suffering post-traumatic stress. She's pretty young to have gone through that."

Clara stared at her for a moment. "Do you have nightmares, too?"

Jill sighed. "I've had some. It's a hard thing to get over."

Clara got tears in her eyes. "That must have been horrible for Dan, to feel that building come down on him, to be thrown and buried." She brought her fingers to her chest. "How in the world did he survive?"

"God was looking out for him." But even as she uttered those words, she remembered Ashley's question.

I wonder why my mom didn't get a miracle?

She regarded Clara. The woman stared into space as if a veil had just been lifted. Jill wondered if she would have more compassion for Ashley now. Would she be gentler with her?

But she knew better than to expect too much.

"Well, I guess I'll go back to bed," she said. "Do you need anything?"

"No, dear, I'll be fine."

Jill watched her go back into her room, before Jill closed the door to her own.

Chapter Fifty

● ● ●

Jill rose early the next morning, hoping to get to the hospital by the 7:00 A.M. visitation. It would take her forty-five minutes to get there, and she wanted to make sure she allowed for any traffic glitches. Just before she left at 5:30, she looked in on Ashley.

To her surprise, the girl was already up, sitting on the chaise beside the window, reading.

"You're up early," Jill said.

Her eyes were puffy and red. Jill wondered if she'd slept at all after her nightmare last night. "It's a big day," Ashley said. "My mother's funeral day. Couldn't sleep it away."

The tragic acceptance in that statement impaled Jill's heart. She sighed and went to sit on the bed. "You know, I lost my mother when I was a freshman in college, about the age you are now."

"What did she die of?"

"Heart attack. And I remember waking up that morning, the day of the funeral, and the house was teeming with relatives and people were running around getting dressed and chattering like it was Christmas or something. And I remember thinking, this can't be. I can't really be going to my mom's funeral. I had this urge to run ask her what I should wear, if these shoes looked all right with this dress. I had never even *been* to a funeral before."

Ashley looked down at the notebook in her hands. "I went to my dad's when I was five, but I don't remember much about it."

"Well, I'll walk you through it," Jill said. "I'll be there with you the whole time. I can meet you there, or you can pick me up at the hospital."

"You shouldn't come," Ashley said. "You should be with Dan."

"Dan will understand," Jill said. "Don't argue, because I'm coming."

Ashley let out a ragged sigh. "Good." She drew in a deep breath and wiped her eyes with the heel of her hand. "I know it's stupid, me needing you like this and all when I hardly even know you. It's kind of like you're my angel. The one my mom prayed for."

"What do you mean, honey?"

Ashley turned a few pages in the notebook she held. "Right here," she said. "It was a prayer. She wrote, 'Send her godly people who can love and guide her. I'm asking for a miracle, Lord.'" She looked up at Jill. "I guess that miracle would be you."

Jill wished she was worthy of that. But God was clearly working in this as he was probably working in the life of every person who'd been touched by that explosion. Miracles didn't always come as expected or wanted.

She only hoped she'd have the wisdom to be the answer to Debbie Morris's prayer.

Chapter Fifty-One

● ● ●

Dan had grown used to the poking and prodding, but he hated it when they turned him over to examine the incision on his back. It was then that he realized the extent of his paralysis. His arms were still strong and had full mobility, but his legs lay there like lead pipes, too heavy to move.

Always before, he'd been able to overcome physical problems through the sheer force of his will.

But this was more serious than anything he'd ever faced, and he realized now that the strength of his will was not going to be enough.

The physiatrist stood over him next to the thoracic surgeon who had stabilized his spine, moving his legs in various positions and scratching him with instruments.

"Do you feel it now? How about now?"

He felt like he was living through some bad cellular phone commercial, and he got tired of saying no. Every time they poked him and he didn't feel anything, he sank deeper into despair.

Finally, they turned him back over and moved his legs into what should have been a comfortable position.

"Tell me, Dan," the physiatrist said. "How are you doing, really?"

"I feel like somebody operated on me and put the wrong bottom half on. Like my legs belong to someone else."

"That's understandable. We have counselors available, who are used to dealing with paraplegia. If you need to talk—"

Anger surged through him. "So—what are you saying? That I'm a paraplegic and I need to deal with it? Have you guys given up? Is this paralysis permanent?"

The doctors exchanged looks. This time, Dr. Grist spoke. "Dan, the injury to your spinal cord was pretty severe. We're giving you drugs to help with the swelling. Until the inflammation is completely gone, we can't know for sure whether it's permanent."

Dan realized the doctor was evading. He was tired of playing games. "Tell me the worst-case scenario, Doc. I need to know what I'm dealing with."

Dr. Dalton, the physiatrist who specialized in physical medicine and rehabilitation, patted his leg. "There are degrees of paraplegia, Dan. Yours may not be complete. For example, you could have paralysis in your legs but still have hip control and bladder and bowel function."

He felt as if someone had shoved a solid object down his throat, and he tried to swallow. "You mean this catheter and bag might not be temporary?"

Dr. Grist sighed. "Dan, we've begun to feel that there will be some degree of paralysis. We're hoping this is an incomplete SCI, but we won't know for a while. As soon as we get you moved into your own room in a couple of days, you'll be starting intensive physical and occupational therapy. First they'll work on getting you into a wheelchair—"

Dan felt the blood rushing to his face. "A wheelchair?" The words knocked the breath out of him.

"After that, they'll begin working with you to maximize the mobility you do have."

Dan just stared at them. "I'm a fireman. That's what I do. I have to be able to walk. Are you telling me that I'll never walk again?"

The doctors exchanged looks again. "In all probability, you won't," Dr . Grist said. "But there's a chance that you could. We don't want to give up hope."

Damaged goods, he thought. He was damaged goods. He wondered what Jill was thinking about her husband who would be wheelchair-bound for the rest of his life. Big, strong Dan, who could bench-press more than anyone else at Midtown, confined to a wheelchair.

Tough Dan, the rescuer who would never rescue again. Fireman Dan, who would now be put on medical disability and replaced with someone who had use of his legs.

Oh, God, what have you done to me?

Tears burned in his eyes, and he hated himself for them. If he was going to be weak physically, he couldn't afford to be weak emotionally, too. He wiped his eyes and forced the tears away. When Jill came in for her 7:00 A.M. visit in a few minutes, he would smile and laugh and pretend that he was fine.

He would be a man, even if he didn't feel like one.

Chapter Fifty-Two

● ● ●

The doctors updated Jill before the visit.

"You told him—when I wasn't there to help him through it?" she asked. "Why would you do that?"

"Mrs. Nichols, he knew we were testing his feeling in his legs. He understands the extent of his injuries."

"No, he doesn't! Until now, he thought the paralysis was just temporary. He had hope. How could you have taken that from him?"

The doctors hadn't given a satisfactory answer, and she supposed there wasn't one.

The damage was done, so she was filled with trepidation as she went in to see him. He lay still with his eyes closed, as if he slept.

She went to his side and touched his shoulder. "Dan?"

His eyes opened, and he smiled up at her as if she was the only bit of color in a black-and-white world. "Hey there, beautiful." He chuckled and touched her face. "Going home agreed with you. You look rested."

She hadn't expected such a bright greeting. She had expected anger, sorrow, despair. "How are you?"

"I'm good," he said. "Can't wait to get into my own room. These people are driving me crazy. They wake me up in the middle of the night to take my pulse. The hospital is a terrible place for a sick person to be."

Jill wasn't fooled. She knew what he was doing. "Dan, I just talked to the doctors. They told me—"

He set his fingertips over her lips. "Shhh," he said. "Those guys don't know what they're talking about."

So it's denial, she thought. Dan was pretending that it wasn't true.

"They just don't know me," he said. "They don't know how hard I'll work. They don't know what I'm made of."

A flame of hope flickered inside her. It was true, they didn't. Dan wasn't an ordinary patient. He was an athlete, a competitor. He loved a challenge.

Maybe he really could beat this.

"So tell me how things went last night, what with Ashley and my mother there together."

She knew he was trying to change the subject. She sat down next to his bed and leaned on the mattress. Gazing at him, she saw that his eyes were red. Was his nonchalance about all this just a façade for her?

"Were there any casualties?" he asked.

Jill wanted to talk more about his paralysis, but she decided to defer to him. "Well, things were fine until Ashley woke up in the middle of the night with a terrible nightmare. She was reliving the whole thing. Screaming for her mother."

His bright façade faded. "Yeah, I know those dreams."

"Me too," she said. "I've had them every night since the building fell."

He took her hand. "In mine, I'm always looking for you."

"At least I'm here. Ashley never did find her mother. Not alive, anyway." She sighed. "She's just a kid."

"Funeral's today?"

"Yeah," she whispered. "She's going to come by here and get me. She was up before dawn."

"I'm glad you're going with her."

"Yeah. God must love her a lot, because he's poured it into me." Her eyes glistened. "I want you to meet her soon."

"Me, too. What about my mother? Is she coming to see me today?"

"Of course." Jill hoped her dread wasn't evident in her voice. "She insisted on being here while I'm gone, although they won't let her in until visiting time."

He sighed. "Well, that's fine. It won't hurt to catch up."

That surprised her. She would have expected him to express dread, as well. "She's just . . . a little outspoken. Sometimes she says things . . . that are hurtful."

He smiled. "You don't think I can take it?"

"I'm just suggesting that you might want to brace yourself."

"I may not have been around her in years, but I'm well aware of my mother's level of sensitivity. I had a dog that got out of our fence and was hit by a car when I was ten or so, and I was broken-hearted. My mother responded by lecturing me about fence maintenance and the irresponsibility of our gardener, who should have fixed it. Then she bought me another puppy."

Jill winced. "She meant well."

"I guess. But I doubt she's changed that much in all these years."

"Maybe not. But she loves you, and that's the main thing."

His eyebrows lifted. "She said that?"

Again his reaction surprised her. "Well, not in so many words. But she dropped everything and came here, and she's been throwing her weight around. . . . Wouldn't you agree that that's how she loves?"

He stared at the air and seemed to think that over. "Maybe, though that might be a stretch."

"She wouldn't be here if she didn't," Jill said. "She's not the type to just go through the motions."

"No, I guess not."

Was that a longing in his tone? It occurred to her for the first time that he might be glad his mother was here. Maybe he needed for her to be.

They brought Dan his breakfast, and since he could not sit up, she fed it to him, chattering the whole time to get his mind off of his helplessness. She could see from the strained look on his face that he resented the help yet knew he couldn't do without it.

His paralysis was going to be the greatest challenge he'd ever faced, she thought. And his biggest battle would be accepting this new phase of his life.

Chapter Fifty-Three

● ● ●

Jill was battle-weary by the time Ashley came for her at the hospital.

But when she saw how the girl had groomed herself for the funeral, her strength was renewed.

Ashley had combed her hair down and had a silver barrette on one side, pulling it back from her face. She wore a tasteful black dress, its collar covering her tattoo. Her black pumps had a slight heel, and she wore a delicate chain with a gold locket that hung gracefully below her throat. She had taken out her eyebrow and nose rings and only wore a few gold studs in her ears.

Jill almost came to tears as she crossed the room to the girl. "Honey, you look beautiful. Your mother would have been proud."

"She should be," Ashley said with a weak smile. "She bought all this for me. First time I've ever put it on."

Jill's throat constricted, but she told herself not to cry. Ashley seemed to be holding together by a thread. One tear might just do her in.

Ashley followed her to get her purse. Clara looked up as she recognized Ashley. "Well, you look very nice, young lady."

Ashley didn't meet her eyes. "Thanks."

They left the hospital and got into Ashley's Subaru, and Ashley was quiet as she drove to her mother's church. They went in the back way, and Ashley opted to stay in a room with just Jill and the coffin, unable to greet her mother's friends. The preacher came in and prayed with them, and when it was time, the funeral director ushered them into the packed sanctuary.

Ashley's face was gray-white as Jill walked with her to the front row and sat down with her. She put her arm around her, but the girl was rigid as stone. She sat like a statue as a church member sang a hymn. The preacher spoke of Debbie Morris's commitment to Christ and her prayers for her daughter, and quoted the psalm about the death of a saint being precious to God. But Jill feared Ashley did not hear a word. Even when her mother's closest friend got up and tearfully told happy stories of Debbie's life, Ashley didn't shed a tear.

She rode quietly with her in the funeral home's limousine as they followed the hearse to the burial plot next to Ashley's father.

When they reached the cemetery, they waited as the pall-bearers carried the coffin to the tent set up for them.

As the cars pulled up and the people began to surround the tent, Jill noticed a rugged group of young people. They looked as if they were dressed for a heavy metal concert, with their hair tousled and spiked like Ashley's usually was, and their clothes a combination of nightclub glamour and crack house.

But they were here.

Jill tapped Ashley's shoulder and pointed to them. Her rock-hard façade finally cracked, and for a moment Jill thought Ashley was going to shatter.

They came toward her, and Jill put her arm defensively around her.

"Hey, baby," one of the guys said and reached down to hug her.

"Chris." Ashley returned the hug stiffly. "How'd you guys know about this?"

"The church lady told us," one of her girlfriends said, and gave her another hug.

"Yeah," Chris said. "We were floored, babe. Why didn't you tell me?"

Ashley swallowed hard. "Couldn't."

The crowd was gathering around, and the funeral director was motioning for them to come and sit in the folding chairs in front of the coffin. Jill didn't know whether to whisk her away or hold the director off.

"So where have you been, babe?"

Jill saw the discomfort on Ashley's face, so she intervened. "She's been staying with me." She extended her hand. "I'm Jill Nichols. You guys can talk later, okay? After the burial."

"Yeah, sure. We'll talk after, Ash."

Ashley nodded and allowed Jill to lead her to her seat.

She sat staring dully at the coffin as the preacher said the final words for her mother, then ended with a prayer. The pallbearers each came by to hug her, then took the roses off of their lapels and set them on the coffin.

Finally, the director ushered Ashley and Jill out of the tent and left them there for well-wishers to approach. She accepted all of the condolences with whispered thank-yous, then finally turned to her friends.

Jill heard her agreeing to call them later.

By the time they were back in the car, Jill could see that the girl was completely drained. They were silent again as they were driven back to the church.

When Ashley was back behind the wheel of her own car, Jill sat quietly in the passenger seat. Ashley stared through the dirty windshield for a moment. "Well, it's over," she said.

Jill knew better, but she didn't say so. "It was a nice funeral. Very honoring to your mother."

"Yeah. They did a good job. I never could have done all that."

"God's good to send helpers when we need them. Your mother sounds like a fun person. I wish I'd known her."

Ashley started the car and pulled out of the parking lot. "I wish I'd hung out with her more."

"I wished the same thing about my mom."

Ashley glanced over at her. "But I bet you weren't like me. You've probably always been a straight-and-narrow kind of person. The kind parents brag about."

Jill decided not to take that as an indictment. She wished the girl could forgive herself for her rebellion. She needed the forgiveness of Christ, she thought. Then maybe she could start healing.

Her mother's prayer for a godly person to love and guide her reminded Jill of her mission. Ashley had been sent to her for a reason. She hoped she wouldn't fail Debbie.

"Chris wants me to come hang out today."

An alarm went off in Jill's heart. "Are you going to?"

Ashley seemed to think that over for a long moment. "I don't know. Going back there just seems like throwing it all back in Mom's face somehow. She wanted me to stop using drugs. She wanted me to quit hanging out with that group. And now that she's gone, it seems like I ought to do what she asked for once."

"Honey, you can stay with me as long as you need to. And as soon as your head's clear, you and I can work through all the legal stuff with your mother's estate."

Ashley looked over at her as if she hadn't even considered that. "Oh, yeah. I guess I will need a lawyer, huh?"

"Just to handle the probate and all. It won't be a problem. It just might take some time."

Ashley just shook her head. "Five days ago I was a sixteen-year-old kid. Now I feel like I'm eighty."

Again, Jill could relate.

Chapter Fifty-Four

● ● ●

Clara was in top form when Jill got back to the waiting room, ranting about the lukewarm coffee and the cafeteria food. Ashley left, and soon after, Jill decided she had to get out of there as well. It was a good time to visit Gordon.

His door was partially open, and she knocked lightly and heard a grumbled, "Come in."

She stepped inside and saw him standing up, trying to walk on crutches as a nurse walked beside him.

Jill smiled. "It's good to see you up, Gordon."

Sweat glistened on his forehead. "Wasn't my idea," he said in a hoarse, phlegmy voice.

"We're letting him go home tomorrow," the nurse said, "and he's got to be able to get around."

She could see the pain on his face with each step, and his breathing sounded wheezy and heavy. The smoke inhalation had done a number on Jill and Ashley. She could only imagine what it would do to someone who was out of shape and Gordon's age. It wasn't going to be easy for him to go home to an empty house with no one to cook or clean for him and nothing to do with his time.

"So how's your old man?" he asked her.

"He's still in ICU, but he's doing great." She decided not to mention the paralysis.

Gordon looked genuinely pleased. "Now that's good news. And what about that other young lady that was helping me on the stairs?"

"Ashley? We buried her mother this morning."

He sagged on his crutches. "You're kidding me. She died?"

"She was actually the first one to see the bomb and report it. She was probably right there in front of it when it exploded."

The intensity of compassion on Gordon's face surprised her. He hobbled back to the bed and sat down. She thought he was going to cry. "That's just wrong. How old is the girl?"

"Sixteen," Jill said. "Her father died when she was five, so she really doesn't have anybody now."

"Sixteen." He swallowed hard and rubbed his face. "Being alone is a very hard thing. I wouldn't have wished it on her, not for anything. She seems like a good kid."

Jill sat down and leaned her elbows on her knees. "Gordon, are you going to be all right when you go home?"

"Oh, yeah," he said, "I'll be fine."

"How are you going to get there?"

"I'll call a cab. No big deal."

"A cab ride from New Orleans to Newpointe could be pretty expensive," she said.

He shrugged. "Well, you do what you got to do."

"You need someone to help you, Gordon."

He waved a dismissive hand. "Naw, I'll be all right."

Jill thought of all the people at her church who would probably rush to help one of the Icon victims. They would love to know there was anything they could do for one of them.

She got to her feet. "Tell you what. I'm going to check back on you tomorrow morning. If I can, I'll take you home myself. But if I can't get away, what if I got some of my friends from church to come and help you? They'd love to do it. They'd consider it part of the rescue effort, in a way."

He looked genuinely moved. "Well, if there are people that kindhearted, I sure wouldn't turn them away."

She went to his bed and bent down to hug him. "Well, I'd better get back to ICU. You'll be hearing from me tomorrow."

"You're a sweetheart," he said. "A God-given angel."

Chapter Fifty-Five

● ● ●

The sheer volume of the debris the detective teams sifted through made Stan wonder if his work here would have any impact at all. But someone had to do it. Somewhere under all the ashes, there was evidence that could link them to the killer.

Donning safety goggles and breathing masks, and wearing rubber gloves, the investigative teams sifted the ashes and powder into boxes that were later discarded. Big pieces were left behind and sorted into lines and lines of evidence laid out on the floors for the forensics teams to follow up on. Occasionally, someone found something that had higher importance, and the forensics teams would examine it immediately.

But it was a slow process.

So far, they'd found hundreds of pieces of car tags, jewelry, computer parts, but nothing that could definitively point to the origin of the bomb, who had made it, or even what it was made of.

"If I gotta dig through ashes," Sid said, "I'd rather be looking for bodies. Look at this." He pulled out a set of car keys. "This goes in the evidence pile, only how can they know if it belonged to some poor soul who worked in the building, or the bomber himself? It's like looking for a needle in a haystack, only we don't know it's a needle we're looking for."

"You got any better ideas?" Stan asked him.

Sid shook his head. "No, man, I don't. But my talents are wasted here. Let me out there to hunt down Merritt. Now, that would get us somewhere."

Stan had thought the same thing himself. It was maddening doing such menial labor, but it had to be done. And not too many were qualified to do it.

"Well, this is where they need us," he said. "I guess if we really want to help, we have to do what's needed."

"Thing is," Sid said, "we could dig through this stuff for months and still not finish. We're talking thirty floors' worth of ashes and debris."

"Maybe we won't have to go through all of it. Maybe we'll find exactly what we're looking for and it'll crack the whole case."

Sid didn't look convinced, but Stan knew he didn't plan to slack off on his work. This was an investigation like any other, and every piece of evidence counted.

Chapter Fifty-Six

● ● ●

The firehouse at Newpointe's Midtown Station was a somber place as the crew on duty came for supper. Aunt Aggie had tried to lighten the mood when she'd first come here today, but she had soon realized that she couldn't combat their moods. They were grieving several of their own. Truth be known, she was grieving too, but busyness was the best antidote to grief she knew.

She had boiled a pot of shrimp for them today and had made gumbo, which was their favorite because it kept and they could snack on it at night. As she dipped it out of the pot into bowls and passed it around the table, she wondered if any of them would eat a bite.

"Ain't none of y'all need to be at work today," she said in her rapid Cajun tone. "They ought to close down the whole fire department, y'ask me."

Ray looked wearier than the rest of them. "Aunt Aggie, you know we can't do that."

"I'm just saying you boys been through a lot. There ought to be some off time 'fore you start burying your buddies." She put a bowl in front of Nick and stroked his hair. He sat slumped over, staring down at the table. She could hear the wheeze of his breathing. None of them was sucking oxygen like they should today. The whole lot of them needed to be in the hospital, if you asked her. But here they were at work, serving the community who hardly appreciated them at all.

"Eat up, Nicky," she said. "You need your strength, *sha*. You got a lot to do."

"Five funerals," he said, looking up at the men across the table from him. "Five funerals in the next forty-eight hours."

"Least you found them," Aggie said. "You could be still digging through that pile, looking for bodies. Lots of folks still are."

She knew her words weren't helpful, so she bit her tongue and went back to the stove and pulled out the biscuits she had prepared for them. Maybe the food would comfort them, if she could get them to eat. She'd made a big chocolate cake for dessert and had even brought some of that pralines-and-cream ice cream from the Baskin-Robbins up the street. If she could keep their bellies full, maybe their hearts wouldn't feel so empty.

Chapter Fifty-Seven

• • •

Stan was tired of the evidence warehouse. It was filthy work in high temperatures, since so much of the debris still smoked and smoldered, and they couldn't use fans because it would blow the ashes around. He'd logged what seemed like thousands of bits of evidence, yet nothing he'd found seemed of any consequence in the whole scheme of things.

Then he saw a commotion on the other side of the room. He nudged Sid, who worked next to him. "Think they got something?"

Sid stopped working and took his goggles off to peer across the room.

Some of the forensics people had run over to examine something, and people all around that part of the room had stopped working to see.

"I'm goin' over there," Sid said. "It'll do me good to see 'em pull something important out of that pile."

Stan pulled his mask off and followed Sid around the outer perimeter of the room. Others were doing the same.

A crowd of detectives began to form around the forensics team as they turned over a big chunk of metal. Stan saw that there were letters on it. A commerical sign of some sort, he thought.

"It's a part from one of those Budget rental trucks," one of the lead forensics guys announced. "Inside's charred, metal's melted. Looks like we might have the point of origin of the third bomb."

Stan started to laugh, and Sid slapped him a high five.

"Now we're talking," Sid said. "We can run down a rental truck."

Stan went to the pile from which that piece had been found. "Let's work over here for a while," he said. "Maybe we'll find more pieces."

And as he resumed his work, Stan felt as if it wasn't wasted after all.

Chapter Fifty-Eight

● ● ●

Allie Branning had expected her time with Gordon to be more of a chore than a blessing, but when Jill had asked them to help him, she couldn't refuse. As she and Celia and Susan escorted the limping man into his house, she found herself enjoying his wit.

"Ain't much, but it's home," he said. "If I'd known you girls were gonna come home with me, I'd have straightened up before I left. 'Course, when I went up to Icon that day, I didn't plan on landing in the hospital."

"Don't you worry about a thing," Susan said. "Now you just come right on in here and you sit down in your chair. This *is* your chair, isn't it?"

He smiled. "Yes, ma'am. That one over there was Alma's."

"It looks like her." Susan had known Alma before she died, though she had never met Gordon until today. "Your wife was a beautiful woman. I know you miss her terribly."

His face sobered up. "I'm glad she's not alive to see what went on this week."

Susan sighed. "All I can say about that is God's still on his throne. In fact, that's why we're here. We want to take care of you because we know how much God loves you."

The man chuckled. "Let's not get carried away."

Allie went to the adjoining kitchen and started unloading his bag of medicine. "You don't think God loves you?" she asked.

He gave her a disarming grin. "You wouldn't blame him if you knew me better."

Celia walked around the room, picking up craft item's that his wife had probably made. "Well, your wife sure seemed to love you. She decorated this house so sweet."

"She made a lot of this stuff herself. Watched them decorating shows on TV and always had new ideas about how to make the house homier."

"I bet she cooked, too," Susan said.

"Yep. I've lost quite a bit of weight since she died, though you couldn't tell it by looking at me."

"Well, speaking of weight, we have a ton of food out in the trunk," Susan said. "Aunt Aggie made you some of her special recipes that she only cooks for the firefighters, so you can consider yourself privileged. You're having gumbo for supper."

She saw the emotion pulling at his face. "I don't even know what to say. I can never repay you for all this."

Allie looked from Celia to Susan and knew they were all thinking the same thing. The look on his face had already repaid them many times over. Gordon was going to be easy to take care of.

Chapter Fifty-Nine

● ● ●

Issie had never frozen on a call before.

She stood over the patient, who lay on the couch, and watched as her new partner, B.J. Casey, did what needed to be done.

She was useless.

She should have known by the woman's symptoms that it was a diabetic coma. Nausea, vomiting, dehydration, rapid respirations ... She should have started an IV and drawn some blood, checked the glucose level, administered dextrose ...

But she had done none of those things. Her heart had raced as if she were the patient, and her hands trembled as she'd started her primary assessment. B.J., who had years' less experience, had seen her hesitation and had taken over.

It was disgraceful. She had no business in the field like this. She should have stayed home, yet they were down two medics, and she wasn't the only one grieving.

When B.J. had stabilized the patient, they loaded her into the unit. Issie drove her to the Slidell hospital and went through the motions of turning her over to the emergency staff.

B.J. was quiet as he got behind the wheel and drove them back to Midtown. "It's okay, Issie. We're all a little shaken."

"It's not okay," she said. "I'm not going on another call tonight."

"You'll be all right. That's why there are two of us."

"No," she said. "I'm putting people's lives in danger. Someone's going to have to fill in for me."

She hated being so weak. The others had been on the site with her. They had been there, too, when her friends had been pulled out. But they hadn't fallen apart.

When they reached Midtown, she called around to find a replacement. No one seemed to be home. It was as if they were all somewhere together, sharing war stories and talking out their memories.

Joe's Place. Of course that was where they were. It's where she would have been before she'd become a Christian. The bar just yards from the door of Midtown Station would have been her place to unwind, spill her guts, vent her anger, and share her grief.

Now she had Nick and the church. But Nick was grieving the loss of his own men, planning five funerals, performing his duties as chaplain of Emergency Services. Even now, though he was on duty, he'd retreated to the back of the station to work on what he'd say at the funerals. He had his work cut out for him.

She went back out of the station and looked toward the bar. The parking lot was full—too many cars to pick out the few belonging to her friends.

"You find anybody?" B.J. asked from the rescue unit.

She shook her head. "They're at Joe's. I'll go find somebody who hasn't been drinking."

She stepped across the street, hoping Nick wouldn't glance out the window and see her heading to her old haunt.

She crossed through the parking lot, a sense of nostalgia beating through her. When she opened the door, light spilled out, along with the smell of smoke and alcohol.

The truth was, she could use a drink right now. Just one would calm her heart and steady her hands. Then maybe she could trust herself again.

She found her colleagues sitting around a table in the corner, their faces grim as they leaned in, talking in quiet voices. She longed to join them.

Bob Sigrest looked up as she approached. "Preacher's wife, two o'clock." The others laughed.

"Very funny," she said.

Frenchy scooted her chair over to make room for her. "I thought you were on duty."

"I was . . . am. Look, I need one of you to fill in for me. I can't work tonight."

Their smiles sobered again. "What's wrong?"

She thought of glossing over it, pleading illness or something. But she knew word would get around. "My head's not in it or something," she said. "I froze on the last call. If seconds had counted, if someone's life hung in the balance, they might have died."

Twila slid her chair back and got up. "I'll go. I just got here, haven't had anything to drink."

Issie looked at her friend. Her eyes were red, too, as if she'd been crying before coming in. Twila had been Karen's partner. She was sure the deaths had hit her hard too.

"Thank you, Twila. Sorry I had to ask."

"It's okay," Twila said. "I may have to call on you sometime."

She hurried out to get her uniform and join B.J. in the rescue unit, and Issie stood there for a moment, thinking of pulling up a chair and settling in.

"You okay?" Frenchy asked.

She nodded. "I will be."

"Don't feel bad, Issie," she said. "It did a number on all of us. Sit down, have one beer. You need to relax."

Issie looked toward the bar. Would it really be a scandal if she ordered one beer or a glass of wine? If she sat here with her friends and coworkers for a few minutes?

What would Nick say?

More importantly, what would Christ say?

"No, I've got to go home."

"Come on, Issie," Bob said. "Jesus drank. Take off your preacher's wife hat and put on your medic's. This is where you belong right now."

She had heard that argument that Jesus drank before, had even made it herself a time or two. But one drink wasn't the problem. It was the lure of the lifestyle, the temptation of her old self calling her back, the pull that she couldn't explain.

"I'll talk to you guys later," she said.

She hurried out of the place, crossed back over to Purchase Street, and got into her car in the parking lot next to the station.

Finally, she let herself fall apart.

• • •

Nick sat in the TV room, his notes spread out on a small table in front of him. He heard the car door in the parking lot, and glanced out.

Was that Issie sitting there behind the wheel? Why wasn't she on duty?

Worried, he went outside and opened the passenger door. The light came on, illuminating her anguished face.

"Baby, what's wrong?"

She stared straight ahead through the windshield. "I kind of lost it and had to get Twila to fill in for me."

He slipped into the car and closed the door, making the light go back out. He slid his arms around her, and she sank into him. She smelled of cigarette smoke. He wondered if B.J., her new partner, smoked. "Honey, I told you it was too soon for you to go back to work."

"But it wasn't too soon for you," she said. "You went through worse than I did."

"Why didn't you come get me?"

"I'm okay, Nick. Really. I didn't want to give you one more person to counsel."

"Issie, you're my wife."

"I know, but . . . I thought I could handle it. But I can't seem to function. I can't think."

Nick knew just what she meant. He'd felt fragmented for days and couldn't seem to put himself back together. One minute he was numb, and the next he was crying like a baby.

"I've had the same problem. And I've been hearing it over and over from the others."

"I'll start to do something and forget what I was doing," she said. "I walk into rooms and don't know why I'm there. A little while ago, we got a call, and it was so simple, but for the life of me, I couldn't think what to do for her."

Nick reached into the backseat for a box of tissue, handed it to her. She blew her nose, then pulled out another one and dabbed at her eyes.

"Nick, I went to Joe's Place."

Nick stared at her for a moment and felt that cowardly feeling of dread, as if another part of his life might fold over and snap.

"That would explain the cigarette smell."

"I went to get someone to replace me. They were all sitting there around that table, relaxing and swapping stories. And I thought of all the times I'd sat there with Karen and Steve. I thought if I could just have one drink to calm my nerves . . ."

He waited, that dread pulsing through him.

She swallowed. "And then I realized how strong that pull was, too strong, like there was some force that really wanted me to go back to that life. So I left and came back here, and I started thinking what a wretch I am, that one disaster could shake me like that, when I'm the one who has so much to be thankful for. It could be you being buried tomorrow."

The relief shooting through him almost made him light-headed. He kissed her then, a long, grateful, hungry kiss that had healing power for them both.

"I'm sorry I went there," she whispered against his lips. "I'm sure word will be all over town tomorrow that the preacher's wife was in the bar. But I didn't sit down, Nick, and I didn't drink a drop."

So many in town were watching Issie, waiting for her to mess up and show what they considered her true colors. But he knew the changes in her life were real. He pressed his forehead against hers. "Baby, don't worry what they say. You haven't embarrassed me. And what you're suffering is post-traumatic stress syndrome. It's normal."

"I feel like such a loser."

"Well, you're not. There's no sin in being tempted, Issie. And there's no sin in needing time to recover from a trauma."

He slid his hand down her long black hair. In the moonlight, even with these tears on her face, she was the most beautiful woman he'd ever seen.

"We'll just have to give ourselves some time to get over this," he said, stroking her hair. "But God's not mad at you, Issie."

"Well, I'm mad at him." She looked at him, clearly startled at her own confession. "My partner is dead, Nick!" She pulled out of his embrace and slammed her hands on the steering wheel. "There are holes in the whole department, on this very shift. Nothing's ever going to be the same. And don't tell me that God's taking care of everything, because he didn't. I thought it was supposed to be better when you were a Christian, that there was protection and peace, that God would watch over us. Remember the psalm where he said he wouldn't let us strike our foot on a stone, that if we stumbled he wouldn't let us hurl headlong? Some of us stumbled the other day, Nick. And some of us were hurled headlong. Explain that to me!"

It was an honest question, uttered from the deepest pain in an anguished heart.

He just wasn't sure he could answer. Not for the first time, Nick wondered what he was doing posing as a minister. He couldn't think of a single word to comfort his own wife.

"I need for it to make sense, Nick," she said. "Did God cause that explosion?"

"Of course not," Nick said. "That explosion was caused by someone evil. It was an act of terrorism . . . hatred."

"Then why didn't God stop it?" Issie asked. "Why would he let so many people die, innocent people who hadn't done anything wrong?"

"Did he let them die?" Nick asked. "There are 135 confirmed dead so far. There were at least 8,000 in the building that day. If 7,865 people got out alive and 135 died, do you really think Satan won?"

"Some of those 135 people were our friends, Nick! He *destroyed* their families!"

She got out of the car, and slammed the door behind her, and started walking to the yard behind the station. Nick got out and followed.

She walked to the bayou behind the property and stood there weeping into the wind.

Nick suddenly felt very tired.

"Issie, all I meant was that I'm trusting God with this. I believe that there's judgment for the evil ones who did this. We do know that God has punishment for this crime. Evil people do not prevail, even if it looks like they do for a while."

She went to a bench someone had put on the bank of the bayou and sat down, her hair flapping in the wind. He wished he'd brought a jacket out with him to put over her shoulders.

"I read parts of Job this morning," she said, "and Satan comes to God and gets permission to strike Job and take his whole family and his kids and his livestock and everything he owns. And what does God say? He says, 'Sure, go ahead. Just don't kill him. He may *wish* he was dead, but you can't kill him.' Is that what happened here? Did Satan go to God and say, 'Oh, you know that Icon Building over there and all those people in it, those people you love? How about I let one of my men go in and plant a bomb and blow the place up and bury those people alive? How about that?'" She smeared her tears across her face. "And God just looked at him and said, 'Sure, go ahead.'"

Nick sat down next to her and said a silent prayer that the Lord would give him the right answer to this complicated and important question. If he couldn't talk his wife through her anger, how could he hope to talk a congregation through it? And more importantly, how would he give the mourners at five funerals anything substantial to comfort them?

"Issie, God put Job into the Bible to show us that there would be times when we would suffer and would not be able to explain it, no matter how hard we tried. That Satan still works on this earth. That sometimes we're tested, and sometimes we're refined, but that God is still in charge. I don't know why God allowed Satan to wreak havoc on New Orleans a few days ago. I don't know why he allowed September 11. But I do know that many more people got out of those buildings than didn't. God was there for Mark and me when we were buried. He made a pocket for us when there shouldn't have been one. He was there for Jill, and got her out just minutes before it went down. He was there for Dan. It's a miracle that he lived. How can you think God just turned his head and let it all happen?"

She was quiet then, staring out at the water. Moments crept by as she thought that through. "I guess I don't," she whispered finally. "He did come through, didn't he?"

"Yes, he did."

"But why didn't he come through for Steve and Karen and the others?"

Nick sat silent for a moment and set his elbows on his knees. "Before they were born, honey, God knew the number of their days. This was no surprise to him."

She sighed and blew her nose. "I'm not cut out to be a preacher's wife."

He took her hand. "I'm not cut out to be a preacher."

"I just wish things were as clear to me as they are to you," she said.

"I didn't say they were clear. But when I doubt, when I question, I can go back to Scripture. It's all there. And I can stand on it, Issie. I can bet my life on it. God is good, even when things go bad."

"Pray that the Lord will have patience with me as I work through this anger."

Nick put his arm around her and started talking to the Lord as if he sat before them, knee to knee, listening to their hearts' cries. And Nick was certain that was exactly where he was.

Chapter Sixty

● ● ●

The Walgreens across from the Piggly-Wiggly had seen better days. It needed a fresh coat of paint and some repairs to update the building. Potholes marred the parking lot, shaking Ashley's Subaru.

The place was full of Saturday Christmas shoppers, but Ashley managed to find a space as someone else was pulling out.

She went in, felt the warm glow of the heater, and heard the obnoxious choral rendition of "Rudolph the Red-Nosed Reindeer." She passed down the aisle of decorations and glanced at the boxes of gold tinsel, the shelves full of colored lights, the fake trees standing on displays.

It seemed wrong that Christmas was going on at all this year.

She cut across the store to the aisle of hair products and stood in front of the hair dyes. This morning as she'd looked in the mirror, she had hated what she'd seen. It was time for a change, she thought, time to turn a corner, time to become someone new.

She grabbed the color she wanted off of the shelf and made a beeline for the cash register. As she walked back out to her car, she felt as desolate as a Middle Eastern desert. Maybe instead of dying her hair, she should just check out entirely, she thought. Ending it was preferable to hanging around in this void where her mother used to be, leeching off some stranger she'd met in a stairwell on the worst day of her life. She knew where she could get the pills to do it. She could just wash them down with a bottle of Mountain Dew, fall into a gentle sleep, and never wake up.

But did she really want to do that?

Maybe she would just hold that option open, secure in the fact that this desolation she felt didn't have to be permanent.

For now, she would just dye her hair and see what came of that.

Chapter Sixty-One

• • •

By Saturday afternoon, the team of detectives sifting the debris for evidence had found enough pieces of the rental truck to determine the serial number. They had traced the truck to the Budget Truck Rental in Newpointe, and Stan had been dispatched to find out who'd rented it.

The young man behind the Budget counter wore a dress shirt and tie tucked into a pair of Levi's with a frayed hole in the knee. His hair looked tousled by design, and while it seemed to be oily and dirty, Stan knew that it was probably just hair product globbed in it and molded in a way that would make him look as if he'd just walked in from a wind tunnel.

"May I help you, sir?" he asked as Stan came to the desk.

Stan showed him his police badge. "I'm Detective Stan Shepherd from the Newpointe Police Department. I need to know if you have any trucks that weren't turned back in on time."

"We have a few," the guy said, "but sometimes renters keep them a little longer than they'd planned. We don't panic unless they're more than a week late."

"This one was probably rented out about nine days ago, probably the morning of December fifth . . . or possibly a day or two before that."

The kid opened his logbook and flipped to that day. "Let's see, we rented one out on the fourth."

Stan looked where he was pointing. "What was the name of the renter?"

"John Trammel," he said, turning the book around so Stan could see.

Probably an alias. "Were you working that day?"

The kid nodded. "Probably. I'm usually the only one working the front desk."

"I know this was a week ago, but do you remember anything about the man who rented it that day? Age, height, hair color?"

He scratched his head. "No, I really couldn't say. I've rented a ton of stuff since then. A lot of the Icon survivors lost their vehicles, and our New Orleans stores ran out of cars, so we've taken the spillover. The faces are all running together."

"What about copies of his driver's license and credit card?"

"We just have the numbers," the kid said. "We don't have copies."

Stan took the numbers. The name was probably fake, but it was possible that the DMV would have the culprit's picture.

"Do you have a record of when he said he would bring it back?"

He looked back down at his notes again. "Well, this one was kind of open-ended. He rented it for a week but said it might be a few days longer. So technically, it's not late yet."

Stan thought as much. "I need to see the serial number on that vehicle."

"Sure thing." The guy checked the four-digit number next to the man's name, then pulled out another large notebook and found the number. "Here it is, right here."

It was the same number Mills had given him. Stan drew in a deep breath and pulled the picture of Merritt out of his coat pocket. "Was this by any chance the man who rented the truck that day?"

The kid looked down at the picture, then took a step back. "Isn't that the Icon dude, the one who was in so much trouble?"

Stan didn't answer. "Was it him? Have you seen him in here?"

"No, man. I would know him if he came in. As much as he'd been on the news before the bombing, I wouldn't have forgotten."

"So you're sure it wasn't him?"

"Positive, man."

Now what?

If Merritt hadn't rented the truck, who had? Someone with ties to Newpointe? Had they come here because it was convenient?

If it was at all in his power—or even in his town—Stan would find the mystery suspect.

Chapter Sixty-Two

● ● ●

Clara's horrified scream shook the house.

Jill had followed her home and had just come in the door when she heard her mother-in-law's cry. She bolted through the house and up the hall . . .

. . . and saw what Clara saw.

Ashley had dyed her hair jet black, a stark contrast to the pale face it framed, and she'd circled her eyes in thick black eyeliner. Even her lips were colored black, and she wore a black turtleneck and tight black pants.

Jill didn't quite know what to say.

Clara didn't have the same problem. "A vampire!" she cried. "You look like a vampire! What is *wrong* with you?"

Jill touched Clara's shoulder to calm her and tried not to look shocked herself. Struggling for words, she told herself that this was not the disaster Clara made it out to be. Ashley was the same girl she had met on the stairwell at Icon. She just looked different.

"What do you call that, Ashley?" Jill asked. "Gothic?"

Ashley folded her arms. "Just Goth."

Jill swallowed and touched Ashley's hair. "It's soft," she said. "Must have included a good conditioner." It was an absurd comment to make when the girl really did look like a vampire. But it was the most benign thing that came to her mind.

Clearly, Ashley wasn't going for "soft." She wanted to look hard and heartless, cold and dark. Jill wondered if this was her expression of what her soul felt like these days.

Ashley thrust her chin up. "Do you like it?" It was a challenge, meant to provoke.

Or maybe it was a test. "Well . . . let's just say it's different."

"Different?" Clara cried. "It's evil looking. For heaven's sake, she looks like blood ought to be dripping out of her mouth!"

Jill sighed and looked back at Clara. "I could use some coffee. Would you mind making a pot, Clara?"

Clara was still breathing hard, her hand against her chest. Clearly glad for an escape from the girl, she headed back up the hall, muttering under her breath.

Jill turned back to Ashley and decided to cut to the chase. "Honey, why'd you do this?"

Ashley went back into her room and dropped down on the bed. "I was sick of the way I looked," she said. "Couldn't stand myself in the mirror. It was time for a change."

Jill sat down on the edge of the chaise. "I can understand wanting a change. But are you sure this is the direction you want to go?"

"Pretty sure," Ashley said, looking up at the ceiling. "If you have a problem with it, I can leave."

It was a dare, no question about it, but Jill couldn't stand the thought of Ashley walking out of here, wearing the darkness of her soul on the outside. What would she do with it then? How would she fulfill the fantasy of this dark mood?

She remembered the prayer Debbie Morris had written in her prayer journal, for someone to guide her daughter.

Lord, give me the right response.

"Of course I don't have a problem with it." She got up and went to the bed, rubbed the girl's shoulders. "Have you eaten?"

Ashley looked surprised that Jill had dropped the subject. "Not hungry."

"I want you to eat, anyway," she said. "I picked up a pizza on the way home. Come on. Don't tell me you want to miss Clara's face as she bites into pepperoni."

"She expects me to sink my fangs into her neck."

Jill grinned. "Don't pretend you don't like that."

The comment seemed to send Ashley back into her thoughts. She fixed her eyes on a spot on the wall.

"Ashley?"

She shook out of it. "Maybe I could eat a little."

"Then maybe we can sit together and watch a movie."

Ashley looked up at her. "You don't have to go back to the hospital?"

"Not tonight. Dan's getting moved to a room tomorrow, and I'll be staying with him constantly after that. He wanted me to sleep at home tonight. And who knows? Maybe I'll dye my hair too. Got any more of that color?"

Ashley smiled then. It was the first real smile she'd ever seen on the girl. "No, I used it all."

Jill snapped her fingers. "Darn it."

"We could buy more."

Jill laughed and looked at her watch. "We'll never make it before the stores close. Too bad."

The girl was giggling under her breath as she followed her to the kitchen.

Jill thought it would be worth dying her hair to keep that smile on her face.

Chapter Sixty-Three

● ● ●

Dan was sick of lying on his back.

He couldn't sit up or turn over, and the catheter and colostomy bag robbed him of his last bits of dignity. As they moved him from ICU into his own private room Sunday afternoon, friends from the waiting room met him in the hallway, high-fiving him and cheering as if he'd just crossed the finish line.

Some of them stood looking through the door as they moved him like a sack of cement from the gurney to his bed.

Clearly, Jill couldn't understand why he wasn't happy about getting out of ICU. He couldn't explain it to her without looking like some wimp who couldn't take the hand he'd been dealt.

"Are you sure you're feeling all right?" she asked him, fixing his covers and hovering over him as if he lay on his deathbed. He almost wished he did.

"Yeah, fine."

"Honey, what's wrong?"

"Nothing." He felt sorry for her, really. She hadn't signed up to nurse a vegetable for the rest of her life.

He hadn't signed up to *be* one.

"Dan, tell me what's wrong. I don't want you pulling into your shell and hiding your feelings from me. It's a bad habit, and it's self-destructive."

"I'm fine," he said. "It's just that it's Sunday and you haven't been to church."

She frowned down at him as if he'd just insulted her. "I wanted to stay with you."

"I think you should go," he said.

"Of course I'm not going. I've been looking forward to getting you in here so I could be with you all the time. Why would I leave?"

She looked hurt, so he tried to soften his face and reached out for her hand. "There are people you need to thank for their prayers."

She let out a hard sigh. "You're trying to get rid of me, aren't you?"

He pulled her hand against his face. "No, of course not."

"No, you are." She sat down beside him and leaned her elbows on his mattress. Touching his face, she said, "Talk to me, Dan. I need to understand what's going through your mind."

He swallowed and fixed his eyes on the ceiling. "I'm just . . . I need to have a little time alone tonight. I need to have a talk with God."

She stared at him for a long moment, and her eyes filled with tears. "Can't you do it with me here? I could pray with you."

"I'm not a little kid," he said. "I can be left alone for a couple of hours."

"But if you need anything—"

"If I need anything, I can buzz for the nurse. I'm not *completely* helpless."

The silence that hung between them was painful.

Finally, she cleared her throat and got up. "Okay, I guess I could go and take Ashley and Gordon. They need to get acclimated, anyway."

"Take my mother, too."

"She won't want to come. When she hears I'm leaving, she'll insist on staying with you."

Just what he needed. "Find a way to make her go."

"I'll do my best." She came back to his bed and slid her soft hand across his arm. "Honey, are you sure?"

He met her eyes then, and he hated that he was hurting her. "I'll be all right by the time you get back. I promise. I just need some time to get my head straight."

"You want me to leave your Bible by the bed?"

He couldn't imagine wanting to read it, not until he said what he needed to say to God. "Yeah, leave it there." He looked at the clock. "You should go, or you'll be late."

She looked as if he were asking her to walk into enemy fire. "Yeah, I guess so."

"Do me a favor, and put out the 'no visitors' sign."

She hesitated again and looked at him with worried eyes. "If you need me, call Susan or Allie's cell phone. I've got to get another one, one of these days."

"I'll be all right," he said.

He was certain she was crying as she left the room, but he couldn't make himself call her back.

Chapter Sixty-Four

● ● ●

Jill dreaded telling Clara that she was leaving Dan to go to church. She would explode with allegations of neglect and insist on making up for Jill's failures.

Clara had gone home for a little while this afternoon but had intended to come back tonight. Jill couldn't let that happen before Dan was ready.

She wiped the tears from her eyes and told herself that Dan's mood wasn't about her. Being a paraplegic in ICU had been one thing, but now that he was in a regular hospital room, she knew he was dealing with the permanency of his condition.

She couldn't take it personally. He just needed some time. Maybe he would pray and peace would fall over him. Prayer always centered and calmed her.

She went to the pay phone and called her home number. Clara answered it quickly. "Nichols residence."

"Clara, I'm glad I caught you."

"What is it, Jill?" she asked. "What's happened?"

"Nothing. I just . . ." She paused and cleared her throat. "I was wondering if you would do Dan a favor before you come back to the hospital."

"Of course. Anything."

She hated lying, but she told herself it was for Dan. "He's cold, and he needs another pair of sweatpants. He especially likes the fleece kind." She didn't even know if there was such a thing in sweatpants.

"Of course. I'll go right now and buy several pairs. What size is he?"

"Large. Do you mind, Clara? Also, he could use some more wool socks."

She knew there wouldn't be a department store open in Newpointe on Sunday night. That should keep Clara busy at least until she got back.

"Of course. I'll go right now."

"Thank you." She thought she was going to be sick. "Uh, could I speak to Ashley, please?"

"She's locked in her room, no doubt painting blood drops on her mouth. I'll get her."

Jill waited. As she did, her eyes drifted to Dan's hospital room. She saw a nurse go in, and she wondered what she would think about her leaving him alone. She would think she was a terrible wife. But again, it wasn't about her. She had to give Dan what he needed.

"Hello?" Ashley's voice was low, as if she didn't want Clara to hear.

"Hey, Ashley. What are you doing?"

"Reading."

She knew she was probably reading her mother's journal. She wished she could cut herself down the middle and be there for both Dan and the girl. "Dan wants me to go to church tonight and thank our friends for their prayers. I'd like for you to come with me."

"Church?" she asked. "I don't know, Jill."

"I was thinking of asking Gordon, too. I'm going to need help getting him to the car. We make a good team, you and me."

There was a moment of silence, then, "Okay, I guess."

"Great. Look, if you don't mind, don't tell Clara I'm coming home to get you. She wouldn't understand."

"Don't worry. She just ran out of the house like she saw a roach or something."

"She's on a mission. I'll be home in about forty-five minutes, okay? Be ready."

She hung up the phone and looked at Dan's room again. The nurse came back out and didn't look as if anything was wrong. So Dan must be all right.

She called Gordon and made arrangements to pick him up.

Then she forced herself to do what Dan had asked her to do.

Chapter Sixty-Five

● ● ●

Ashley made no attempt to change her look for church. She
met Jill at the door with her slicked-back, soot-black hair
and black eyeliner a quarter of an inch thick, outlining her eyes.
Her skin looked as if she'd applied a lighter powder, just to make
herself look more pale. Her lips were colored black, and she'd
polished her nails to match them.

She got into the car, chewing her gum as if it was a piece of
taffy, and slumped down, like a child being forced to do something against her will. Jill began to wonder whether it was wise
to take her.

But she knew that Ashley was still challenging her, waiting
for her to react in anger and throw her out, maybe even wanting a reason to go back to her friends.

And Jill was not going to give her one.

Instead, she chattered about Dan's move and all the friends
who had come by the hospital today. Ashley answered in mono-
syllables. When they reached Gordon's house, Jill looked over
at her. "Why don't you come to the door with me so we can help
him out together?"

Ashley didn't argue. She got out of the car and followed Jill
up to his door.

Jill rang the bell and looked over at her. "He's not going to
recognize you." She stroked her hair out of her eyes.

The girl didn't recoil at her touch. She just chewed her gum
harder.

The door opened. "Hello there."

Gordon dropped a crutch and wobbled on the other one. Jill felt guilty for getting him up. She grabbed it and handed it back to him.

"Thank you, darlin'," he said.

"How are you feeling?"

"Doing okay," he said. "I'm hobbling around pretty good." He looked at Ashley. "Who's this young lady?"

"Ashley. You remember. She's the one who helped me get you down that day."

Gordon gave her another once-over. "You look different."

Ashley crossed her arms in that defensive gesture she had. "I am different."

Jill smiled. "She's changed her look a little bit since that day."

Gordon looked as if he didn't quite know what to say. "Well, change is good now and then." His face sobered. "I'm real sorry to hear about your mama, hon."

Ashley was silent.

She walked on one side of him, helping to steady him as he hobbled to the car, and then she helped him get into the back-seat and turn sideways, propping his casted leg.

As they drove to the church, Gordon chatted about all the people who had come from the church to bring him food. "I can't believe it," he said. "I've never had this kind of outpouring of love in my whole life. I don't know what I was thinking all these years, refusing to go to church. If that's the kind of people you have there, then I don't mind going at all. I'm glad you asked me."

Jill smiled. "How about you, Ashley? How long since you've been in church?"

She blew a bubble, popped it. "Couple of years. My mom used to take me all the time."

"Why'd you quit?" Jill asked.

Ashley shrugged again. "Outgrew it, I guess."

Jill hoped she would find out soon that she couldn't out-grow God.

• • •

The service was somber, following in the wake of five funerals that Nick had preached over the last two days. Nick looked beaten down, completely spent.

When he asked Jill to come to the front and say a few words about Dan's condition, she couldn't say no. She went to the pulpit and looked out on the weary, grim faces of the congregation.

"I want to thank you all for your prayers for Dan. So many of them have been answered. I feel such gratitude every day, that he was pulled out when by all rights he should be dead. And then you prayed for him while his life hung by a thread in the hospital. He could have died again, or stayed unconscious on the respirator. But God is gracious to answer our prayers, and he has a plan for my husband."

She sighed and thought of the pain Dan was experiencing right now, lying there alone, wrestling with God. She chose her words carefully.

"Now Dan faces some other challenges. He's dealing with paralysis, and we're being told that he may never walk again." Her voice broke off, and tears pushed to her eyes. "Please pray for him. He's a proud man, Dan is, and this is not easy for him. And pray that I'll know how to support him through it."

She couldn't go on, so Nick came to her aid, putting his arm around her. "Thank you, Jill. Know that we're all constantly praying for both of you. And we want to welcome your guests, Ashley Morris and Gordon Webster. I know our members will make them feel as welcome as they are."

Jill stepped down from the pulpit and went back to sit between them. Gordon reached for her hand, held it tight. Ashley kept her arms folded tightly across her chest.

"Many of you have asked what you can do for the families of the grieving," he said. "And now there is something. We've decided to hold a rummage sale next weekend, to raise money to help the grieving families of the Icon disaster, particularly those from Newpointe. If you have anything you can donate, please contact Aunt Aggie, who'll be heading the whole thing up."

Aunt Aggie sprang to her feet and waved around at the congregation. "We be taking donations too, *sha*. Shame on you if you don't help!"

Jill smiled, knowing that if Aunt Aggie had anything to do with it, it was going to be a raging success.

After the service, church members rallied around Gordon, treating him like a hero because he had survived the explosion. They surrounded Jill too, wanting more news of Dan and his progress.

But as she updated someone for the tenth time that night, she looked across the room and saw Ashley sitting in a corner, chewing her gum with a vengeance, her arms and legs crossed as if warding off any evil that might come her way.

The youth seemed afraid of her; the adults seemed disgusted.

So she sat alone, watching as Gordon became the man of the hour.

As soon as Jill could break free, she went to sit down next to her. "Why are you over here all alone?"

Ashley blew a bubble. "Where else would I be?"

"With me. I could introduce you to people. You might get to know some of the kids and want to come back to Sunday school."

Ashley shot her a look. "I don't do Sunday school."

She wanted to tell her that she had to do it if she lived in her home, but then she looked around and realized that she wouldn't want to come either, if she were ignored like this.

She almost couldn't fault the reaction of her church friends. Ashley hadn't exactly made herself look approachable. Yet the Bible had clear instructions about not showing partiality. She knew that God saw the true Ashley and had his arms open wide for her. But these people couldn't see past her carefully constructed image.

Maybe that was the point of it—to keep everyone at arm's length while she climbed into her cocoon of grief.

Her heart broke for the girl, and she vowed not to be pushed away, no matter how unlovable the girl pretended to be.

Chapter Sixty-Six

● ● ●

Dan hated his tears. He hated that he was alone, and he hated even more that Jill would come back, not leave his side, and watch him regress from a man into a helpless child.

"So what was it all for, Lord?" he said through tight lips, staring up at the ceiling tiles, as if the Lord sat just behind them. "All those years of pumping iron and pushing my body to be in the best physical condition it could be? I thought you blessed that. I thought you took pleasure in my self-discipline."

He grabbed his covers and flung them back, revealing his useless legs. "And now you've left my body half-dead, and the legs that used to be so strong, that still have the muscle I built up in them, that still have all the tissue and the blood, and the strong bones . . . everything they need . . . why won't you heal them? Why won't you let me move my toes? Just my toes for now. That would make all the difference. Then I'd know that there's hope."

He looked down at his feet and willed his toes to move. Grinding his teeth, he felt the strain in his face and his neck, his fingernails cutting into the palms of his hands.

But his toes remained still.

Finally, he let out his breath and wilted wearily back on his pillow. Putting his hand over his eyes, he whispered, "I don't know how to be this way, Lord. You didn't prepare me. You didn't give me any warning."

He twisted his face and let the tears flow, wiping them from his cheeks as fast as they came. "Please, Lord, let me walk again."

A knock sounded on the door, and he grabbed his sheet and covered himself again, and quickly wiped his face with the edge of the sheet. Hadn't Jill put the "no visitors" sign out? Could people not read?

The door came open, and his mother stepped inside. "Danny? I didn't hear you say come in. I thought you might be sleeping."

He looked at her with dull eyes. "Yeah, I was sleeping."

"Where's Jill?"

He drew in a deep breath and wiped his face again. It was still wet. He could see from the look on her face that she hadn't missed the tears.

"I made her go to church. I wanted her to thank the people for their prayers."

Clara came further inside. She was carrying two shopping bags. "You mean to tell me that she left you here alone?"

"I told her to, Mother. I wanted her to go."

"Well, that's crazy. You can't be left alone. For heaven's sake, you can't even walk. What if you needed something? What if there was an emergency?"

"I have a buzzer. I can call the nurse."

Clara set the bags down and came to his side, straightened his blanket. "Well, I'm certainly glad I came when I did. Just in the nick of time, I see. Anything could happen. I thought Jill was more responsible than that."

"She is responsible, Mother. She was just doing what I asked." He sighed. "Truth is, I wanted to be alone for a little while."

He hoped that would clue her in.

"Well, that doesn't even make sense. You were alone for days in that ICU." Her voice softened as she looked into his face. He wondered if his eyes were red. He didn't have that much experience with tears. He didn't suppose they became him.

Thankfully, she didn't mention them. Instead, she grabbed the bags. "I brought you some things," she said. "Jill asked me to find you some fleece sweatpants. Well, you would think that would be easy to find, but for heaven's sake, there wasn't a single department store still open in Newpointe. I had to come all the way to New Orleans."

Amusement cut through his grief. Had that been Jill's way of keeping Clara busy so she wouldn't come here? He wondered why she hadn't taken her to church.

"Mother, you didn't have to do that."

"Of course I did. Once I knew what you needed, you didn't think I was going to ignore it, did you? So I came back to New Orleans and went to the Riverwalk, and got there at six-thirty, and of all things, they close at seven on Sundays. It's almost as if they don't *want* to sell anything! And let me tell you, customer service is a thing of the past."

He pictured his mother prancing into that huge mall, rushing from store to store demanding fleece sweatpants. He started to grin.

"First store I went to had never carried fleece *anything*, and frankly, I wasn't surprised, since I'd never heard of it, either. I actually pictured sweatpants that were fuzzy like sheep."

Dan laughed. It surprised him. He would never have dreamed his mother could cheer him up, purely by accident.

She seemed encouraged by his amusement. "I must have run through five stores, for heaven's sake. You would have thought I was one of those wild sale-crazed women in those commercials, knocking people down to get to the fifty-percent-off rack."

Dan's belly laugh made her laugh too. "So what did you buy?"

"Well, at seven o'clock, I reached a store and asked the first clerk I saw if they had fleece sweatpants, and he said they did, but that they were closing. So I threw a hundred-dollar bill at him and told him there were three more where that came from if he would just keep the store open until I was finished. I can tell you, that changed his tune."

She grabbed the bags and proudly withdrew the sweatpants she had bought. He took one pair from her, checked the size. "You did good, Mom."

He hadn't called her that in a very long time, and her smile trembled slightly. Then smiling even more broadly, she pulled out three more pairs of pants, some wool socks, and a few fleece zip-up jackets in gray, brown, navy, and burgundy. Finally, she pulled out a pink one.

"Whoa, wait a minute," he said. "I'm not wearing pink."

She winked at him then and held it in front of her. "This one's for me."

He had never seen her dressed casually. "Really?"

"Yes. This material feels so comfortable and warm. And—" she pulled out a pair of women's Nikes "—I bought myself these."

He laughed again. "Say it isn't so. My mother in tennis shoes? Is the world ending?"

She dropped them back into the bag. "We'll see. Meanwhile, are your feet cold?"

His smile faded. "I really don't know."

She stared at him for a moment, as if aware that she had shattered the moment. "Of course you don't," she said finally. She pulled his blanket up and checked his feet. "Yes, they're quite cold. I'll put your socks on."

He looked at the ceiling as she worked the wool socks over his feet. He didn't feel a thing.

When she was finished, she stepped back and covered them again. "There now."

"Thank you, Mother," he said.

She stood looking at him, and it seemed that her eyes were glistening. And for the first time, he got the sense that she really did love him.

He let that sink in deep, in that lonely place he had kept locked up since childhood.

"So, let's see what's on television," she said as she took the remote control. "You probably like those Discovery shows like your father did. Maybe there's something on about dung beetles or the mating habits of snakes."

He laughed again as his mother began to channel surf.

Chapter Sixty-Seven

● ● ●

Jill had prayed about Dan's mood all the way back to the hospital, but she hadn't expected to hear laughter when she pushed through his door.

She stepped inside and saw his mother standing just outside of his bathroom, modeling a pink sweatsuit as if she walked a Parisian runway.

Dan was applauding and whistling like a sports fan.

Jill laughed. "Clara?"

Clara spun around and struck a pose. "What do you think?"

Jill looked at Dan. The pain was gone from his eyes, and his laughter was genuine. "It's you," she told her mother-in-law.

"Mom brought me several pairs of fleece sweatpants," he said with a wink. "And she liked them so much she bought one for herself. I made her model it."

"I could get used to this," Clara said.

He reached for Jill, and she bent down to hug him. "Hey, check out the Nikes."

Jill laughed again. "Clara, I just don't know what to think."

She seemed very proud of herself. "Well, I'll have to change now. I can't let the hospital staff see me like this."

"Why not?" Dan asked. "You have to let you hair down now and then."

"Maybe later," she said. "I'll have to get used to it. Plan for it. This is not a change you can make in a flash." She shot Jill a teasing look. "After all, I'm not Ashley."

She closed herself in the rest room, and Jill turned back to Dan.

He was chuckling. "What do you think?"

"I think . . . I'm stunned. Absolutely stunned."

"Pretty good scheme," he said. "Making her go looking for pants. But you underestimated my mother. She always gets what she wants."

"I guess I did."

She said a silent thank-you to God, and asked forgiveness for underestimating him, as well.

Chapter Sixty-Eight

• • •

Ashley sat in Jill's living room, staring at the television and thinking about those high school kids she'd seen at church tonight. They had all sat together in their own section, all buddy-buddy and cliqueish, as if they'd grown up together. Several of the girls had shot looks at her when Jill paraded her in. She had seen them snickering at the way she looked, and she had chomped on her gum and taken grim satisfaction in their whispers.

They weren't so different from her, with their highlighted hair and their Mary Kayed eyes and their haughty, holier-than-thou looks.

A news report flashed on, and the words "Icon International" caught her attention. She turned it up.

"*... breaking news on the investigation into the bombing at the Icon International Building last Monday. Sources tell us that the FBI is interviewing a former temporary employee of Icon, a twenty-three-year-old named Amber Williams, in regard to the money missing from Donald Merritt's bank account. The former CEO of Icon is rumored to have had an affair with the woman, and speculation abounds that she may have actually had access to his accounts.*"

Ashley pulled her bare feet up and hugged her knees. A news reporter solicited responses from people on the street.

"Nothing would surprise me about those people," a chubby postal worker said. "That Merritt was a piece of work."

Another citizen had tears in her eyes as she spoke into the microphone. "I don't believe he's even missing, what with all the witnesses who saw him on the stairs that day. I wouldn't be surprised if Donald Merritt himself hadn't set that bomb."

Ashley caught her breath. Was it possible that her mother's boss had set the bomb that had killed so many of his own employees? Jill had been with him right before the evacuation. Would he have been so stupid as to hang around in his office until just seconds before the bomb went off?

The possibility made her nauseous.

She heard Clara's car pulling up in the driveway, and quickly she turned off the set and went back to her room. She couldn't stomach that woman on top of everything else.

She closed the door and turned off her light, and wished she had a dark cave she could crawl into to die. Instead, she hunkered down in the corner between the chest of drawers and the wall. She sat on the floor, arms around her knees, and wondered where her mother was. If she'd been right about heaven, she was there right now, probably making some kind of holy pitch to God that her daughter wasn't really as evil as she looked.

But if she'd been wrong and there was no heaven or hell, then her mother had ceased to exist at all.

Whichever it was, Ashley longed to join her.

Why had she run when her mother told her to? Of all times, why had she chosen that one time to obey? If she had just died there like her, it would all be over.

The news would have profiled her like a celebrity who would be missed. Those same people who'd acted as though she was invisible tonight would know her name and put roses and teddy bears on her grave.

But wasn't that what she wanted, for people to ignore her and leave her alone?

She honestly didn't know what she wanted. She thought about going back to her friends, letting their drugs numb the pain, finding laughter in a vial of cocaine. But something kept her from it. Grief, she thought. How could she go and get high when her mother was dead?

She heard the clomp of Clara's high-heeled shoes on the floor as she came down the hall. They stopped outside Ashley's door.

She knocked.

"What?" Ashley asked.

"I'd like to speak to you for a moment," Clara said through the door.

Ashley didn't say anything, and finally the door came open. Light spilled into the dark room.

Clara looked around for her, then finally saw her on the floor. "What on earth are you doing?"

Ashley sighed. "Thinking."

"In the dark, on the floor?"

Ashley didn't appreciate her tone, as if she'd been caught tunneling through the Sheetrock. "Did you need something?"

Clara turned on her light, flooding out the darkness. So much for her cave. Ashley got up and faced her stiffly.

"Actually, I came to talk to you about our relationship."

Ashley was slightly amused. "We have a relationship?"

"Well, no. But I thought since we're going to be living here together for a while, that we should make the best of it."

"So what, exactly, brought about this sudden burst of good-will? Did you get caught up in the Christmas music on the way home?"

Clara came into the room and perched on the edge of the chaise. "Actually, I was just looking forward to the day my son comes home. And I was trying to think of ways to make things easier for him. If he's coming home to two new people in his home, we could certainly make an effort to be cordial to each other."

Ashley was suspicious. "So ... I could be more cordial to you ... how?"

Clara's face tightened. Ashley knew her tone had set her off. "Respect would be a good starting place."

Ashley got up and sat down on the bed. "Yeah, whatever. Like you respect me."

"Young lady, you need to understand that Jill has invited you into this home out of the goodness of her heart. It is a privilege, not a right, for you to be here at all. And while she hasn't asked any payment from you, I think respect is not too much to ask."

"I do respect Jill."

"Oh, do you now? You call your behavior respectful? It was bad enough when your hair was pink and sticking out all over the place."

"Burgundy," Ashley muttered. "My hair was burgundy."

"Young lady, the last time I looked, there's no such color hair as *burgundy*."

"I got it out of a bottle," Ashley said, "just like you."

The barb hit home. "You see? *That's* the kind of thing I'm talking about. *That* kind of disrespect."

"Oh, I see," Ashley threw back. "You can talk about the color of my hair, but I can't talk about yours?"

"You are not my equal, young lady. I am your elder. Have you never been taught to be respectful of your elders? Did your mother just completely overlook that in your upbringing?"

Ashley felt the heat burning her ears. "You leave my mother out of this."

Clara huffed. "I'm trying to make a point about this blackness that you're wearing all over your body like some kind of cloak. It looks ridiculous and frightening, and it has to be embarrassing to my daughter-in-law. And my son, God help him, has an overwhelming amount to deal with, without worrying about the cult wanna-be living in his house."

Ashley's mouth trembled. "Jill didn't tell me it was embarrassing her. She doesn't have a problem with it."

"*Everyone* has a problem with it, young lady, and you know that! That's why you do it. I'm telling you, you've got to clean up your act before my son comes back to this house."

Ashley just stared at her. "Don't worry about it. I'll be gone long before then."

Clara's face suddenly changed. She actually looked happy. "Really? You're leaving?"

"Yeah, I'll be checking out before you know it. Then Dan will only have you to contend with when he gets home."

Clara's thin lips tightened. "So where are you going? You don't have a job or an education. How do you suppose you'll support yourself?"

"My mother had some money," she said. "Jill's going to get it for me."

Clara got up and dusted her slacks off. "I might have known you weren't here out of some grand sense of bonding that took place on that stairwell."

That did it. Tears came to Ashley's eyes, and she sprang up. "What do you want? I haven't done anything to you."

"I don't like to see my family abused. When they've extended mercy to you, you should be more conscious of how you respond to it."

"It's *you* they've extended mercy to, lady. They should have thrown you out the day you walked in!"

Clara's mouth fell open. "You have no right to say that to me!"

"I'm just making observations," Ashley said, "just like you seem to be doing."

Clara pointed at her chest. "I am Dan Nichols' mother," she said. "You are no relation to this family."

"You don't even have the right to use the word 'mother,'" Ashley cried. "You hadn't even *seen* your son in ten years. You didn't even come to his wedding." Ashley slapped at her tears, despising them. "I don't understand why good mothers like mine have to die, and mothers like you . . ."

Her words broke off and hung in the air.

"How dare you?" Clara whispered.

"Get out of my room!" Ashley screamed. "Get out of here or I'll call Jill and tell her you're harassing me."

Clara stood there a moment, her eyes blazing. Finally, she slammed out of the room. Ashley heard her heels clomping into her own room, and another door slammed.

Ashley turned the light back off and went back to the corner of her room. Hunkering down in a little ball, she wept and tried to make a plan.

Chapter Sixty-Nine

● ● ●

Ashley ran up the staircase, taking the steps two by two. At the top she could see her mother standing in front of the bomb, and she knew that if she could just get to her, she could change the fate of both their lives. But as hard as she ran up those stairs, she couldn't get to the top. A super-speed escalator sped her down as she ran up with all of her might.

So she screamed out, "Mom!"

But her mom only smiled and mouthed, "Ashley."

"Mom, get away!" she screamed. "Get away! Please, Mama!" But the stairwell only grew longer, and there were more steps. The faster she ran, the farther away her mother was.

Then the world exploded, and she watched her mother vanish in a wave of flames and smoke, and she felt herself falling down a canyon, falling, falling, with no place to land.

She saw her mother falling next to her and screamed, "Mama!" Debbie waved her arms as if she were a bird flying, but her wings were clipped. She fell faster than Ashley. Ashley couldn't reach her mother. She watched her hurl headlong into the earth and explode like the bomb had, sending up a mushroom cloud that cradled Ashley and softened her fall.

Mama! Mama!"

She woke suddenly and sat upright in bed. She was covered with sweat and trembling all over, but the mushroom cloud was gone.

She turned on the lamp next to her bed and pulled the covers up around her, trying to stop crying. Trembling, she pulled the pillow to her face and sobbed into it with all the anguish she felt for her mother, with all the rage and hatred and anger she felt at whomever had done this to her life, and all the self-disgust she felt for not loving her mother more while she was alive.

It wouldn't have taken that much. If she had just stayed at home, finished school, brushed her hair once in a while—her mother would have been so pleased with her. But it was too late now, and life was just too long to endure these memories in her head. Somewhere there had to be relief. Somewhere there had to be an end to all this.

··· ···

From the other room Clara lay awake in bed, listening to the sound of the girl's sobs.

She should get up and go in there, she told herself. Maybe the girl just needed human contact—any human contact. Maybe she should do what Jill had done the other night. Hug her and hold her still.

But she still nursed the sting from her indictment tonight.

I don't understand why good mothers like mine have to die, and mothers like you . . .

She could prove Ashley was wrong about her by going into her room. But what if the girl recoiled from her efforts? What if she said more hurtful things?

What if she spoke more truth?

Clara closed her eyes and wished the things Ashley had said hadn't cut so deep. But she knew that truth was the sharpest blade. Clara didn't have normal maternal instincts. How could she go in there and hug Ashley now when she hadn't even hugged her own son since before he was ten years old?

Why was that?

She thought of Dan as a boy, leaping with excitement when she and his father had returned from one of their important trips. He would throw himself at her, strangling her with his hug.

She thought of how crushed he would be when they left again. His hugs then had been desperate, clinging.

Why hadn't they broken her heart?

At some point, he'd grown more stoic about the whole thing and, sometimes, didn't even show up to say good-bye. Eventually he had stopped welcoming them home. He had been in good hands, she'd told herself then. His nannies had been more maternal than she. They'd been more organized, more resourceful. They had known what a boy like Dan needed. Unfortunately, none of them had stayed more than a couple of years before she had found fault and fired them. The replacement had always seemed like an improvement.

I don't understand why good mothers like mine have to die, and mothers like you . . .

Ashley's words played through her mind like some kind of evil mantra bent on her destruction. Maybe the girl was right. But for the life of her, Clara didn't know what to do with that knowledge.

•••

The night was long, and finally, as morning began to shine through the blinds on Clara's window, she got up and went into the kitchen to make a pot of coffee. She was just sitting down to drink it when Ashley's door opened and the girl walked out, fully dressed, carrying her stuffed bag over her shoulder.

Clara wondered if she had slept at all that night. Guilt spiraled through her at the thought of how she had failed to go and help her, but now she didn't know how to cross the divide between them.

"Good morning," Clara said gently.

Ashley tossed the house key on the counter. "Tell Jill I appreciated her taking me in." She headed to the door.

Clara got to her feet. "You're leaving? For good?"

"That's right," Ashley said.

"Ashley, I wish you'd reconsider. Wait until you talk to Jill."

"I've waited long enough." The words sounded hollow, lifeless.

Clara followed her to the door, racking her brain for the right thing to do, the right thing to say. "Ashley, I didn't mean to hurt you last night. What I said about your mother and your upbringing was wrong."

But the confession came too late. Ashley opened the door and trod across the lawn to her car.

"Do you at least have any money?" Clara called after her.

The Subaru's motor choked to life, and Ashley drove away.

Chapter Seventy

• • •

Dan's brooding had gotten worse, and Jill felt that the slightest thing could set him off. She'd had trouble sleeping on the hard extended chair in his room, and several times when she'd awakened, she'd found him staring into the darkness.

For the life of her, she didn't know how to help him.

When a man knocked on the hospital room door at midmorning, Jill was relieved for the diversion.

"I'm Mills Bryan, Special Agent with the FBI." He came into the room and showed them his badge.

Jill got up and reached for his hand. "We've met before, Agent Bryan. The Newpointe Post Office bombing."

Recognition dawned on his face. "Yes. I thought the name sounded familiar. I hope I'm not disturbing anything."

Though still flat on his back, Dan seemed to come to attention. He shook the man's hand. "Not at all. What brings you here?"

"Is it about Icon?" Jill asked.

"Yes, actually," he said. "Mrs. Nichols, Stan Shepherd told me you were in a meeting with Donald Merritt when the building was evacuated."

"That's right."

"I need to ask you a few questions."

"Sure," Jill said. "If there's anything I can tell you that would help you figure out who did this, I will. As you can see, our lives have been drastically affected by what happened."

"Yeah," Dan agreed. "It's real personal."

"I can understand that." Mills Bryan was a heavyset man with a deeply receding hairline and buzz-cut gray hair. He had intelligent eyes. Jill had the feeling that he didn't miss much.

"Mrs. Nichols, I understand that you came out of the office right in front of Merritt. Is that right?"

Jill had tried many times to recall it exactly as it had happened. "I evacuated with his office staff. He went to the south stairwell, and I went to the north. Later, I crossed to the south, after the second bomb went off."

"Did you see him after that?"

"No, I didn't. That's not to say that he wasn't there. I was trying to help someone so I was slowed down a little. If he didn't have any obstacles, he could have gotten out way ahead of me."

"Where would you say he was in relation to that first bomb?"

"It's hard to say. The bomb went off so quickly after we began to evacuate. I hadn't gone more than a couple of flights."

He seemed to process that. "You didn't by any chance hear the call he got about the bomb, did you?"

"Just his side of it."

"Did you catch a description of the bomb?"

"No," she said. "Just that it was in the stockroom directly beneath us." She tried to remember if there was anything else she could offer him.

Suddenly she thought of Ashley.

"I do know someone who saw the bomb, though."

He looked at her as if he'd hit pay dirt. "Oh, yeah?"

"Yes. Ashley Morris. She's the sixteen-year-old daughter of Debbie Morris, who worked in Merritt's office. Ashley had come to see her mother, and they had walked to the stockroom together. She saw the bomb, then her mother told her to run. Debbie didn't make it out."

Bryan got a notepad out and jotted her name down. "The security guard told us that Debbie Morris reported the bomb, but we didn't know about her daughter. Did you report this to the police?"

"Well, no. We've all been so busy. I've been focused on Dan, and she's been grieving. It never occurred to us."

"So where's the girl now?"

"She's staying with me."

Bryan looked relieved. "I need to talk to her as soon as possible."

"Sure, fine," Jill said. She gave him her address. "She's probably at home now. I can call and make sure, if you want."

"Yes, if you don't mind."

She went to the phone next to Dan's bed, and Dan made small talk with the man as she called home.

There was no answer after six rings. Finally, she gave up. "I don't know where she is, Agent Bryan. She may be on her way here, but she doesn't have a cell phone or anything."

She saw the frustration on his face. "Would you call me as soon as you locate her? It's very important that we interview her as soon as possible."

"I will," Jill said. "Trust me, she'll want to do everything she can to help you find the bomber. It's personal to her, too."

• • •

Not long after Agent Bryan left, the physical therapist came in with a wheelchair. Dallas was a tall, athletic man who'd obviously had a little too much caffeine. It was clear he had excelled in his motivation classes, and nothing—not paralysis nor amputation nor anything short of death—would deter him from expecting great things from his patients.

Jill could see that his attitude only irritated Dan. Before Dallas could move Dan into the wheelchair, he had to first get him sitting up straight in the bed. And when that didn't go well, Dan was even more aggravated.

"There are balance issues we have to deal with in paralysis cases," Dallas told Jill. "He's been lying flat for over a week. He'll have to adjust to sitting up again."

"Don't talk about me like I'm not here," Dan bit out.

Jill felt helpless as Dan forced himself through the nausea that assaulted him when Dallas sat him up. But after several minutes, it passed.

"Great," Dallas said. "You're doing great, man. I'm really proud of you."

Dan wasn't impressed. "I sat up. Don't act like I just won the Boston Marathon."

"But this is a big accomplishment. Some patients take several sessions to—"

"Don't patronize me. I'm not some kid."

Jill gave Dallas an embarrassed look. "Dallas, he didn't mean—"

"Don't apologize for me, Jill!" Dan turned back to Dallas. "Let's go. I'm ready to get in that chair."

Dallas seemed undaunted by Dan's mood. Jill wondered if he was used to taking the abuse of angry patients.

"No problem," Dallas said. "I think you're ready." He looked up at Jill. "You think you can help me lift him?"

"Sure."

"No!" Dan shook his head. "No way. I don't want my wife to lift me!"

Tears came to Jill's eyes even though she knew that he didn't mean to hurt her. It was simply that his own pain was so deep. And her being here, watching him struggle, was causing him even more pain.

"Dan, maybe I should leave until you and Dallas finish."

Dan was beginning to sweat. "I think that would be good."

"All right then. I'll be in the waiting room down the hall."

Dallas smiled at her. She wondered how he did it. "I'll come get you when we're done."

She stepped out into the hall and tried to stop her tears. This wasn't about her, she told herself again. It was about him, and if he needed her to leave him alone, she would do that.

She didn't have to like it.

· · ·

"Jill!"

Jill looked up and saw Clara getting off the elevator. She tried to pull herself together.

"Hi, Clara," she said as his mother approached. "You can't go in right now. His physical therapist's in there with him."

Clara accepted that. "What are they doing?"

"He's trying to get him wheelchair-trained. Apparently it's more complicated than I thought."

Clara seemed to run that through her mind. She was wearing her sweatsuit and Nikes, and her hair was pulled back and clasped at the nape of her neck.

"Clara, I was trying to call Ashley a little while ago, but no one answered at home. Do you know where she is?"

"Yes," Clara said, lifting her chin. "She left."

Jill stared at her. "What do you mean? Where did she go?"

"She didn't say. She just left the key and told me to thank you for taking her in. She said she wasn't coming back."

Jill stood there a moment as a tide of rage rose up inside her. "What did you do?"

Clara stepped back. "Me? I didn't do anything. I'm just the messenger, Jill."

Jill's face burned. "You said something to her, didn't you? You ran her off! How dare you?"

"I did not run her off!"

Jill pushed past her and started down the hall. Clara turned and followed. "Where are you going?"

"To find her!" she bit out. "To undo whatever you did!"

"Jill, you are jumping to conclusions!"

Jill stopped and turned on her. "No, I'm not! You've hated her since you first laid eyes on her. She's not good enough for you. She looks different! And she has problems that make you uncomfortable." She started to cry and brought her hand to her forehead. "Don't you have any compassion, Clara? Don't you care about anyone but yourself?"

Clara looked as if she might cry, as well. But she stood straighter, her chin higher. "For your information, I tried to talk her out of leaving. I told her to wait until she had talked to you. I even tried to give her money." Her voice broke off, and suddenly the woman looked very small. "I don't know why I came here," she said. "Ashley's right. I've been a failure as a mother. I had no right to waltz in here and try to be one now."

Jill hadn't expected that response from her.

Had Clara really tried to stop Ashley? Had Ashley told Clara that?

Clara searched her purse for a handkerchief and dabbed at her eyes. Jill realized she probably didn't have much experience with public displays of emotion.

"I'll leave," Clara said. "I'll go home and pack and take the next flight out to Paris. I don't belong here." She started to the elevator.

Jill stood there, trying to imagine the conversation in which Ashley had accused Clara of being a failure as a mother.

Even if it was true, she wished Ashley hadn't said it. And now, if Clara left . . . how would she explain it to Dan? He was angry enough. If he thought his mother had let him down again by breezing into his life and back out again, how would he respond?

But what had Clara done to Ashley? The child had no place constructive to go. She had already hinted at suicide. What if Clara had pushed her over the edge?

The elevator came, and she watched as Clara got on it. She made no move to stop her as the doors closed.

Jill wilted against the wall. Clara was right on the edge herself. Jill hadn't considered it before, but Clara might have as many problems as Gordon and Ashley did. It was just harder to see them. And she was family. Talk about compassion—where was Jill's for Clara?

She was Dan's mother. When Jill and Dan had children—if that was even possible now—Clara would be their children's grandmother.

Suddenly, Jill missed her own mother with all her heart. She would have been a terrific grandmother.

She felt like a bereaved child.

How could she send Dan's mother away?

She couldn't. Quickly, she went to the elevators and pushed the "down" button. Thankfully, the doors opened quickly.

She stepped into the empty car and pressed "ground floor." When the doors opened again, she burst off and looked around in the big lobby. She saw Clara across the floor, going through the double glass doors.

"Clara!" she called.

Clara turned. Fifty-dollar mascara ran down her face, and her pink lips trembled with her pain.

Jill went toward her. "Clara, please don't go."

"Why not?" Clara asked. "I'm not doing anyone any good here."

"Yes, you are," she said. "Please don't make me go up there and tell Dan that you left."

"He's used to it," Clara said.

"No, he's not," Jill said. "He'll never get used to it. Never." She stopped and tried to regroup. "Clara, I'm sorry I jumped on you about Ashley. I don't know what happened, and I'm really worried about her. But please . . . I don't want you to go. You're the only one who's been able to cheer Dan up. God knows I can't do it."

Clara's face changed. "I've cheered him up?"

"Yes! I don't know how you did it, but last night Dan was in a terrible mood when I left, and when I came back, he was totally different. You made him laugh, Clara. He enjoyed having you here."

"He did? Really?"

"Yes!" She sucked in a sob. "Oh, Clara, I'd give anything to have my mother here. Dan *has* you."

Clara wiped her handkerchief under her eyes. "But I've been a disappointment as a mother. I was never there. I left it to nannies to raise him. I can't undo any of that."

"You can be a mother to him now, Clara. He may be a grown man, but grown men and grown women still need their mothers. And Dan needs you."

Clara's face softened. "If I thought it would help him—"

"I wouldn't say it if it wasn't true, would I?"

"Well, I . . . I don't know why you would." She sighed. "I want to stay."

"Good," Jill said. "That's good." She reached out and hugged the woman. It wasn't something Clara was used to, and she returned it stiffly.

When Jill let her go, she looked at Clara and realized she'd worn the sweatsuit and tennis shoes she'd bought last night. "I'm so glad you wore that, Clara. Dan's going to need a grin when he gets finished with his therapy."

Clara was finally able to smile again. "Anything I can do."

Chapter Seventy-One

● ● ●

Dan's mood lightened somewhat when he saw his mother in her casual combo, but he still seemed to brood all afternoon. When Dallas came back in later that day for another therapy session, Jill took the opportunity to try to find Ashley.

She found the girl's mother's address in the phone book. The modest brick house sat in a lower-middle-class neighborhood. The yard looked neatly landscaped, with carefully trimmed holly bushes and well-placed perennial shrubs. It looked as if much love had gone into the maintenance of the house.

Ashley's car was not in the drive, but on the off chance that she was inside anyway, Jill went to the door and knocked. As she waited, she scanned the other houses. She wondered how many of the neighbors realized that Debbie had died. Had any of them been at the funeral?

When Ashley didn't come to the door, Jill went back to her car and sat behind the wheel.

She wondered where she would go if she were a sixteen-year-old girl, orphaned and grieving with nowhere to turn.

"Lord, please watch over her," she whispered. "Don't let anything happen to her." She pulled a pad out of her glove compartment, found a pen, and began to write.

Dear Ashley,
    If you see this note, please call me immediately. I'm not going to rest until I find you. I know things look grim right now. I can't even imagine how grim. But whatever you may think, you are not alone. Please come back and stay with me.

She wondered if she should add anything about the FBI wanting to talk to her, but she didn't want to frighten the girl. She would tell her that herself when she heard from her. She added, "Love, Jill," and stuck the note on the door. As she pulled away, she prayed that she would hear from Ashley soon.

Chapter Seventy-Two

• • •

Another dead end. Stan sat at his desk in the Newpointe police department, staring at the computer screen.

John Trammel, the man on the driver's license Budget had recorded, had died two years earlier of renal cancer.

So had the cards been stolen?

He checked the credit card account, saw that someone had opened that account in the last six months. The statements were made to a post office box, which was registered under the dead man's name.

Who had the key to that box?

He wondered if the perpetrator looked like John Trammel's picture. If so, he wasn't Middle Eastern but a balding Caucasian. Could he be a relative?

Was he at all connected to Donald Merritt?

He checked the charges on the credit card, saw that there had been several purchases at an agricultural store just outside town. Fertilizer was a known bomb-making substance, and Stan had a hunch he would find that on the receipts. There were two or three purchases at hardware stores, several small purchases at different gas stations.

He would start with the agricultural store, he decided, and see if any deliveries had been made to the man claiming to be John Trammel. That would give him a starting place.

Chapter Seventy-Three

● ● ●

Nick was with Dan when Jill came back to the room. They seemed engaged in quiet discussion, and she hoped he was getting some of his frustrations off of his chest, even if he didn't want to talk to her about them.

"Am I interrupting anything?"

Dan lay on his back, but the head of his bed had been slightly inclined, so that he was no longer flat. That was progress, she thought.

He smiled and reached for her. "No, honey. Come in."

She came to his bed and kissed him, then rose up and started to greet Nick.

But Dan cut in. "You've been crying. Is it because of my mood? I've been treating you awful."

"No." She rubbed his shoulder. "You have a lot to deal with. I understand." Those tears assaulted her again, and she grabbed a Kleenex and swabbed her nose. "I was actually just a little upset about Ashley."

Nick took off his glasses and rubbed his eyes. They were still bloodshot from the Icon site. "The girl you brought to church the other night?"

"Yes," Jill said. "She took off this morning. She told Clara she isn't coming back."

"Did you call the FBI to let them know?" Dan asked.

She sat down in the chair next to the bed. "No. I don't want them to think she was trying to avoid their questioning. I'm hoping I'll find her. That she'll call or something."

"The FBI is looking for her?" Nick asked.

Jill sighed. "Ashley saw the bomb. She was with her mother when she discovered it. If it weren't for that, hundreds more people would have been killed. Her mother alerted security and started the evacuation. It cost her her own life."

Nick sank back. "Wow. I had no idea."

"Yeah, and they want to talk to her about what she saw. I went by her mother's house, but she wasn't there. I'm afraid she went back to the friends she lived with before, and from what she's told me, they're no good for her. She's just trying to Band-Aid her grief. I almost don't blame her." She closed her hands into fists, and her face twisted. "The thing is, she needs the Lord more than anyone I know. And when I brought her to church the other night, I hoped that the people would embrace her and that the youth would draw her in. But it didn't work that way."

"I'm sorry," Nick said. "We should have done better."

"The thing is, I brought Gordon too, and he's a sweet old man. He's easy to be warm to. He looks like any other member of our church. Everybody rallied around him and wanted to cook for him and do things for him. And I'm glad, because he needs it. But they didn't do the same for Ashley."

Dan kissed her hand. "It was the way she looks," he said. "Our church isn't used to Goth. Isn't that what you said she looks like?"

Nick nodded. "He's right. She didn't look very approachable."

"I know," Jill said. "She does look kind of creepy with her hair and lips painted black. She's not the kind of kid we're used to in our congregation. But maybe those are just the kind of kids that we should be drawing into church. And for heaven's sake, once we get them there, we sure shouldn't alienate them by treating them like they're outcasts. She came to us just as wounded as Gordon was, probably even more, but I don't know how to make the church care about her."

Nick seemed to deflate with the indictment. "I'm sorry, Jill. It's my fault. I should have led the effort more. I should have embraced her, pulled her in, made her feel welcome. But you're right. I was a little put off by her."

"She's a sweet, mixed-up kid." Jill got up and went to the window, pulled back the curtain to let in some light. "She's just expressing herself, and she *feels* so dark. She's empty right now, in misery. I know a little bit about how she feels because I lost my mother when I was younger, but it was nothing like this . . . so violently, with so many regrets."

Nick sank into a chair. "We really messed up."

Jill sighed. "It's not your fault. I'm just saying that we could do better. Didn't James tell us not to show partiality? If I get her back, we all have to do better. Her life may depend on it."

Nick got up and slid his hands into his pockets. "If you get her back, Jill, I can promise you she's going to be loved at our church. She'll never walk through those doors and be ignored again."

"Fine, but it has to be real," Jill said. "She's too smart for anything else. She'll know immediately if she's being patronized."

"Trust me, Jill. We'll do it right this time. Find her and I promise we won't fail her again."

Chapter Seventy-Four

● ● ●

Ashley parked her car as close to her mother's grave as she could get. She got out and stepped carefully between the mounds, her eyes on the fresh new plot among all the others. Her mother did not have a headstone yet or any kind of marker to let observers know what kind of woman had been laid to rest here.

But Ashley knew.

Treading across the grass with her black hair stringing into her eyes, she went to the mound where green sod struggled to take root over the freshly filled grave. She sat down on top of it, hugging her knees, and tried to feel the closeness of her mother.

But all she felt was the cool breeze.

Ashley knew that if her mother could speak right now, she would have told Ashley she wasn't here anymore, that she was dwelling in the house of the Lord, walking on streets paved of gold, and worshiping God like it was church camp, her cup overflowing.

But Ashley's cup was empty.

She tried to formulate words to say to her mother, but it felt silly and fruitless. It was too late to say any of the things on her mind.

She sat there for a long time, the crisp wind drying the tears on her face as fast as they fell. Finally, she got up, moved to the tree near the grave, and leaned back against it. It was peaceful here. All around her death lay lined up with an order that life did not have. There was no pain in this graveyard, no dread, and no fear.

Wouldn't she be better off lying here among them? There was just room enough beside her mother's grave for her own. She wondered if she would feel close to her, lying side by side with her, all the pain and recriminations ended and put to rest. It felt like her only hope.

Looking up at the sky, she saw the leaves blowing on the wind. Up north, the trees were probably already bare, but in the south, they still fell. Soon all would be cold and dead.

She wondered if her mother had been right, if there really was a God, if he looked down on her and cared in the least about the pain she felt right now.

It was a dilemma. If there was no God, only suffering and then death, then she'd never have hope of seeing her mother again. And there was no point in going on. But if there was a God who cared about her, as her mother believed, then he would have to show Ashley that her life was worth living.

Right now she just couldn't see it.

Ashley returned to her car. She drove around for a while but didn't know where to go. If she spent the night at her mother's house, Jill would find her and convince her to come back. She didn't want to deal with Clara.

And she didn't think she could handle being in her own house alone.

Finally, she pulled her car into a park and hunkered down on the seat to sleep there.

Chapter Seventy-Five

● ● ●

Dan urged Jill to go look for Ashley again when Clara got back to the hospital after lunch. He also asked her to go home to get his tennis shoes so that he wouldn't have to begin using his wheelchair in his socks.

Jill drove by the girl's house and saw her note still on the door. She obviously hadn't been home. Where on earth could she be?

She hoped she would find her in Newpointe, waiting on the porch of Jill's house again, but forty minutes later, when she pulled into her driveway, there was no sign of her.

Then she thought of Gordon. He was the only other person in Newpointe that Ashley really knew. She doubted she would have gone to his house, but maybe...

She decided she needed to check on him anyway, so she drove across town. Ashley's car wasn't there.

Near tears again, she went to the front porch. The screen door was closed, but the front door was open. Gordon sat in his chair with his casted leg propped up. She knocked, and he looked up at her with delight.

"Come in, Jill! What a surprise! I thought you'd be at the hospital."

"I was." She came in and gave him a hug. The television blared, but he didn't turn it down.

"To tell you the truth, I was looking for Ashley," she said, sitting down. "She left my house this morning, and I haven't been able to find her. She hasn't by any chance been by here today, has she?"

"No, I haven't seen her. Can't imagine her wanting to come see an old man. Is everything all right?"

"I don't know." She let her gaze drift to the television set. It was another news broadcast about the Icon Building. They came frequently and rarely offered new information. "She's pretty depressed," she went on. "I'm a little worried about her. But how are you?"

He chuckled and patted his stomach. "I've never been better taken care of in my life. All those sweet people from your church have been coming by, bringing me food, warming things up for me. I haven't hardly had to even get up from this chair. It's unbelievable how good they've been to me."

She smiled. "I'm sure they're getting as much out of it as you are."

Donald Merritt's picture flashed on the screen, and their attention shifted to the set.

"... *Sources tell us that the FBI is still investigating Merritt's disappearance. Speculation abounds about whether the Icon CEO really died in the bombing. Some say he may have had a part in planting the bombs that killed so many people. The latest death toll is a hundred and fifty-three.*"

Gordon picked up the remote control and turned it off. When Jill looked at him, his face was red, and his hand shook as he threw the thing down.

"If anybody deserved to die, it was Donald Merritt," he said through his teeth. "Instead, he's probably off sipping margaritas somewhere and spending my retirement money with half a dozen of his cohorts."

Jill thought of the man she'd been deposing the morning of the bombing. Yes, he was a jerk, all right. He had no regard for his employees' retirement or for the stockholders who had supported him. But was he a killer? A thief maybe, but she found it hard to believe he could deliberately murder all those people. And if he'd known that there was a bomb in the building, wouldn't he have missed that meeting?

No, she couldn't imagine that he had anything to do with it. But she knew Gordon wasn't going to buy her defense of the man.

Chapter Seventy-Six

● ● ●

Before going back to the hospital, Jill went by a cell phone company and bought two new cell phones to replace the ones she and Dan had lost at Icon. When she was back in her car, she called to check on Dan. Clara answered and handed him the phone.

"Hi, honey. I just wanted to let you know that I'm on my way back. I'll be there in about forty minutes. I got a new cell phone, so if you need to reach me you can use the same number as my old one. I replaced yours, too."

"No need to hurry," he said. "I have physical therapy again at three, so I'll be busy at least for the next couple of hours. Take your time."

Jill knew he didn't want her there when he was struggling. "Is your mother going to stay?"

There was a heavy pause, then, "I hope not."

She smiled. "Just tell her what you told me. That you'd rather do it alone. She'll understand."

"Did you?"

Her smile faltered. "Sure, I did."

"It's not you, you know. I just have a problem with pride. Guess it's a guy thing."

"Hey, you don't have to explain it to me."

She heard voices, then Dan said, "Well, they're here. Guess I'll let you go."

"Okay. I think I'll run by the office for an hour or so. I'll be back by the time you're finished."

Dan hung up, and Jill turned her car around and went back to her office. Maybe with the resources she had there, she could come up with a plan to find Ashley.

Her secretary, Sheila, sat at the front desk with her feet propped up, reading a *Ladies Home Journal* and talking on the phone. She caught her breath at the sight of her boss, dropped her feet, and tossed the magazine aside. "I got to go," she told whoever was on the other end of the phone. "Incoming."

Jill rolled her eyes. Sheila was so dramatic. "Hi there," she said.

"I didn't know you'd be in today." Sheila got to her feet and came around the desk. "Good grief, you look like death warmed over. *You* ought to be in the hospital, not your husband. How is he, anyway?"

"He's as well as can be expected." She knew it was an evasion, but she didn't feel like going into it now.

"You're not honestly going to try to work this afternoon? I mean, it's okay if you don't because I've postponed all of your meetings for the next week or so."

Sheila was efficient, even if she did drive Jill crazy. "I appreciate you handling everything."

"Hey, no problem."

"I just came in to work on a case for a friend," she said, "a girl whose mother was killed in the bombing."

"So is it going to be a full day?" Sheila asked. "I've been knocking off at about three o'clock."

Jill bristled. "How about staying until five today, since I pay you for a full day?"

Sheila shrugged. "No problem. I'm just happy I have a job. If you'd bought the farm the other day, I'd be out of work."

Jill shot her a dull look. "It was that thought that kept me alive."

She went into her office and closed the door behind her. She had thought of firing Sheila a number of times for her flip attitude and smart-aleck remarks. She had even managed to do it a time or two. But no one could help her run the small legal office better, so Jill had always wound up keeping her on.

Jill sat behind her desk, where she got her best ideas, and flipped through the phone book of the church where Debbie Morris's funeral was held. They'd said that they had contacted Ashley's friends when they'd been looking for her. She wondered if they still had the number.

She called the church and waited as the secretary did her greeting mini-speech. "New Way of Life Community Church, where the love of Christ is a verb instead of a noun. Annie speaking. May I help you?"

Jill wondered if she'd written the greeting herself. She hoped the pastor hadn't penned it. "Yes. This is Jill Nichols. I'm a friend of Ashley Morris—"

"Yes, Mrs. Nichols! I met you at the funeral. Ashley's living with you, isn't she?"

"Well, that's why I'm calling. Ashley took all her things and left my house this morning, and I've been trying to find her. I was wondering if you still had the numbers of any of her friends."

"Hold on, hon. Let me give a quick look through my Rolodex."

Jill waited, praying that she found something.

"Okay, hon. I have a number here. It's the house where she was living before her mama died."

Jill wrote the number down and thanked her. Quickly, she dialed it.

Someone picked it up, and she heard loud music blaring in the background. "Hello?"

Jill decided not to identify herself to the girl. "May I speak to Ashley, please?"

"We haven't seen Ashley," the girl said in a sleepy voice. "She, like, strung out after her mother died, and she hasn't been around."

"You're sure she hasn't been there today?"

"I've been here all day, lady. But she may have gone by to see Chris at work."

"Where is that?"

"At the Fixation Tattoo Parlor," the girl said. "She works there too, but she hasn't been in in a week. Chris is probably there now, though."

Jill decided to go by there instead of calling him, since she feared he might not be honest with her if Ashley was with him. She looked it up in the phone book and got the address.

It took forty minutes to get back to New Orleans and fifteen more to navigate her way to the tattoo parlor. She finally found it—a tiny hole-in-the-wall with a neon sign flashing over the store. On the windows were dozens of images that patrons could have permanently etched on their skin.

She stepped into the small shop that smelled of cigarette smoke and rubbing alcohol. No one was out front, but she heard music playing behind the beads that hung over the door to the back part of the store.

"Hello!" she called to the back.

She heard someone curse, then Chris, the young man Ashley had spoken to at the funeral, came scuffing out. "Hey. Sammy's busy doing a tattoo, but you can use the time to pick out what you want. Do you know where you want it?"

Jill cleared her throat. "Uh . . . I didn't come for a tattoo, actually. I came to talk to you. Chris, isn't it?"

He finally looked at her. "Yeah. You're the one who was with Ashley the other day at the funeral."

"That's right," she said. "Chris, have you seen Ashley today? I really need to get in touch with her."

"No. She hasn't exactly shared her life with me since what happened last week. It's almost like she blames me for it or something. I can understand her being strung out about her mom and everything, but she doesn't have to, like, turn her back on me and her friends."

"She's really mixed up right now. So she hasn't been by here at all?"

"No. I wish she would. Besides missing her, I want my money back."

"What money?"

"She owes me thirty bucks," he said. "I wouldn't be that worried about it if she was around, you know, but when she vanishes like this, it makes me mad. I really need it."

If Jill hadn't understood Ashley's reluctance to contact him before, she did now. She pulled a piece of paper out of her purse and jotted her cell phone number on it. "If she does contact you, would you ask her to call me, please? It's very important."

"Yeah, sure. If I see her."

Jill started to leave.

"Hey, if you find her," he said, "tell her to call me too, will you? Tell her it's only right after all we've meant to each other."

As Jill went back to her car, she prayed that the girl wouldn't get tangled up with him again.

Before going back to the hospital, she went by Ashley's house again. The note was still there. She added her cell phone number to it, hoping Ashley would use it.

Chapter Seventy-Seven

● ● ●

I can do it." Dan shook off Dallas's hands and tried to move himself into the wheelchair. As weak as he was from his injuries, the strength in his muscular arms should have made it easier.

But it wasn't. It required sideways movement, and with no help from his legs at all, it was like bench-pressing two hundred pounds in the wrong position.

"Come on, Dan. You can do this. You're practically trained for it. You have the strength."

Sweat ran into Dan's eyes as he struggled to move himself. His arms shook, and his body felt as if it was sliding . . .

Dallas hurried to correct him, then repositioned him on the bed.

Dan thought of giving up, but he couldn't. He had to move forward. He couldn't just lie flat on his back for the rest of his life.

"Come on, Dan. Don't give up. You've come this far. Yesterday you couldn't even sit up. Now you've got your balance. And you're lucky, man. You've got good hip control. A lot of paraplegics don't have that. And your abs are tough, which helps a lot."

Dan found it hard to be grateful for those things.

Finally, gritting his teeth, his arms bulging with the effort, he managed to grab one arm of the chair and reached for the other one behind his back. Slowly, he put himself into the chair.

"Way to go, Dan! That was great!"

"I told you not to patronize me," he gritted. "Couple weeks ago I was bench-pressing two-eighty. Now I have trouble lifting myself."

"It's a different set of muscles, man. You're getting it, though. It'll be easier for you than most of my patients. You should see the ones with scrawny, wimpy arms trying to do it. You're way ahead of where you could be. Now, let's see if you can wheel yourself around."

Dan managed to move the chair around the room, turn it around, come back. By the time he'd done it three or four times, he was exhausted.

"I think that's enough for today," Dallas said. "Man, I'm really proud of you. You want to stay in the chair or move back to the bed?"

As much as Dan wanted to stay in the chair, he felt he would pass out right here if he didn't get into a reclining position. Summoning up all the energy he had left, he managed to get back onto the bed.

He lay there after Dallas left, flat on his back, staring up at the ceiling and cursing the day he had responded to the Icon disaster. Why hadn't he recognized the signs that the building was unstable? Why hadn't he gotten out before the third bomb went off?

Why hadn't he just died in the rubble? It would have been easier for everyone.

The door opened, and Clara hurried in. "Dan, Dallas tells me you moved yourself around in the chair. Why didn't you come out and let me see?"

Dan just kept his eyes on the ceiling. "It's not something I'm all that proud of."

"Well, why not? It's tremendous progress." She came to the side of his bed and straightened his covers.

"It's a wheelchair," he said. "It's like being proud of going back to training wheels."

"Dan, for heaven's sake, you need to look at how far you've come since the accident."

"That is what I'm looking at. I could run five miles before the accident. I could take fifteen stories of a building in minutes, carrying sixty-five pounds of equipment, wearing turnouts, and braving 110-degree heat. Now I'm supposed to celebrate if I can roll the wheels of my chair."

Clara grew quiet. "Would you like for me to turn on the television?"

"Yeah," he said. "I think I'm missing Jerry Springer. Let's see, today the subject is 'My Child Has a Gay Alien Priest for a Father,' or something equally stimulating."

Clara didn't recognize the sarcasm. "You could watch Oprah."

"Forget it." He finally looked at her. She was wearing her hair down in a ponytail clasped at the nape of her neck. She looked much more maternal than she had before. He liked the new look.

But he really wanted to be alone.

"Look, Mom, do you think you could give me a few minutes? I need to be alone for a while. I need to think."

She studied him for a moment, as if trying to decide if thinking was the best thing for him. "All right, dear. I'll wait out in the waiting room down the hall. When should I come back?"

"Half an hour," he said. "Or forty-five minutes. I don't know."

She looked hurt. "All right then." She patted him awkwardly. "Buzz the nurse if you want me to come back."

He waited for her to leave and, gritting his teeth, turned his thoughts to God. He was angry. Angrier than he'd ever been.

"Why didn't you let me die?" he asked. "It would have been better than this."

Tears ran onto his pillow, and he realized, for the first time in his life, that he hated. But his hatred shot without a target. It was hatred toward some faceless person or group of people who had destroyed his life in this way.

He hoped that wherever they were, some unseen spiritual knife was twisting in their gut, repaying them according to their deeds. He hoped they would suffer a long and miserable death, then burn in everlasting hell.

But none of that would restore him to the way he was before.

He would probably never walk again. He would never father children.

All of his dreams were dead.

"It's unacceptable!" he told the Lord. "All of what you've done to me is completely unacceptable. I didn't sign up for a life in a wheelchair. I refuse to accept that!"

But he knew his refusals carried little weight with the Almighty who heard his prayers.

Chapter Seventy-Eight

● ● ●

Jill hoped that Dan's physical therapy had been productive, but when she saw Clara in the hallway, pacing as if she didn't know what to do with herself, she had a bad feeling.

"Thank goodness you're back!"

Jill looked at the woman with dread. "What is it, Clara? Has something happened?"

"No, of course not. It's just that Dan is ... well, depressed."

She thought of asking her what was new about that. "His PT didn't go well?"

"No, it went very well," Clara said. "That young man who does his therapy said he had moved from the bed to the chair himself and had rolled himself around the room several times. He thought it was amazing progress. He reminded me that a week ago Dan was buried. To be up and around in this amount of time is something to be proud of."

"But Dan didn't see it that way?"

"No. Do something, Jill. He's extremely down. He asked me to give him some time to think. But I'm worried what he's in there thinking."

"Me too." Jill looked at his door. "I'm not sure I know what to do for him, Clara. About all any of us can do is hold his hand and try to encourage him."

The woman looked helpless—out of her element.

"Well, I guess I'll go home for a while. I might be back later tonight, after dinner." She looked up at Jill. "Did you find the girl?"

Clara's concern surprised her. She supposed she had made a lot of progress in the last week, as well. "No, I don't know where she could be. I have a cell phone now. I'm just praying she'll call."

"I'll let you know if she shows up," Clara said.

"Well, I guess I'll go on in." She sighed and prayed a silent prayer for strength.

••• •

Jill was not able to pull Dan out of his lethargy, and he didn't want to talk about his condition or his depression. Feeling rejected, but again reminding herself that it wasn't about her, she slept fitfully that night in the chair next to his bed.

The night was long, and she woke several times. Some of those times he slept; others, she found him awake, his eyes fixed on the ceiling.

"Want to talk?" she asked him a couple of those times.

"Nope," was his reply, cutting off any hope of communication between them.

Another time, she asked him if he'd like to pray with her. He told her he saw no point in that, since God had refused to answer his most recent prayers.

Jill lay on that uncomfortable chair and prayed silently that God would change his heart and show him just how many prayers he really had answered.

Chapter Seventy-Nine

● ● ●

I want everybody's minds off the Icon disaster." Jim Shoemaker, the Newpointe police chief, paced in front of his men and women for their 7:00 A.M. briefing. His face was sunburned from the hours he'd spent at the Icon site, but now he was ready to get back to business. "The FBI's handling that investigation, and Stan and Sid are assisting, but the rest of us need to settle down and crack this car theft ring in town. We still have a job to do. The perpetrators seem to be targeting grocery store parking lots . . ."

Stan jotted some obligatory notes on his legal pad, and his mind wandered back to John Trammel. So far, he'd found no connection between the dead man whose identity had been stolen and the Icon CEO. But he wasn't finished. He had gone himself to interview Merritt's pilot. The man claimed he had not heard from his boss but indicated that he would turn him in, in two seconds flat if he did.

"That man needs to be locked in a cage if he had anything to do with that bombing," he said.

Stan didn't think he would have lied to protect Merritt—not unless a lot of money had changed hands.

The door opened, and a sergeant stuck his head in. "Excuse me, Chief. Stan, you have an urgent call."

Stan got up, slipped out of the meeting, and hurried to his desk. "Stan Shepherd."

"Uh . . . Detective Shepherd . . ." The woman's voice was halting, soft. "This is Amber Williams. I thought of something about Donald, and I need to report it."

Stan leaned back hard in his chair. "Amber, why didn't you call the FBI?"

"Because I didn't have anything to do with that bombing, yet I felt like they thought I did somehow. And then someone there leaked my statement to the press, and next thing I know I'm considered an adulterous home wrecker who stole his money, and my own parents won't even speak to me!" Her voice broke off and she sat there a moment, trying to go on. "I know you and trust you, Detective Shepherd. So I decided to call you instead."

Stan felt sorry for the girl, even though she had brought so much of this on herself. "All right, Amber. What is it?"

"Well, I've been thinking a lot about where Donald might be if he's still alive and all. You know, hiding places. And something came to me."

He sat up straighter. "Yeah? Go ahead."

"On one of the times we met, he had the key to a cabin. It belonged to one of his coworkers, Ansel James, I think. He said he had a deal with him that he could use this cabin whenever he wanted. We spent several different weekends there. No one knew we were using it, no one but Ansel and me. But Ansel was killed in the explosion."

Stan grabbed his pen and started writing. "So you think Merritt might be in that cabin?"

"If he still had that key, maybe so."

Stan grabbed his sport coat from the chair where it hung. "Tell me how I can find the cabin, Amber."

Amber explained where the cabin was and how to get there. By the time Stan got off the phone, he was ready to burst out of his skin.

He rushed out without explaining to anyone where he was going. The last thing he needed now was for the chief to stop him.

In his car, Stan tried to call Mills from his cell phone, but another agent answered and offered to take a message. "Tell him it's Stan Shepherd." He thought of telling him about the possible hiding place, but Mills was the only one he trusted to handle this correctly. The wrong move could alert Merritt that they were onto him.

"Tell Mills to call me on my cellular ASAP. I have some important information for him."

"Anything I can take down?"

"No," he said. "But please, express the urgency to him. It's very important."

He hung his phone back on his belt and decided he'd go to the cabin himself. If Merritt was there, Stan could make sure that he stayed there until he heard from Mills.

Chapter Eighty

• • •

Ashley awoke in her car, shivering with the sudden drop in temperature. It was morning, and a thin layer of dew lay over her windows.

She pulled her denim jacket around her. It wasn't very heavy, but that was all right. Ashley didn't plan to be around when the weather got colder.

She started her car, hoping the heater would warm her up. The Subaru was almost out of gas, but she couldn't waste what money she had left on filling it up.

There was something else she needed to buy.

She thought of Ty, the drug dealer who hung out at the convenience store near Eddie's house. He was a storehouse of treasures. She knew she could get sleeping pills from him.

She only hoped he hadn't taken the day off.

She found him leaning against a garbage can, talking trash with some of his patrons. Unintimidated, Ashley pushed through them and made her purchase.

Armed with new purpose, she went back to her mother's house. She pulled her car into the driveway and looked down at the little bag of pills Ty had given her. There were just enough.

She sat there a moment, wondering if she had the strength to take her own life. Her courage faltered, but then she realized she was too weak to go on. Either way, she lost. It was better just to get it over with.

She got out, grabbed her duffel bag, and went to the door. Jill's note hung there, stuck between the doorway and the casing. She took it down and read it.

She thought of calling Jill, giving life one more try. But it seemed hopeless and futile.

Wadding the note in her fist, she unlocked the door and pushed inside. The sense that her mother was alive surrounded her again, pulling her into the warmth of the room. It was funny how the thermostat made the heat come on even though no one was in the house to warm.

Life went on, she supposed. It was a cruel fact, but one she could not escape.

Weary and chilled from the night in her car, she went into her mother's room, pulled back the cover, and slipped inside the bed. She laid her head on the pillow that her mother used to sleep on. Oh, how she missed her. She would give anything to turn time back and do things better. Why had she been so stupid as to think there would always be time for repentance and restoration? For her, time had run out.

Lying in the bed, curled up and warm beneath the covers, she noticed the light blinking on her mother's answering machine next to the bed. The tape was probably full by now, she thought. She reached over and turned it on, hoping to hear her mother's outgoing message and pretend just for a moment that she was still here, speaking into her ear, stroking her hair, and kissing her awake.

"Hi, this is Debbie. Ashley and I aren't home right now, but if you'd like to leave a message, we'll call you back as soon as we can. God bless you and have a nice day."

Tears sprang to Ashley's eyes.

Beep. "Debbie, this is Sara. I heard what happened at the Icon Building. I'm praying you got out okay. Please call me as soon as you get this message."

Beep. "Debbie, this is Anna. Are you okay, honey? I'm desperate to find out if you're all right. Please call me back."

Beep. "Debbie, this is Jim. I'm trying to account for everybody in the office. Call me back as soon as you get this message and let me know if you've seen anybody else."

Ashley opened the bag of pills, dumped them out on the pillow next to her.

Beep. "Debbie, I'm hoping against hope that you're going to hear this message and call me back. Please. This is Sara. I can't stand much more of this."

Beep. "Hey, Ash, if you're there, call me." It was Chris, probably the night of the explosion, when she hadn't come home.

Beep. "Ashley, this is Sara." She could tell her mother's best friend had been crying. "I heard about your mother and I wanted to tell you that I'm so very sorry. If you get this, please call me."

She squeezed her eyes shut.

Beep. "Ashley, this is your great-aunt Cecelia from Oklahoma. Please call me. I need to talk to you immediately."

Beep. "Oh, Debbie, I heard the news today, and I can't believe it's true." There was a sob, then, "I just wanted to hear your voice one more time."

Ashley couldn't take any more. She turned off the machine, dropped her head on the pillow and wept until all the black mascara and eyeliner dripped from her eyes and onto the pillowcase, saturating it.

Her mother had a life. She had friends. People were grieving over her. Ashley wasn't the only one. But she didn't know how that helped her in any way.

She could take these pills, and the pain would end. It would be so easy.

What choice did she have, anyway? She had no place to go, no anchor to hold her anywhere. She could go back to her friends and dull her pain with drugs and alcohol, but what kind of future would that give her? Before long, most of them would be in jail or dead themselves.

She gathered the pills into her fist and held them as she worked up her courage.

Soon it would all be over.

Chapter Eighty-One

● ● ●

Stan found the cabin exactly where Amber had described, sitting alone in a cluster of pines near a lake. Fog rose from the water as the cold wind crept in. He left his car far back in the trees, for he didn't want any occupants of the house to hear him coming.

Using his binoculars, he scanned the windows for a sign of life. Someone was definitely inside. He could see smoke coming from the chimney. Behind the house he could see that some wood had recently been split and stacked.

But for all he knew, someone in Ansel James's family could be occupying the cabin, nursing their grief over the death of their loved one.

Setting his phone on vibrate, he moved carefully between the trees until he found a window that had no drapes pulled over it. He could see someone standing at a sink washing dishes, but he couldn't make out who it was. He put the binoculars back to his eyes, tried to zoom in and focus.

Donald Merritt!

It was him, all right, though he'd dyed his gray hair brown, and it looked like he was working on a beard. Still, he was unscathed and looked as healthy as ever, biting into an apple as if he had nothing to do with hundreds of people dying.

Stan looked around and saw a pickup truck tucked away in the bushes.

His phone vibrated. Quickly, Stan answered it. "Shepherd."

"Stan, this is Mills. What have you got?"

"I've found Merritt," he whispered.

"No kidding?"

"Do me a favor. Run this car tag through." He read off the truck's tag number.

He heard Bryan typing the data in. "Reported as stolen last week," he said.

"Guess who stole it."

"Where is he, Stan?"

Stan gave him directions to the cabin. The FBI was on its way.

All he had to do was stay out of sight and make sure Merritt didn't leave until they got there.

Chapter Eighty-Two

● ● ●

Jill waited until Dallas came for Dan's physical therapy session before she headed out to look for Ashley again. Before leaving, she gave Dan the cell phone she'd bought him. He hooked it onto the waist of his sweatpants and told her to call him directly on that number rather than going through the switchboard. That way, if he happened to be in his wheelchair, he could easily answer.

Jill drove to Ashley's house to see if the note was still on the door. When she saw the girl's car in the driveway, she almost yelled for joy. She ran to the door and rang the bell.

There was no answer. She knocked, then banged on the door.

Finally, she heard Ashley's aggravated voice on the other side. "Who is it?"

"Jill," she called. "Ashley, please open the door!"

There was a long hesitation.

"Ashley! Come on, let me in. Please!"

Finally, she heard the bolt clicking, and the door came open. Ashley didn't wait to greet her. As Jill stepped inside, she watched Ashley retreat from the room and head into one of the bedrooms.

Jill followed her.

"Ashley, I've looked all over for you. Where have you been?" She caught up to the girl and turned her around.

Ashley had black makeup streaking her wet face, and as Jill reached for her, she crumpled into sobs.

"Sweet Ashley," Jill said, crushing her against her. "I'm so happy I found you. Honey, it's going to be all right."

Ashley just wept her heart out as Jill held her.

• • •

After a while, Ashley pulled back and wiped her face on her sleeve. She hadn't expected Jill to hold her like that, as if she had some personal stake in her life.

As if she actually loved her.

That would be too good to be true. Ashley had barged in on her, after all, and practically forced herself on the woman. They were strangers, really. Why would Jill care so much?

She thought of her mother's prayer.

. . . send her godly people who can love and guide her.

What would her mother have said if she'd known about the pills she had almost taken? It would break her heart, she knew.

It would break Jill's, too.

"I'm not leaving you here, Ashley. I want you to pack up whatever you need and come back to my house."

"That's crazy," Ashley said. "You hardly even know me. I've never even met Dan. And Clara—"

"Don't worry about Clara. She's changing, Ashley. And she's been worried about you. I think she regrets the fight you two had." She took Ashley's hand. "Come on, Ashley. Please. What do you need? I'll help you pack."

She turned to the closet, and as she did, her gaze swept the bed. She saw the pills scattered across the dark green comforter.

Ashamed, Ashley went to the bed and started picking them up.

"Ashley, what are those?"

"Aspirin," she said. "I had a headache, and I spilled the bottle."

Jill took one of them, turned it over in her hand. "That's not an aspirin, Ashley."

Ashley didn't have the energy or will to convince her. "What do you care? It's my life."

"Your life has impact on others, honey."

She wasn't sure why that comment amused her, but she breathed a mirthless laugh. "Oh, yeah? Whose?"

She could almost see the wheels turning in Jill's mind, as if she racked her brain for an answer. "How about all those grieving loved ones of Icon victims?"

Ashley hadn't expected that one. "How does my life affect them?"

Jill took the bag from her hands. "Ashley, the FBI interviewed me yesterday about the morning of the explosions. I told them you had seen the actual bomb. It turns out you're the only one living who saw it. They want to interview you, honey. They think you might be able to tell them something that will help them catch the killer."

She was right. That would make a difference to those who grieved. "Really? You're not just making that up?"

"No. I'll take you there right now. It could make a difference."

Ashley looked at the bag Jill clutched. She would flush them, she knew. But she supposed she could get more where she'd gotten those.

But not now. There was time for suicide later—after she'd helped put the killer behind bars.

Ashley glanced in the mirror. Black makeup still streaked her face. She really did look like a vampire. "Just let me take a quick shower and change," she said. "I want them to take me seriously."

"Okay, honey," Jill said. "I'll wait right here."

Chapter Eighty-Three

• • •

Stan heard the back door opening, and he backed into the bushes, drew his weapon, and waited.

Merritt loped out, whistling. He wore sunglasses, a pair of sweatpants, and a baggy T-shirt.

Stan watched as he headed for the pickup.

He was going to have to act. No way could he let this man get away.

He stepped out of the forest. "Freeze!"

Merritt swung around and saw Stan coming toward him, his gun trained on him. Panic flashed across his face, and for a moment he did freeze.

Then he decided to run for it. He leaped into the truck, turned the key, and began to back out.

"No, you don't!" Stan fired at two of his tires, crippling the truck.

Merritt leaped out and took off on foot.

Stan fired over his head, but the man kept running.

He wasn't going to get away. Stan knew he could hit him with one shot, kill him instantly. But he wanted the man alive.

If he'd planted those bombs, he wanted to see him suffer like Dan had suffered, like George and Jacob and the others had suffered. He wanted him to know the kind of anguish that the grieving families felt. He wanted Merritt to face his own family with his deadly deception.

He launched after Merritt. When he caught up, he threw himself on the man's back, knocking him to the ground.

"You haven't got anything on me!" Merritt shouted against the dirt. "I haven't broken any laws!"

Stan cuffed his wrists roughly and searched him for a weapon. Quickly, he radioed for backup, then called Mills Bryan to tell him what had happened. With the element of surprise no longer necessary, he heard sirens not far away.

"You, my friend, are under arrest. . . ."

"For *what?*" Merritt cried.

"For one hundred and fifty-three counts of first-degree murder, and still counting, pal. That's just for starters." He pressed the barrel of his firearm to Merritt's skull. "You have the right to remain silent . . ."

Two police cars and a SWAT team van screeched to a halt nearby, and several armed men jumped out and surrounded them.

Stan got up and left him lying there on the dirt as Mills Bryan took over.

His hands were shaking as he returned his weapon to its holster.

Chapter Eighty-Four

• • •

Jill called the number Mills Bryan had given her, and he asked if she could bring Ashley to the Newpointe Police Department, since that was where he and his agents were currently occupied.

When she tried to turn onto Purchase Street, Jill caught her breath.

Press vans glutted the road.

"What's going on?" Ashley asked.

"I don't know," Jill said, "but I'm going to park somewhere else." She pulled her car into Allie's flower shop parking lot. Ashley got out and ran her fingers through her hair. She had combed it down and left her face free of makeup, and had removed the black polish from her fingers and toes. She wore a pair of faded jeans and an LSU T-shirt. Even though she still wore her nose ring, she looked as close to normal as Jill had ever seen her. Ashley followed her across the street, up the block, and through the press members lining the sidewalk as if they were waiting for a statement from someone.

They stopped as they came to one of the New Orleans correspondents making a live remote broadcast. "We don't yet know where they found Donald Merritt, but we're told he is inside at the Newpointe Police Department, being interviewed by the FBI at this very moment."

Jill looked at Ashley. "Donald Merritt."

Ashley's face changed, and Jill saw her pale face go red. The girl pushed past the reporters and started up the steps of the police department.

Sid Ford let them in. "Jill, I didn't expect to see you here."

"I brought Ashley Morris," she said. "Agent Bryan wanted to interview her."

"Yeah, go on in. Tell Stan. He's at his desk. I'm trying to keep the press out."

"Where is he?" Ashley demanded. "Where's Donald Merritt?"

"Being interrogated," he said. He pointed to the closed door at the back of the room. "Feds got him in there."

Ashley cursed and shot for the door. Jill followed her. "Ashley, you can't go in there!"

Stan looked up from his desk and got to his feet.

The girl reached the Interview Room door and bolted through it. Stan caught up to her before Jill did and grabbed her to pull her back.

Some of the agents reached for their guns, and Donald Merritt shrank back.

"It's okay," Stan told them. "I've got her!"

"You killed my mother!" Her scream shrieked out over the building, silencing everyone who heard it. She cursed again. "You murdered her!"

Stan tried to move her out of the doorway, but she fought to break free. "If I had a gun, I'd kill you myself!" she screamed. "I'd blow you into a million pieces! I'd bury you alive!"

Merritt looked shaken. "I didn't plant the bomb!" he yelled back. "I didn't kill anybody!"

Stan wrestled Ashley from the room, and one of the agents came out to help calm her. Jill tried to help.

"Why are you talking to him?" Ashley sobbed. "He's not a person! He's a monster! Why can't you just kill him and get it over with?"

"Honey, calm down," Jill cried. "Please, calm down."

Stan pulled her into another interview room. He led her to a chair and bent over her. "Look at me, sweetheart," he said. "I want you to try to calm down and look at me."

Ashley's face twisted as she looked up at him.

"We're going to prosecute him to the full extent of the law," he said. "I promise you, if he's guilty, he's not going to get away with it."

"*If?*" Ashley cried. "Of course he's guilty, or he wouldn't have faked his death! He killed a hundred and fifty-three people! He killed my mother!"

Someone handed Stan a glass of water, and he gave it to her. Then he pulled up a chair and sat knee to knee with her. "If we prove he did it, you can bet he'll get the death penalty, Ashley. And you can help us prove it. You can tell us what you saw that day."

"I just saw the bomb!" she said. "I didn't see him with it. It's not like he'd written his name on it. If he walks free—"

"He won't," Stan said. "But the things you tell us can help us trace the things he made the bomb with. We can find out where he bought them, search his property for them. Everything you can give us can help us connect him to the crime."

Ashley drank some of the water. Hiccuping her sobs, she locked into Stan's gaze.

"Can you calm down and help us, Ashley?"

She looked up at Jill, and Jill nodded, reassuring her.

"You're one of the only witnesses so far," Stan said. "We need you, Ashley, if justice is going to be done."

Finally, Ashley drew in a long, deep breath. "I'll tell you whatever I can."

Chapter Eighty-Five

● ● ●

When Ashley had finished telling her story, Jill took her out of the station. Stan went with Mills to finish his interrogation of Merritt.

"Funny thing happened after that girl came in," one of the agents with Merritt told them. "He started wanting to talk."

Merritt was trembling. "I didn't do it," he said. "I really didn't do it. I know this looks bad. But I didn't plant those bombs. You've got to believe me. All I did was take advantage of the opportunity."

"What do you mean, you took advantage?" Mills asked.

"I didn't even think of it when the explosion happened. I was just like everybody else, running down the stairs, trying to get everybody out when the first bomb went off. I was one of the last ones out of the building, and then it collapsed, and I was in shock like everybody else, just standing in the dust and trying to figure out what in the world had happened." His voice broke off.

"I realized my whole world had come crashing down. There was nothing left. And finally the thought occurred to me that I could just start walking and never come back. They would think I had died in the collapse. All my problems with the law, all my financial worries, my family problems, everything. I could leave them all behind and just start over."

"But then you took money out of your bank account."

"I thought no one would know. I didn't even know my family knew about that account." He looked into the agent's face. "I know I've done some horrible things that have caused problems for a lot of people. But I've never killed anybody. And I sure wouldn't have killed that many innocent people."

As the interrogation went on, Stan began growing angrier. The man was a liar, as well as a bloody killer.

Chapter Eighty-Six

● ● ●

Itold you he wasn't dead."

Gordon's reaction to the news of Merritt's arrest didn't surprise Jill. She and Ashley had decided to go by his house before going back to the hospital, just to make sure he knew. He had already been watching the news updates when they came in.

"Well, you hit it right on the money," Jill said.

She looked at Ashley, who had been quiet since they'd left the police station. Seeing Merritt had almost pushed her over the edge. Jill thought of those pills she had flushed down the toilet. How hard would it be for Ashley to get more?

"Of all the people to have survived that blast." Gordon rubbed his red face and looked at Ashley. "You okay, honey?"

Ashley didn't answer. "They said I might be called as a witness in his trial. I'll do anything to make sure he pays."

"If he lives that long." He shivered.

Jill realized it was cold in the house, so she got an afghan off of the couch and laid it over his legs. "What do you mean, if he lives that long?"

Gordon pulled the blanket up to warm himself. "There are some angry people out there who lost loved ones, like Ashley here. Or your husband, whose life may be changed forever. Some angry soul is going to take that man down. I wouldn't give a plug nickel for his life right now."

Jill knew he was right.

The doorbell rang, and Jill sprang up to get it. Stan Shepherd stood there, looking grim and thoughtful.

"Hey, Jill," he said. "I saw your car."

"Were you looking for me?"

"No, I just came by to talk to Gordon."

She let him in, and Stan smiled at Ashley, then shook Gordon's hand and told him not to get up. "Gordon, I met you at church the other night. Detective Stan Shepherd of the Newpointe Police Department."

"Yes, I remember you," he said. "Have a seat."

Stan sat down next to Jill. "The reason I'm here is I'd like to take a statement from you, since you were near the top floors of the building when the bomb went off."

Gordon shrugged. "I don't know what I could add to what they've already told you. I practically can't remember anything. I hurt my leg after the first bomb went off. If it weren't for these two young ladies, I'd probably be dead right now."

"Well, I'd just like to ask you a few questions, if you don't mind."

Jill got up and nodded to Ashley. "We'll leave you two alone. I really need to get back to the hospital."

"No, don't go," Gordon said. "You might be able to fill in some of the blanks for me. I'm not sure I remember everything."

Stan nodded that they could stay, so they both sat back down.

"Gordon, if you don't mind, tell me what took you to the Icon International Building that day."

Gordon swallowed and looked down at his hands. He began to rub them on his trousers. Jill could see that the memories made him just as tense as they made her.

"I went up to clean out my desk. You see, my wife had died two weeks earlier. While I was out for her funeral, they laid me off. Pretty crummy thing to do, if you ask me. They're selfish and hateful, the whole lot of them. The ones who were left were the ones padding their pockets. They're all in cahoots."

"What floor did you work on?"

"The twentieth," Gordon said. "I had boxed up the stuff from my desk, and then I ran upstairs to human services for my exit interview. Before I got there, the evacuation started, and I turned to go back down."

"Before the evacuation, did you make it up to the twenty-ninth floor, by any chance?"

"No, not quite. I think I was about to twenty-five or twenty-six when the alarm went off."

"Could you tell me if you saw Donald Merritt on those stairs?"

"No," he said. "I don't remember seeing him."

"Even on the stairs on the way down, do you remember seeing him run past you?"

"I was pretty tied up," Gordon said. "I don't remember noticing anybody's faces except for Jill's and Ashley's."

"We're just trying to establish when and how he got out of the building, whether he seemed to have foreknowledge of the bombs on the lower floors . . ."

"He had foreknowledge, all right," Gordon bit out. "Planted all three of those bombs and left those people to die."

"Do you have any information to prove that?"

"The fact that he's alive with two suitcases full of cash is all the evidence you need," Gordon spouted out.

Stan frowned. "How did you know we found suitcases?"

"Heard it on the news. They said it was a confirmed report from the FBI."

Jill noticed that as the wind blew harder, the living room grew colder. She shivered. "Stan, I hate to interrupt, but Gordon, I'd like to turn the heat up. Can you tell me where the thermostat is?"

Gordon shook his head. "Don't bother. The furnace is broken."

"Broken?" she said. "But it's going to get below freezing later this week. You'll need heat."

"Can't help it," Gordon said. "I haven't been able to afford to get it fixed. But it won't be cold for more than a couple of days, then it'll warm up again."

Stan frowned and got up. "Well, you've got to have heat. I've been known to fix a few furnaces in my time. I could come by tomorrow and take a look."

"No, you've got enough on you, what with Merritt and all. Don't worry about it. I'll be fine."

"The FBI just about has this under control. I can take a few hours tomorrow afternoon. Meanwhile, I can get you some space heaters for tonight."

Gordon rubbed his mouth again, masking his emotion. "You people are good to me. I don't deserve it. You've done enough." He cleared his throat. "I was thinking how I'd like to give something to help with that fundraiser your church is having, where they're donating money to the families. I don't have money, but I was thinking that somebody might get some use out of my wife's clothes. They're worth something."

Jill was moved. "Gordon, are you sure?"

He rubbed his mouth again. "I'm sure. I just don't think I can clean out her closet myself. It's just . . . kind of hard."

"I could do it." Ashley's words surprised them both.

Jill looked at the girl, stunned. "Really, Ashley?"

"Well, yeah. I could come tomorrow. I don't have anything else to do."

"You wouldn't mind?" Gordon asked. "Darlin', that would be a godsend. That way somebody can make use of her things before the holidays. It might fill somebody's needs like you people have filled mine. And it might raise something to help those poor grieving people."

Jill looked back at Stan. He was smiling gently at the girl. "That's nice of you, Ashley."

She looked embarrassed. "I just know how it is."

Jill hoped that when Ashley had to clean out her mother's house, she could help her do it. But for now, helping Gordon was a perfect way to pull the girl outside her own grief.

As they got ready to leave, Gordon reached up to hug Ashley. "You're a blessed angel. You know it? I don't care if people *are* afraid of you. You look right nice today, though."

Jill caught her breath and shot a startled look at the girl. Ashley just grinned.

Chapter Eighty-Seven

● ● ●

Ashley's silence on the drive back to New Orleans worried Jill. The girl was still fragile, even more so than she'd been when she'd found her at her mother's earlier. She feared leaving her alone again, yet she needed to be with Dan.

Torn, she called Dan as they made their way across Lake Pontchartrain. It rang several times before Dan picked up. "Hello?" He seemed out of breath.

"Hi, honey. It's me. Everything all right?"

"Yeah, fine. How'd it go at the police station?"

She had called him on the way there to let him know why she'd been delayed. "It went okay. I'll tell you about it when I get there. Was therapy all right?"

"It was fine."

She knew from his tone that it hadn't been fine at all. "You sound out of breath. Are you all right?"

"Everything's all right, Jill. Everything's fine. When will you be here?"

Jill wasn't sure if he was anxious to see her or just irritable about her being gone. "Soon. I have to take Ashley to get her car. I was . . . thinking I might bring her by to meet you . . . if you feel like company."

"Sure, if you want."

That was no help. She wondered if this was the time. "Are you sure you're up to it?"

"Yes, I'm up to it."

There was no question about it. He was irritated. She hoped she wasn't the cause of it. When she hung up, she looked over at Ashley. "He's looking forward to meeting you."

Ashley wasn't buying. "Are you sure? Because I could come another time."

"Of course I'm sure."

"I'm sorry I kept you away so long."

Jill squeezed her hand. "Don't be sorry, honey. It was important."

The girl let go of her hand and gazed out the window at the concrete railing over the lake. Was she thinking of suicide again?

"I'm worried about you, Ashley."

Ashley shrugged. "There's nothing to worry about."

"You were going to take those pills. I'm afraid to leave you alone, but I know that I can't be with you all the time."

"Don't worry about it," Ashley said. "I've found a new reason to live."

"You have?"

"Yeah. I plan to stay alive long enough to see Merritt fry."

Jill felt sick. "Honey, that's no reason."

Ashley breathed a laugh. "Well, it's the only one I've got."

Help me give her a reason, Lord. The prayer came from deep in her gut.

"Ashley, your mother made a sacrifice that day. A big one. She gave her life so that others could live."

"It's not like she had a choice. She didn't wake up that day and decide to be a martyr."

"No, she didn't. But when she saw that bomb, instead of saving herself, she alerted the building so they could evacuate. Jesus said, 'Greater love hath no man than this, that he lay down his life for his friend.'"

"It wasn't love. It was responsibility. What else could she do?"

"She could have run. Then there might be five hundred people dead instead of a hundred and fifty-three. She had a choice, and she did what she had to do."

"So my mother's a hero. Nobody cares."

"I care. I would be one of the dead if it weren't for her."

Ashley's body language was closed tight—her arms crossed over her chest, her legs crossed at the knee.

"Ashley, what your mother did was similar to what Christ did for you."

"So you're making my mother a Christ-figure now?"

The girl's cynicism didn't daunt Jill.

"No, I'm just using her as an example. It's like if Christ knew where the bomb was and threw himself over it, to keep it from killing the very people who'd built it. In a way, I built it with my sins, and you built it with yours. And he knew that, but he didn't want us to be destroyed by our own actions, because he loves us."

Ashley pulled her feet up on the seat and hugged her knees. "My mother loved me. She's the only one who ever has."

"No, she's not, Ashley. Christ has loved you since before you were born. And he made me love you."

For the rest of the ride, Ashley didn't say a word, but silent tears ran down her face.

When they reached her mother's house, Jill pulled in behind her car. Ashley didn't make a move to get out.

"Tell me something," she whispered finally. "Tell me how you can keep trusting God. Your husband is paralyzed. A building fell on him. In my mind, that's grounds for waving your fist at God."

Jill cut off her engine and shifted to face the girl. "Honey, my faith can't depend on my circumstances. If God was good before the disaster, then does he stop being good because this happened? Isn't he the same God he was before?"

"Maybe he isn't the God you thought he was. Maybe he never was. Or maybe he likes you better than me, and that's why Dan didn't die."

"Ashley, on September 11, a lot of people died while I sat in my living room crying, thankful that I was safe in Louisiana, where nothing bad ever happens. You could say that he loved the people in Louisiana better than the people in New York or Washington or Pennsylvania, but it wouldn't be true. And last week, did God love the people who weren't in the Icon Building better than those who were? Did he love Dan more than your mother? Did he love our friend Mark more than he loved Dan?"

"Maybe."

"Honey, we all die. The time comes for every one of us. Not because God hates us, but because of that ticking bomb that we built with our sins, that bomb that's guaranteed to go off someday. Jesus didn't build the bomb, but it's like he threw himself over it to keep it from killing us. Like your mom, he gave his life to save us. That's love, Ashley. That's the God who doesn't change even when our circumstances do."

Ashley sat there for a moment, staring up at the house where she'd lived for most of her life. Jill saw the longing on her face.

Finally, Ashley opened the door, slid out. "I'll meet you at the hospital."

"Room 328," Jill said.

Ashley just nodded and went to get into her car.

Chapter Eighty-Eight

● ● ●

Sheer determination had kept Dan in the wheelchair for over an hour as he'd waited for Jill to get back.

It was absurd, all this effort just to sit up. He had hoped his therapy sessions would focus on getting him to walk again. But he couldn't even move his little toe. And staying in this chair took more effort than any physical conditioning he'd done in his entire life.

"You look exhausted, dear," his mother said. "Why don't you get back on the bed and lie down?"

"I want to be in this chair when Jill comes in."

"But she's taking so long."

He grabbed a towel off of the bed where he'd flung it and wiped the sweat from his face. "She'll be here soon."

It amazed him that such debilitating fatigue could overtake him. His mother got up and poured him a glass of ice water. He drank it gratefully.

He heard the door opening, and he rolled the chair around. Jill's joy made it all worth it. "Dan, you're up. Look at you!"

He tried to smile, but the relief of finally seeing her seemed to add to the pressing fatigue. "Been in the chair over an hour."

She bent over to kiss him, and he saw from her eyes that she had been crying. Her nose was red from wiping it.

"You okay?" he asked.

Had she been crying over their broken lives?

"I'm fine." She sat down on his bed and looked at him. "You look like yourself, Dan. Sitting up, wheeling around."

"He needs to get back in bed," Clara spouted. "He's utterly exhausted, but he insisted on being in that chair when you came back."

Jill's joy faded, and she looked at him with those misty eyes. "Honey, if you need to lie down—"

"No, I'm fine," he lied. "Tell me about your meeting with the FBI."

Jill quickly filled him in on Ashley's outburst with Merritt and her grief on the way back to New Orleans. His heart softened, and he saw in Jill's eyes that she was grieving for her, too. He wished he could put his arms around her, hold her, and tell her that things would be all right.

But he was pretty sure they wouldn't be.

He glanced across the room and saw that his mother's eyes were moist, as well. She had come a long way in the last few days.

"Ashley followed me here to meet you. She's probably out in the hall already. Do you mind if she comes in?"

He was glad he was sitting up. "Yeah, of course. I've been looking forward to it."

Jill got up and went to the door, and he used his arms to straighten himself in the chair. Then he rolled around to face the door.

"Come in, Ashley," he heard Jill say.

The girl stepped in.

She didn't look exactly like he'd pictured. Her face was washed clean of makeup, and her black hair was parted on the side and combed down. She had her nose ring in and several loops hanging on her ears.

But she looked very young and fragile.

He smiled and reached a hand out to her. "Hey, Ashley. It's good to finally meet you."

Her hand was as cold as ice, and he felt her trembling. He wondered if she felt his, as well.

"You, too," she said.

"I'm glad Jill found you. She's been a wreck looking for you."

Ashley just looked up at Jill, and Jill stroked her back protectively.

He felt it too, that protective instinct. That inexplicable anger at what she'd been through. That determination to make things better for her if he could.

Clara stood up and came around the bed. "I'm glad she found you, too," she said. "You're coming back to the house, aren't you? I've found I'm terrified to stay there alone."

Ashley looked surprised. "Yeah, I guess."

"Good. I'll follow you back when you leave. Maybe I'll pick up a pizza or whatever it is you teenagers like to eat."

Ashley looked at Jill, as if to ask if Clara had hit her head or something. Jill just smiled.

Yes, Dan's mother had made great progress.

He studied the girl for a moment, forgetting his own exhaustion. She looked as if she was ready to break and run.

"Ashley, I want you to know that you have a home with us as long as you need it."

Her mouth trembled slightly. "Thank you."

"I'm serious," he said. "You're welcome for the duration. Two years, three years, five years, whatever. We have that big house, so we might as well fill up the rooms."

The look of gratitude on Jill's face warmed him.

He hoped Ashley would be warmed, as well.

• • •

As Jill walked Ashley and Clara to the elevator, she said a silent prayer that they would get along tonight. Though they still seemed awkward together, she hoped they would both be on their best behavior.

When she got back to Dan's room, he had moved his chair next to the bed.

She leaned over and kissed him. "Thank you for being so sweet to her."

He tried to smile. "She seemed like a sweet kid. I don't know what all my mother's vampire talk was about."

"She looked a little different today because she wanted the FBI to take her seriously. I hope you'll still like her when she's in full makeup."

"I will," he said. "And I meant what I said."

"That's one of the reasons I'm in love with you."

His reaction to that startled her. His face tightened, and he looked as if the comment made him angry. She couldn't imagine why.

"I've got to get out of this chair," he said.

"Okay, what do I need to do?"

"Nothing," he said. "I can do it." He positioned it next to the bed and locked the wheels. Then he tried to lift himself.

"Do you want me to go get someone to help?"

The question only seemed to make him angrier. "I'm okay," he said, as more perspiration broke out over him. His arms shook with the strain, and veins burst out on his forehead.

"Here, let me help you." She reached out, but he pushed her hands away.

"I *said* I could do it."

The words were so hostile, so cold, that she stepped back, her arms at her sides, and watched him try again. When he failed, she could see that he was near tears.

"Please let me go get someone to help."

"I don't want help!" Dan shouted. "Don't you get it?"

She shrank back. "Dan, don't yell at me. I don't know what you want."

"I want to walk!" His voice whiplashed across the room, and she felt the impact of them. The words were like daggers, pinning her to the wall. Silence fell in their wake, and she stared at him through her tears.

With herculean effort, he managed to move himself to the bed. She stood still as he pulled himself further onto the mattress, then lifted one leg at a time, dead useless limbs. When he'd gotten them positioned, he finally fell back on his pillows.

She saw his chest rising and falling as he tried to catch his breath. His face was red and soaked with sweat.

She thought of grabbing his towel and wiping off his face, but would that be help where he didn't want it? Could she get him water? Help him out of his sweaty clothes? Would he accept that or snap at her again?

"I don't know what to do for you, Dan."

He just stared up at the ceiling, shaking his head. "I don't want anyone to do anything for me. I just want to be left alone."

She stood there, hating the tears that rolled down her cheeks. This wasn't about her, she told herself. His rejection was not meant to hurt.

Yet it did.

Had she lost her husband, even though he'd lived?

Finally, she pushed away from the wall and came closer to his bed. "I was talking to Ashley in the car before. She asked me how I could continue to trust God after all that had happened."

He kept his eyes on the ceiling. "What did you say?"

"I said that our circumstances can't determine what we believe about God. That he's still good, even when bad things happen."

"Nice pat answer," Dan said.

"Was it? Don't you think it's true?"

"It's a little harder from where I sit," he said. "After what God's done to me."

Jill's sympathy and hurt faded, and a slow anger began to burn in her chest. "What he's done *to* you? Dan, what about what he's done *for* you?"

His face reddened again. "Forgive me if I'm not grateful for being a cripple."

"Well, are you grateful to be alive?"

"No, I'm not!" he shouted. "I'd rather be dead!"

Shocked silence fell between them, and Jill gaped at him for a long moment. Her confusion gave birth to anger. "How dare you!"

It clearly wasn't the reaction he'd expected of her. "How dare I *what?*"

"How dare you wish you were dead after all the prayers that went up on your behalf! After the *miracles* God gave you when you were buried? When your lung collapsed and you couldn't breathe without help?" She bent over him, pointing a finger at his face. "When you were lost, I begged God, *pleaded* with him, to save you. And he did. And then when you were lying in ICU unconscious, hanging by a thread, I made bargains with him, Dan! I told him that I'd take you any way I could get you, as long as he let you wake up! Are you telling me that was a foolish bargain?"

"Yes," he said through his teeth. "It was a very foolish bargain."

She straightened then and backed away. "So you're saying that you wouldn't have made the same bargain for me? If it had been me buried under that building? If I'd been the one dying in ICU?"

He got quiet then, and his face twisted. Tears began to run down his face. She wanted to go to him, hold him, but she feared he might push her away.

Finally, he looked up at her. "I would have," he whispered. "I would have made that bargain for you."

"Then how can you say that God's answer was wrong? How can you say that you'd rather be dead? I thought your faith was stronger than your own physical ability."

"I don't know if it is."

That confession broke her heart.

"Only you can decide that, honey." She wiped the tears off her face. "This isn't about your weakness, Dan. It's about your strength. Are you strong enough to be weak? Even if you never stand again, will your *faith* be able to? After all these years of building all that strength, how strong are you, really?"

He was sobbing openly now, and she wanted to stop his pain. Forgetting her fear of being pushed away, she sat down on the bed next to him and put her arms around him.

He pulled her against him and held her as he wept.

After a moment, he let her go, and she sat up and looked down at him.

"I don't think you . . . understand all the repercussions of this," he said. "Do you realize that my paralysis might mean that you and I never have children? Are you ready to deal with *that?*"

"Dan, if that's part of the bargain, so be it. I told God I wanted you *any way* I could get you. It's worth it to me, honey."

"But you want children. I want them."

"So we could adopt. We don't even know all the options yet. All's not lost, Dan. Not unless you give up hope. Not unless you live your life wishing to die."

He reached for her again, and she laid her head on his chest and held him, praying silently that God would bring healing to Dan's spirit . . . if not to his legs.

Chapter Eighty-Nine

● ● ●

Late that night Dan woke in his hospital bed. He looked at Jill and saw that she lay twisted on the vinyl recliner she'd been sleeping in. She couldn't be comfortable.

He stared up at the ceiling, thinking of their talk tonight. Her question for him had hit dead center.

Are you strong enough to be weak?

He honestly didn't know the answer.

What about when they sent him home? When people stared and children whispered, when he had to park in disabled parking spaces, when he had to give up his job? When his wife had to watch him struggling and had to help him with the simplest tasks? Was he strong enough to withstand all that?

He reached for the Bible lying on his bed table. For a moment he stared at it, wondering what he should open it to. The passages where Christ healed the lame? Or the ones where he didn't?

He turned to 2 Corinthians and turned the pages, scanning, looking for one particular verse. He found it, highlighted in chapter 12. He had made notes beside it, as if he had a clue what it was all about. He really hadn't known anything when he'd written those notes.

But he knew now.

"For when I am weak, then I am strong."

Trying to remember the context, he went back to verse seven and read hungrily, desperate for something that would speak to him in Paul's words.

To keep me from becoming conceited because of these surpassingly great revelations, there was given me a thorn in my flesh, a messenger of Satan, to torment me. Three times I pleaded with the Lord to take it away from me. But he said to me, "My grace is sufficient for you, for my power is made perfect in weakness." Therefore, I will boast all the more gladly about my weaknesses, so that Christ's power may rest on me. That is why, for Christ's sake, I delight in weaknesses, in insults, in hardships, in persecutions, in difficulties. For when I am weak, then I am strong.

He read those words over and over, analyzing them in his mind, wondering if he really understood what true strength was. All these years, he'd been so proud of his strength. He'd worn it like a royal robe. He'd endured teasing and jeering from his friends, but all the while he'd known that they really did admire him.

And that admiration meant everything to him.

Maybe it all boiled down to pride.

He turned to the concordance at the back of his Bible and looked for the word "weak." He scanned the listing there and decided to turn to 1 Corinthians 1:27.

But God chose the foolish things of the world to shame the wise; God chose the weak things of the world to shame the strong. He chose the lowly things of this world and the despised things—and the things that are not—to nullify the things that are, so that no one may boast before him. It is because of him that you are in Christ Jesus, who has become for us wisdom from God—that is, our righteousness, holiness and redemption. Therefore, as it is written: "Let him who boasts boast in the Lord."

Had he boasted before God? Had he put his faith more in the strength in his own body than he had in the power of Christ in him? *For when I am weak, then I am strong.*

Maybe that power of Christ within him would surpass any physical strength he'd had before. People were watching him, pitying him, probably expecting the worst.

Was it possible that God could use him through this? By being confined to a wheelchair, could he become an even mightier soldier in the Lord's kingdom?

Hope sprang up inside him, a young, fragile bud.

Jill had been right. How dare he wish he was dead when the Lord had answered so many prayers for him?

Maybe it wasn't that God was finished with him but that he had a new task ahead. Maybe God was merely sending him in a new direction. Maybe he should think of it as the beginning of a new era instead of the end of his life.

"My faith in you doesn't rest on whether you heal me," Dan whispered. "But I'd sure appreciate it if you could give me the strength ... the strength to be weak." Tears ran down his face again. He wiped them away. He was getting so tired of them.

Jill stirred and looked over at him. "Dan? Are you okay?"

"Yeah." He wiped his face on his sleeve. "Come here."

She got up and came to his bed, bent over him.

"No," he said. "I mean here." He patted the mattress beside him. "Help me scoot over, then lie down with me."

A smile softened her lips, and she helped him move. Then she got onto the bed and stretched out next to him. He pulled her head onto his chest and held her the way he used to do at night before they fell asleep.

"It's going to be all right," he whispered. "Everything's going to be all right."

He felt Jill's tears warmly wetting his shirt. "You have no idea how I've wished I could hear those words."

He knew. He had long wished he could say them. "I love you," he whispered.

"I love you too." She kissed him, then laid her head back down.

Dan kept stroking her hair, and after a while, he felt her body relaxing into restful sleep.

And he felt strong again.

Chapter Ninety

● ● ●

Gordon's wife's clothes smelled of mothballs and old perfume, and Ashley could tell by the condition they were in that few of them were new. Still, someone would be happy to get them, and they would help raise money for the families.

Stan had come shortly after she'd shown up and was working on the furnace near the back of the house. She felt the heat come on and was glad that the rooms would warm up soon. The temperature outside had dropped ten degrees in the last couple of hours, and the house felt refrigerated.

She took an armload of clothes to one of the boxes she had on the bed and began folding them and putting them in. As she did, she looked around at the framed pictures Gordon had of his wife. She had been a pretty woman when she was young.

She saw a scrapbook on the bed table. Sitting down on the bed, she opened it and began to flip through. She saw pictures of the two of them when they were her age, so many years ago. Alma was laughing in almost every one. There had probably been lots of laughter in this house before she died.

She turned the pages and found memories of vacations on the beach, in the mountains, at the Grand Canyon.

And then she saw a naval unit, decked out in uniform. She studied the faces until she found Gordon, seventy-five pounds lighter and thirty-five years younger. At the front of the group was a sign that said "NAVEODFAC."

"Is it getting warm in here yet?" Stan came in and raised his hand to the vent.

"I think so. You must have fixed it."

"Good." He looked around at all the boxes she'd packed. "You've done a good job. I'm glad you're feeling better, after yesterday."

"So where is Donald Merritt now?" she asked.

"He's in jail. No bond is being set. You don't have to worry." She didn't say anything, but just kept folding.

"If you want, I can load these into my car and take them to Aunt Aggie's for the rummage sale."

"Yeah, that'd be good."

He picked up the photo album next to her. "Pictures of Gordon?"

"Yeah." She pointed to the naval photo and picked him out. "I think that's him."

Stan chuckled.

She heard Gordon hobbling up the hall, coming to check on them. Gordon stopped at the door and leaned on one crutch. "You did it, Stan. It's actually warming up."

"Glad to do it," Stan said. "Hey, Gordon, when were you in the Navy?"

"Back in the sixties," he said. "Fought in Vietnam, as a matter of fact."

"You look very dignified here."

Gordon took the photo album and chuckled. "Musta been 1965. Before my bride started feeding me so good."

"So what did all those letters stand for?"

"Naval EOD Facility. It was an electronic maintenance division." He closed the book and looked at his wife's dresses laid out on the bed. "Her church dresses," he said. "Somebody oughta really enjoy those. I hope they hang them up real nice, so folks can see what good shape they're in."

• • •

Stan loaded the boxes into his car and left Ashley to finish sorting the rest of the clothes. He would take them to Aunt Aggie when he got off work this afternoon. For now, he needed to get back to the station.

The old man's emotion over all of his wife's things being boxed up and taken away kept playing through Stan's mind. He wondered what he would be like when he was old, if Celia went before he did. How would he stand to be alone?

The pictures in Gordon's photo album kept flashing through his mind, snapshots of a life well lived. He wished he'd met Alma Webster. She seemed like a bright and pleasant woman.

And Gordon looked as if he'd always been pleasant, too.

He thought of that Naval picture again, and the sign in front of the division—NAVEODFAC. Gordon hadn't really explained what the letters stood for. Stan told himself that he'd ask him when he saw him again, but as he went into the station, he found that his curiosity had gotten the best of him.

He went to his desk, turned his computer on, and checked all his messages. But his mind went back to that picture.

Finally, to satisfy his curiosity, he opened his search engine and typed in the letters NAVEODFAC.

Several things came up, so he opened the first one.

And then he understood why his mind had refused to let it go.

The letters stood for Naval Explosive Ordnance Disposal Facility. Gordon had served in the Navy as an explosives man.

He knew how to build bombs.

Stan's face grew hot. He got up, staring down at his monitor, as a new paradigm of possibilities lined up in his mind. Could it be that Gordon had something to do with the bombs at Icon?

He had been in the building that day, even though he was no longer employed there. He was angry, resentful . . .

And he'd lied to Stan about what he'd done in the Navy.

Stan had to think. He sat back down and pulled up all the information he had at his disposal on Gordon Webster. There were no arrests, his driver's license was current. . . .

He printed out Gordon's driver's license picture and tore it from the printer. If he showed it to the guy at Budget Truck Rental, would he recognize Gordon as the one who'd rented the truck?

Could it be that Merritt was telling the truth?

No way. Stan was racing up the wrong road. Gordon couldn't have had anything to do with the bombing. Not that humble grandfatherly man, with his gentle smile and his kind face.

Then again, he'd had a lot to be angry about. The death of his wife, the loss of his job, the unjust disappearance of his retirement. What if he'd been so angry and upset that he'd schemed to get even?

He could imagine someone in Gordon's position targeting Merritt, maybe, but not an entire building full of his coworkers. And the fact that Gordon had ordnance experience certainly didn't prove he was a killer.

Still, Stan had to investigate and see what he could find out. He took the picture and headed to the rental company.

As he drove, he tried to remember what Ashley had told the FBI yesterday.

She had described water jugs surrounding the bomb itself, and they had concluded that it was some kind of fuel that had probably been dollied in, a few jugs at a time. Whoever had brought them in had not been noticed. Merritt could have done it at night, but none of the security guards had seen him bringing anything unusual in.

If the bomber had done it in broad daylight, it must have been disguised. Anyone who'd seen it had probably believed it was water for the coolers. It had to be someone familiar, some-one people were used to seeing there.

There had been a large amount of fertilizer used in the construction of the truck bomb. The company that sold it had no record of delivering it. Could Gordon have bought it himself and delivered it to some hiding place?

Part of him hoped it wouldn't be true. He could live with Merritt being the culprit.

But no one would believe that Gordon Webster had done it.

Chapter Ninety-One

• • •

S tan hurried into the Budget office, anxious to show the desk clerk Gordon's picture. A couple stood in front of the desk, and a man waited for his turn. Stan stepped in front of them.

"Dude, you're back," the guy said.

Stan leaned on the counter and handed him the copy of Gordon's license. "Do me a favor and tell me if this is the man who rented that truck."

He studied the picture, squinting his eyes, as if trying to remember. "Yeah, man, I think that's the dude all right. Sweet old man. You don't think he—?"

"Thanks," Stan said. "That's all I need to know. I'll need you to come in and give a statement later today."

"No problem, man. I'll come as soon as I get off." As Stan started toward the door, the kid yelled behind him. "Hey, did this dude help that Merritt guy blow up the building?"

Stan didn't answer him as he raced back out to his car. The moment he was in it, he called the FBI. "Mills," he said when the agent answered his phone. "I think you've got the wrong man."

As he explained what he'd learned, he raced back to Gordon's. Afraid for Ashley's safety, he called Gordon's house as soon as he'd hung up. The old man answered.

"Hello?"

"Hey, Gordon, Stan here." He hoped he sounded natural. "I need to tell Ashley something. Could you put her on?"

"Sure, hold on."

Stan's heart raced faster than his car.

"Hello?"

"Ashley, I want you to listen carefully. Tell Gordon that you forgot to leave the key for Clara and that you have to run to Jill's. Then get out of there immediately. Do you understand?"

There was a long pause. "Why?"

"I can't explain it now. Please, just do it. And act as naturally as you can."

"Okay."

As he hung up he prayed that she would get out before Gordon knew they were onto him.

Chapter Ninety-Two

● ● ●

Ashley hung up the phone and looked around for her keys. "Uh . . . I have to go. I forgot to leave Clara a key."

Gordon seemed to stiffen. "Stan called to tell you you'd forgotten to leave a key?"

She swept her hair behind her ears. "No . . . uh . . . he was talking to Jill or something, and she asked him to remind me."

She started past him. "I'll come back and finish later . . . after I do this."

She heard Gordon hobbling into the bedroom, heard a drawer being pulled out. What was going on? Why would Stan insist that she leave like this?

"Ashley."

"Yeah?" She turned around. Gordon was holding a gun.

She sucked in a breath and stepped back.

"Honey, I hate to do this," he said, and she could see on his face that he truly did. "I wouldn't hurt you for the world, but I see how things are playing out."

"What do you mean? Nothing's playing out. I just have to go."

"Stan told you to get out of here, didn't he?"

"No. He just said—"

"He knows." His finger was over the trigger, ready to squeeze. "You're not going anywhere, honey. I need you to drive me somewhere. You and I, we're going to get out of this town. I want you to walk with me out to your car."

He abandoned his crutches and walked on his cast toward her. Sticking the gun in her ribs, he turned her around.

"What are you doing?" she cried. "I don't want to go anywhere."

His face was red now, and he spoke through his teeth as he ushered her out the door. "I'm not taking the blame. They can't pin this on me." He got her to the car, opened the passenger door, and made her slide over behind the wheel.

"Start the car and let's go," he said, keeping the gun in her ribs.

She did as she was told and backed the car out. "Pin what on you?"

"I'm not going down for killing a hundred and fifty-three people! It was that picture. You shouldn't have been snooping through my stuff, Ashley."

Ashley almost lost control of the car. "A hundred and fifty-three people?" she repeated. "You helped Merritt kill my mother and a hundred and fifty-two other people?"

"No, I didn't. But they'll think I did because of my background."

He was guilty. She knew it with sudden, absolute certainty. Why else would he have a gun in her ribs? She thought of running the car off a bridge, crashing it into a brick wall, driving headlong into an eighteen-wheeler. She would gladly die for the honor of killing him.

"Turn here," he shouted, pointing to a dirt road in a wooded area.

She turned without slowing, letting her tires slide on the gravel.

"Stop the car!"

"No!" she shouted. "I'm going to kill us both."

He fired the gun across her, shattering her window. She screamed and let go of the wheel.

"I said, 'Stop the car!'"

She slammed on the brakes, afraid he would fire it again. The fear made her angry. Didn't she want to die? Wasn't it worth it?

Her survival instinct kicked in, and she realized that what she wanted most was to get out of this car and run for her life.

"I don't want to have to use this, honey," he said in a breathless voice, "but I will. I'm driving. Move over."

She watched through the blur of angry tears as he came around the car to her side. He put the gun to her head, so she scooted over. He had trouble getting his casted leg in, but he managed.

He started the car, turned it around, and started taking the back roads toward New Orleans.

"If Detective Shepherd figured it out, they'll find you," she said. "They'll hunt you down like a rabid animal."

"They won't find me." His voice was softer now, almost calm.

She wondered if Stan would realize that Gordon had kidnapped her. If not, then when Jill realized Ashley had disappeared again, she would be certain she had run off with a bottle of sleeping pills. This time, she might finally realize that Ashley wasn't worth chasing.

"Where are we going?" she said.

"New Orleans," he said.

"Where in New Orleans?"

"Your mother's house," he said.

Horrified, she thought of jumping out. "I won't tell you where it is."

"You don't have to, sweetie. I looked it up days ago. I know right where it is. They won't think to look for me there."

Chapter Ninety-Three

● ● ●

While Dan went to the hospital's rehab center for his therapy session, Jill drove back to Newpointe to help Ashley at Gordon's.

But when she turned the corner onto Gordon's street, she caught her breath. Police cars were lined up on the front of his property, their blue lights flashing. She pulled up behind them. What on earth had happened? Had Gordon died? Was Ashley in trouble?

She bolted out of the car. "What happened?"

A cop with an ATF jacket stopped her. "Ma'am, you can't go any further."

She fought him out of her way. "Please! I have to know what happened!"

She saw Stan then, standing at one of the cars. He hurried toward her, calling to the cop to let her go.

"Stan, what's going on?"

"Jill, I hate to break this to you, but we have strong reason to believe that Gordon Webster planted the bombs at the Icon Building. And I think he might have Ashley."

"*What?*" She couldn't have heard him right. "No, that can't be. He was in there himself. He was a victim."

"I have a witness who says he's the one who rented the truck that was used in the bombing. The FBI just searched the property he used to own outside town. It was foreclosed on last week, but they found evidence of bomb-making materials in an old barn on the property. Now he's vanished, and I'm afraid she's with him."

"No!" She hit Stan, shoving him back. "If you knew, why didn't you tell us?"

"I called her and told her to leave the moment I knew, Jill. And maybe she did—maybe she got away safely. But I'm afraid the call was a mistake. The phone call may have made him suspicious. I raced over here, but they were already gone. Do you know how to reach her?"

"No! I called my house on the way over and she wasn't there." Numbness bled through her, and she stared up at the house. Was it really possible that the old man she had helped down the stairs, injured and needy, the one who had lost his wife and his retirement and his job, could really have killed over a hundred and fifty people in a cold-blooded act of murder? Had he taken Ashley hostage?

"If you called her, don't you think she might have left? Maybe he has an accomplice. Maybe someone picked him up."

"It's possible."

She turned back to her car. "I've got to go find her."

"Be careful, Jill. He could be dangerous."

Jill wept as she drove away. Ashley couldn't be with Gordon. If Stan had warned her, maybe she had listened. Maybe she was home by now.

Jill drove by her own house but didn't see Ashley's car. She tried to think.

If Ashley had left as she was told, then figured out that Gordon was involved, what could she be thinking? Would it destroy her trust in everyone? If she had gotten away, would she buy some more of those pills and carry out her suicide plans?

She pulled her cell phone off the waist of her jeans and pressed number one—the speed dial number she'd programmed for Dan.

He answered quickly. "Hey, babe."

"Dan, pray!" she shouted into the phone. "They figured out that Gordon is the one who planted the bombs, and they think he may have Ashley!"

"Gordon?" he said. "The man you've been helping?"

"Yes! I'm driving to New Orleans. I'm hoping she's at her mother's house and not with him after all. But pray, Dan! Please!"

"I will. Jill, be careful!"

"All right. Keep your phone on you."

She flew across Lake Pontchartrain and into New Orleans, and then she raced to Ashley's neighborhood.

As she turned onto Ashley's street, she saw her Subaru in the carport.

"Thank you, God!" she cried out. "Oh, she's here!" Screeching into the driveway, she bolted out and went to the door. It wasn't locked, so she burst inside.

Ashley sat on the floor in a corner of the living room, her hands, feet, and mouth taped up with duct tape.

Gordon sat on the couch, a gun pointed at her head.

"Come on in, Jill," he said. "We started this out together. We might as well finish it together."

Jill froze. "Put the gun down, Gordon. Put it down now."

"I'm afraid I can't do that, Jill," he said. "Get over there with her."

Jill ran to Ashley and threw her arms around her. Ashley fell against her.

And as Gordon got the duct tape to tie her up, Jill pressed the number one on the cell phone hanging on her waistband and quickly sent the call.

Chapter Ninety-Four

● ● ●

Dan was wheeling himself back to his room when his phone rang again. He grabbed it. "Hello, Jill?"

There was no answer. He thought maybe Jill had reached a bad area and lost the signal. He started to hang up, but then he heard voices.

"Gordon, think about what you're doing! We saved your life on those stairs. You want to kill us now?"

"I didn't ask you to save my life!" he cried. "I told you to go without me. I had planned to die there! But you kept dragging me down those stairs."

Dan closed his eyes, clutching the phone. Then pressing his hand over the receiver, he looked up at a passing nurse. "Hand me another phone! Hurry! I have to call the police!"

Chapter Ninety-Five

● ● ●

Gordon tore off a strip of tape and wrapped it around Jill's hands. "Gordon, why did you do it?" she cried. "Why did you kill all those people?"

He started on her feet. "I was desperate," he bit out. "What would you have done? My wife died because we didn't have the insurance to pay for her treatment. Then she died a horrible, suffering death, and I got this phone call. It was my supervisor, and I thought he was calling to tell me how sorry he was, give me his condolences and all that. Instead, he told me I was on the list of layoffs."

He set the duct tape down and lowered himself painfully into a chair, keeping his gun trained on them.

"He told me about severance packages and all that, but I didn't believe a word of it. I knew that the people who had already been laid off were having trouble getting their severance. And then all that stuff came out about Donald Merritt on the news, how he'd stolen from his employees, robbed the 401K accounts, committed fraud, and lied to the stockholders. It wasn't just Merritt. They were all involved. Everyone still in that building was in on it. They were padding their pockets at our expense. And all of a sudden, I wanted revenge." He broke off and started to cry. The gun trembled in his hand. "They shouldn't have been able to get away with it, Jill."

"They weren't going to, Gordon," she bit out. "I was in a meeting that morning trying to fight for the employees. He was about to be indicted. He would have paid."

"But don't you see?" he said. "It wouldn't have brought my retirement back. It wouldn't have given me a job. It wouldn't have brought my wife back to me."

"Icon International was not responsible for the death of your wife," she said.

"Oh, yes they were," he said. "One minute the doctors were talking about aggressive chemo treatments. Then when they found out we didn't have insurance—because those frauds had not paid the premiums—they suddenly backed off and said that they didn't think the chemo would help. They would have done it if we'd had insurance. Then when she died, Icon rubbed salt into my wound, twisted the knife. I decided that I was going to get even, so I made the bombs. I used my dead brother-in-law's ID and rented a truck, and I packed it full of explosives and parked it in the parking garage. I had a dozen water jugs of gasoline in the truck, and it took me four trips with my dolly to get them to the tenth and twenty-ninth floors. No one asked what I was doing. Then I carried the bombs up in crates and set them in the middle of those jugs."

Ashley began a muted wail through the duct tape. Jill prayed that Dan was listening—that he had notified the police.

"I was supposed to die in the explosion. That was my plan. I didn't have anything else to live for. All I could think about was the fact that Donald Merritt was in that meeting. The bomb was right below him. I never counted on anybody finding it and warning him in time to get him out."

Jill shivered. "If Ashley's mother hadn't warned us, there might have been thousands dead."

"They were all frauds!" he shouted. "Don't you see? The ones who were still there, the layoff survivors, they were all getting rich off our misfortune! Everybody there deserved to die. And I was going to die with them."

"So why didn't you?"

His face twisted, and he started to cry. "I panicked! I took off running when the alarm went off. When I got injured, I thought it was poetic justice. Only you came along and insisted on getting me down. But I got you out, too. After the second bomb, I told you how you could get out, remember? I knew that when the truck bomb went off the building would come down. I directed you to the other stairwell so you could get out before it did."

Ashley's muffled screaming got louder, and she fought to break free of the duct tape.

"It was a horrible thing I did," Gordon said. "I realized that later. And then you were so kind, Jill. You kept coming by the hospital, and you had all those church people feeding and caring for me. I never had people provide for me the way you and your church did. They made my life worth living again."

Jill thought of all the people who had served this dangerous man. They had ignored Ashley to embrace him. Had believed he was the one most lovable.

"And then I started to realize that maybe what I had done was a desperate thing, and I really didn't have to do it. Maybe life would have been all right if I'd just given it more time. Merritt deserved to be blamed for the explosion."

He watched Ashley for a moment. Her face was crimson, and she screamed into the duct tape that locked her mouth shut.

"I'm sorry for you, young lady," he said, rubbing his face. "I really am. I don't blame you for hating me like you do. I suppose you'd kill me if you could."

Ashley fought and screamed muffled threats.

"You were right, you know. If I leave here, they *will* hunt me down like a rabid animal. And you two have been good to me."

He started walking toward them, that gun shaking in his hand. "Gordon, please," Jill said. "Just go. You can take my car. Just walk out of here and leave us. You'll get a head start before the police start looking for you."

He kept hobbling toward them, wincing as he stepped on his cast. He stopped over Ashley, and she looked up at him with murderous hatred in her eyes. Jill knew she was daring him to kill her.

Instead, he pulled out a pocketknife . . . and cut her hands free.

She came at him, but he thrust the gun at her. "Here, darlin'," he said.

She froze and stared at that gun.

"I know what you want to do," he said. "Take the gun, Ashley. It's only fair you should have the honors."

Ashley took the gun.

Chapter Ninety-Six

● ● ●

Stan was with Mills when he got Dan's frantic call. They had quickly discovered the location of Jill's cell phone.

"It's my fault," Stan said. "I should never have called her. I should have just gone there and got her out myself."

"You did what you thought was right, Stan."

Stan held on as Mills flew through traffic. "Can't you go any faster?"

The blue light on his dashboard was flashing, and his siren blared, but people were slow to get out of their way.

He held his cell phone to his ear, waiting for the FBI to patch into Jill's call so he could hear what was going on.

Suddenly, voices came across the line.

"Gordon, please, just go." It was Jill's voice. "You can take my car. Just walk out of here and leave us. You'll get a head start before the police start looking for you."

There was a long pause. Stan closed his eyes and prayed. *Lord, please . . .*

"Here, darlin'." Gordon's voice. What could he be doing? "I know what you want to do. Take the gun, Ashley. It's only fair you should have the honors."

"He's giving the gun to the girl!" Stan shouted. "She'll kill him, just like she wanted to kill Merritt!" He thought of that poor, hurting kid, with vengeful murder on her hands to top everything else.

"We're almost there," Mills said.

Stan hoped it wouldn't be too late.

Chapter Ninety-Seven

●●●

Ashley ripped the duct tape off of her mouth, then leveled the gun on Gordon. "You murdering monster!" she screamed. The gun trembled in her hand.

Jill struggled to break free of her own tape. "Ashley, don't pull that trigger," she said. "Untape me, and I'll call the police. They can lock him up!"

Ashley's teeth ground together. "Why shouldn't I kill him?" she cried. "He has no right to live!"

"Ashley, cut my tape and give me the gun."

"No! You'll turn him over to the police! He'll sit in some cushy jail cell for months before he even goes to trial. I'm going to pull this trigger and blow his head off, and then some distant relative of his will have to come to the morgue and identify his disfigured body."

The words were uttered with such pain that Jill almost hoped she would do it.

But she knew what it would do to the girl.

"Honey, untape me. Give me the gun."

"No, I want to do it!" Ashley shook so hard that Jill thought she might drop it.

"Your mother wouldn't have wanted this," Jill cried. "She wanted you to be okay. She didn't want you to have a man's blood on your hands."

Gordon was weeping openly now. "Come on, Ashley," he said. "It's the only thing that'll give you peace."

Ashley closed her finger over the trigger.

Chapter Ninety-Eight

● ● ●

Dan had made it to his room, clutching the phone to his ear and listening to every gut-wrenching word. Clara had followed him in and stood over him, waiting for word.

"What's happening?"

Dan held out a hand to silence her. "Oh, dear God. He gave Ashley the gun." He heard Gordon taunting her, urging her to pull the trigger.

Where was Jill? Was she in the line of fire? Was she fighting Ashley for the gun?

Suddenly the gunshot cracked across the line.

"Oh God, no!" Dan cried. "Please, God!"

Clara caught him before he fell out of his chair. Throwing her arms around him, she held him and tried to calm him down.

Chapter Ninety-Nine

• • •

Stan burst through the door, his gun drawn.

Gordon lay on the floor in a pool of blood, clutching his arm.

Ashley and Jill sat just a few feet away. The girl dropped the gun. Hysterical screams shook the house.

Jill sat next to her, wailing out her own terror.

The room filled with agents and cops, and Stan got the gun before Ashley could go for it again. Then he bent down and cut Jill's hands free. She reached for the girl and pulled her into her arms.

Stan turned back to Gordon. The gunshot had merely grazed his arm.

As police swarmed around him, he stooped down and looked into Jill's face. "I know you're upset," he said, "but, Jill, you might want to get on that phone and let Dan know you're all right."

Sobbing, Jill pulled the phone off of her belt.

"Hi, honey," she said.

Chapter One Hundred

● ● ●

Ashley couldn't stop shivering. She sat curled up on the couch, her mother's handmade quilt draped around her, long after they had taken Gordon off in the squad car. Jill held her, just the way her mother would have, as the police swarmed the place.

She couldn't believe she had shot him. And she couldn't believe she had missed.

Rage still rippled through her, but the sorrow was deeper, more intense. Her mother had died because of a disgruntled employee with a messed-up idea about who had been responsible for his problems.

And to think she had helped save his life.

"It's okay, honey. It's all over," Jill said.

"How could he do it?" she whispered. "How could he do that to my mother? To all those people? How could he let us help him when he'd caused it all?"

"I don't know." Jill laid her head over hers. Ashley felt as if Jill's arms were the only things holding her together.

"He'll say he was insane. They'll probably put him in some institution, and he'll never pay."

"Oh, no," Jill said. "Trust me, honey. He's going to pay."

Stan came over and sat on the coffee table across from them. "Ashley, I'm so sorry," he said. "I never should have called you at Gordon's. I thought I was getting you out of danger, but I wound up causing it."

It wasn't his fault, she thought. He had been trying to do the right thing. If he hadn't figured it out, they might still be pampering Gordon and bringing him food. "It was my fault," she said. "If I'd been a better actor, I could have walked right out of there. But he knew something wasn't right."

"I hope you can forgive me," he said.

"It's okay. Really."

They hadn't said anything about her pulling the trigger. She wondered if she was in trouble. She looked up at Jill as Stan went back to work.

"Are they going to arrest me?"

Jill looked surprised at her question. "I don't think so, honey."

"Why not? I would have murdered him if I hadn't been shaking so. It threw my aim off. I would have killed him in a minute. I didn't even care what happened to me."

Jill closed her eyes, and Ashley saw the pain on her face. "You'll be okay, honey. You've got a really good lawyer."

She heard a commotion outside, then Stan went to the door. After a moment, he wheeled Dan in.

Jill let her go and sprang up. "Dan!"

He reached for her, and she ran into his arms. "What are you doing here?"

Clara clicked in behind him. "He made me bring him, Jill. He made me roll him right out of that hospital."

"Are you all right?" he whispered, not letting her go.

"I'm fine. I told you on the phone I was."

"I had to see for myself."

Ashley watched them, wondering at the love they seemed to have for each other. She was glad Dan wasn't dead. Jill didn't deserve that. And he seemed like a good man.

Clara came toward her, and Ashley's defenses went back up. But this time, the woman didn't look threatening. Instead, she lowered herself to the couch where Jill had been sitting.

"Are you all right, dear?"

Ashley was still shivering. "I'm fine."

"That was a horrible thing." She set her hand on Ashley's leg, patted it gently. "A very horrible thing."

The woman was about to cry, and as she struggled not to, she reached up and pushed Ashley's hair back from her face. "We need to get you home," she said. "We'll start a fire to warm you up. I'll make some hot cider. Maybe we'll order some more Chinese takeout."

Ashley felt herself warming up already.

She watched the men swarming through her mother's house, taking pictures and fingerprints as if they didn't already know that Gordon was guilty.

She wondered if her mother was watching from somewhere, still praying for her. Someone was. She had come too close to death too many times in the last several days.

Maybe her mother's prayers really were being answered.

Her gaze drifted back to Jill and Dan again. The fact that either of them were in her life at all was a miracle. Yes, God had answered her mother's prayers. There was no doubt about that.

She thought of Jill's analogy of the bomb and Christ's death. Gordon had built a bomb, but according to Jill, she had built one too, with her own sins. Today she would have committed murder if her hand had just been steady.

Her mother had prayed for her salvation. It had probably been her dying prayer.

And through the loneliest, darkest of her days, God had sent people to love her.

It was a miracle, indeed.

Thank you, Jesus. Maybe she did need to think about what Christ had done for her. Maybe she needed to let God answer her mother's last prayer.

Chapter One Hundred and One

● ● ●

Jill sat on the side of the bathtub and stared down at the test strip in her hand. Three minutes was a very long time.

She watched the second hand on the clock she'd brought in with her, shaking her foot with nervous energy.

Please, God . . .

It was Christmas morning, after all, and Dan had been released from the hospital yesterday. She had slipped out of bed while he still slept and pulled out the box she'd gotten at the drugstore.

Thirty more seconds.

She counted them down, thinking what a wonderful day it would be if the test was positive. But it would be a wonderful day, anyway, she told herself. She had spent the last week making sure that the morning would be grand for Dan, Ashley, and Clara.

She had never expected this gift of her own.

So much had happened since Gordon's arrest. She had taken Ashley to her first counseling session and had hope that she could help Ashley heal over time. Gordon had pled guilty to planting the bombs, and everyone was certain he would get the death penalty for his crimes.

Donald Merritt had also been indicted for his crimes committed before the bombing. He, too, sat in jail pending trial. No bond had been set, since he'd proven to be a flight risk.

And she had watched Clara and Dan's relationship blossom from one of strangers to that of mother and son. There might be hope for the woman, after all.

As she'd rushed around packing Dan's things to bring him home, it had hit her that she hadn't had a period since mid-November. Had the stress changed her hormones, or did God have a special gift for her?

Five ... four ... three ...

She refused to look until it was time.

... two ... one.

She looked down at the strip. There were two pink lines.

What had the instructions said? She launched across the bathroom and grabbed the box to read the directions again.

She threw her hand over her mouth and burst into tears.

Flinging the door open, she ran to the bed. "Dan, wake up!" she cried. "It's Christmas!"

Dan opened his eyes and sat up. "What? Did it snow or something? Are we having a white Christmas?"

Jill started to laugh. "No, a pink one! Look at it, Dan. Two pink lines."

He frowned and took the test strip. "What is this?"

"It's your gift!"

He grinned up at her. "You shouldn't have."

She laughed again. "It's a pregnancy test, honey. We're going to have a baby!"

The look on his face was enough to last her the next forty Christmases. "We're what?"

She touched his face. "Yes, sweetheart."

His amusement faded, and a sweet, poignant look came over his face. "Really?"

She nodded and smiled through her tears. He pulled her into his arms as he began to cry, unashamed and full of joy.

And she knew that everything really was going to be all right.

Afterword

● ● ●

As I wrote *Line of Duty*, America was preparing to go to war. Duct tape and plastic sheeting were top-selling items in the stores. Families were saying good-bye to their sons and daughters, their fathers and husbands. Yellow ribbons were adorning our streetlights, trees, and fenceposts. I looked ahead with uncertainty as I wrote, realizing that by the time of publication, many of you could be grieving or suffering. The potential for nuclear disaster was on the horizon. The very air we breathed could turn into poison.

But it strikes me now, looking back, that even though the worst part of the war is over, the threats remain. They're the same threats we had on December 7, 1941. The same ones we had on September 11, 2001. The same threats we will have this time next year. Yet one thing is certain: though we may not know exactly how it will come about, God has given us the end of the story. He will prevail. And at the end of time there will be a separating out of God's friends from his enemies. Have you decided what side you'll be on? Are you sure?

We in America live in a prosperous society. Most of us live in comfort. Many of us assign little significance to our acts of worship. We show up in church, sing our hymns or praise songs, bow our heads for public prayer, then go on about our lives, leaving our convictions and our Christianity behind, as if it's something bulky that we can't manage to carry with us. We tell ourselves that if push ever comes to shove, we will stand for Christ to the point of death. But will we really, when we don't even stand for him behind the wheels of our cars or in our offices or as we do our taxes?

What would we look like if we truly stood for Christ? Would we look like travelers laden down with heavy bags and awkward packages, unable to use our hands because they're so full of the Lord's things?

Maybe not. Romans 13:14 says, "Put on the Lord Jesus Christ" (NASB). Put him on? Like a robe? Could this mean that when people look at us, they're to see Christ? We're to stand for him, bearing "fruit in keeping with repentance" (Matthew 3:8), and as Christ said in John 9:4, "We must work the works of Him who sent Me, as long as it is day; night is coming, when no man can work" (NASB).

Night is coming indeed. But we know how the story ends. Whether you're a pre-tribber or a post-tribber, a postmillennialist or a dispensationalist, or any of those other words that only theologians can define, anyone who's read the Bible knows that this earth is a temporary home. It will come to an end. And we will be caught standing on one side or the other.

Will we be caught wearing his robe? "And it was given to [the bride] to clothe herself in fine linen, bright and clean; for the fine linen is the righteous acts of the saints."

Christ will ride in as the conqueror, with us, his army, behind him.

"... and the armies which are in heaven, clothed in fine linen, white and clean, were following Him on white horses" (Rev 19:14 NASB).

His clean linen.

His righteousness.

Mine through his grace.

I can't wait to be a part of that Army flanking the Lord as he takes what is his ... and shares it with me.

About the Author

Terri Blackstock is an award-winning novelist who has written for several major publishers including HarperCollins, Dell, Harlequin, and Silhouette. Published under two pseudonyms, her books have sold over 3.5 million copies worldwide.

With her success in secular publishing at its peak, Blackstock had what she calls "a spiritual awakening." A Christian since the age of fourteen, she realized she had not been using her gift as God intended. It was at that point that she recommitted her life to Christ, gave up her secular career, and made the decision to write only books that would point her readers to him.

"I wanted to be able to tell the truth in my stories," she said, "and not just be politically correct. It doesn't matter how many readers I have if I can't tell them what I know about the roots of their problems and the solutions that have literally saved my own life."

Her books are about flawed Christians in crisis and God's provisions for their mistakes and wrong choices. She claims to be extremely qualified to write such books, since she's had years of personal experience.

A native of nowhere, since she was raised in the Air Force, Blackstock makes Mississippi her home. She and her husband are the parents of three children—a blended family which she considers one more of God's provisions.

#1 Bestseller!

Cape Refuge

Terri Blackstock

Mystery and suspense combine in this first book of an exciting new 4-book series by best-selling author Terri Blackstock.

Thelma and Wayne Owens run a bed and breakfast in Cape Refuge, Georgia. After a heated, public argument with his in-laws, Jonathan discovers Thelma and Wayne murdered in the warehouse where they held their church services. Considered the prime suspect, Jonathan is arrested. Grief-stricken, Morgan and Blair launch their own investigation to help Matthew Cade, the town's young police chief, find the real killer. Shady characters and a raft of suspects keep the plot twisting and the suspense building as we learn not only who murdered Thelma and Wayne, but also the secrets about their family's past and the true reason for Blair's disfigurement.

Softcover: 0-310-23592-8

Southern Storm

Terri Blackstock

The second book in the best-selling Cape Refuge suspense series.

Police Chief Cade disappears without a trace after accidentally hitting a man with his patrol car and killing him. While the rest of the police force looks for him and chases a series of clues that condemn Cade as a murderer, Blair Owens can't believe he is guilty of such a crime. Instead, she conducts her own search for the truth.

Softcover: 0-310-23593-6

We want to hear from you. Please send your comments about this book to us in care of zreview@zondervan.com. Thank you.

GRAND RAPIDS, MICHIGAN 49530 USA

WWW.ZONDERVAN.COM